SEVEN
PHOTOGRAPHS

ALAN ROSSMAN

SEVEN PHOTOGRAPHS

iUniverse books may be ordered through booksellers or by contacting:

iUniverse
1663 Liberty Drive
Bloomington, IN 47403
www.iuniverse.com
1-800-Authors (1-800-288-4677)

ISBN: 978-1-5320-6529-3 (sc)
ISBN: 978-1-5320-6531-6 (hc)
ISBN: 978-1-5320-6530-9 (e)

Library of Congress Control Number: 2019900779

Print information available on the last page.

iUniverse rev. date: 02/11/2019

SEVEN
PHOTOGRAPHS

Acknowledgments

Puddled delusions? Sure, I've had a few. But no delusion is more vociferous than the one banging around in my head at this particular moment in time. Make no mistake—there is no way I would be composing these words were it not for the love, encouragement, and guidance of others. Where to begin? I owe a deep debt of gratitude to the talented authors of the Wesley Writers Workshop, especially Sharon Fiffer, who taught me what it means to think like a writer. Thanks too to the friends and family members who endured early drafts of this book and those who patiently sat by as I tried to convey this thing that I loved in hopes that they might find a thing that was in it to be loved by them as well: Stephen Taft, Katy Buoscio, Henry Moss, Wendy Beigler, Ivan Hernandez Salinas, Diane Salmon, David Ardis, Bill Levin, Chris Halverson, Mark Antonucci, Howard Kaplan, and Jeremy Rossman, to whom I now must bestow a lifetime supply of tacos. Special thanks to the guy on the Virago by my side, my brother Howard, whose unwavering support, careful reading, and generous words have been the wind at my back throughout this project. The updraft created by his confidence in me—no matter the endeavor—has always been inspiriting. It turns out that my kids—Matthew, Madeline, and Meredith—were my harshest critics *and* my most ardent fans. I could never be more grateful. But it was their steadfast belief in their old man, that not only could he really do this thing but he *must*, that will forever bring tears to my eyes. And lastly, my heart goes out to the girl of my dreams, my wife, Cindy, who knows this story better than anyone. From that windswept beach at the Cape to the edge of the farthest horizon, you never know what may come from a tuna noodle casserole.

For my father
Maybe now we can both get some rest

A tear contains an ocean. A photographer is aware of the tiny moments in a person's life that reveal greater truths.
—Anonymous

In photography there are no shadows
that cannot be illuminated.
—August Sander

Photography is truth.
—Jean-Luc Godard

Contents

Prologue

The first thing Owen did when the letter arrived was send three texts. The first was to Hannah. He made sure to attach a picture of the envelope along with the message letting her know how proud they all were of her accomplishment. The second was to Janey: just the picture, no words. He knew that would be enough to ease her mind after weeks of edgy anticipation. And the third was to the group. There was to be an official family gathering that evening to celebrate the news of the newest addition to the University of Wisconsin's class of 2018. Their attendance was requested. He spent the rest of the afternoon cleaning the grill and sweeping out the patio and wondering at the passage of time.

They ate quickly without much gaiety until it was time for the toasts and everyone's glass was filled. "To Hannah," they cheered. "Madison will never be the same." And after the plates had been cleared and left to soak in the sink, he walked back out to his family as they gathered around the smoldering fire.

"Jesus, Owen. Again with the camera? Really?" The tone of Janey's voice was kinder than her words. It didn't feel like an indictment at all. Still, when he glanced up from the viewfinder, he was relieved to see that her smile was tinted with tolerance, the gentle kind that accumulates around a long marriage like warm spring rain. She raised her glass and blew him a kiss that carried the assurance she meant him no harm despite her sloppy choice of words.

"But, Jane, this light is just too perfect," Owen insisted. "I don't want to miss it. Nobody minds, right?"

It was a gorgeous evening. All along the far horizon, the sky phosphoresced with the dying cinders of a glistering sunset. He could trace an uninterrupted progression of color from blue to purple to violet to black as his eyes scanned the heavens. The gauzy smoke from the fire pit veiled the backyard in a soft-focused haze that scoured away serrations. It was the kind of light that longed to be captured, and he was sure it would never last.

"Not at all, sweetie. Go for it," Janey said.

Owen knew that the Nikon was too much camera for him. Most of its potential would never be claimed. There were just too many ways to see. But he loved the way it felt in his hands. Billeted. Deliberate. Sincere. It had been a gift to Aaron several years ago, bestowed with all the best intentions of loving parents. And some frantic hopes as well.

Like other good parents, Owen and Janey indulged their children's interests with meticulous care. But the rules of indulgence were blurred with Aaron, whose soul could never calm. Just as it was with the bird watching and rock climbing and beekeeping and skateboarding and stargazing before, his zeal for photography was frightening at first. It was always like that. It burned on a fuse until it erupted in a flash, and then it was gone; the raw material that drove his desires would be all used up. Obsessive passion disorder, some of his doctors called it. Or "frenum frenzy." But Owen and Janey kept trying. They were sure that one day they would land on the right channel and the world would be set on fire.

Owen found the discarded camera gathering dust in the basement. He began carrying it around to document the shifting sands of his family as his kids left childhood behind. He liked looking at the photographs, especially at night, sitting alone at his computer. On some of those nights when the house was silent, he would tilt his ear to the screen and eavesdrop on the voices carried by the pictures. He was drawn by the promise of what they might say. But the sounds were muffled and difficult to discern, masked by static like shreds of music from a distant radio station. Someday, perhaps, he would be ready to listen. In the meantime, the Nikon was usually there, and the celebration of his daughter's acceptance to college was an event worthy of some shutter time.

"Hey, Hannah," he said while squinting through the camera. "As the guest of honor at this shindig, you're up first. Let's get a shot of the new college girl on the day she got the letter."

Hannah held up a painted finger while continuing to text with her thumbs.

The realization that other plans were being made left him wistful. But Owen knew that the drama of the lens would be irresistible to his eldest daughter. She soon put down the phone and began to pose like the models she adored in her glossy magazines. He snapped away like a paparazzo. Then he leaned over and softly kissed the top of her head. "Congratulations, honey. We are all so proud of you. You're going to have a great time in Madison."

She was already reaching for her phone.

"All right, Sara. You're next." He thought about asking her to put down the book, but the impression she cast on the coated glass lens left him breathless, so he just let her be. Her eyes reflected the flames. They blazed with the plight of a heroine's trial and the untrammeled wants of her innocence. He composed the shot to highlight those eyes and the inkling of secrets they hid. And when she looked up, the shutter kept clicking until he knew he had what he wanted. "That was beautiful, honey."

"Thanks, Dad," she sighed, returning to her story with a faraway smile.

"Okay, pal. Your turn." Owen was untroubled when his son did not reply. It usually took a couple of tries to get a response, especially lately. They had all grown accustomed to repeating things until the attention that seemed so splintered could congeal around the moment. Owen removed the heavy camera and sat down on the steps next to his son. He put an arm around the boy and gently rubbed his back, just like he did on all the troublesome nights. And he waited for him to return.

Eventually, Aaron's eyes cleared, and he glanced absently at the father who was suddenly by his side.

"Son, can I take your picture?"

"Sure, Dad. You can take my picture. How would you like me to be?"

More and more frequently, Owen did not know what to say to his son. Aaron's questions had that effect on everyone. It was almost as if the things he said were transmitted on a separate wavelength or required a spell of decoding to understand. And so too, Owen knew that he often overthought his replies, just as he was doing then. He yearned for the days when things were easier.

"However you want to be is good with me," Owen said at last, satisfied with the sound of his reply.

Aaron stared directly into the camera.

Owen shot from various angles, but he failed to find the proper perspective. Just when he thought he should stop, the fire pit crackled and sent a shower of sparks to sprinkle the night air, seizing Aaron's attention as they rose. Owen kept shooting, compelled by the premonition that these were the ones that mattered.

At last, he put the camera down, tucking away until later the pleasure he knew would come when he could sit alone with his photos. He pulled up a chair next to the fire and peered at his family unfiltered. For a second or two, everything was all right.

"I think I'm going to go up if nobody minds," Aaron said as the last of sparks flickered away into the tangled branches above. The final remnants of light had faded from the sky, and darkness gathered around them. The air snapped with an unexpected chill that numbed the warmth from the fire.

"You feel okay, sweetie?" Janey asked. She had been watching her son with a bead of concern as he followed the trail of sparks. Hearing no reply, she collected herself and came to sit beside him. She laid her head on his shoulder and enfolded him too easily in her arms. What had become of their strong, young son?

"Are you okay?" she whispered again, more urgently in his ear.

By then, the phone, the book, and the camera were all but forgotten as they each waited anxiously for Aaron to respond.

He nodded once, and his body softly imploded. When he finally stood, Janey's arms withered away, and she sank into the crater left behind. Without a word, Aaron opened the sliding doors that led into the house and wound his way upstairs.

Owen took note of the look that passed between his daughters. He had seen that look before. It made him want to cry.

They had planned to spend the following day hiking the trails at Starved Rock.

Owen woke early to pack the car with sandwiches and snacks and their gear. He had a large pot of coffee brewing by the time Janey and the girls came downstairs. As they warmed some toast to go with their coffee, Owen scrolled through the photos from the night before, taking note of several shots he wanted to save. Ideas raced in his head, and he began sketching some on paper. *Something special should be done with those shots,* he thought, *something with the impress of permanence.*

"Anybody know where Aaron is?" Owen asked as the others were finishing their breakfast. He didn't think they should wait much longer. Leaving late would cut into their time on the trails, and the day would get off on the wrong foot. He knew that negotiating family events could sometimes be a finicky affair. One false step like a late departure, and the day could easily detonate.

"Let's give him a few more minutes," Janey suggested. "We've got time."

Owen shrugged and poured a second cup of coffee. He sneaked another peek at his watch and then looked over again at Janey. Something unsettling had twisted her face even as she stared through the curlicues of steam that rose from her cup. "It's getting a little late," Owen said stiffly. "We better get him up. You want to give it a try this time?"

Janey reluctantly nodded. "Aaron, honey, let's go. Rise and shine!" she called from the bottom of the stairs.

They all waited like church mice to hear the sound of his steps as he lumbered his way out of bed, their four faces apprehensively angled upstairs, but nobody heard a thing.

"Aaron. C'mon, sweetheart. We need to be on the road in five," Janey called out again after taking a tentative first step on the stairs.

That was the moment that loosened the dread. When she turned back around, Janey's eyes were empty and flat, just two white ovals. The flesh around her cheeks was drawn like a mask. Her countenance had been supplanted with an expression that Owen could never describe. He held up a hand to allay her fear.

Then he heard her calling as she made her way upstairs.

"Aaron, sweetie, time to get up. We're burning daylight here."

And he heard her calling from the second-floor landing.

"Aaron, let's go!"

And the howl he heard as she opened the door was a sound he would never forget.

EQUINOX

And the sky dripped puddles of blue from
the infinity pool of sapphires above.

Chapter

1

Winter was coming. Winter was coming and would soon settle in for the long haul, laying in roots that run all the way down to the center of the earth. There was nothing Wilson could do to deny the fact that winter, most certainly, was coming. He didn't need to see the gunmetal sky suspended above to tell him that winter was near. Nor did he need to feel the newly frozen ground beneath his feet, unforgiving as concrete at dawn. Neither the northerly winds that stabbed his skin with chips of broken porcelain nor the shards of frost that clung like lichen to downspouts and drainpipes were required. None of those were necessary. And most unnecessary of all was the interminable darkness that shadowed him throughout the day.

"Christ, it's always dark."

It was dark when he woke up and brushed away the liquid dreams that had returned to enervate the night. It was dark when he sat down for dinner; the dusty chandelier and even the smell of warm pie—bought at the local Qwik-Mart and reheating in the microwave as a hedge against dinner—were unable to dispel the gloom. So much darkness. Sure, all these signs indicated that winter was coming, but they weren't really necessary to tell him that winter would soon be here. He knew it because of the sadness.

Wilson Lacy was fast becoming an old man. He was turning old and tired and sour like yesterday's meat loaf with the same moldy fuzz sprouting in tufts wherever it found purchase on his long and careworn face and that vinegary stink of decay.

Now, our world is replete with tired and sour old men. There are legions of them, battalions of old bones on patrol, dampening down the threats posed by the exuberance of youth with the force of their obsolescence. You see them everywhere, especially around midday, shuffling along with their stooped shoulders and threadbare trousers, starched stiff at the cuffs with stains of salt and trailing contrails of woe behind them.

And deep down inside, Wilson feared he was becoming one of them, an unwilling recruit in the army of the old. But what set him apart from the others, what Wilson Lacy liked to think distinguished him from his cohort of curmudgeons, was the source of his senescence. It wasn't just his age that made Wilson old. It wasn't just the grave toll that so many years aboveground had taken on his soul. And it wasn't just the aloneness that had plummeted down around him like nightfall. What was making Wilson old was more peculiar than that—and maybe a tad more romantic too; think more Dorian Gray, less Ebenezer Scrooge. What was turning Wilson Lacy into an old man was the arrival, every winter, as reliable as the morning paper, of the sadness.

"It is so tiresome, isn't it?"

For as long as Wilson could remember, the onset of winter was accompanied by a deep dive into despair. He knew its rhythms with a lover's intimacy, intuiting the tidal pulls of sorrow that heralded its arrival. He once told me that if there were a silver lining to be found in his circadian affliction, it was that the descent into the sadness didn't happen all at once. It wasn't as if a light switch simply shut off, leaving him paralyzed by the dark and grief.

Instead, he could feel its approach looming at the tail end of the astronomical calendar and gathering steam as the days grew short. He could see it out there, skulking at the edges of the sky, as the last flicker of flames that had lit the fiery autumnal canvas drained from the trees and his world became dipped in a tincture of gray. He could smell it coming as the lusty spice of rotting apples and molding leaves slowly gave away to the coppery tang of wet wool. The sadness encroached on tiptoes, like a spider stalking its prey, wrapping itself around him with a mummifying web of silk, insulating him from the pleasures of the world, and depositing a gnawing pit of anguish to fester like a canker in his gut.

Yeah, I know that sounds awfully bleak. In fact, it reeks of desperation. Fair enough. That last paragraph especially depends upon a somber palette to paint a dreary picture of an unsettled soul staring down the Panzer-like incursion of a troubling time. No lapis blue seas or laurel green fields here. Not even close. But I do believe Wilson would agree that this was an accurate description of the way things stood as another winter prepared to lay siege. After all, he was a realist, a member in good standing of the Empiricism SIG of the American Philosophical Association with the John Locke coffee mug and David Hume hoodie to prove it. He knew stuff. And like the experimentalists before him, he had some pretty strong ideas about *how* he came to know the stuff he knew. Consider this ...

Knowledge, Wilson surmised, is most reliably constructed through our experiences in the world. He believed that the senses are like antennae, enabling us to tune in to all the rich stimuli around us and the means by which we make *sense* of our experiences. Consequently, Wilson approached his world with a stout, unshakable, incontrovertible scientific bias. He would make observations about the world around him ("Winter is coming"); he would use those observations to generate questions ("Just how bad is this going to get?"); he would pose hypotheses that could be investigated with rigorous experimental methods ("Nope, even this expensive, imported, freshly brewed beer tastes flat"); and he would apply the very best evidence skimmed from those experiments to draw meaningful conclusions ("I'm well and truly screwed—winter is almost here"). Then, when those conclusions were kissed by the wand of imagination, they would spark new questions for further explorations and on and on it goes.

For Wilson, the *truths* that emerged from this way of thinking—from his own personal epistemology—were the highest expressions of human consciousness and understanding. And the truth was simply this: Winter was coming, and he was sad.

We live in a neighborhood of small houses, neatly parceled into quarter-acre lots in one of the suburban enclaves that propagated like buckthorn around Chicago during the Eisenhower years. The owners of these houses are a demographer's dream of diversity. There are young couples just starting out, siphoned off from the magnetic pull of the city in search of green space and ease; growing families enticed by the promise of community schools and fresh breezes off the lake for the kids; empty nesters emptying out their homes to fit their newly scaled-down lifestyles; and elderly retirees frantically trying to keep pace with the waves of blight that seemed to constantly invade their lawns, crumble their foundations, rot their window frames, and de-shingle their roofs. But despite all the different reasons they had for settling in our area and regardless of their particular station in life, the residents of our neighborhood all seem to have one thing in common when it comes to their homes: we cherish the stories they tell.

Our houses don no makeup. They are ungilded by pretension. What they lack in square footage they recoup in an affluence of charm that exudes from their resiliency, their constancy, and their grace. They sprouted like wildflowers in the rich soil and favorable conditions of postwar America, reflecting the sunny nonchalance of the moment and the dreams of their designers to fit the more modest needs of a simpler time. Ever since, they have been lovingly tended by generations of families, cultivated with scrupulous care, and have thrived like the living things they are. Although the maples have replaced the ash, which replaced the elms, which once canopied the streets with a tangled mosaic of lace, the views down Poplar Lane or Hawthorn Drive have remained otherwise unchanged for decades. Tudors still stand next to Colonials. Georgians and Cape Cods share driveways. The lawn of a ranch merges unfenced and unbroken with that of a bungalow. And the stately old Victorians that have survived since the town's settling over a century and a half ago anchor an exquisite garden that is the pride and joy of those who call our neighborhood home.

On most days then, the streets and parkways and yards of our lovely few blocks are home to a kennel of activity. Over on DeTamble, kids spill past driveways and out into the street like excited particles skyrocketing in space. The small park at the corner of Forest and Lincoln is the turf of the tribe of the neighborhood's young moms, trading mysteries and quiet desires while keeping a watchful eye on their toddlers. Runners stretch and make their way to the trails. Bikers and skateboarders zoom by in small wolf packs. Others are tackling chores—raking, mowing, planting, painting, fixing, washing—burdened or not by the work of keeping disorder at bay. And some, alone or in pairs, simply walk the allees and avenues just to take in the air and the cadence of the stir. I belong to that last group. I'm a walker, and during my thirty years in the area, I have covered a lot of ground. It's one of the things I love best about living where we do. There is a bit of magic brewing in the chance and happenstance that occasions an encounter on these walks, casting spells of possibility on us all, and it leaves behind a faint but unmistakable trace of the bonhomie of belonging. Walking is how I got to know Wilson Lacy.

The truth is I had seen Wilson around town for many years before actually getting to know him. He was a hard figure to miss, tearing up and down the lakefront boulevards in his sleek, midcentury sports car. I'd often spy him at work in his garage, tucked into the setback of his property, during my walks. The times when our paths would cross—him on his way to mail a letter, me picking up some items at Waltons—we'd nod or attempt an awkward wave, and maybe trade a few words, complicit in nothing more than sharing the same street and similar ages, and at least on my part, a warm coal of curiosity about the other guy. But for a long while, that's where we stood; our relationship could go no further, hamstrung as we were by the strict rules that guide the courtship of neighbors as dictated by the laws of social custom.

These rules had been revealed to me over time, seeded by careful observation and validated by numerous trials conducted over the course of a lot of long walks around town. They outline a series of stages—I like to think of it as a trajectory—that defines the widely accepted norms and expectations of neighborly engagements. The trajectory goes something like this: Upon completion of several random encounters with the same neighbor, eye contact between two individuals is permitted. Eventually, if acknowledged by both parties through silent displays of mutualism, the pair may begin the perfunctory exchange of small greetings *but only while still in passing motion* ("Hey, what's up?"). This is known as stage 1. Any further progress along the continuum depends on the habituation of such greetings over a significant period of time, and a favorable chemistry of companionability, the precise molecular structure of which eludes me still, though I know it when I feel it. And I bet you do too.

With those preconditions met, the participants may then advance to stage 2. Now, upon meeting, the two parties are free to suspend their nonrelational activities (walking, pruning, etc.) in order to exchange more complete sentences ("Hey, did you watch that Packers game on Sunday? That Rodgers, huh?"). With repeated exposures, these proto-conversations may slowly begin to reveal details of increasingly intimate nature. Each revelation paves the way for the next, more personal ones as the tenuous bond between the two neighbors strengthens and solidifies.

This second stage of the trajectory can be persistent as it entails several gradations of growing affinity. And it is often chronic. This is where most neighborly relationships plateau since, thus far, the necessary encounters that drive the trajectory have been conducted only on the dance floor of fate. A chance lapse in meeting due to a change of schedule or illness often implies a regression back to stage 1 and the long Sisyphean march through the chutes and ladders maze of sociability. Stage 2 can be a pleasant place for neighbors to be, a comfortable way station that carries no liability of interpersonal messiness, entanglement, or fatigue. Up to this point however—*and this is critical*—there has yet to be the interjection of intention (i.e., intention of action), the volatile catalyst that is essential for advancement to the third and final stage. Once introduced, it sparks a combustible reaction out of which a true friendship may synthesize from the ether of chance.

Wilson and I had been following this trajectory for years. In the months leading up to that winter, we were contentedly mired in an advanced phase of stage 2. I knew, for instance, that he lived alone, though I suspected he had, until recently, been married. He loosely referenced a couple of kids who were successful, grown, and gone. I knew he was newly retired from a job doing something in science and that he liked sports but, for reasons I never really understood, he absolutely despised the hometown Cubs.

"The fury of a thousand burning suns is nothing compared to how much I detest those goddamn Cubs."

Pure Wilson.

He had an engineer's understanding of the way things worked and a mechanic's knack for fixing them when they didn't. That sports car of his (a 1959 MGA twin-cam roadster, I now know) is a testament to his considerable skills. On most topics, he spoke freely and openly and listened with a generous ear. Whenever I saw him, there was usually a smudge of grease or paint or oil that stained his clothes or the roughly chewed tips of his fingers, a well-worn tool of some kind fidgeting in his hand, and a slight insistence to his stance as if he could never quit thinking about whatever problem he was working on and was anxious to get back to it. I enjoyed our conversations and suspected he did too, and I believe we would have called each other friends. And I often noticed something else whenever we spoke; there was a peculiar quiet that sometimes filled the spaces between his words, like an eclipsing shadow that concealed the things unsaid. Even in the beginning, that shadow was often there. It would loom like overcast to cloud his gaze and tear him adrift in the middle of a thought. There was a touch of sadness about those quiet spaces that often left me hollow. It could spark a mournfulness that lingered in me long after our small talks had ended.

The trajectory stipulates that every relationship needs a catalyst in order to grow: an act of willful, deliberate, calculated intention designed to alter the conditions necessary for a reaction to proceed. That's just the way it works. *Our* catalyst—the one that signals the start of *this* story—was introduced in the fall of Wilson's sixty-second year, on an absolutely gorgeous day in mid-October when winter was nothing more than a rumor whispering in the cooling breeze. Sure, every once in a while there would be a tremor of menace to remind you which direction the seasons were heading, the way the wind mercilessly incised the leaves from their branches and the Rorschach-like patterns of frost, guillotine edged, that lay stenciled on car windshields in the morning. But on that particularly magnificent day, when the light from the sun still radiated enough warmth to inflame the soul and the sky dripped puddles of blue from the infinity pool of sapphires above, winter was safely encamped, hundreds of miles away, gathering strength, preparing its assault. It was time to up the ante. And so, impelled by the force of an obscure intention and awash in the allure of such a perfect day, I turned away from my regular route, taking instead the path of flagstone steps that led up the driveway, toward that open and floodlit garage, straight into stage 3 and the heart of Wilson Lacy's sadness.

Chapter

2

The first thing that hit me was the smell—
though really, in hindsight, that sounds a
bit lame. After all, this was no aerial blend
of wispy scents. There was no tender caress.
This was a lead fist of stench that enveloped
the garage with venomous smog. It would
take the sophisticated nose of a world-class
aromachologist to fully decant the range of
tones that pummeled my senses. There was
gasoline and motor oil to be sure. But lying just   beneath   was
an assemblage of more minor notes: phenols of carburetor cleaner
in aerosol form, astringents of lacquer-based paint, the oaky
nuttiness of metal polish paired nicely with the fat, flamboyant
brightness of WD-40 and other penetrating fluids, esters of beer,
and underlying it all, a slight yeasty finish of sweat. My first
instinct was to scan the area for sources of open flame that might
ignite this unstable cloud. But just as that threat had been safely
retired, my balance returned, and with it came a rogue wave of
nostalgia. Smell-induced memories are fragile things. They can
bend time just enough to displace the present with a chimera of
the past. For just a moment, in the brief few seconds that it took
for that wave to crest, walking into Wilson's garage was like
stepping back in time, back to the garages and service stations
and workshops of my youth where the air was laden with the
same perfume and mechanical things were fixed by the laying

on of hands and the careful application of experience, instinct, and intuition.

The garage was ablaze with light. A combination of fluorescent fixtures suspended from the ceiling and several halogen towers chased away the shadow scraps from every ledge, nook, and cranny. The entire interior volume was rinsed with a crisp, natural brilliance. In fact, I could discern no difference in moving from the sunlit area outside the garage to the artificially lit area inside. I even proceeded to test this illusion several times—stepping in, stepping out, stepping in, stepping out—and was befuddled on every attempt by a perfectly seamless transition of light with each border crossing. Incredible.

Still, my befuddlement grew as I continued to look around. Wilson had somehow achieved an odd geometric anomaly that had the effect of making the space inside the garage appear far larger than what I had expected on my approach. It was baffling. The only way I could reconcile this visual quirk was to attribute it to the colossal collection of stuff that was improbably crammed within and the solicitous way it all contended for the favor of my eye. Where to begin?

The MGA stood centerstage, held aloft at the moment by jack stands with all four wheels removed. Several other large projects of indeterminate origin were scattered around. Some were partially covered in cloths with only their outlines to hint at their genus. Others were immodestly bare, splayed like disemboweled cadavers in a ghoulish lab patiently awaiting resurrection. There were tools everywhere: hanging on pegs, carpeting the floor, stowed in open cabinets, and others, momentarily at rest atop any horizontal surface that would hold them. Books and manuals, some opened to pages that were heavily marked, several with covers that were grease stained and worn, lay scattered across a workbench. Parts in various states of assembly or disassembly, supplies in asymmetrical containers—bottles, boxes, jars, tubes, and cans—and a thousand other unidentifiable oddments filled the gaps and lent the space an exquisite veneer of chaos and disorder. The low-frequency hum from the lights and the wheeze of a moribund fan were no match for side two of *Let it Bleed*, which came in booming from an unspied source. And the walls. Oh my god, the walls.

The garage was constructed of concrete cinder blocks, but those walls were covered with so much ephemera—posters, photographs, diagrams, banners, signs—that not even a dusting of gray could show through. Clearly, the long, hard slog of evolution was at work here. It must have taken decades for the garage to arrive in this state, time enough for layer upon layer of mechanical sediment to be deposited in strata like some wondrous geological formation. It was mesmerizing.

I wanted nothing more than to simply stand there and take in my fill of this sensory jambalaya when Mick and the boys ("If you try some time, you just might find …") resuscitated my focus and restored my intent in coming up the driveway. Stage 3. Yet despite the obvious signs of activity, Wilson was nowhere to be found. After one more look, I resolved myself to the reality of a failed first attempt and the resumption of my daily walk. But hold on. Not so fast. We're only on chapter 2. Because sure enough, just as I was leaving, the squeal of tired metal casters pinged across the room, and an old hardwood creeper scrabbled out on crab legs from under the car.

"Hello? Who's there? Oh, hey Owen … is that you?" He was wearing the kind of magnifiers favored by watchmakers for close, detail work. They made his eyes look like koi.

"Hey there, Wilson. How's it going?" I replied, swaying from side to side to stay within his wobbling line of sight. "I was just walking by and saw your lights on. Thought I'd stop by. I hope that was okay. Holy cow, man. This is some garage!"

Despite the thick lenses that still covered his eyes, Wilson scanned the garage from wall to wall as if he too were taking it all in for the very first time, or perhaps straining to see it through another person's eyes. "Yeah, I guess it just kind of grew up around me over the years. The den of a crazy man, I suppose."

Cautiously, he lifted his long, stringy frame from the ancient creeper and exhaled with the relief of being vertical again. Then he removed the magnifiers and was now better able to home in on my location. Without the goggles, I could see that his face was streaked with greasy black smears as if he was getting ready for a night game under the bright lights at Wrigley. I pictured him wearing that war paint for the remainder of the day, never even noticing it was there until he caught his reflection in the nighttime mirror. And maybe it was the contrast with that dark, smudgy tar, but I saw something else in his eyes that I had never seen before; they shimmered like wave caps in the late afternoon sun, catching the glint of the overhead lights and reflecting it outward in all directions. Their sparkle was drawn, I assumed, from the sheer joy of doing a thing he truly enjoyed. I wondered if that too would be something he'd notice later on, at day's end, in his reflection held by the nighttime mirror.

He pulled a dirty rag from the pocket of his overalls and managed to remove a layer or two of grime from his hands. He then proceeded to describe what he was working on under the car, something having to do with the brakes, which, he confessed, were never much more than a rumor. At first, he spoke rapidly, without taking a breath, as if he were finally free to voice a long-repressed plea, but a timer was callously counting down. He told me that the brake pedal felt mushy on his last outing and that any confidence he had in the car's stopping power was slowly leaking away along with the hydraulic fluid he was endeavoring to replace. All this was apparently part of his efforts to keep the car running in top form for what he said was the heart of the driving season, the last few weeks of autumn when the cool days and more open roads were exactly what the MG craved.

"There really are only three or four weeks of good driving left," he estimated. "Then I'll have to retire the car for the season. So, I'm thinking I better do whatever I can to get the most out of the time that remains."

As he was talking, I noticed that a new disc had yet to be cued up in the player. In the small space of silence left by the Stones, a refrigerator cycled on over in a corner. I suppose it was the unit's activation that caused the lights in the garage to flicker as they struggled to keep up with the voltage drain. Whether it was the shadow of that flicker or something else entirely, I'm not exactly sure. But it seemed as though the candescence of Wilson's eyes also dimmed, just a bit and just for a moment in communion with the lights, as if their voltage too was diminished by some equivalent system drain.

"You know, really, to be honest, the brakes were probably fine," he quietly admitted while running a hand over the curve of a fender. The words sounded remote and detached like they were worn from a great journey, and I wondered if they were really intended for me. "Sometimes I just take these things on to keep myself busy, maybe chew up another day and get my hands dirty. It's something to do, I guess."

He then walked over to the workbench and started rummaging through a box of CDs. For just an instant—probably no more than a heartbeat or two—I had the ticklish feeling of being forgotten or left behind somehow, as if my presence beside him had slipped from his mind. Only once a new disc was selected and the garage again filled with sound, did Wilson's distraction subside.

"Oh, yeah, right. Are you a beer drinker, Owen?" he then asked more brightly.

Let it be noted that one of the accepted codicils amending the rules of neighborhood courtship allows for the introduction of beer as a class 1A lubricant for greasing the often-precipitous transition between stages 2 and 3 of the trajectory. Its utility lies less in the effect of the alcohol to uncouple inhibitions (though those benefits should not be overlooked) but rather in providing a tangible totem to hold attention when the delicate threads of conversation begin to fray; in such times, it's always good to have a beer in hand. In any case, I gladly replied that yes, I did indeed drink beer.

Two summer ales were pulled from the same small fridge and deftly opened with the flick of a screwdriver, a neat trick that must have required hours of practice to perfect. We then stood around for a few minutes without saying much, clutching to the longnecks like buoys. But there was nothing to indicate that either one of us considered the interlude as anything awkward. There seemed to be no rush to fill the silence between us. Instead, it just felt like a quiet moment of simply savoring the taste of a really good beer, one that blossomed with the effervescence of high summer and trailed an aftertaste that was tinged with the slightly sad sorrow that such an ale, just like summer itself, was at the tail end of its run. I know that's how it was for me.

Anxious to hear more about the garage, I asked Wilson for a tour and some of the backstory on how this all came to be. He told me that the car came to him from the estate of a distant uncle in upstate New York with whom he stayed for a few summers back when he was a young boy. Apparently, at the start of every summer, the uncle would create a to-do list of repairs that the two of them would tackle together. No job was too big or too small to wind up on the list. If the work on the car was completed—and he assured me it always was—they would reward themselves with a road trip to take in the races at Watkins Glen. It sounded like a pretty great way for a kid to spend his summers. Sadly though, Wilson's visits to the uncle ended as abruptly as they began, and while the closeness between them lasted only for the duration of those brief summers, it left a lasting impression on them both. He never did see the uncle again, an admission that was freighted with a heavy dose of remorse and remained stubbornly indifferent to the shock of learning, many years later, soon after the uncle's passing, that the car not only had survived but was to be his.

The MG arrived in Wilson's garage nearly twenty years ago as a complete, but nonrunning car having sat in that upstate New York shed, unused and untouched for more than a decade. So too, it sat in Wilson's garage for a couple of years more before he began the recommissioning work. Eighteen months later, he had coaxed it back to life, though it continues to exact constant attention in order to maintain turnkey reliability. The records of this vigilance were displayed to me in the form of a thick file of paperwork on the car—receipts and running notes and other documentation, registrations, photographs, parts brochures, and even the car's original build sheet—all neatly organized in a massive binder.

Sorted separately in one of the binder's pockets was that bundle of to-do lists that prescribed each year's maintenance tasks, a practice passed down from master to apprentice. They were ordered chronologically with the 2015 list on top. Thumbing through that bundle was archival. It read like a canticle of time. Except for the gap from that period of dormancy, they stretched all the way back to 1959. But it was the lists that were dated from 1968 to 1971 that most drew my attention. Of the entire set, only these four included a small box, hand drawn at the bottom in heavy black marker. A dotted line ran inside each box with a caption that read: "Work completed by ..." Though the signature on those lines was clearly that of a child and had mostly faded away, there was no mistaking its provenance; they each bore the autograph of Wilson H. Lacy.

"I found those in the trunk when I began redoing the car," he said, buying a moment and clearing his throat with a swig of beer. "They still carry the smell of that sweet old shed. For a while, it felt like there was nothing we wouldn't tackle, nothing we couldn't do to keep this car running. We were fearless back then." He sighed deeply and scratched his head as the memory of those days seemed to stir something inside him. "You know," he then added a little reluctantly while returning the lists to the binder, "someone once told me that these old cars are about as close to time machines as we're ever likely to get. Nothing could be truer in my estimation."

The other projects in the garage turned out to be a small collection of antique motorcycles in varying states of decay, the balance of the uncle's bequest. Wilson had no memory of ever seeing these in the shed during his summers in New York, and they arrived in his driveway with no clues whatsoever as to his uncle's motives for acquiring them, their history, or his intentions for them. To this day, they wear a shroud of mystery as well as tattered drop cloths to keep the mice away. They stand—or more accurately, they lean—in queue, awaiting Wilson's attention. He had been steadily accumulating the parts he figures he will need for the restorations, ticking them off one by one from the detailed inventory hanging alongside the workbench.

He showed me some old magnetos he discovered in Austria and had already rebuilt, rare headlights sourced from a guy in Spain, as large as dinner plates with tiny silver medallions emblazoned in the shell, and carburetors of fantastic design that looked like they were hatched from the dreams of a steampunk artist, all exceedingly rare finds prospected like gold from around the world, each essential to the work that lay ahead.

"So tell me," I asked while inspecting an eighty-year-old gearbox that looked as good as new. "How did you ever get to be such an expert with these things? It all seems like voodoo to me."

"Well, Owen," he began through the small flecks of a smile, "just as soon as I get anywhere near the neighborhood of expertise, I'll be sure to let you know." And then, after downing the last of his beer, he modestly deferred to his uncle. "Now he was a real expert. He believed that anyone could go out and buy some new part or take something to a specialist and have it fixed. But fixing things is a whole lot different from restoring them, from safeguarding their spirit and preserving their souls. That sort of work is a completely different kind of endeavor. It doesn't come so easily. Or so surely, I'm afraid."

While we waited for the heft of those words to settle, Wilson put his beer bottle down and gazed off vacantly to the side. I watched his eyes glaze over with an invisible film, making it seem like he was looking at nothing at all. Instead, I felt him drifting away as he rode a deep-water current back to those languorous summers in upstate New York, to those times when there was nothing to fear and when every problem came with a straightforward solution. It was from the impressions left by that long-ago time that he then finally added, "He used to tell me that to be any good at restoring things, I would need two important qualities. The first, he said, was courage, the courage just to dig in and try no matter how complicated or impossible or daunting something might seem, to let go of the worry of making a mistake. And the second was compassion, to be able to forgive the machine—and myself—when I do. Seems like pretty good advice, don't you think?"

Do you remember those books of stereogram images that were popular years ago? For a while, you'd see them everywhere. Magic Eye books, I think they were called. I suppose it's my background as a visual artist, but I just loved those books. We would stare at them for hours, our eyes glued to the pages of colorful, two-dimensional designs desperately hoping to unlock the surprise that everyone was talking about. They'd whisper advice, "Try squinting a little more." "Keep at it, it'll happen," they promised. And then there was that moment, maybe you know the one, when you would tilt your head a certain way or adopt a peculiar kind of angle to your gaze, and then suddenly—*yow*! That very same image you had been staring at was completely transformed. It awoke from its slumber as if enchanted by some optical sorcery and a riot of three-dimensional grandeur leapt from the page. At first you didn't know it, but that grandeur lay hidden behind the chaotic and disordered patterns in the book. Only once unveiled did you realize that it had been there all along; you just needed to know how to look.

In much the same way, my perception of Wilson's garage was undergoing an equally remarkable transformation. Gone was the sense of befuddlement that first ambushed me at the door. I could feel that melting clean away. In its place was a new sensation, a new aesthetic enabled by a different way of looking. I was beginning to see the garage through the eyes of a fabulist—or an ethnographer—whose view of things, thanks to a proper tilt of the head or special sort of squint, allows him to piece together an authentic human story from the discordant terrain in front of him, even while some of the elements of that story remain hidden behind chaos and disorder and even sadness, patiently waiting for his wits to grow sharper.

By then, the beers were long gone as was the hint of summer they carried, evaporated into space like a flimsy illusion. Neither one of us alluded to another. Instead, we exchanged that silent acknowledgement of guises that passes between friends to signal that it was probably time to move on. I figured Wilson wanted to get back under the car to see about those brakes, and I knew that Janey was likely wondering what happened to me on my walk. I left my bottle on top of the fridge, thanked him for the tour, and began to make my way out.

"Hey, Owen," I heard him holler just as I was leaving. His voice cast dark shades of doubt to every corner of the garage as if a vague force inside him was compelling the words that followed. And though their glaze had mostly receded, his eyes stayed anchored to the wrench he spun in his hands. "If all goes well, I ought to have this job buttoned up by tomorrow. I don't know if you'd even be interested, but if you ever want to go for a drive, maybe just let me know—now that you know where to find me."

I said that sounded terrific, confessing I'd like nothing more than a ride in his time machine and that I would definitely take him up on the offer. "And hey," I suggested while lagging in the doorway, "maybe we'll stop somewhere along the way so I can pay you back for that beer and even get something to eat."

"Um, yeah, sure," he replied without much conviction. "Maybe we could do that too."

And there it was. Boom. Done. Stage 3.

I remember a lot about my walk home from Wilson's garage on that October afternoon, but I recall no portents of sorrow, nothing to foreshadow the anchors of gloom that might weigh down an old man, or any harbinger of the sadness that I would soon get to know so well. That sadness, like winter, was still a ways off. What I do remember is the streets teeming with activity as skeletons were hung and ghosts were strung, as witches were nailed to trees and pumpkins bristled with bees, as lawns were raked in a race against time, as pint-sized Bradys and Mannings ran plays conceived in the dirt, and as young parents safely guided their kids on bikes and scooters and strollers through the lush maze of it all.

I remember that as I approached my house, I saw Janey getting the grill lit for what we had planned as a late-season barbeque on the back porch, a beer of her own in hand. I remember noticing that the boundless autumnal skies that greeted the day had surrendered their turf to carpet rolls of gray that made everything feel just a bit more squeezed, a bit more pinched, and a bit more fraught than when my walk began. I remember that the wind picked up as I turned down my drive, scissoring through my shirt, and I thought I could almost smell snow. And I remember too that for the first time that fall, I felt cold.

Chapter

I used to go to these meetings. In the beginning, after my world fell apart, I used to go all the time. But I've recently cut back. I like to think of that as a sign of progress. It's no exaggeration to say that these meetings were my salvation. So, before going any further with the story of Wilson and the winter that loomed, allow me to set the scene of this particular November meeting. It may seem like a glaring departure but it's not.   It's important. Trust me on this.

I am sitting in an old classroom in the basement of a local church. Folding tables are off to the side and hold store bought cookies sealed in cellophane wrappers. An ancient coffee machine—a percolator—stands beside a tower of paper cups and bleeds a bitter aroma. Tiles of yellow linoleum, cracked and embedded with grit, scratch underfoot and the concrete walls perspire. You get the idea. There are twenty people seated in plastic chairs. It would be difficult for an outsider to tell what we all have in common or what brings us together to this nondescript room. Bill, in his mid fifties and greying in loose fitting clothes, is the only one wearing a nametag. And sandals in the middle of November. The clipboard he carries is splintered along the edges and plastered with stickers. He is leading the group through some opening remarks.

"And lastly, our annual Thanksgiving pot luck over at Orrington House will be on the 20th at 4:30. We're asking everyone to bring a dish or two to share with the folks in the shelter and any warm clothing you may be able to donate. I'll be sending out a reminder to your emails in the next day or two. If you could get back to me right away, that would be great. We're hoping for a strong turnout again, so please people, do what you can to make it.

"Right, that covers tonight's announcements. We'll hold off on questions for now but, as always, I'll stick around for a while afterwards. If anyone would like to talk with me about something privately, I'll be here. Just let me know. Okay, good, so as you can see from your agenda, Owen is our scheduled share tonight. So without any further delay—Owen, you're up."

Sure, it's true, I had done this before. Several times in fact. It's the way the group runs. The plainspoken share is an essential part of the survivor's therapy. But that didn't make what was about to happen any easier. It will never be easy. It's not *supposed* to be easy. Bill tells us that all the time. As usual, I tried to hide my discomfort as I made my way to the front of the room. Those steps seem to take forever. Everyone knew how hard this would be. I'm sure they all saw the strain on my face. But that's okay. They had all been there themselves at one time or another. And would be again.

"Yup, okay, thanks Bill. Hi everyone. It's nice to see you all again and, just for the record, my name is Owen Conway, and this is my forty-third SOS support group meeting and my ninth time sharing."

"Hi, Owen."

"Ha! Yeah, hi. I thought I'd start with a quick update if that's okay. So, things have been going pretty well lately. Generally speaking, I guess. I've been able to dig in a little more at work over the past couple of months. I've even surprised myself by coming up with a few decent layouts for some new accounts. So that's good. It's nice to feel like maybe I'm contributing again. Not just going through the motions. And sometimes, just lately, I even lose myself in the work like before. Now I don't know whether that's a good thing or a bad thing, though from what I hear from some of you, it's a pretty normal thing. My colleagues have been great. Some still tiptoe around me, but I can't really blame them for that. Everybody there continues to be supportive, and for that, I really am grateful.

"Janey seems to be doing okay. I'm not sure how she manages, but she has always been the stronger one of us, so maybe I shouldn't be too surprised. I do see her struggling every once in a while, trying to keep everything together, and that kind of concerns me, but here we are, about a year and a half later, and I think that's mostly because of how tough she is. She's also working full-time even though I still think it would have been better to keep the shorter hours and take some more time for herself. I don't know. I think she'd agree that the really bad days are rarer now than they used to be, and our routines feel a little less excruciating. These all seem like good things, right? And we're still there too, still together. I know that a lot of couples fall apart, and I totally get that, but whatever we had before seems more or less intact and keeping us together and for that too I am truly grateful.

"Let's see. What else, what else. The girls are all settled in up at Madison. I find it hard to believe that the end of the semester is already in sight, but that's what they tell me. They're both busy with classes and friends and living the college dream, which is wonderful, I suppose, but I do miss them an awful lot. We just found out that they won't be coming in for Thanksgiving, so we won't get to see them until winter break. Janey and I feel lucky that they're there together. They really do seem to take care of each other, and that's as much as we could ever hope for. I guess for me that's the hardest part of all this. It's that moment of walking into the house on nights when Janey is working and Hannah and Sara are gone. I walk in, and it's so quiet and cold in there. It makes me feel tired, dead tired and worn out, like I'm always a little behind or a little late or ... just slow. That's it—like I'm slow. My limbs feel like wet clay, and the world is moving by at its usual pace, but it just seems so fast I can't ever catch up, and the faster it all goes, the harder it is for me to hold on, and I think maybe I should let go, I mean really just let go and finally be done, and that feeling can be very hard to shake off. How the hell can the world keep spinning?

"Look, the way I've been thinking about it lately is that the light in our lives is dimmer now than it was before. That's just a fact about which I can do no goddamn thing. It just is. Everything is a little darker, a little colder, and a little harder than it used to be, and we are all still adjusting to that as best as we can. And yes, Ethan, I am still walking—as often as possible, thank you very much.

"So, I know that look from Bill; that's the look that means it's probably time to get on with my share. Okay. I'm ready. I'm sure this comes as no surprise to the regulars, but I chose to bring another photograph for my share tonight. For the new folks in the room, let me start by saying that over the last year or so, I have found some comfort in the stacks of old photographs we have collected as a family.

"Of course, I'm always thinking about how that sounds. Some people might find that kind of morbid—a grieving guy in a dark room staring at old photographs of a better time, maybe some Joni Mitchell playing in the background. Yeah, I get it, but it's really not like that at all. I've always been a very visual person. I tend to understand things by seeing things, and I've noticed lately that the way I look at these old pictures is different now from the way it used to be. It's changed in some way, like I'm able to see things in these photos that I never noticed before. It's like if I stare at a photo long enough, all sorts of new thoughts about the moment in which the picture was taken just bubble up in my mind. It's pretty amazing. And when I do this, I often find something new, some new meaning in that photograph that lets me think about that moment a little differently.

"It reminds me of something that an old professor of mine once said in a design class I took in college. I'm paraphrasing here but it went sort of like this: 'Visual images are embedded with layers of meaning. Uncovering that meaning often requires a different way of looking; one may stare vacantly at an image and find that the elusive threads tangled deep below begin to disengage themselves and find their way to consciousness.'

"That's the goal! I guess that's exactly what I'm trying to do with these pictures. I stare at them vacantly—such a perfect word—and then I just let come what will. Impressions. Reflections. Questions. Whatever. I find that some of these photos speak more loudly than they used to. In fact, the more I look, the more I hear, and when I allow myself to really listen, what I discover is often very revealing. It helps me cope with everything that has happened.

"So anyways, here's my photo for tonight. I'll pass it around. This picture was taken maybe ten years ago? The girls are about eight or nine, and Aaron would have been around twelve. We're all outside on some fall day, and it looks to me like we must have been doing a bit of yard work. You can see the piles of leaves on the grass and the rakes leaning against the house. I think Halloween must have been a week or two away from the look of the pumpkins on the steps. I love the colors in this picture; everyone is wrapped in a different shade, and the leaves—look at the leaves—stuck to their sleeves and hoods and their hair. Just beautiful. It's just a simple picture of an ordinary family outside their home on a random Saturday in October. We're not on a beach in the Caribbean. We're not tracking lions on safari in Africa. We're not standing on top of the Eifel Tower and looking down at the lights of Paris. It's not a graduation, or a birthday, or an anniversary, or any kind of celebration or event. There is absolutely nothing special about this picture at all, and that is precisely what makes it so damn special now. A sweet, normal, unassuming day in what was supposed to be a lifetime of such days in the story of our small family.

"I don't really remember the moment, but I do remember those times. I can imagine that we were probably getting ready to go inside, feeling in our bones that delicious kind of fatigue that comes from doing work outdoors. God, I used to love that feeling.

I know that, no matter how tired we might have felt, the house would soon be lit up; it would be bursting with life and noise and light and motion. I can hear the sounds of the TV mixing with music from CDs. I can hear laughter and trash talk over the life and death battles of some video game.

"We'd carelessly bump into each other as we wove our way through the house—colliding like billiard balls—and hanging over it all would be the smell of Janey's cooking sifting through the air and holding us together as the sun went down. Nothing but normal. A simple slice of life. We'd eat with wolfish appetites and Janey and I would finish our wine at the table as the kids rushed off to who knows where. A little later we'd all head down to the basement, into that dark, hushed room, the girls in pajamas with stuffed animals in their hands, smelling sweetly of bath soap and shampoo, Aaron in his sweats, for a family movie night, and we'd huddle together on the couch with blankets and pillows for warmth and comfort but for something else too, and when that was over, we'd sleep, the five of us, all cradled under the same roof and the house would sigh with relief all night long. Truly nothing special, just an ordinary day captured in an ordinary photo—one of hundreds—sitting forgotten and neglected at the bottom of a drawer, humdrum and mundane, undeserving of a second look. And yet I can't stop looking at it.

"I can't stop looking at Aaron in this picture, and I can't stop wondering what was going on in his mind as this most ordinary day unfolded and as this particularly ordinary moment was frozen forever. I can't stop looking at his eyes and the way they're focused just a bit off-center from the camera, though everyone else has their eyes fixed right on the lens, almost as if he was tuning in on another frequency from the rest of us and maybe never even heard me count down for the snapshot, or at least didn't hear me call out like the others did. I guess he was always like that, both part of us and apart from us all at the same time. Janey and I used to think of that as the core of his peculiar charm, a touch of dreaminess that we thought was sure to be a sign of his creativity, really of his greatness we knew would come, and we prayed he'd never outgrow it.

"But now I don't know. Now I'm not so sure. Maybe it was something else, something we should have thought about more deeply or more clearly or differently or—I don't know—paid more attention to before things starting getting bad. And yeah—I know, I know—that's the devil's hindsight talking, but this picture makes me wonder whether he ever felt the peace and refuge and comfort, the safe mooring, that comes from the ordinariness of an ordinary day in October, and if he couldn't feel it then, how likely is it that he ever did any time after, and just how utterly sad that is.

"I don't know. I really don't. But here's what I do know. I know that on this day, at the moment when this picture was taken, he was loved as much as a son and a brother ever could be loved. He was adored by his mother, cherished by his father, and worshipped by his sisters. He had to feel that ... that love had to have gotten through even as he drifts off here and then later as he drifted away from the rest of us. I look at his face in this picture, the loose, easy way he's standing, and I know that he felt it. I can see it in his smile, it's right there, and I like to believe I can still feel it in the way we hugged good night on that ordinary night in October. He always gave the best hugs, and I know that despite the torments or storms or misery he was about to go through, that love had to be there inside him, even then, and it had to shed at least a little light and maybe a little comfort in his times of darkness, right? I just know it. It had to. Right?"

Silence.

It's always like that at the end of a share. Absolute silence. For me, that's the worst part. I don't know if it's out of respect or something that hides even deeper, but I always find the silence a little troubling, a little difficult to bear. It feels so poignant somehow. Theatrical almost. There's just too much empty space to think. So I quickly moved to wrap things up and return to the safe haven of my seat in the back.

"Well, anyways, there it is. Another short thesis about the power of photographs and how even the most ordinary image—when you really look at it—can disengage the threads tangled below. And, hey, thanks again for listening. I know we all know how valuable this sharing is but for what it's worth, it bears repeating. I could never be here like this without the support of everyone here. So, really. Thank you for that. I truly appreciate it."

It was several hours later when I finally got home. There are some things I always must do after I share—things that have to be done if I'm ever going to get any sleep. That evening, the streets were dead quiet. Nothing moved in the black, crystalline air. The velveteen dark. Tinsels of light glistened above while a full moon ladled a lustrous glow that spilled onto the sidewalk and paved the way home. My footsteps felt heavy, not with fatigue, though the walk had been long, but something like contrition, its source as secret as the night.

Once inside, I was greeted by the same darkness, the same silence, and the very same cold that I had worked so hard to avoid. But they were there nonetheless. Before replacing the photograph in its drawer, I held it again to my lips, just briefly, but long enough for something inside me to come undone. Upstairs, as I undressed, I couldn't help but notice all the ways my body continues to betray me, with its aches and sounds and slack. I crawled into bed and curled up close next to Janey. The warmth of her body soothed my own, and I felt myself relax for the first time that day. She woke slightly, just enough to drape an arm around me and feel the wetness of my tears on her shoulder.

Chapter

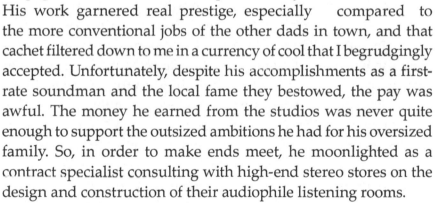

Leland (aka "Con Man") Conway was an audio engineer by trade who handled the recording and mixing responsibilities at two well-known studios during the sixties and seventies. He was highly sought after for his precision in the control room, and his balanced ear is said to have left a lasting impression that can still be heard in the deep grooves of some semi-important vinyl. His work garnered real prestige, especially compared to the more conventional jobs of the other dads in town, and that cachet filtered down to me in a currency of cool that I begrudgingly accepted. Unfortunately, despite his accomplishments as a first-rate soundman and the local fame they bestowed, the pay was awful. The money he earned from the studios was never quite enough to support the outsized ambitions he had for his oversized family. So, in order to make ends meet, he moonlighted as a contract specialist consulting with high-end stereo stores on the design and construction of their audiophile listening rooms.

For a while during high school, my brothers and I would accompany him on his trips to these stores and help him take the detailed measurements as a first step in the design process. We would listen as he talked with storeowners about reverberant spaces and Helmholtz-type resonators, how to minimize resonance and maximize scattering diffusion, and how subtle changes to the textile surfaces of the room would optimize the acoustic field to create a soundstage of sound that would leave the customer in a state of aural awe—and nicely tenderized for the closing sales pitch. And most passionately of all, he churched us on the egregiousness of confusing hearing with listening, a sermon for the blasphemous that he evangelized like the Holy Gospel to his congregation of children and clients alike. So, it was with a touch of filial tenderness that I caught myself listening to the sibilant fizz of the radiator as I sat in a state of unproductive dreaminess, adrift in my small home office on a dreary Saturday in November, doodling out the sound's reverberation signature all over the incomplete—and soon to be overdue—layout drafts in front of me.

My studio is tucked inside the third-floor dormer of our old house. Thanks to some weird acoustical imaging and questionable construction practices, it has become the ideal place to listen to the fusion of sounds that heralds the change of seasons. With my eyes closed, I can easily identify the sustained glissando of the radiator's hiss as hot water moves through serpentine lengths of cast-iron pipe. There too, in the foreground, is the crescendo of loose storm windows banging angrily against their frames in a gusty, atonal beat. The pizzicato pops and chirps of building materials thermally expanding and contracting at different rates stands in harmonic dissonance to the *whoosh* of induction as boiler pumps turn on and off with a brooding rhythm. It plays like a requiem to the farewell of summer, an ode to winter's arrival. The sounds are hypnotic, and they induce a lazy haze to my afternoon that my neighbors, in their more modern homes built of twenty-first-century materials and laser-tight tolerances, never get to hear. For more than a moment, they lulled me away from the exigencies of work and set me to wondering what phonic witchery the Con Man might have wrought with all this wonderful noise.

But the changing seasons brought more than just a range of new sounds. The dwindling daylight also forced me to cut back on my walks around town. The times when I did get out, it was easy to tell which way the wind was blowing. The evidence teemed. There was a bold starkness to the landscape now, as if

Mother Nature had been rudely stripped of her frippery. The trees had long shed their soft summer finery and a skeletal armature had been exposed with a peekaboo immodesty. I always imagine that the sudden denuding would be a little embarrassing to the neighborhood flora, but apparently, it's not. Instead, it's almost as if the trees are saying, "Go ahead. Look all you want, fella. That's it, baby. Take a good long look. This is how it's gonna be for a while, so get used to it. It's November, and you might as well buckle up. Spring is a long way off."

That drive with Wilson never did materialize. I'm not exactly sure why. I suppose it had something to do with the clay feet of inertia. The few times that I would walk by his house, ruffled with the intention of shoring up the amity of before, the garage was always shuttered, and I just wasn't sure we were far enough along in stage 3 to hazard a knock on the door.

With each passing day, that knock seemed more and more implausible. I could feel the link we had begun to form—as well as any prospect for that ride—rusting away as autumn waned. But at the time, I was dealing with a few challenges that had hijacked my attention. My boss read my return to full-time status as an all clear to reboot my workload. And Janey and I found ourselves clinging to each other with grave desperation as the shadow of a shared darkness continued to seep through the cracks of our composure. At times, the exhilaration of that October afternoon in Wilson's garage seemed like nothing more than a ghost memory.

So there I was, sitting in my studio, mindlessly sketching sound patterns and contemplating roll-off frequencies, engrossed in anything that wasn't work related or came stamped with a Monday deadline. I was stuck in the muck of a nasty creative block. The source of my impasse was a proposal for a new account that had been handed over the previous week. I smelled trouble from the very beginning when an endless litany of "nonnegotiable" demands was presented to me that included far too many design elements with no functional cohesion. Attempts to streamline the request fell flat, and for days, I had been cooped up in the studio, alternating between drifts of distraction and fruitlessly jigsawing doomed compositional ideas. Every draft came out unbalanced. The prospects were not good. I was getting nowhere, and agitation churned.

And then, just as arguments for an extension began forming in my head, I was roused by a change in the room. The symphony of sounds that had filled the studio was gone, and in its place was a deep, heavy silence. Satisfied thermostats finally shut down. Blustery gales had calmed. The acoustic space was dead, and the contrast woke me from my drifts with a cold slap. It braced my attention, and I refocused on the work in front of me. But the view from my desk was disheartening. The few, uninspired ideas I had been able to generate were overrun with doodles that did little to chill the heat of my growing panic. And a glance at the clock was all it took to bring that panic to a boil. Nearly a full day was lost with no progress to show for it, leaving only a handful of hours to pull something together before Monday morning's meeting. It was time for a drastic maneuver. Time to change the game. Time to get out. Time to take a walk and put the right side of the brain on low simmer for a while.

I left the silence of the studio and headed downstairs to grab my coat. The more I thought about it, the more I was sure that a walk was just what I needed. *Keep it simple,* I thought. *No phone. No pen. No notepad. Just a good, brisk walk to put things right.* I found Janey in the kitchen making fast work of a sandwich. She was thumbing through the pages of her *Fodor's Travel Guide to Australia.* One of Aaron's old sweatshirts was draped over her work clothes, and a mostly empty wineglass was in her hand.

"Hey, Jane, I think I'm gonna go out for a while," I delicately proposed as I buttoned my coat. "I'm getting nowhere upstairs so I thought I'd take a walk and try to clear the head."

She looked up from the last few bites of her tuna melt, a blotch of mayonnaise whitening her chin. Though her eyes were aimed directly at mine, I could tell she was off on her own, on a ramble maybe, across the barren Outback. "Okay," she said absently. "Oh, and hey, if you're going anywhere near Waltons, could you pick up a couple bottles of red? I told you that Mitch and Susan may be stopping by tomorrow, didn't I? We have nothing in the house. And listen, Owen, don't forget to take a key this time. Sophie needs me to fill in for Maggie, and I have to be there at four."

I acknowledged that I would, she did, I will, and okay, but I did not have the heart to mention anything about the mayo. Or the sweatshirt and the wine. Instead, I went back upstairs for my wallet and keys, checking to make sure the credit card was in its usual place. A sharp chill triggered a last-minute decision to add a sweater under my coat, and by the time I got back to the kitchen en route to the front door, Janey was already gone.

I left with no particular route in mind, only the wish to empty my head of the frustrations of work and maybe make room for a new inspiration. Still, I was a little surprised to find myself standing across the street from Wilson's house, peering up the driveway at a most unexpected sight. Because on that late November day, when the whole world was lacquered with a varnish of gray, the view that ran from the street, up the drive, and into the wide-open garage was unimpeded. It came delivered to me like a fortuitous invitation, and those, I've learned, ought never be rebuffed. So, for the moment, I put aside all other thoughts and turned to tread again on the rocky path of flagstone steps that led straight back toward Wilson's garage.

Even from several yards away, I could see him foraging around inside. There was a small wooden ladder laced to a shoulder as he paced along the back wall. Every few steps, he would stop to glance up at a tall arrangement of shelves while furiously rubbing his chin. After several scrubbed trials, he set down the ladder and finally began to climb. Heavy metal things groaned like dead spirits as he shoved them out of the way. Then it took a long blind stretch and a few loud grunts before a roll of fabric could be dragged from one of the shelves. He tucked the roll under his arm and climbed back down, somehow managing to keep his balance on the spindly ladder while wielding his cumbersome load and was utterly unmoved to find me standing there by the door.

"Hey, Wilson." I waved as I took a step deeper into the dim garage.

"Oh, hi, Owen." The thick bolt of black cloth was in his gloved hands. Its corpulence deadened the sound and turned everything into a muffle. Several ribbons of nylon belted the bolt together to keep it from unraveling. Wilson bent his head and started to untie the ribbons while the silence lengthened between us.

As he worked, I let my eyes adjust to the gloom and then roam over the scene. How different it all seemed from the last time I was there. How could so many changes have taken place in so short a time? The sunny brilliance of my October visit was gone. In its place, leaden glare wept glumly from the ceiling. The cinder block walls vented a graveyard dampness that penetrated my jacket like gamma rays. It left an aching frost in my bones and the stink of something like formaldehyde on my skin. And the magnificent chaos that had once stitched everything together into a harmonious jumble had been replaced with rigid, Teutonic order. I was standing in a tomb filled with relics being readied for their eternal rest. Only the MGA was still exposed, but that too seemed like merely a temporary condition.

"Hey, so, I've been wondering, did you ever get the brakes sorted out?" I asked in an attempt to break through the muddiness.

"Yeah, I guess they were okay." He shrugged indifferently while untying the last of the ribbons. "They'll never be great, but they got me through the season in one piece. And that's about all I can ask of those old drums." Though I assumed there was more to be said on that subject, nothing further was forthcoming. Instead, he just stood there, the bolt of heavy black cloth still in his hands.

"So what's going on then?" I asked, a slight bite of worry in my voice.

"I was just getting ready to cover the car."

"Well here, why don't you let me give you a hand?" I made the suggestion entirely unaware of what was entailed or whether an extra hand would even be welcomed. I only knew that Wilson looked like he could use some help.

He held the roll in front of him, laying it flat across his outstretched arms. I stood just a few feet away, wholly unsure what to do. From that distance, it was easy to see the cobwebs of red in the whites of his eyes and the eggplant bruises just beneath. The lines at the corners of his mouth tugged downward, and that formaldehyde smell continued to swirl. And in place of the charmingly fidgety stance that had always betrayed his desire to get back to work, Wilson seemed unmoored, as if the pressure of some heavy atmosphere had extracted a toll of some kind—perhaps of spirit—over the past several weeks. Standing there, it seemed that the affinity we shared on my previous visit had left behind only the slightest trace of a graceless smudge, like smoldering ash. Sure, time might explain the modest fade in rapport, but how to explain the more material differences inside the garage and in Wilson himself?

He handed me one end of the cover, and we started to unroll it, stepping back from each other with every turn of the bolt. When it was completely unwound, we raised it over our heads and slid into position behind each end of the car. At his signal, we slowly lowered it down until the body of the MGA had been draped, leaving only a vague profile to allege what lay beneath. Small metal clips where then affixed to each of the four corners and to the frame rails below both doors. Another job completed.

It was as if we had just performed the final scene in the last act of a play at the tail end of its run and the klieg lights were about to be switched off for the season. Right on cue, I watched Wilson hit his mark and take a last, long, appraising look around the garage. At that moment, if ten or even twenty more people had been inside, lathering the space with their collective vim, he still would have seemed all alone.

One at a time, he pulled the cords that dangled from the lights, sinking the garage into a cavernous pitch that would not be easily evicted. As we made our way out, he grabbed a padlock that hung on a nail and sealed the door shut with a *wumpth*. Carefully threading the lock through the hasp, he snapped it tight and gave it a shake before finally turning away. And though I had already taken a few steps down the driveway, I still heard him whisper under his breath, to himself only, in sotto voce, a final soliloquy before an empty hall. The words were unmistakable.

They cut like a knife through the cold, dense air: "As darkness rains from the skies, I drown on wings of dragonflies."

With a vast sigh, Wilson turned up his collar, dug his hands deep into the pockets of his coat, and left the garage behind.

In the months that followed, I often thought about those words. And though I am still unsure of their meaning, at that moment, their implication was clear: *Winter,* I thought to myself, *is finally here.*

We stood outside a while longer, not really saying much but not making any signs to separate either. Nervously, I noted that neither one of us mentioned anything about the ride we had agreed to but never managed to arrange. In light of all the doleful changes, it seemed like a good idea to tread lightly in approaching the topic and give it a generous berth. But I also remember thinking that if I left now, with so much unsaid, it could be a really long time before we would see each other again, and neither one of us would be happy with that.

And then, as if to seal winter's arrival, the first few flakes of snow started to fall: large, wondrous flakes that amplified the silence around us. They landed in our hair and on our shoulders and were, for the briefest instant, the most delicate things in the universe.

"Well, that's just perfect. Absolutely perfect. Extraordinary timing," Wilson seethed. "Yet another sign that the season is truly over. Did we really need *another* sign?"

And that's when it hit me. It was right there in the gently falling snow, flanked by the slumbering garage on one side and this curious new friend on the other. The small pieces of a story I didn't even know I'd been puzzling over finally began to fall into place. Those story pieces were like clues. And though I had been blindly gathering them all along, only then did they seem so obvious and expose so much. That was the moment I first felt Wilson Lacy's sadness: the corporeal, material, anatomical fact of it. It surged in waves that pulled me toward him with an urgent undertow. True, there were no moans of misery or tears of despair—no great revelations of grief or lamentations of woe—but the sadness was there as real as the snow. And I know sadness when I see it. It isn't so easily explained. I know the suffering it inflicts and the slick stain of gloom it casts over everything in one's life. I know how it grinds you down, compressing you into the earth with a force that overwhelms your ability to resist. I also know that the only way to lessen the sadness is to diffuse it by sharing it with someone else. I have Janey. Janey has me. The girls have each other. I wondered if Wilson had anyone to share his sadness with.

The lure of his sadness was gravitationally strong. It moved me. Sadness often does. I surrendered to its sway and let its currents steer the course of what followed next between Wilson and me.

"So, I guess we never did get it together for that ride, huh? That's really too bad. It would have been fun," I cautiously offered.

"Yeah, I'm sorry about that, Owen. I'm not sure what happened, but the last few weeks just slipped by. Truth is, I'm not so good when it comes to things like that, never have been, even when my intentions are sincere. The fault was with me."

The snow then began to fall more heavily, in even bigger flakes, the kind that lets you glimpse the frill of nature's byzantine lacework. It filled the air between us with a translucent curtain and, in kinship with the weather, I too picked up the intensity. "I do still owe you that beer though. You know, from the last time I was over. And I'm a guy who hates to be in debt."

He flinched when I said that, and a pained expression burned his face. *Perhaps,* I thought, *he is unaccustomed to such persistence—or maybe he just wants to be left alone.* My reasons for believing in the former explanation instead of the latter remain inscrutable to me.

Then, raising his right hand, he proceeded to touch his forehead, his chest, and finally both shoulders while muttering something that sounded like Latin. "There," he claimed, his face nearly white. "You have been officially absolved of your debt."

So I dug in.

"No, really, you don't get it," I pleaded. "If I don't pay you back soon, I'll never again get a good night's sleep. It's called debtor's insomnia. I'm not making that up. That's a real thing. You can Google it. How about this: Are you free Tuesday night?" I chose not to wait for an answer. "What do you say I come by around six and pick you up? We can grab some dinner, and I can finally pay you back and make things right with the world once again."

The offer wasn't given much thought. "Nah, thanks," he quickly replied. "It really isn't necessary. And besides, now I owe you for the help today so that must make us even."

But I pressed on. Like the encroaching winter that was descending all around us, I would not be dissuaded. "Listen, I insist. We'll work out who buys what later, but I'll be here at six sharp on Tuesday, and while my old Corolla has a cool factor hovering around zero next to that sweet MG, it'll get us where we're going. I'm not taking no for an answer."

I could see how heavily the invitation weighed on him as he rocked on his heels in self-debate, balancing all the options and implications within the framework of his own secret calculus. In the course of the waffling, his hair turned white with snow, a frosting that refused his tousles and gave him the aspect of a much older man, making it seem as if years had passed in fretful deliberation. In time though, it was clear that his search for an exit strategy was fruitless. He finally relented, nodding his head and agreeing to be ready at six. I extended my hand as if shaking on it would make it so, and he grasped it with something that felt very much like longing. "Okay, Owen. I'll be ready. See you Tuesday."

I went straight home after that. My head was clear, and I was anxious to have another go at those layout ideas. Something about scale and proportional space kept cropping up as I walked. At least it was a place to start.

Along the way, I marveled at the hurried rate at which the snow was accumulating. It always seems so miraculous at the start of the season. By the time I turned up my walkway, my shoes had begun to leave shallow prints in tender drifts, but there wouldn't be enough snowfall to call for the shovel. Surely though, that day was not far off. And even though the house was empty when I entered, it didn't feel quite as cold as I expected. Or seem as dark.

I marked down my dinner with Wilson on the kitchen calendar so Janey would see it and then headed upstairs to the studio with a renewed sense of optimism. I thought I would do some brainstorming on the computer and then maybe grab a drink to shore up my courage before facing the design problems that still covered my desk.

As I emptied my pockets and laid my wallet on the table, I realized with a twinge of chagrin that I had forgotten to pick up the wine. *Janey's wine. For tomorrow. Shit.* Though Waltons was just a few blocks away and I'd already passed it twice that day, I decided this time to drive. It looked like winter outside, and I was pretty sure that my problems would still be there, patiently waiting for me whenever I got back.

Chapter

5

The clock in the Corolla read 5:47. Too early as usual. No bombshells there. For reasons that have forever eluded me, I am one of those people who always arrive early. I offer this admission with no lump of pride or dash of conceit, actually quite the opposite. It's a bit of a problem. When *you* enter a movie theater at a reasonable time, perhaps as the previews are about to begin, I'm the guy you see camped out in the back row. I'm the patient you wonder about in the waiting room—the one you notice when you arrive, the one you pass by as you go in, and the one you nod to as you leave. And, yeah, the guy loitering in the lobby of a restaurant who won't be seated until the rest of his party arrives? That's me. So, I admit to not being too surprised to find myself a little early as I drove past Wilson's house on that Tuesday evening, succumbing to the realization that a few loops around the neighborhood were most definitely in order.

Though it was still before six, the streets were saturated with late November ink, the kind that always seems a shade or two darker than the color of night in other months. The snow from Saturday's dusting was mostly gone, but the puddles of slush it left behind made travel sloppy. The tires howled with resentment as they lumbered through. Along Judson and Kimball, the homes were warmly lit, glowing from the inside like a mother-to-be and buttoned up snug.

Turning west and driving along Greenleaf, the houses all looked empty. They sat impassive in the early night, awaiting the return of the working couples with their flocks of kids, and then they too would stir with life. The first signs of the holiday season were already on display as the more devout homeowners had strung lights and put up decorations, but it all needed more snow to really shine. And while the car's emphysemic heater struggled to keep up with the frigid conditions outside, I lolled in comfort, warmed by the sight of my neighborhood.

5:52 by the watch on my wrist. I turned south on Sycamore and lined up for the straight shot down Linden when a vanguard of tremors roiled my belly. I suppose that was to be expected. You see, up to that point, my conversations with Wilson had been mostly adventitious. They arose spontaneously from nothing much more than chance. There was usually enough common ground to excite our talks with sufficient momentum to carry us over and through any floundering moments we encountered. And though, at times, the weight of our words could encumber the flow, our conversations never felt forced. They were free from contrivance. But this? This was something different.

This time, there would be no shiny objects to snare our attention, no handy life preservers to buoy us up if we flailed about, and no easy exits. This time, there would only be the two of us with our burgeoning bond and whatever thoughts, stories, experiences, problems, and dreams we might bring to the table. Under such conditions, before the loose threads of friendship can knit together to support the freight of two people, a few nervous tremors don't seem unreasonable. I worried over what we would talk about away from the garage and the familiar neighborhood touchstones. I fretted about whether there would be enough to say to make it through an entire meal. And, if I'm honest, I'll even concede to a momentary pang of regret for ever bringing this dinner up in the first place when instead I could be safe at home, sitting in front of the TV, a beer in hand, with nothing unknown to fear.

I pulled into Wilson's driveway at 5:55, pleased with myself for not landing the Corolla too early. My old Radiograph pen, two receipts from Waltons, an overdue cable bill, and thirty-seven cents in change were rescued from the folds of the passenger seat before I switched off the ignition and was swallowed by darkness. The interior of the car vanished into the black surround with an abruptness that made me cringe and left me fumbling for the handle and a way out.

For the next few minutes, I stumbled around like a drunk feeling my way around to the front of the car while my eyes worked to accommodate the pitch. Even the flashlight from my phone was no match for that deep well of darkness. Its narrow white cone penetrated only a few feet before surrendering entirely. Cautiously, one small step at a time, I made my way forward.

The front of Wilson's house was completely unlit. "Desolate" doesn't even come close. Double-hung black holes substituted for windows on both stories. They sucked the light from the adjoining houses and cast it into oblivion. A tarpaulin of murk draped the oversized lot so that only the faintest suggestion of maple trees could be seen. The sharp edges of their leafless branches tore at the moonless sky. I kept my head down and my hands in front of me as I pushed through the gelatinous darkness.

It wasn't until I inched my way to the front step that I spied a more welcoming glimmer coming from the back of the house. I followed it around like a moth. The source of that glimmer turned out to be the phosphorous glow of a mercury vapor lamp, the kind that was used to illuminate large fields and parking lots years ago, an unusual choice for residential lighting. It was hanging just above a back entrance, not nearly high enough to be seen from the street, and its unnatural glow stood the rear of the house in stark contrast with the rest. Standing under the halo of that sallow melon light, I could just make out an impressive collection of bird feeders staked in the grass, though their reservoirs all looked empty. Presuming that this was where I was expected to enter, I reached out my hand and rang the bell.

And ... nothing. Not a sound or any kind of response. The tremors ground on while I ticked off my options and pondered my next move. Do I ring again and risk coming across like an impatient oaf or stand here waiting on the vagaries of fate? After what seemed like a courteous interval, I reached out again, this time pressing down hard enough for any wonky switchgear to engage. Still nothing. And again, more time numbly passed. "Caution meet wind," I muttered under my breath before unleashing an exploratory knock, first on the screen, then on the door, then harder on the glass, then harder still. Nothing.

At that point, I bowed to the nagging fear that maybe the fault here was mine. So I pulled out my phone to confirm that: a) it was Tuesday, b) it was now a few minutes past six, and c) there were no messages of catastrophe that could explain away the situation. Entering the territory of last resorts, I started to make my way around to the front of the house. My plan was to let loose a final cannonade of knocks and rings before heading back to the car. But the slam of the screen behind me triggered a trifecta of signs to fire in rapid succession; first, an inside light switched on; then, footsteps rapidly approached; and at last, a clunky deadbolt slid with a *thunk*. As I raced back around, the toe of my shoe snagged on a root, and I catapulted my way to the ground. That was exactly how Wilson found me when the door finally opened: dazed and a little wobbly, crouched on a bent and bloodied knee, looking like a sprinter on his mark, waiting for the starting gun to fire.

"Yeah, that doorbell has been on the fritz for a while," he explained through the screen. He seemed neither worried by my predicament nor interested in an explanation. He just held the door open and waited for me to enter. "I never have been able to trace the fault. Sorry about that. Nice knocking though. Good resonance. C'mon in. I just need to grab a few things."

I straightened up and brushed off my pants as cool as a ballplayer after stealing third base. Tracking his steps, I followed Wilson through a small mudroom. And then, in a flash, he was gone. He zoomed from room to room in a high-velocity blur, switching on lights all around the house in an effort to shoo away the dark. I was too slow to catch him on his rounds and offer any kind of proper greeting and then lost him entirely as he headed upstairs.

"Make yourself at home, Owen," he called from above. "I'll be down in just a few minutes."

Entering the house of a new friend for the very first time is an experience that never grows old. First impressions are illuminating things. They shine with unparalleled candlepower to reveal essential pieces of a life story. And when that light is amplified through the lens of compassion, the brightness can expose fragments of the story that would otherwise lay shrouded in shadow. That is precisely what happened as I made myself at home in Wilson's house. My walkabout cast flares of luminescence into the dark corners of his life. The shadows had nowhere to hide.

Wilson lives in a very old home. Several small rooms make up the main floor, all connected by a labyrinth of doorways and wainscoted hallways that lends the house a warren-like feel. One room leads to another in a secret circuitry that makes little architectural sense but would have delighted avid hide-and-go-seekers. Weaving my way through these rooms, it was easy to envision a buzzing swarm of activity as family members and friends burbled in and out, crossing along divergent paths, coming and going in tightly packed play. But if that vision were ever realized, I guessed it must have been a long time ago; the warren had been deserted for a while. The abandoned rooms through which I walked were like the ancient palimpsests I studied in college, those manuscripts where the oldest stories are effaced to make room for later inscriptions while still retaining faint, ghostlike traces of the originals.

I have no keen aesthetic when it comes to interior design. I will confess to that. But even to my eye, most everything on the first floor was glazed with blandness. It all evoked the spiritlessness of a model house that had been hurriedly staged with the leftover miscellany of a real estate warehouse. The look is lived-in, but there's no life there. There was no clutter or adornment of any kind. I could find no mark of style. No imprint of taste. No stamp left by the stroke of another. Nothing to reject the drabness or generica that made it all seem so gloomy, so empty, and so lifeless.

Okay, maybe that's a little harsh. Fair enough. After all, there *were* two notable exceptions tucked away in the back of the house. The kitchen was actually quite charming with its wallpaper border of white lilies and acanthus leaves. An old porcelain sink had settled beneath a large bay window. Veins like blue cheese mottled its mint green finish, and the yellow-stained cups in the dish dryer looked like gas station giveaways. There was a small pedestal table set to the side. Its wood glowed richly with polish, and the top boasted an inlay of exquisite blue tiles. Marks of some kind, maybe initials, had been carved into the round fascia. A single chair of matching design was arranged beside the table, and an unidentifiable but not wholly unpleasant odor wafted in the air.

And just past the kitchen was an adjoining den. Here, as I peeked in, I found the thumbprint of existence. Stacks of laundry with paper-cut folds smothered a small love seat, and a plate of graham cracker crumbs lay on the floor. Hanging over the armrest of a recliner was an opened copy of *Nature*. An assortment of neon highlighters had pooled in the cushions. Overstuffed bookcases stretched from floor to ceiling. A flat-screen TV sat atop a stone mantel. These were signs of life. They struck a decisive note of distinction from the rest of the rooms I had seen. But standing in the doorway, waiting for Wilson to return, the house still felt lonesome, and yes, even a little sad—just these two small rooms set aside like a desperate island cut off from a mainland that lay many leagues away as the ghostly impressions left by that once-buzzing swarm simply refused to fade.

And this is where the light shone brightest. It was just as I was getting ready to leave the den to check on Wilson's progress that I turned and caught sight of the wall behind me. In that instant, I felt something change. Imagine a beam resting on a fulcrum. It sits perfectly plumb. The ends of the beam are suspended above the foundation at exactly the same height. The load on one side is offset by the effort on the other. Two possible futures hang in the balance, poised on the pivot of the present. But the weight of what I saw—as I stood there gobsmacked with astonishment in Wilson's den—had shifted the center of gravity. It tilted the beam to favor one of those futures though I couldn't say for sure which one.

How can I describe it?

The wall was covered with photographs. No, wait. That doesn't nearly do it justice. Let me try that again. The south-facing wall of his den—the entire surface of it, *all of it,* by my estimate one hundred square feet of it—was encrusted by the most magnificent montage of still photographs I have ever seen. It was incredible. Hundreds of photos were wallpapered across the length of the white plaster canvas. Some were in frames; others had been affixed to the wall with tape or pins. They dovetailed together so perfectly—so seamlessly—that I thought I could peel it from the surface in a single piece. I was awestruck by the sight of it. It was captivating and pleaded for a closer look.

There were sepia portraits of a man and woman from over a century ago in rigid poses with frigid faces that insinuated the hard times of immigrant life. Were these Wilson's grandparents? There were rectangular black-and-whites, the old kind with scalloped edges, old enough so that the contrasting tones that were once so sharp had mellowed into just a few shades of gray. They showed men in drab army uniforms, women in knee-length bathing suits, the propellers of a DC-3 angled eagerly toward the sky and the mile-long fenders of streamlined Fords yearning for the open roads, fedora hats and fat cigars, wide-open spaces and neon signs, rickety ballparks and ramshackle pool halls, all of it connected in some way to my friend Wilson.

There were the square photos I remember so well from my youth, snapshots we used to call them, exposed on Kodak film and taken with Instamatic cameras that blazed with real flashbulbs. Here was a young couple standing together on the stoop of a newly built house, the skeletons of other houses rising up on either side. Then two became three, then four, then five with that same couple beaming in the midst of beanstalking kids as saplings turned into trees.

And there was one of a young Wilson—I could tell by the eyes—maybe at twelve or thirteen, standing alongside a bearded man in overalls that were stained with grease and holding a wrench in one hand while the other rested gently on the kid's shoulder, and the distinctive contours of the MGA gleamed in the background of some distant field. There were color shots, three-by-five and larger, of Wilson with long, sun-lightened hair laying on the grass, legs entwined with those of a beautiful girl in bell-bottoms and a peasant blouse, or posing in front of a chapel in the center of a college quadrangle and then again, the two of them standing next to a tent in the wilderness huddled in each other's arms, and again leaning alongside a covered bridge backdropped by snowy mountains, and then sitting in the sand with the wide ocean in front of them.

There were more. Thick Polaroids of the same girl in a hospital gown holding a newborn on her breast, and then another. Larger color prints portrayed a swarm of activity buzzing on the front lawn of this very same house, driveway games that gave way to glimpses of the open garage in back, tree house parties with gaggles of kids, and photos of Wilson and the girl, now woman, standing on the shores of some tropical beach, drinks in hand but no longer entwined, and baseball games and soccer matches and birthdays and graduations and Christmas mornings and recitals and a family.

A folding frame held two eight-by-tens of a young man and young woman, each in a cap and gown and wearing a rendition of the same downcast eyes, and there were even a few that looked to be downloaded from JPEGs and printed on filler paper of that same young man and a different young woman lying in bed or at a park or on a walk or at the zoo with a toddler held between them. Individually, they were like small patches of grace, the blending of light and shadow, color and shade, form and substance confessing an urgent story that smoldered inside every single one. But stepping back from the wall and taking it all in, the separate notes that made up the multitude of stories softly blurred together into a spiraling arabesque with tender filaments that stretched across the magnificence of Wilson's life—the categorical, fundamental, axiomatic, unequivocal magnificence of Wilson's life. I was swept away by the tale it begged to tell, and that is how he found me, reeling with awe, when he came down the stairs at last.

"Oh my god, Wilson," I gushed loudly with outstretched arms as he walked into the den. "This is unbelievable. This wall. It's absolutely fantastic. I could look at it for hours. I really could. I just love it."

He took a few steps toward me, and we both stood there, side by side in similar poses, arms across our chests like aficionados appraising an exhibit on display. Ripples of heat curled from the edges of his tomato-red ears. I struggled to stifle a desire to babble. There was so much I wanted to say. Instead, I turned toward him and patiently waited while his eyes scanned the wall from one corner to the other.

"Thanks. Yeah, I like it too," he said, absently picking at something in the palm of his hand. A drop of perspiration condensed above his lip. He wiped it off with his sleeve. "It started a couple of years ago with just a handful. I guess I got a little carried away. I'm afraid that it might look a little obsessive. Not that anybody ever sees it though."

"I don't know," I said. "It doesn't seem so obsessive to me. Not at all. What I love about it is that if you look at it just right, it tells a story. Visually, it's so evocative. It reminds me of the epic poems from ancient Greece, like *The Odyssey*, only better because this depicts something real: the real journey of a regular guy through the course of his life. It is incredible. I would need hours to take it all in, and already I have so many questions. There is so much I want to know about all these people. Who are all these people?"

I worried that my enthusiasm was coming across a little too strong. It occasionally does. Despite my best intentions, it can overwhelm, and I considered taking it down a notch. But I saw no signs of retreat on Wilson's part. Instead, he appeared unruffled and continued to stare at his wall. "Well, thanks, Owen," he said as he began to zip up his jacket, ready, it seemed, to move on. "I'm pretty sure I've never been compared to Odysseus before, but I appreciate the association. Honestly though, I'm not sure there's much mythologizing to do here. Nothing quite so grand, I'm afraid. And if I started now, we'd never get out of here, and then you'd still be saddled with that debt—and I know how much you would hate that."

He was right. The story would take time. We had a reservation to keep and were already cutting it close. So I leveraged his itch to get on with the evening and used it as blackmail to hear more, lots more, as a precondition for leaving. He agreed to my terms, and after one more look at his glorious wall, we headed out to the car. Despite the cold, the engine fired right up, and I left thinking there would be no shortage of things to talk about after all.

Hennigan's is a local pub that had a lot to recommend it as our destination. It's one of the few places around town where you can get a really tasty burger or a really great salad and pretty much everything in between. I knew nothing of Wilson's preferences, but I figured neither one of us would have a problem with the menu. They also brew their own beer, and there is always a fine selection on tap. Dave and Tim, the sibling owners, got in on the microbrewing craze at the perfect time and established a well-deserved reputation for the quality of their craft beers. The Hennigan's label, a riff on industrial midwestern, broad-shouldered themes, was actually designed by me several years ago in exchange for free growlers, an arrangement that has worked out well for all parties. When I described the relaxed, neighborly vibe of the place, Wilson said he was game to give it a try.

What I forgot to mention was the reception I sometimes receive when I enter the place. That omission was sure enough apparent the moment we walked in the door. We hadn't even taken off our coats before Sweet Sassy Sophie, the storied hostess, wrapped her sweet, loving arms around me and planted a kiss smack dab on the check, her customary greeting and lipstick smears reserved for the most regular of regulars.

"Owen, baby, how's it going?" she said, releasing me from a hug that may or may not have lasted a beat or two too long.

I told her I was well and introduced her to Wilson whose hand she warmly took in her own.

"Wilson," she sang, using the legendary glitter of her viridescent eyes to remarkable effect, "it is a pleasure meeting you." She casually grabbed his arm in hers as if it were the most natural thing in the world and proceeded to take us to our table.

Working our way through the crowd attracted the attention of several diners. Sophie's sway has its charms. A few of the busboys and waitstaff shouted greetings or slapped my hand with a high five, and Jim at the bar begged me to explain why the Wisconsin football team was so incapable of putting a game away in the fourth quarter.

"You boys enjoy your dinner," Sophie purred as we finally sat down. "If you need anything, anything at all, just let me know." The menus she left in our laps were still warm from her hands and smelled faintly of ocean spray and sunlight and sand.

"Sheesh, Owen. Do you know everyone here?" Wilson's question hovered in the air between us once we were alone. But it did not hover for long. Before I could explain, a striking waitress in her tight-fitting Hennigan's skirt came by and wordlessly deposited two tall glasses directly in front of us. Each was filled to the brim with the cool frost of amber.

Wilson began squirming uneasily in his seat, thoroughly confused by the unexpected arrival of the drinks. That confusion, I knew, was only just beginning. Because without missing a beat, this very same waitress leaned over my chair and let her hair tumble around me in a shimmering curtain of silk. And then she placed a kiss right on my lips.

"So this must be the famous Wilson Lacy, huh?" the waitress coyly confided as she shook the hair from her face and rested a hand on the back of my chair.

I glanced over at Wilson who looked to be coming undone. The sequence of events he just witnessed—from Sophie's greeting, to the arrival of the unordered beers, to this sloppy kiss from an incorrigible waitress—was a lot to take in. He must have been recalibrating the meaning of a relaxed, neighborly vibe.

"Uh, Wilson," I finally relented. "Sorry for all the commotion. I probably should have warned you, but it's not always like this. Anyways, this is my wife, Janey. Janey, this is indeed the famous Wilson Lacy."

Garbled vowels then belched from his throat, and he exhaled with a convulsive twitch. He started to stand to shake her hand, but Janey being Janey, was too quick. "Hey there, Wilson Lacy," she said, turning the handshake into a hug. "It's really nice to meet you. Owen talks a lot about you. I think it's great that you guys decided to do this." Then, she eased back into her waitress role to inform us that she would soon return to take our orders and that the drinks were on the house, courtesy of Jim. With a watchful eye on the crowd, she stole a taste of my beer, licked the foam from her lips, and then sauntered away. But before she could make it all the way to the kitchen, she turned and called back so that everyone in the section could hear, "You better still figure the cost of those beers into the tip, you old cheapskate."

As the atmosphere cleared, and we were left on our own, I could see Wilson's neck, shoulders, and chest unwind by degrees. He leaned back at last in his chair. "So, that's your wife, huh?" he said, tilting his pilsner toward me with a shy little grin. "You are a lucky man, Owen. How long have the two of you been together?"

And with that question, one end of the loose thread of conversation had shaken free. It was impossible to tell where it might lead. But I picked it up anyway, gratefully, and started to pull in hopes of unraveling things as far as I possibly could. "Well, let's see." I began the mental calculations that never came easily to me. "It'll be thirty-five years next April. We met right after college, at a Cubs game as a matter of fact, and we've been together ever since. Thirty-five years. Jesus, that's a long time, but it feels like the blink of an eye. How the hell did that happen?"

While we considered that question, I took a sip of beer and decided to pull that thread a little more. So far, there had been no resistance. The unwinding was easy. "So, let's see—what else can I tell you? We have two girls, Hannah and Sara, they're both are up in school at Madison. One is studying journalism, and the other is studying boys. And I'm sure I must have told you at some point that I'm a graphic designer. I do layouts and visual design for a small firm in the city. A little freelancing on my own too when I get the chance. I've been doing these same things pretty much forever as the years flew by. And you know, it's funny; I still can't get over how fast the ride is. I try to tell that to the young couples in the neighborhood, but they don't really get it. How could they with their whole lives in front of them? I don't *feel* old, but you can't really argue with the math."

I caught myself tracking the bubbles of air as they danced around in my beer, unsure why or for how long I had been staring at my glass, surprised at how far I had just pulled that thread, how much I had already unwound. I don't think my intention was to loosen so much, and I felt the heat of a blush crawl over my face.

Wilson though, seemed undisturbed by my confessional. Instead, there was an earnest glint in his eyes. He looked ready to pick up the thread. "No, I get it," he said. "I know just what you mean. I'm almost sixty-two for heaven's sake. To me, that is simply unbelievable. Somehow, without even trying, I've become an old man. You're right. The mathematics *are* pretty persuasive. And to tell you the truth, I think I've grown a little tired of playing out the string. It is so tiresome, isn't it? It's like the radiance that made being alive so joyful has diminished somehow, as if our senses have already registered their fill, and it's harder and harder for any of that joyfulness to penetrate through. I think that's the part about growing old that bothers me the most: the numbness."

Now it was Wilson's turn to gaze at his beer. The slow, solemn way he shook his head bespoke disbelief as if, perhaps, he regretted the words. Maybe some of those things were not quite ready to be shared. The raw exposure left very little cover, and I could feel him slipping away as he considered all that he just heard himself say. Those last few words in particular lacked the spontaneity of casual conversation. There was no improvisation there. They sounded practiced and profoundly familiar, drawn like stagnant water from the well of intimacy one has with one's own life.

And maybe it was because I was starting to know him better, but I also noticed that the shadow of his sadness had returned. I saw it again, just as I did the other day, pressing down on him as he sat worrying at his beer. I could see now that it was more than a mood or a state of mind, or it was those but something else too. His sadness was like an avatar that was often by his side, invisible to others but conspicuous by the force it exerted on his life. We sat for a moment in silence, retreating slightly from the heat of the discussion, fearful that the thread might have been pulled too far and needed to be wound back. We fumbled with the menus and small talk while hastily draining our beers, and I found myself wishing that Janey would soon return.

She always knows everything that goes on in the restaurant. It is her sixth sense. That's just the way she is, with her nose in everything around her. She moves back and forth with the pulse of the place, knowing what people need before they know it themselves and then making sure they get it with a garnish of grace. She has always been like that. I guess that's what makes her such an excellent waitress. Also, she has never steered me wrong on her recommendations for what to get on any particular night. She gathers the information like a spy from her friendly reconnaissance with the chefs.

Following her suggestion, Wilson and I both ordered the shrimp tacos; the shrimp, she said, were divine, something she claimed to know from extensive, firsthand experience. "I've been nibbling on them all evening," she admitted after taking our orders. "And that's a thing you don't have to mention to Sophie."

Before Wilson or I could pick up the thread, two more beers arrived, this time delivered by Jim himself who was on a ten-minute break from the bar. "Hey, guys, you gotta try this," he exclaimed while pulling up a chair from the next table over.

Invitations were usually beside the point with Jim. "You're gonna love it. It's the latest from the boys, a really nice Weizenbock that they've been futzing with for the last few months, but I think maybe they finally got it right. Looks good, right? Oh, and be sure to smell it first. That, my fine fellows, is what the nape of a Bavarian fraulein smells like, just below the ear, in case you're wondering. Hey, I'm Jim, by the way," he said to Wilson with an open hand and the hundred-watt smile that comes so naturally to a guy who has spent most of his adult life pulling taps behind a bar.

"Oh yeah, sorry," I said. "Wilson, this is Jim, the local barkeep and armchair braumeister. Jim, this is my friend Wilson Lacy."

"It's a pleasure to meet you, Wilson Lacy, and FYI, partner, there ain't no armchair about it." He turned his chair to square with Wilson's in order to study the lines of his face while helping himself to my beer. "Hey, when you guys walked in, I thought I recognized you. Aren't you the guy with the old MG?"

Wilson raised his eyes, looked more keenly at Jim, and nodded once.

Jim's face erupted, and he nearly jumped out of his chair. "I knew it! Man, oh, man, I knew it! I was just telling Sophie. Dude, that is one seriously fine ride. I love seeing that car on the road. It stands out like a sexy speedboat in a sea of SUVs. It is so nice to meet someone who respects the things from the past. I just wanted to stop by and tell you how awesome that is. Really fantastic. But I'll let you guys get back to it. Again, nice to meet you, Wilson, and enjoy the beers, gents. Let me know what you think." He then carried his chair to the next table over, setting it down to inquire of the gleaming young ladies if they were ready for a refill on their Chardonnay. Wilson and I closed our eyes and breathed in the beer, losing ourselves in the idyllic valleys and towering summits and long lovely napes of the Black Forest. When we opened them again a moment later, we each had another secret to keep.

The action in the place was picking up. Hennigan's often spotlights local bands on a small stage tucked into the back, a popular draw for folks from all over, but it looked like there were no concerts planned for that night. Still, it was nice to see such a great crowd on a Tuesday. Just as always, Janey was spot-on with her recommendation. Wilson and I agreed that the tacos were wonderful, and we signaled over to Jim with four thumbs up to let him know that the next great success story in the ledger of Hennigan's brewery was already being written by the golden Weizenbock of which we had just made quick work.

As we mopped up our plates with the last of the tortillas, Janey came by with three small tumblers of still another beer, this time an experimental, yet-unreleased IPA that we just had to taste. I was happy to have her sit with us while we appraised the ale and considered whether either one of us could handle desert. Apparently, there was a slice or two of a pecan pie she was holding over for us just in case. She moved her chair in close to mine, rested her hands on my arm, and laid her head on my shoulder, a lacy tent of tenderness spiced with garlic and mint.

"So, Wilson," she sighed through a yawn, "tell me, did I do you right on those tacos?"

He pointed to his empty plate in enthusiastic confirmation that she had, indeed, done him right. "They were absolutely delicious, Janey. My compliments to the chef. And I don't know about your husband, but I never say no to pie."

She flashed him a warm smile, polished off her tumbler, and started to stand, giving my arm a last gentle squeeze. Then she stretched like the yogis she secretly admired but would never oblige and gathered herself for the downward slide of her long evening shift. Sidling over to Wilson's side of the table, she crouched down low to meet him at eye level, and I overheard her say, "You know, Wilson, if you liked the meal you had here, you're just gonna have to come over some night so I can cook for you. I make these guys look like punks. Maybe for the holidays? We'll pick a date, and I'll make sure hubby over there checks that you're available. It'll be fun. You'll come?"

Again, and as always, Wilson was too slow. With the kind of formality that proved he had a long way to go before grasping the wiles of Janey Conway—for she was already heading back to the kitchen, leaving him no way out whatsoever—he called in a voice just loud enough to thank her for the kind invitation. She signaled her response with a cool backward wave that made it abundantly clear she expected him there.

With dinner cleared and desert on its way, it seemed like a good time to locate the loose end of the thread we had been following, buried somewhere among the table scraps and empty glasses that still littered our table. I felt confident that the details I shared earlier were ample grounds for asking Wilson to do the same. I realized that the list of things I knew about his life was really quite small, and I was eager to hear more.

But maybe the best way to restart the conversation would not be to pick up right where we left off: the sadness, the numbness, and feeling old. Maybe starting more slowly would be a better idea. I reached again for that loose end and pulled once more, careful not to yank with a jerk but to insist with an even, steady draw intended to carry him along, however far he wanted to go. "All right, Wilson," I opened with a tad of tremolo in my voice. "Your turn. Tell me about yourself. Besides the car, I really don't know much of anything at all."

He began gingerly at first, the way a nimble young skater's airy routine leaves barely a mark on the ice. He talked about his career as a research scientist investigating the dark corners of high-energy physics at Argonne National Laboratory. The work, he said, was thrilling for a while, taking place right at the time when particle accelerators and computer mapping were pulling back the curtain on the mysteries of the universe. While at Argonne, his team won a grant that gained him access to the CERN cyclotron in Switzerland, where he lived for six months, a period that turned out to be the most productive of his research career.

Eventually, governmental priorities changed. Funding dried up, taking with it the pure research work he loved. Wilson became disillusioned. He knew his time at Argonne had passed. A period of soul-searching brought him to a stint at the Adler Planetarium as a science educator. The experience of sharing the adventure of science with the public resurrected in him a long-held desire to teach. And so, taking advantage of his extensive contacts in the scientific community, he landed a visiting professorship in the teacher's college at a small, local university. Fifteen years and several promotions up the academic ladder later, he decided at last to retire; the itch to reinvent his life one more time was an irresistible factor in his decision.

That was nearly three years ago, and he spoke about that decision with remorse. The reinvention had not come. "I was actually a little surprised by my inability to fill the void that was created when I left the university," he explained in a voice that fell a register lower. His eyes were stuck on the empty glass of beer that he fitfully turned in his hand, and the pauses between his thoughts grew longer. "I'm a little upset at myself for not being able to seize the chance to do something great. What a waste. I guess the reinvention is on hold for the time being. You know, I always used to think that retirement was something that *happens* to old people. Now I know it's what *makes* you old—or at least that's what happened to me. It just about knocked me out, Owen, and to tell you the truth, I'm not so sure I'll ever recover." He rested the glass on the table but kept his eyes averted from mine. The avatar, I saw, was bearing down hard, constricting his chest, and he labored for breath.

It was easy to forget that we were sitting in the midst of a bustling restaurant. It took the lapse that followed to remind us of that. Only then did the ambient noise from all the other tables intrude on our talk.

We looked around the room with our heads spinning in different directions, wondering where we might go from there. The longer that lapse went on, the more it would slacken the thread between us. And all that slack would make it nearly impossible to carry on.

So I decided to pull again in hopes of sustaining the tension. "And when I was looking at your photos, I couldn't help but notice a lovely girl by your side in so many of them. Is there a Mrs. Lacy?" I asked, stretching the ~~thread~~ piano wire tight.

Wilson recoiled like he'd been stung by a wasp. It was as if an imaginary line had just been drawn. On one side of that line were all the details of his professional resume that he had just freely shared. On the other side was everything else that went together to make up his life. I suppose he was considering whether to cross that line—whether it made any sense, whether it would be worth it, all things considered—and sometimes I wonder, *If we hadn't just had such a great meal, if we hadn't just enjoyed some terrific beer, and if he wasn't so all alone with another winter snapping at his heels, would he have ever dared to cross?*

"Well, I *was* married," he started to explain while studying his glass for imperfections. "Almost as long as you actually. To the love of my life. But I'm not anymore. See, I also have two kids: a son and a daughter. They both live out East now. We were a close family once, like yours I imagine, happy even. But once the kids moved out into their lives, my wife and I never quite adjusted to the empty nest. We went through all the right motions. We tried to do all the right things. We kept looking for ways to reconnect, but we just couldn't. Somewhere along the way to growing old, we lost track of whatever it was we had when we were young. And there really was something back then. I have photos to prove it. Anyways, after a couple of years of floundering around, we decided to call it quits. Or, more accurately, she did, I guess."

I was reluctant to interrupt. It was unclear whether his words were at an end or just at rest on a temporary stay. The silence lengthened—not uncomfortably, but noticeably—until, after a ponderous few seconds, he shattered it with the swing of a sledgehammer. "But there's something else too."

And now another line appeared. More entrenched than the first, this line was built upon a granite foundation that ran many feet deep to anchor a wall that stretched as many feet high. It was treacherous and severe—a wall of defense—and I was unsure whether it could ever be scaled, but I knew that if Wilson were to try, he was going to need some help. "Yeah?" I prodded.

"Well, it's like this," he started again. "I have inherited two things from my father that I could just as well have done without. I guess that's my birthright. The first is a propensity toward hypertension. But that's easily managed. The other is a bit more insidious."

Here he began shifting nervously in his chair, rubbing his palms on the front of his pants while his brow knitted into a matrix of knots. When he poured himself some water, he poured it into his beer glass by mistake. I watched his hand tremble as he brought the muddled drink to his mouth. After a long, strenuous swallow he put the glass down and leaned in with a conspiratorial air. And while I waited for him to continue, my heart began to race. There was a look of indecision that clouded his face, and I thought he might choose to turn back. All I could do was lean in too and wait a little bit more.

"This is kind of hard to talk about," he stammered. "And I'm not really sure why I'm mentioning it now, but in for a penny—what the hell, right? We've already come this far. You see, Owen, I guess I struggle a little with what is clinically referred to as depression. I don't know if you have any experience with it, maybe someone you know?"

I nodded but offered no reply.

"Yeah, well, no sense in getting too far into the weeds here. Suffice it to say that it comes and goes, but there can be some extended stretches when I get pretty low. I've been dealing with it for a very long time, so I know its rhythms fairly well, though all that knowing doesn't really do me much good. The reason why I'm bringing it up now, in this conversation, is that it can make me hard to be around. My wife—*my ex-wife*—endured it for the length of our marriage, and that was not an easy thing to do. I understand that. And frankly, it wasn't so bad when the kids were there. We were always so busy, but once they left, I guess I became—or I guess the demons became—pretty insufferable. Her patience began to wane. Again, completely justified. I'm not sure this was covered in the 'for-better-or-worse' stipulation of our marriage contract. And then, a couple of years ago, she just had enough. She said she needed a break. She wanted to be on her own for a while and see what happiness she could make in the world. So she packed up and moved out to the Eastern Shore, and we haven't seen each other since."

And here I have no recollection of how I responded. I've tried to remember the things I said, but my words are completely lost to me. I do know that I said *something*, and I know too that he would tell from the tone of my voice that I understood and maybe even knew a thing or two about those demons as well.

After that, he talked with the ease of an unburdening. He spoke openly about his depression and how it always gets worse as winter arrives. He lamented his attempts at seeking help. The therapies he pursued failed to lessen the depression; instead, they fractured his sense of himself in unsustainable ways. He even acknowledged that he could feel it building inside him now, with the season's recent arrival, and asked—with his scientific curiosity and a touch of dread in his voice—whether I had noticed anything unusual. And then came the apology that I knew would follow, the apology I always hear from others once they have reached out to another, the apology that Bill always rails against with such vehemence.

"Anyways, I'm sorry, Owen. I didn't mean to go so dark there. I have no right laying all that on you. Blame it on the beer. I'm sure that's the last thing you wanted to talk about tonight. 'A song guaranteed to bring you right down' as the great Neil Young once said."

Like a kite string that had unraveled from its reel after a long afternoon of flight, the thread of our evening's conversation lay unspooled, tangled, and knotted in a heap upon the table. It would take forever to wind it back up, but there seemed no harm just leaving out in the open for now.

We were talked out. We both knew it. I looked around the restaurant and saw with surprise that we were one of the few parties still left at a table. The plates of pie and glasses of beer and most of the diners were all long gone. The bar was still doing a brisk business, which would continue, I knew, right up until closing and, depending on Jim's mood, maybe even past. I signaled to Janey that we were ready for the check and then laughed as Wilson and I both raced into our pockets, giving rise to the debate over who was going to pay. Before we could achieve any sort of detente, she delivered the news that everything—drinks, tacos, and pie—had all been taken care of.

"The Hennigan boys are interested in a redesign on their label, but they're too nervous to ask you about it. They're using me and a free meal and all that beer to soften you up. Sneaky SOBs, aren't they?" She laughed while tearing up the check.

So the debt would remain unpaid, at least for a little while longer.

We put on our coats and began to make our way out, complaining like old men about stiff backs and firecracker knees and how we both had lost track of time. We bid our farewell to the trusty barkeep while conveying our appreciation for the barmy smell of that fraulein's neck and our fervent desire for more. There could be little doubt that the beer we enjoyed with our dinner had laid its glow of honeyed contentment on everything around us, and I had the wind-changing feeling that Wilson and I were leaving Hennigan's somehow different from when we had arrived. And that wasn't just the beer doing the talking. It was the intoxication that comes with stage 3, and, okay, maybe the beer as well.

Sophie caught up with us at the door, and I girded myself for the gooey goodbye that comes free with every meal. Imagine my amazement then when she passed me over like yesterday's news to wrap a thunderstruck Wilson in one of her sweet, loving hugs, the kind that could make a strawberry blush. Jammed as we were inside the tight foyer, it was easy to hear the whisper she lightly laid in his ear.

"Hey, Wilson Lacy, it was awfully nice to meet you. You're welcome back here anytime you like, you hear me? Don't be a stranger now." I'm even pretty sure she gave his back a tiny little squeeze before finally letting him go.

Feigning the resentment of a petulant child, I asked her where the hell my hug was.

"Hey now, Owen," she began with a smirk. "This one here doesn't come with a wedding ring, and that wife of yours is a jealous floozy." And when she smacked my ass with a sweet, sassy slap (that may or may not have been a bit too hard), it started me thinking: *Could it be that we're all secretly ensnared in epic poems of our own?*

It took the entire length of the car ride home for the Corolla to warm up, owing as much to the glaciers up north as to the malaise of my old blower motor. The Blackhawks were hosting the Blues, and we listened in for a while to the play-by-play, taking pleasure in the commodious elbow room granted us by the safe return to the breeziest of conversational topics. We wrangled over the dysfunction that had long beleaguered the sports franchises in our city, and we reminisced with joy about the glory days— though any mention of the sunny prospects for the baseball team from the North Side was strictly forbidden. I pulled up to the curb outside Wilson's house, and we both agreed that we had a good time.

Still, the impression left by his photograph wall had not faded. I mentioned again my wish to have a good long look and hear more about the odyssey of his life that it portrayed. We made a tentative plan to do just that the following week.

As he got out of the car and walked toward his door, I was reminded of the other indelible impression left by my time in Wilson's home. I wondered how it would feel to walk into that house so late on an early winter's night—with nothing but the ghosts buzzing around those empty rooms to welcome him home.

Would the cold be a little sharper after our talk tonight? Its grip a little tighter? Would the darkness seem bleaker for having conceded so much? The sadness more dreadful? Would it have been better to have left the threads as they were, wound tight on their spools, rather than invite the mess of their unraveling? These were the thoughts that occupied my mind during the final stretch toward home.

And when I turned into my driveway and shut off the car, I was left with the sensation that I too was being pulled along into something, willingly and freely, but pulled nonetheless by the threads that bind two friends together—that the strings we had left on the restaurant table were just a fragment of the longer strands to come—and I was just fine with all that.

But truthfully, by the time I found my way into my own empty home, the only thing I could think about was the way Janey looked in her tight Hennigan's skirt, and I was just fine with that too.

PERTURBATION

Eastham, May 13, 2016

Chapter

6

Eastham lies in what is commonly referred to as the Lower Cape, bounded by the Atlantic Ocean on one side and Cape Cod Bay on the other. It owes much of its enduring allure to the protection it receives by falling safely within the boundaries of the National Seashore, a legislative act of natural preservation championed in 1961 by the area's most famous resident. While the terrain is now mostly salt marsh and sand, Eastham once boasted towering stands of precolonial oak that have long since gone to make up the walls and floors of homes all the way down to Boston. The town's storied New England history traces an unambiguous path back to its founding in 1651 as settlers from Plymouth Colony were drawn there by, among other things, the abundance of shellfish. That surfeit still exists today.

Richie's Lobster Bar has been an Eastham fixture for twenty-seven years. Its clapboard construction and gabled roof exude Cape Cod charm. It lies directly on Route 6, under the umbrella of Nauset Light, and attracts locals and tourists in much the same way as did Mac's Shanty, The Beachcomber, and The Sea Shore Diner before it. That venerable old building has dished out a lot of crab cakes over the years.

To help make ends meet, Richie rents out the loft above the restaurant on an annual lease. Converted from an old storage space, the apartment is now open and sunny and runs the full length of the restaurant's footprint below. Exposed beams, perhaps culled from those presettlement oaks, shelter the entire span of the living area beneath its forested canopy. East and south-facing windows let in sea breezes seasoned with the mysteries of the ocean and grant the sun full reign as it glides across the sky.

Rachel has been the steadiest tenant Richie has ever had, moving in two years ago after coming from out West and staying put ever since. She loves the place—the first she has called her own since college—and no longer shrinks from the smell of fried fish.

On this cloudless Friday morning in May, she lies in bed, awake but dreaming, waiting for the alarm to sound and the night to end. She watches the shadows come and go as newly leafed branches swirl in warm winds. Adrift in the quiet of her own private thoughts, she clutches loose pebbles of awe and marvels again at the life she has carved out for herself, all the way out here at the end of the world. And she stills the stubborn voice inside her that wonders why.

Ben lies next to her, unmoving and unmoved. Though his presence in her bed has grown familiar, she can locate no imprint of his presence on her life. She knows that he and his pile of clothes now scattered on the chair will soon be gone, and there will be nothing left of Ben to linger. This realization comes unbidden and hued with disquiet, and she leans in closer to try to awaken.

After a few more moments, she reaches over to silence the alarm as well as her thoughts and, at last, the day begins.

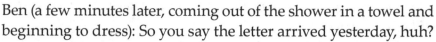

Ben (a few minutes later, coming out of the shower in a towel and beginning to dress): So you say the letter arrived yesterday, huh? I still can't get over that. Who writes letters anymore? Did he say what he wanted?

Rachel (lying in bed, still watching the light cavorting above her): I left it over there on the desk. You can read it if you want to. Something about how he'd been doing a lot of thinking over the winter and had come to some important realizations. "Insights" he called them. But he didn't offer a whole lot more than that. He said he was going to call in a day or two to fill me in. I guess the letter was his way of preparing me for whatever it is he's just now realized or decided to share.

Ben (picks up the letter from the desk and glances at it briefly before putting it down unread): Huh. So, any predictions? You must have some idea.

Rachel: No. Not really. Of course, the first thing I thought of was that he's sick and trying to find some way to let me know. But he must have anticipated that reaction because he went out of his way to say that he's fine and that there is nothing to worry about. So, what does that leave? I don't know. Maybe he needs something. Or maybe it's simpler than that. Maybe he wants to sell the house. I really don't know. I honestly can't figure it out. I mean, why now, after all this time, does he decide to reach out? And why like this? It just doesn't seem like him at all.

Ben: What do you mean?

Rachel: Well, he was always very precise in his planning. Very methodical and meticulous. About everything really. But the way he sounded in the letter made me think that there was something more spontaneous behind all this. Like an idea had just come to him and he was going to follow up on it right away, whatever the cost. That's not his style. He was never impulsive. There were always a lot of steps between an idea and the eventual follow-through: so many details that had to be figured out first, listed on paper, and then checked off one at a time. But this feels different somehow.

Ben (tying his shoes and then appraising himself in the mirror): Well, look, I know I am in no position to say this, I mean, all I know about the guy is from what you've told me, but I gotta say, the whole thing does seems a little strange: a letter from out of the blue, the mention of some big reveal to come in a follow-up phone call. It's a lot of drama if you ask me. I thought you said the only time the two of you ever talk is when something comes up with William or Nora?

Rachel (turning on her side and gazing out the ocean-side window): Up until yesterday, that was pretty much true; those *had* been the only times we communicated. I think the last time I actually spoke to him was back in January to let him know about William and Amy's ultrasound. Yeah, look, there's no doubt about it, everything about this is a little weird. But I don't really know what more there is to say about it or what more we can make of it right now. All I know is what's in the letter. And like I said, you're more than welcome to read it. I guess we'll just have to wait until he calls. In the meantime, I'd rather not dwell on it, okay?

Ben (still looking at his reflection in the mirror, making minor adjustments here and there): Yeah, sure, babe. No problem. (He takes a couple of steps closer to the bed and then glances at his watch.) Oh, shit. Look, I gotta run. I'm gonna be late for my meeting, but maybe tonight, you can tell me why the two of you split up in the first place. I don't think I ever heard that story. I mean, after all those years? Jesus. He must have done something awful for you to leave all that life behind and then put so many miles in between. I'm curious to hear what happened—just so I don't make the same mistakes, you know? Who knows, maybe I'll learn something. (He laughs weakly.)

Rachel: I don't know, Ben.

Ben: All right. Well, whatever. I'll call you later. Think about if you want me to pick something up for dinner or if you'd rather just go out. I'm good either way. Hey, are you okay, hon?

Rachel: Yeah, I'm fine. So long, Ben.

She stays in bed a little longer—until she too is late for work. She cannot pull away from the silence. Carried by the salt breezes, it winds its way through the empty loft, filling every corner and flooding her soul with

peace. She spreads her arms across the empty bed and beholds her heart and, as expected, finds no trace of Ben.

⤙⤚

Night of the same day. Candlelight has replaced sunlight as the shadow's source; its faint flicker reveals the empty loft. The clamor below of the Friday diners has finally ebbed. The shadows and the quiet and the solitude have mingled with the wine to intensify a state of dreaminess that has dogged her all day.

With a soft sigh of surrender, she moves to the hope chest that rests by the door and takes out the old keepsake box hidden within. Its Swiss maker's mark is stamped in bronze and tarnishing in the salt air despite her vows. She lets her thumb trace over the initials he once carved into its base. The collection of photos she keeps inside greets her with a force she still cannot explain. This time though, rather than look through them all as she occasionally will when the alchemy of wine and solitude gets the better of her, she knows exactly which one she wants to see.

They are sitting at a picnic table that once sat in the sand not far from here nearly forty years ago, the very same ocean before them. They are so young. Her hair glistens like satin and rushes down past her shoulders, bare, brown, and smooth in her white sundress. His is long as well, curled and lightened by long days in the sun, and their eyes shimmer with the electric current of youth. But that's not what she's looking for. The same thing that always draws her to this picture draws her again, and she looks once more to where she always looks, down there in the corner. She smiles at the way their fingers are entwined, the lightest of touches sealing the strongest of bonds, for she remembers this as the moment she realized she loved him, that he was the one, and she could see the long story of their future about to unfold.

The imprint of that moment still lingers, and she guesses it always will. It overcomes her with hurricane strength. A tear she didn't know was coming stains the inside of that beautiful keepsake box, then another, and she says aloud to no one, "Enough. That will be enough. No more now."

She gathers up the stack of old photos and holds them briefly in her wide-open hands. Before any more tears can fall, she places the pile back inside the box and secures the tiny silver clasp. All but this one, she thinks, and instead, pins it to her wall before climbing into bed, reminding herself to get a frame for it first thing in the morning.

SOLSTICE

The cold, dead heart of winter had arrived at last.

Chapter

7

"Hey, wait. I just thought of something!" My exclamation came blurted out in between bites of thick, cheesy pizza. "You know what this reminds me of? It's like something you see on TV. You know, where the savvy secret agent has mapped out all the details of the apocalypse he's trying to prevent. C'mon, you know what I'm talking about, right? The wall is covered with the small pieces of a case he's trying to crack. And they're all connected like a spider's web with strings and pushpins so the audience can see the unbelievable complexity of the case that only 007 or Jack Bauer or Jason Bourne could ever solve and how it all, eventually, points to one logical conclusion. That is *exactly* what this wall reminds me of."

It was the week after Thanksgiving, and the day had been sunless and cold. Wilson and I were sitting in his den on a pair of folding chairs he brought up from the basement. They provided a perfect perch from which we could sit back and admire the effluence of his photograph wall. Behind us, the TV flickered on mute, silenced during halftime of the Kentucky-Duke basketball game that had been the more overt object of our evening's intention. I had been confused about how a guy who hated the Cubs with so much passion could ever wind up rooting for the loathsome Blue Devils—until I learned about his undergraduate days in Durham, right over there where the gothic chapel and bell-bottomed girl loomed so large in several color shots.

The remnants of a Giordano's deep-dish lay in the kitchen as did the last two bottles of the six-pack of Stella I picked up at Waltons. The game was a blowout. The Wildcats had too much length, and really, it was too early in the season for any nonconference matchup to hold our attention. I think we were both relieved to tune it out at the half.

Leaving him to mull over my sharp, pop culture observations, I went to the kitchen to grab the beers. When I returned a minute later, he was standing at the wall and staring like an astigmatic at a couple of aged black-and-whites. The furrows in his forehead conveyed deep concentration as if some detail in a photo had unveiled a previously untrodden thought. He took the beer from my hand and tiredly shook his head before settling back down in his chair. That thought, it appeared, would remain concealed, at least for the time being.

Several clicks of the thermostat, and the room had finally begun to warm. The quiet and the stillness were nice. The wall had our full attention. We were in no rush. I was certain that the story, if we let it, would unfold at its own pace, and we both sat back as if we had all the time in the world.

"I'm not crazy, right? You see that, don't you?" I continued trying to make my point. Now that it was out in the open, it seemed more obvious than ever.

"Yeah, well maybe," he said with more skepticism than conviction, "but without the strings or any kind of logical conclusion though. And whatever happened to the epic poem? The journey of Odysseus, remember? I think I liked that analogy better."

"Look, sure, I'll grant you the strings aren't there. We'll just have to imagine those. That's easy enough. But I'd hold off just a little while more before assuming that there's no logical conclusion to be drawn here. I have a feeling we may find that yet. In fact, I'd be willing to bet that last piece of pizza on it. We just need to figure out the right way to look at it—what lenses to use, what angles to take. That sort of thing. It'll come." I tried to sound credible but worried that my confidence was coming across like empty bluster. I needed to reload with more persuasive ammo. So I doubled down.

"You know, this *is* what I *do,* right? For a living? Connect images to stories? Remember, Wilson, I'm a pro. When you see that sultry model getting out of her cherry-red Lexus with all those shiny raindrops on the hood and suddenly all you can think about is how you gotta get yourself a Lexus even though you never once before in your entire life ever gave a single thought to buying a Lexus—you think that's an accident? A coincidence? That's me! And if my suspicions about this wall are right, there *is* a really good story here. If we follow it, I'm pretty sure it will lead us to some kind of conclusion; the best stories always do. We may not be able to predict what that conclusion will be, we're just getting started, but I'm thinking that when we're done, the story may come out sounding like the saga of an everyman's journey after all, at least to us."

"Or a tragedy," he said.

"Why do you say that?" I asked.

"Ah, I'm just kidding," he replied before downing his beer.

I think we both knew that he was a thousand miles away from kidding. But maybe, in a way, he was right. What is a tragedy, after all, but a particular kind of story? The kind that follows a brave and courageous hero as he wields an indomitable spirit in the face of formidable obstacles, regardless of whether they come from outside or within. Was that what Wilson meant? I wasn't so sure.

We sat for a while more, drinking our beers and looking at the wall, inviting its sharp imagery to come and disencumber our thoughts and perhaps insinuate a further impression or two. We didn't have to wait long.

"But really," he continued, "when you step back and think about it, objectively, there is something tragic here. You can't deny that. I mean look at it. All these photos of all these people over all this enormous span of years—flashes of time that were once so precious someone decided they'd be worth preserving forever, but now they're all gone and would be completely forgotten if they weren't hanging on this wall. Who knows? Maybe they are linked together according to some complex set of equations that has something to do with fate or destiny or poetry or chance. And maybe there is a story embedded somewhere in there. But what if there's not? What if they're just the silver halide distillate of desultory chaotic connections? And what if the harsh reality is that whatever brilliance was captured in those flashes is gone, forever, as if they never happened, and how tragic is that?"

The silver halide distillate of desultory chaotic connections? What? There was no time to unscramble that statement. Wilson was gathering steam like an old locomotive, brutishly building momentum with every stroke and running headlong toward what looked to be a treacherous stretch of track. "It's like I've lugged the weight of all these moments around with me for so many years and toward what end? In fact, the only logical thing I can conclude is, so what? What was it all for? Where did it all lead?" His eyes moved rapidly over the wall even as he savagely wrung his hands.

"I have a feeling you're about to tell me," I calmly submitted, but I don't think he heard me.

"Well, I can tell you where. It led to here and now, to this time, to this exact point in time when a weary and lonesome guy who wasn't always this way now no longer cares about his beloved Duke Blue Devils or the taste of his beer or the sound of Springsteen's voice or the way Sophie's hand felt on my back, because it's harder and harder for him to feel anything at all, just sitting in his empty house, growing old all by himself and not doing much of anything about it except whining to his kind and patient friend because he feels like the only thing he can do anymore, other than just go to sleep, the only way he can feel what it felt like to be alive, is to look back to the past, to a time when he was different and every day was a surprise. Look, I don't want to sound overly dramatic here—I guess it's too late for that though, huh—but it really does make you wonder, what the hell was the point of all *this*?" He spread his arms to their widest span, waving them like a bird that was trying to take flight but instead only attesting to the messy sprawl of his life as represented by the photos on his wall.

I didn't object. How could I? From a certain perspective, I could see his point. I suspect that most everybody has, at one time or another, felt the yoke of the large, existential questions—the *Being and Nothingness* questions—weighing them down with darkness and contorting their way in the world. For centuries, the "point of it all" has been a topic that tested the wisdom of philosophers and college freshmen alike, and I knew the chances were slim that Wilson and I would make any significant contribution to the discourse that night.

But I also knew that Wilson's darkness was of another order entirely, a more virulent strain that resisted the enchantments that come freely to others, compliments of simply being alive. I hoped that the tapestry on his wall could serve as a cipher which, when viewed in just the right light, would enable him to decrypt important themes in the story of his life—themes that remained coded within the photos' glossy surfaces. Maybe that's what the strings on the secret agent's wall were meant to symbolize: the connective links between the story's constituent parts that need to be lace-worked together before any meaning—*or point*—can emerge. I was starting to think of those pictures as individual pieces of evidence that could be relied upon to testify to some semblance of truth about Wilson's life. And maybe that truth would be enough to dent the anguish in his voice and push back against the avatar that was so often by his side. Anyways, it was worth a try. I got up from my chair, seizing upon the tracery of an idea, and stood in front of the wall looking for a place to begin.

"Let me make some guesses here. Is this the uncle you told me about, the one from New York?" I said pointing to a black-and-white of the two of them in a shed.

"Yeah, that's him, probably around 1969 or so."

"And I would wager that this fine-looking couple here would have to be your folks, right? Mr. and Mrs. Lacy standing outside their very first home?"

"Yeah, I think that was right after my dad's discharge from the navy, must have been around '45. Elmira, New York. They really loved that house. Elmira, not so much."

"And this—this has got to be your wife?" I asked, hopscotching over to another section of the wall with a forward leap in time.

"Yep."

"Wow. She is gorgeous. The love of your life, isn't that what you said the other night? I can see why. And this must be you next to her, right, with the Peter Frampton hair? All you needed was the white jumpsuit and Les Paul guitar. By the way, didn't everybody have that album in the seventies? I must have played those songs a million times. Side four especially was like the soundtrack of my youth. "Lines on My Face" followed by "Do You Feel Like We Do?" I tried to sing a few lines, even adding the talk box distortion I remembered so well from so many years of listening to that album, but my efforts, like my voice, fell flat.

"Yeah, nice one, and by the way, you're not the first person to notice the resemblance. My glory days. Yours too by the sound of it."

"And speaking of resemblances, I'm guessing these are your kids, right? They are really beautiful. They both have your eyes. It's actually quite striking. I do want to hear more about them. But first, who is this little guy?" I asked, with another crisscross through time to select another picture on the wall.

"That—believe it or not—is my grandson, my son's son. The young Trevor Lacy. I guess he must be about six or seven by now. Cute kid, huh? Everybody said he was the most beautiful baby they had ever seen. He takes after his grandmother on that score, lucky kid. You might be interested to know that he is, apparently, quite the artist too."

Abruptly then, like he had taken a step too far, he stopped. It seemed that yet another thought, perhaps also untrodden, had just made itself known. As he weighed the costs of this new thought, Wilson slowly rose from his chair. His eyes were filled with the image of little Trevor and the small germ of a tear. "I haven't had a chance to get out there for some time now, but I hear him on the phone every so often. Once again, as it most always does, the fault for that lies with me. In a life burdened with a litany of so many regrets, that may be the loss that I regret the most."

We continued on for several more photos, meandering back and forth across the wall and ambling through time as we wove a lattice of random connections. With each picture I pointed to, Wilson moved closer to the wall. It was like I was reeling in a twenty-pound marlin on the open sea, tightening the drag a little more, then a little more, releasing the tension as needed, working cautiously but surely lest he make a run and I'd get spooled.

With each question I asked, he would extend his hand toward the photo and lightly touch it with his fingertips like it was encoded with braille and as if feeling was seeing and seeing would be believing. When we traced our way back to another picture of Trevor, this time dressed as a baseball player with a Halloween bag on his arm, Wilson reached out his hand to caress the edges of the photo just as he would with the child's tender cheek. I recognized that move. That was my move. I knew what it meant. I knew that the photo was speaking to him as they often do to me, and I knew the emotion that was brewing inside him. I felt it brewing in me.

Watching him embrace that photo of Trevor dislodged something else in me that, up until that moment, I didn't even know was there. I'll call it a misgiving. And as my misgiving rose, it grew feverishly like a tumor until it eclipsed my awareness of everything else. It surged without forgiveness until it overwhelmed my ability to suppress it and demanded release.

"You know, Wilson, there's something I need to tell you. I wasn't completely honest with you the other night."

The force of my words splintered the spell that had been cast by his grandson's photo. He turned from the wall and waited for more.

I held up a finger in a bid for patience and to quell the doubt that dawned on his face. And then I reached for my wallet. Hidden in the billfold was a photo of my own. It had been there for years. I used to depend on it whenever questions about my personal life would surface at work. And I relied on it to keep me grounded when I was alone. Over the years, I lost track of how many times it had been pulled from my wallet, just as I was doing then. But for phantomlike reasons that remained vaguely unsettling, it seemed like forever since I last held it in my hand.

Time had not been so kind. All those years buried in the folds—all that incessant rubbing and chafing against the leather—had stripped away precious microns of matter and left it threadbare and ragged. It sloughed a papery powder that accumulated like dust in the bottom of the wallet until the threaded sutures that had for so long sewed the image together lay exposed along the edges. It felt like a butterfly in my hand. I passed it to Wilson and watched as he examined it closely, struggling to reconcile what he saw in the photo with what he knew of me.

"That was taken a long time ago. We're all out at Benison's Farm for some family apple picking. I remember that day like it was yesterday. You never forget apples in September, the way they drape the branches and the smell before they turn. That sweetness. It was cold for late September, but no one seemed to mind. Janey's dad had a stroke about a week before, and she didn't really want to go. I had to convince her by invoking the 'sanctity of family traditions' argument. That always worked. You can see Hannah and Sara there, counting all the apples we had picked and moving them from bushel to bag. By rights, that was their job. And that right there is Aaron. Our oldest. He must have been around ten or eleven in that picture. You can see him there, holding on to Janey's hand and looking up at the trees, probably counting all the ones we'd missed. My son Aaron. Always traveling on a different wavelength. He died about a year and a half ago."

Wilson's eyes remained fixed on the image as he worked to accommodate the dislocation that must have followed my words.

I imagined the fragments of what he thought to be *my* story disassembling in his mind in order to make room for this new revelation. There would be places where my confession might explain some things more clearly and places where it would force a revision of others. Strangely though, his deliberations were mute; he did not say a word.

Usually, when someone hears about our loss, the response is to rush in and fill the silence with a fulsome declaration of sorrow. I certainly do not begrudge that. It seems only natural. I'm sure I would do the same if confronted with the discomfiture of hearing such news. But Wilson's reaction was different. He took the photo with him and silently sat down in his chair. Time passed while I fought the need to apologize for not mentioning it the previous night, or for making him uncomfortable, or for shifting the focus of our conversation to my problems, or for just complicating things in general. But I was tired of apologizing. Instead, I sat down next to him and let the silence smolder.

The stillness stretched on. I returned my attention to the wall while Wilson kept looking at the photo in his hands. Eventually, he passed the picture back to me, and I buried it again into my wallet, wondering when and under what circumstances it would next be seen.

"I don't know what to say," he finally began in a whisper. "Jesus, Owen. My god, I am so sorry. That is just awful. I cannot even begin to imagine what you and Janey and your daughters must have gone through, *are going through*. I don't know how you live with a loss like that. How does a parent survive the death of a child? How do you keep going? And you—you always seem so together. You always have such a positive outlook on things. I don't think I'll ever be able to understand that. I think I would just die."

So together? *If only he knew*, I thought to myself.

Bill talks about the breach that divides the way others see us from the way we see ourselves. He encourages us to bridge that gap by being honest with the people we care about. So I tried to explain. I told him that survival hadn't been easy and that, in fact, there were plenty of times when I thought I too would just die. Far from "together," I admitted to drowning in sorrow and feeling besieged by the painful questions and unmerciful guilt that never let up. I talked about loss and pain and my own spirals of sadness and that the only way I know how to hold on is to know that I'm needed. I mentioned the help I get from the support group and the importance of being with others. And I told him about the photographs. I described the solace that comes from looking at old photos and the lessons they have taught me about my life.

The solace that comes from looking at old photos. The phrase rang out like an invocation. Once uttered, it conjured the erratic energy that had been whirling around the room, and the air began to sting with a static charge. I could feel it crackling as it goose-bumped my skin like the overture to an August thunderstorm. The unbound electricity churned with unstable current and touched off tiny sparks of vision. A flash here. A glimmer there. Nothing more than that just yet.

Now, I've been around enough curious people to know that when their interest is sparked, there is a perceptible click that signals their abrupt engagement with the world. They instantly turn keen. They look outward with the fierce awareness of a predator chasing down an object of intrigue. This is the preferred state of curious people like Wilson: rustled, alert, and thrumming. So, I wasn't at all surprised when he looked at me with an inquisitive face and asked, "What does that mean—the solace that comes from looking at old photos?"

"Well, not to oversimplify," I started to explain, relieved to ride a cooler line of conversation even while the sparks continued to flare around us, "but the old adage that a picture is worth a thousand words is not a bad shorthand for this idea. Essentially, it's about finding meaning in images by looking at them, interpreting them, and reflecting on them. That's how it was presented to me in college. It's called visual literacy. The idea is that there is meaning engraved in all visual images. Some of the meaning is obvious and straightforward and lives right on the surface. That meaning is easy to extract. But much more—what I like to think of as the good stuff—is often hidden below the surface, and that meaning can be far more elusive. It takes a patient and perceptive observer—a visually literate observer—to ferret that out, to uproot it and then make sense of it. And here is where it gets really interesting. When those images have personal significance, like these photos on your wall for instance, there may be layers and layers of meaning that you never even considered, some of it deeply buried and stubbornly resistant. Once harvested though, it can be surprisingly rich. So, I do a lot of looking and reflecting and thinking about some of my own old pictures, trying to understand the meanings that arise. I even do some writing, which lets me express my thinking more clearly. It's helped me cope with my grief. That's what I meant by the solace that comes from looking at old photos. It hasn't always been pretty, but that's okay, I knew when I started that it wouldn't be so—"

And then, BANG! Fireworks exploding like the Fourth of July. Bursts of brilliance blinded my eyes. Colors. Patterns. And all sorts of grand designs.

Wilson rocked back from the concussion and stared at me with a blend of wariness, confusion, and concern.

"Whoa, whoa, whoa! Hold on a second!" I sprang out of my chair with a discernable shriek, unable to harness the excitement that was suddenly convulsing within me. I was shaking so much my knees nearly crumpled, and it was all I could do to keep standing. "Hang on. I just had a much better idea. I really do think there is a great story here. In fact, I'm surer of that than ever. But I think we may have been looking for it the wrong way. I don't think it's going to work by jumping around and randomly selecting photographs on your wall, just hoping that we stumble on some important themes. We'll never get anywhere that way. It would be like trying to catch a fish by convincing it to jump in the boat. No, forget the spy wall idea. That's all wrong. Why don't we try a different approach?"

True epiphanies are rare events. They appear like rainbows out of thin air, heaven-sent to stun the senses. Disparate particles converge in a favorable atmosphere, and something spectacular arises from nothing. Somehow, I had become a lightning rod for attracting all the wayward current that had been coursing through Wilson's den. It struck like a thunderbolt from out of the blue, delivering a jolt of energy that left me bedazed. And in the single breath that followed that strike, my perspective was transformed. The air was rinsed clean, and the view for miles ahead was free from obstruction. The clarity was breathtaking. I stole one more look at Wilson's wall and *knew* that we'd been going about this the wrong way. The grain size was all wrong. There was simply too much there. No, if we were going to use these photos to compel the story of Wilson's life, surveying this massive collage wouldn't do. The story would only come from a different way of looking.

I was on a crusade. I felt unstoppable. I had been called upon to convince Wilson of the righteousness of my vision. No objection, hesitation, confusion, or doubt could withstand the power of my compulsion. To this day, I think he agreed to hear me out because he recognized the insurmountable force he was up against. Or maybe he was just curious. Maybe he was beginning to see something else in his photographs that could be used to shed some light on his darkness—and that glimmer moved him with an amalgam of desperation and hope. Or maybe, Wilson Lacy is just a generous soul who did not want to disappoint a friend. Whatever the reason, the implication of his next statement was lost on neither of us:

"Okay, Owen. I'm all ears. Let's hear it."

"How about *you* try the visual literacy idea! Think about that for a second. It would be perfect. You could approach it like an experiment, an investigation to see what happens as a result of the process."

I could tell by his leery expression that it would be better to dial it down just a bit, to try and tame the tumult that continued to rage inside me. I wanted the next few words to sound as compelling to him as they did to me. And that required a moment to put my whirling thoughts into more coherent order. *Breathe, Owen. Breathe.*

"Sorry, look, I think I might have gotten too distracted by the brilliance of this wall. And that's on me. Let's reverse the field of vision. Let's narrow the bandwidth. What if, instead, you selected a small number of these photographs, just a handful, whatever amount feels right. We can decide that later. Let's say you pick a few for the way they stand out to you right now, *in this particular moment,* and at this point in your life as you face the prospect of another winter. You could choose them for the way they stir your imagination, or grab your attention, or for how you respond to them or how they make you feel … whatever. You could think of them as flashes in time that you would like to revisit, to explore a little further or unpack more deeply. And then, you could use the techniques of visual literacy to reflect on those pictures, one at a time, just to see what happens. Who knows, maybe you'll find some solace too. What do you think?"

It began with a series of nods. Just the smallest of bobs. Barely perceptible signs of regard. Then he walked over to the far side of the den, pivoted sharply on his heels, and looked again at the wall. This time though, the angle was different. *His* perspective was changed. He scrunched up his eyes to varying degrees like he was searching for something shrouded in fog. A sound like the buzzing from high-tension power lines leaked from his lips. And when he began stroking his chin in a profoundly contemplative state, I knew I had him.

"Ah, so now you're appealing to the scientist in me. Well played, Owen. Well played. You just shifted the lens we had been using from a deductive one to an inductive one. Very clever. I'm impressed. And you know what? I get it. That approach makes sense to me. To be honest, I've always preferred inductive methods of investigation with all their inherent messiness over the more prescriptive methods of deduction that seem so beholden to a strict interpretation of a singular scientific method. After all, science *is* fundamentally inductive by nature. At its best, it uses observation as a basis for generating laws and theories about how the universe works, and if I hear you right, I think that's what you're proposing here, yes?"

Was it? "Uh, okay, whatever, sure, if that works for you. I'm not sure that was my intent, but yeah, that sounds right, as long as we're talking about replacing observations of the universe with observations of a few pictures on your wall here. Keep going."

"No, that is exactly what you're proposing. And it's the right paradigm to apply to this problem. That was good thinking. I guess I could see maybe conducting a trial under those sorts of conditions. At the very least, it might be an interesting exercise. I do like the idea of approaching it as an experiment—a visual literacy experiment. I might even frame it around some kind of testable hypothesis, and I could record the results as findings. I'll have to think more about that, but the idea is provocative. By focusing on a few discrete moments across the length of my life—flashes in time captured on film—I ought to be able to extrapolate meaning in a focused and empirical way."

He was moving quickly, but that was Wilson's way, always wishing to get on with things when there were so many things to be done. He strode briskly throughout the room, alternating between the front of the wall where he would stare at something up close and then back to the rear of the den to peer again through the wide-angle lens. Each revolution generated more ideas about his experiment. They geysered effortlessly and without reservation as he molded the contours of the visual literacy concept to his scientist's sensibilities, and we rode that enthusiasm as far as we could.

"But how to choose the right photographs for the experiment? What's the methodology?" he wondered aloud on one of his swings to the back of the den. My assurance that "you'll know 'em when you see 'em" was met with a contemptuous look of suspicion. That, apparently, would never do.

"No, no, no. Come on Owen," he forcibly argued. "We can do better than that. Clearly defined selection parameters will be absolutely necessary in order to impose a systematic and consistent framework for investigation. We need that to ensure the reliability of the experiment." That is exactly what he said. Word for word. I'm not even kidding.

He proceeded to formulate several "selection benchmarks" that were jotted down in shorthand and taped to the wall. With that accomplished, there was nothing left to do but the choosing. Once again, he demurred at the idea of slowing down claiming that he saw no gain in delaying and that his will to proceed might never be greater. So I left him to it. There was still that last piece of pizza in the kitchen, and I wanted to let Janey know that I'd be out a little longer than expected.

He was standing where I left him when I came back to the den about twenty minutes later. But the collection of photos that graced his wall was now pockmarked with holes. Seven blank spaces had been carved into the canvas by the removal of the photographs that were now in his hand. "Seven seems like a pretty good number to me," he said, passing the stack of pictures to me. "Enough to ensure the culture of meaning without being too overwhelming."

I looked through the photographs one at a time. Of the seven images he had selected, six were color shots; one was black-and-white. Most included other people; a couple did not. Wilson appeared in five, but only once by himself, and the time period they represented stretched from infancy to late-middle age. I could find no algorithm that would have explained the selection of those seven photographs nor one thing they all had in common other than the simple fact that they were part of the story of Wilson's life. And that was enough. I handed the pictures back and asked if he had any thoughts about which he would examine first. He wasted no time in replying.

"It will be this one here. I knew it immediately." He held up a three-by-five color shot that showed an agile-looking teenager ablaze with the moxie of youth standing beside a sun yellow car in what looked to be the height of a long-ago, coppertoned summer.

"And why that one?" I asked.

"Well, I have always loved this picture. Even today, so many years later, I find that it evokes a lot of emotion, maybe what you would call meaning. I thought that would make it an easy point of departure and allow me to gain some confidence with the process." Then his eyes took on that same glassy sheen as he dipped into the bottomless lagoons of reverie. I felt him slip away, gliding on the rails of sweet recollection as his heart and his mind went shimmering back even as he stood steadfast beside me with his hand grasping his photos.

"It was the summer after high school, right before I left for college. We were probably getting ready to go out for the night. An adventure was waiting. The air bristled with it. That's what it felt like every night. It was a time when anything was possible and everything was new. Literally anything might happen that night. Do you remember the times when you could say that—and it was true?

"I remember feeling like I was leaving something behind, like I was casting off a troubled part of myself and was about to embark on my halcyon days. I sometimes think of that as the high point of my life—the sweet spot—and I see myself in this picture standing on the cusp of something magnificent. I mean, Christ, look at me. I was transcendent. You can see that in my face. I was hopeful, happy, alive, longing for whatever was coming—the exact opposite of how I am today. It's just so difficult to reconcile all of that with how I feel now. How can the same person be so different within the span of a single lifetime? How is that even possible? I guess I would like to think about that. So, why not start there?"

Why not indeed? In fact, I think it was obvious to both of us that he had already begun.

He turned his back to me to lay the photographs down but also, I think, to hide his face as he wiped away a tear. And really, who could scroll back over four decades of their life to recall themselves as they were in their rapturous prime and not be touched to shed a tear or two of heartache? I reached out to grab his shoulder, knowing that the journey ahead would not be easy, that more tears were sure to come, and to let him know that he would not be traveling alone.

"Hey, do you remember what you told me in the garage a while ago, those lessons from your uncle about courage and compassion when taking on a difficult challenge, whether it's restoring an old car or saving a soul? That seems like awfully good advice to keep in mind as you start rooting out the meaning from these wonderful images. Courage and compassion, my friend. Let's see how the story unfolds."

The Blue Devils got crushed, brutally stomped, raising all sorts of questions about their toughness heading into conference play. It was late. Coach K's fiery postgame exhortations were likely nothing more than chilly echoes rumbling around in the heads of the Duke starting five. Time had slipped its gears and ticked by unawares. But despite the late hour, I could tell Wilson was eager to get on with it, and I knew it was time for me to go. I headed toward the kitchen to find my coat and then remembered one last thing.

"Oh and I'm supposed to tell you that you are expected to join us for dinner next Saturday. That's tree-trimming night, another in a long line of Conway family traditions. The girls will be in town, and Janey and I would love for you to meet them. I'm told that under no circumstances am I to leave here until you accept so just plan to be there, okay? Believe me, neither one of us wants to face the consequences. Say around five?"

Though I'm sure he tried to disguise it, there was a noticeable droop to his shoulders just then, the slenderest shade of a slump caused by the weight of another invitation. But it lasted only a second or two until he could pull himself together and offer up a response.

"Um ... well ... okay ... sure. Thanks. Tell Janey I'll be there. And tell her too that I'll bring the wine. Enough already with the beer."

With that safely resolved, I reached out for a parting handshake. And just as he did on that snowy day before, he grasped my hand with longing. I could feel it right there in his grip. But there was something else there too in the way he shook my hand that night, something that I hadn't felt before: something that felt like resolve.

"Some evening, huh, Owen?" he said as he released my hand and began kneading the back of his neck.

"Indeed it was, Wilson. Indeed it was. I'm not sure either one of us could have predicted all that or how we wound up where we did. But for whatever it's worth, I had a great time, and I look forward to being along for the ride." I underlined my assertion with an unswerving look in the eye. It was a look I hoped would convey my allegiance.

"Yeah, hey, about that. Before you go," he added as we made our way to the door. "Please don't take this the wrong way, but why all the concern? Why all the compassion for someone you haven't known very long? Why would you want to spend your time doing stuff like this, especially given the heartbreak that you're going through on your own?"

I floundered in search of an honest reply, bollixed a bit by his question. Up until then, my motives were something I never considered. I knew I didn't have much of an answer. "You know, Wilson, it's an interesting question, and to tell you the truth, I'm not really sure. But I'll definitely give it some thought. If I come up with any great insights by next Saturday, I'll let you know. Five o'clock. Don't forget. See you then, my friend."

The door closed behind me, and the dark chocolate stain of early December was smeared upon everything. Despite the cold, I was glad I had left the Corolla at home. The walk would be nice.

Along the way, my mind churned with all that transpired over the winding course of the eventful evening inside Wilson's home. And as I replayed the moment of my leave-taking—that final moment of farewell—I was struck with the realization that I saw no sign of the avatar that often lurks beside him. That's not to say that Wilson was free or that the shadow of his sadness had departed. The story doesn't end here. Not by a long shot. I knew, of course, that the avatar hadn't gone far and would soon reappear to impose its heavy burdens on my friend time and again during the interminable winter that lay ahead. But for the moment, Wilson Lacy was alone in his old and empty house, with his photographs, his memories, and a plan.

Chapter

8

Janey and I met on a blind date in the spring of 1980. A pair of mutual friends thought we would make a good match and arranged for us all to meet for beers at the Cubby Bear Lounge before taking in the season opener across the street at Wrigley Field. For me, it was love at first sight.

This tall, willowy beauty from the pasturelands of Wisconsin stole my heart before the first pitch, and by the time the last batter was retired, I knew she would one day be mine. Throughout the rest of that spring and into the summer, we confirmed the intuition of our matchmaking friends by adhering to each other with a fierce attraction. Any remnants of prior entanglements were joyously jettisoned as we swooned in each other's company.

By the fall though, a malaise had set in. We were both naïve to the rhythms of romance and suddenly seemed unsure about what to do next. I guess, in some weird way, I owe the best parts of my future to the directorial talents of Robert Redford. For it was when we were leaving the theater on a raw November afternoon—having just seen the movie *Ordinary People*—that Janey, aroused by all the cinematically gorgeous family drama, took my hand and suggested that maybe I should come home with her for the Christmas holiday. This, I sensed, was the way forward, the tread upon which we would take the next step, and replied that yes, of course, I would love to accompany her to Chippewa Falls and at last meet Barb and Ted. To this day, I often wonder what would have become of us if we had seen *The Elephant Man* instead.

The Walkers were born with a Christmas spirit that courses through their veins like soda pop to vitalize their blood. That spirit peaks at the start of December as the holiday decorations are liberated from storage. The ornaments are unpacked with military precision and then spread like warm syrup according to blueprints passed down from generation to generation. For the next thirty days, these Yuletide fanatics adopt a seasonally specific language featuring perishable words like poinsettia, Blitzen, and frankincense. They obey arcane rituals involving mistletoe, Advent calendars, and angel chimes. They eat mincemeat, gingerbread, and plum pudding. And their auras burnish with a holiday sparkle that lures strangers into their homes—even a stranger like me who had been blithely debauching their only daughter—to enlighten them in the ways of Christmas. The Walkers—Ted, Barb, Janey, and brother James—were all born with that brand of Christmas spirit. I, on the other hand, was not. In the Conway home, Christmas just kind of came and went without much fanfare or noise.

For several years, Janey and I would return to that old two-story house on the shores of Lake Wissota, but I never did grow comfortable with the liturgy of the Walker family Christmas. Instead, I ended up feeling clumsy around so much holiday grace, always bumbling my attempts to arrange the fireplace kindling or violating the code-approved practice for the Hanging of Tinsel. Even when my place within the close-knit family was assured, still I endured the stings of their Seagram's-laced rebuke, laughing along with everybody else whenever a seasonal infraction occasioned the jab: "So, *this* is the guy she finally brings home?"

When our kids came along, it soon became clear that their genetic disposition toward the holidays came from their mother. Their arrival triggered an insatiable maternalism in Janey who managed to have the family Christmas migrate south to Chicago where it remains to this day. In the first few years under this new management, the Walker clan would descend upon our home bringing the Seagram's and their rollicking holiday ways to be resettled in our living room, transplanted from the Northwoods like a tender sapling in a new-growth forest. Well, that sapling has taken root. It has grown resilient under Janey's loving care, and for a few days before Christmas and a few days after, our house sparkles with a Rockwell-like holiday feel.

The Putting Up of the Conway Family Christmas Tree is scheduled midway through the sequence of preparations, falling squarely between the Hanging of the Outdoor Lights and the Appearance of the Holiday China. Traditionally, this effort is marbled with tension; it's a fidgety job. Ted and James always made it look so easy, as they did with everything else during the holidays: the scenically roaring fire, the tastefully placed garlands, the ambrosial hot toddies. In my hands though, the trunk of the tree wants to put up a fight ("Are you nuts? I'm not going in *there!*"). The hardware is always a little more rusty than the year before ("Ha! Turn *this* sucker!"). And my knees consistently choose *that* day to stage an uprising ("Bend? Who are you kidding?").

Adding to the tension this year was Hannah's surprise announcement that she was thinking about not returning to Madison for spring term. "I'm not sure I see the point of college anymore," she explained as she enameled a layer of bright purple polish on each of her nails, leaving Janey and me speechless.

Now, I suppose our house is not that much different from other houses with college-aged kids. It is elastic. When they leave for school, the house slowly shrinks to envelop us in a cozy, vacuum-packed seal. A new pace settles in. And then becomes routine. Their return for holidays and summers is marked by joyfulness to be sure, as well as a period of adjustment as the house must expand once again to accommodate the force of their kinematic pressure. A period of adjustment is always necessary; reestablishing equilibrium takes time. That period was currently underway. We were adjusting, and we would be fine. In fact, in short order, we'd be great—and getting the tree in the damn base would be a terrific first step.

Hannah was in charge of the stand. Sara was ready with the thumbscrews. I was holding the tree and driving it up and down, silently praying that I might chance upon the requisite—but stunningly elusive—degree of alignment. Several desperate attempts left me gasping for air. A cold slick of sweat puddled along the back of my neck. The girls were exchanging withering looks. Finally, after a particularly mighty thrust and quarter turn to the right, our luck paid off with the piney *plunk* that signaled success. And then the doorbell rang.

"Hey, Hannah. Can you get that? I don't want to let go of the tree until Sara gets those screws tightened up." Though my view was blocked in every direction by seven and a half feet of white pine, I could hear Wilson's voice as the front door swung open.

"Hi, you must be either Hannah or Sara, right?"

"I am indeed," she replied, beaming I knew, with a wide grin of mischief. "And you must be Mr. Lacy. Come on in. My dad is teaching this tree to dance. At the moment, things are not going so well."

With my left hand still clinging to the tree, I waltzed around to where I could see Wilson teetering in the doorway. "Yo, Wilson! Welcome. Come on in. That right there is Hannah, and this over here is Sara. Girls, this is my friend Wilson Lacy."

Courtly greetings were exchanged all around—followed promptly by Hannah's artfully timed question: "So, Dad, I'll bet you and Mr. Lacy can take things from here, right? Is it okay if Sara and I go back upstairs for a while?" The phone she kept in the back of her jeans had been buzzing nonstop.

"What do you say, Wilson? Think you could give me hand getting this thing set up?"

"Of course," he assured me.

And with that, the Conway girls vanished, poof, dematerializing like a mirage. Wilson laid his coat and a Waltons bag on a table nearby and then knelt to the floor to gain access to the fastening hardware. He evinced the same native comfort working flat on the floor as roofers do on a steep pitch, thirty feet in the air; it's like they're born to it. In a matter of seconds, he had the tree secured with an earthquake-proof solidity and standing perfectly straight—from *every* angle! A Christmas miracle.

"Well, that was certainly impressive," I said, cautiously loosening my grip but not quite ready to move away from the base just yet. "You really do have a knack with these things. Hey, welcome by the way. I'm glad you came."

"Thanks," he replied, whisking loose pine needles from the palms of his hands as he lifted himself from the floor. "It's nice to be here. Though, honestly, you really didn't leave me much choice. You can be pretty persuasive, you know." He turned to the table to recover the bag and then humbly handed it to me. The sharp creases ingrained in his sweater had yet to relax, and a dried dollop of shaving cream dotted his collar. He smelled faintly of powder and Old Spice. "I hope red is okay."

"It's perfect," I said. "C'mon, let's take these to the kitchen and get one opened up. Christmas treeing is a thirsty business in the Conway home. I could use a drink."

In our house, the route from the living room to the kitchen winds through a short hallway. The kids used to call it "the tunnel." Hanging in that hallway, just before a pair of pocket doors, is a series of portraits that rest in large brass frames. Aaron, Hannah, and Sara are captured in a triptych of photographs shot in the backyard as we sat beside a springtime fire pit and dusk settled around us. As I opened the doors that led to the kitchen, I noticed that Wilson was rooted in place. He was standing in front of those portraits, staring at them each, one at a time, with his hands laced tightly behind his head.

"Yeah, I took those a while ago, but we just got around to hanging them up," I said, returning alongside him so we both could admire the images. "We're all still getting used to them being in here. Nice though, huh? Even a ham-fisted hack like me can get it right every so often, and these three are about as good as it gets." It really was true. They are beautiful. Somehow, they manage to accentuate the subtle distinctions between the three Conway children—Aaron's abstraction, Hannah's mirth, Sara's grit—while affirming their congruity at the same time. When

I look at them now, after everything, I marvel at my luck. The light from the fire was just enough to expose the resplendence of their faces while keeping safely secret whatever dreams and disquiets were simmering behind their eyes. They are timeless. And heartbreaking too.

"These are remarkable," Wilson quietly avowed as his eyes gripped the photos. His words came slowly, ruminatively, laden with reverence. "They're like windows into their souls. They tempt your gaze. It's almost as if they're each making a silent disclosure of some kind, inviting the observer to imagine what it might be. They are truly riveting, Owen—beautiful images of a beautiful family." We stood there a while longer looking at the photos, and I let my perceptions fluctuate between seeing and listening. I knew my eyes were up to the challenge; seeing was easy. I wasn't so sure about my heart. I wondered if I would ever be able to hear the silent disclosures that lay behind the abstraction, the mirth, and the grit. And what would they reveal? As my fixation grew, I felt Wilson's hand patting my chest and then heard him confess in a suddenly more pressing tone, "You know, Owen, come to think of it, I could use that drink too."

The warmth of the kitchen hit us like a desert wind. We felt its full force on our faces, a hot, dry sirocco that nearly abraded the senses.

But still, the medley of aromas that saturated the air was just too wonderful to miss. It entered our noses and trickled down our throats like the juice from a holiday swizzle stick. Janey was pulling a pie from the oven as we entered, her Irish hue flushed with the charm of her exertions. Strands of hair had fallen loose from their bonds and, in a gesture that always set my heart aflutter, she bent a shoulder to brush them away. At the sight of us standing by the door gaping in awe at the bustling scene, she broke out in sweet laughter, flustered by the chaos that surrounded her.

"Wilson Lacy," she gasped as she searched for a place to deposit the pie. A well-placed elbow cleared some countertop and she laid the burbling pan to rest. At last unencumbered, she walked over to Wilson but refused his hand to give him a hug, leaving the outline of baking powder fingers on the back of his sweater. "Hey, it's good to see you again. I sure hope you're hungry."

"Janey, I'm not sure anyone could walk into this kitchen with all these great smells and feel anything other than hungry. Thank you again for asking me. It's nice to be here," he replied.

For a modestly sized house, our kitchen is unusually large. That was a real plus for Janey as we were looking to purchase our first home all those years ago. She held fast to the idea that the kitchen is the heart of a family home, and she immediately fell in love with the way this one pulsed. On the opposite end from where we just entered, there is a large pantry and then, right beyond that, another set of pocket doors that open to the dining room. As I was brushing the powder from Wilson's sweater, those farthermost doors opened, and Sophie walked in to grab the Christmas china. It could now be used to adorn the table she had been setting.

"And, Wilson, you remember Sophie, right?" I cringed with the fear that perhaps Janey was right; maybe it would have been better to let him know she was joining us. In my defense, I first heard about the plan the previous day and never had the chance to tell him. But Wilson showed neither discomfort nor much surprise at the appearance of our additional guest. Instead, he simply slid away from my brushing, quickly adjusted the sleeves of his sweater, ran a hand through his dark, wavy hair, and then glanced at Sophie with a mostly unassuming smile. "Of course," he said. "Nice to see you again, Sophie."

"And it's nice to see you too, Wilson," she replied, offering the tips of her manicured hand in greeting.

It's a long-standing joke that Sophie came with the house. Over the years, she has become the sister that Janey always longed for, the confidante she never had, a coconspirator in schemes of the heart, and—after a few of their signature gin-and-vermouth martinis—both confessor and confessant. Sophie has that way about her, discharging a radiance that burns like the Mediterranean sun, drenching those lucky enough to be nearby with a midsummer's ease. She is also not one to pass up an occasion as evidenced by her magnificent dress. It sculpted her curves in a luxurious sheath of soft shimmering silk that glittered with sequins of starlight. The magenta color inflamed her eyes and showed off her pale shoulders to great advantage. She looked like she stepped out of the pages of *Vanity Fair* and lent a welcomed festivity to the air. But when her demur greeting caused me to nearly blurt out some remark of protest, Janey flashed me a look that suggested maybe I'd better stand down.

So there we were, the four of us in the kitchen with only the ticking of the oven to mark off the seconds as we adjusted to the geometry of the situation. *Four discrete points are located on a grid in a coordinate plane. Given that the space extends infinitely in all directions, how can the distance between any two points be determined?* As the various angles were being measured and mapped, I realized I was still holding the bag with two bottles of wine.

"Oh, hey, look what Wilson brought," I chirped with relief. "A pinot and a cabernet. It's almost like you left him a list. Which should we open first?" Everybody agreed to go with the pinot now and save the cabernet for later, an insinuation of optimism for the evening ahead. I reached for some glasses, Wilson did the honors, and Janey proffered a toast.

"To Christmas, with good friends both old and new. May we use the blessings of a new year to shed some light into the lives of others." Then, as if the situation's geometry had all at once been solved, our four glasses clicked in perfect symmetry, resounding at just the right wavelength to completely shatter the ice.

Dinner was still an hour away. Janey and Sophie assured us they had the preparations under control, so I offered to give Wilson a tour of the house. We grabbed our wine and began in the basement, working our way up floor by floor. Each room compelled a story or two culled from the annals of Conway family lore. The stories tumbled with ease, and we marveled that so much life could be contained by the elasticized walls of a house that measured roughly two thousand square feet.

With the tour nearly complete, we climbed the narrow staircase that led to my studio on the third floor. "This," I proclaimed as we entered, "is my favorite room in the house." It was easy for Wilson to see why. Like childhood pirates, we peered through the window to survey our neighborhood from that cozy crow's nest in the sky. It all looks so different—so much more tractable—from that unique point of view. More pliable somehow. The radiator was scrubbing away the chill, and the intensity of our isolation from the rest of the house doused the room with a slumbersome calm. I showed him some of the sketches I was working on, and we talked for a while about the connections we had been uncovering between my world of art and his world of science. And then we sat back to enjoy the wine.

"So, I hope you're not uncomfortable with Sophie being here. Kind of unexpected, huh? Sorry about that. Janey just mentioned it, and well, I wasn't quite sure how to bring it up. I guess I just punted. I hope it's okay."

"Oh, Owen, that's no problem at all. It's fine, really. Actually, I haven't been feeling much of the old holiday spirit lately. I keep thinking I'm going to look in the mirror one of these days and the ghost of some Dickensian humbug will be staring back at me. It all just seemed so much easier to come up with some excuse and beg off. I almost did, in fact. But your house—all these preparations, the way you all are around each other—it's pretty wonderful. It's nice to be part of something."

"Well, Christmas runs deep in this family, my friend. And now your name has been entered into the Ledger of Traditions. I'm sorry to say that there is no way out—ever. You might as well go ahead and pencil us into your December calendar from here to eternity. And I am glad you're okay with the guest list. That should entitle me to a reasonable plea bargain with the wife later on. So tell me—I'm dying to know—what's going on with the photographs? Is the experiment underway?"

"Actually, it is," he answered. He bent slightly forward in his chair and took a small drink of wine. It seemed as if he were trying to narrow the space between us so his words would not have to travel so far and not lose their edge. In turn, I moved my chair a few inches closer. "You remember that first picture, right? Well, it turns out it was a good move starting with that one. There really is so much there. I quickly understood that the only way for me to conceptualize my thinking about all that meaning was to write about it, just as you suggested, like in a memoir of sorts. And here's something you may find interesting. As I was looking, I came up with things to write, and as I wrote, I found there were more things to see. That was very surprising to me, the recursive nature of the process, how the looking informed the writing but also how the writing informed the looking. That was something I truly did not expect, a function of the constraints of my own linear thinking, I suppose. After that, layers of meaning just seemed to peel back one after the other, simply by looking and writing, and writing and looking. It was like I was excavating something—the source of my sorrow, it seems."

At that point, his ability to continue came brusquely to an end. It appeared that he had just exhausted his daily dose of good feeling that had been roused by the work and would allow himself no more for the day. The reflex to return to the confines of his sadness appeared autonomic. I was ready to greet the avatar, but it never showed. Instead, Wilson reached into his pocket and pulled out another photograph. I remembered seeing it the other night. I assumed this was to be photograph number two and that his curiosity about what it might contribute to the experiment was enough to keep the sadness at bay. At least for the moment. He handed the photograph to me.

"That one's next," he began, casting his eyes to the floor and resting his chin on top of a fist. There was a more plaintive tone to his voice right then, and it carried the unmistakable tune of reminiscence. "It was taken by a student of mine a few years ago during a class I was teaching at the university. We were doing an activity to come up with a working definition of momentum by dropping contraptions they had designed for the purpose of keeping an egg from breaking. We were exploring the way NASA engineers figured out how to land delicate rovers on the surface of

Mars. Anyways, when I looked at this picture the other day, I saw that so much of my professional life—so much of my thinking—is wrapped up in the subtext of this moment, not so much in the action but rather in the reasons *why* that action is taking place. And that *why*—all those unexamined assumptions that seem so central to my life as a scientist and a teacher—is what I want to explore in this second photograph. I thought it would make a good place to go next. What do you think?"

"I think it's perfect, Wilson. I really do. I also think it's obvious that you are off and running with the experiment. You're on a roll. It looks like my work here is done!" I handed him back the picture but saw that he wasn't quite ready to put it away.

Instead, I watched as he idled over the photo a little longer. And then I witnessed again the power of a visual image—even a simple photograph—to transport a person to another place and time. There is nothing that compares with that power, nothing that has the same convoluted salience—the same visceral force—to fold time like origami. I watched his gaze disperse and his head assume that odd angle, signs that augured his departure as he withdrew from the studio—just for a moment—swept away by the stroke of another reverie to that teachable moment back during his days at the university. There was no way of telling how long he drifted there. It can seem like hours are impossibly fit within the narrowest arc of a second hand's sweep. The heaviness that accompanied his return slammed against his chest with enough gravity to cause him to gasp for air.

"Thanks Owen," he uttered through the choke of a fretful cry as his eyes cleared once more, "but the work, as you put it, is far from done. Hang in there with me a little while longer if you can. You see, I seem to have forgotten just how much I loved the work, the interaction with students, generating that sense of discovery. It makes me wonder what I am supposed to do now that I don't do that anymore. What is there left in this world for an old man to do? To be honest, I haven't a clue. Yet another sad regret, I suppose." He stood from his chair and turned again to peer out the window, at the bitter black night before him. Then he slid the photograph back into his pocket, and when he turned back around, his eyelids were heavy with mourning.

Mining the meaning of such memorable moments is neither easy nor for the faint of heart. That's just the plain, unvarnished truth. You can take that from me. I was just about to say something along those lines when Sara's voice came thundering up the stairs: "Yo, men of the third floor, the holiday feast awaits. Let's do this." Instead, Wilson and I finished our wine and smiled in silent agreement that such platitudes would probably be redundant.

The dining room was bathed in candlelight when we arrived downstairs. The spell it cast upon the scene was enchanting. The room danced as if it were alive, animated by the flickering flame that itself seemed alive, changing shape and painting silhouettes on the walls as if by whim or fancy. I could not help but think that even the coldest, Scroogiest heart would melt at the sight of that table and all that sumptuous candlelight. Its glow swathed us all with the firmness of faith that if this room and these people were the only things left in the world, that would be okay, at least for the night.

We gathered around the table and stood behind our chairs—Janey at one end, me on the other, Hannah and Sara on one side across from Sophie and Wilson on the other—each reveling in the jewellike settings before us.

"Wow, you guys really outdid yourselves," I said.

"Yeah? You like? I guess Sophie and I make a pretty good team, huh?" Janey replied before indicating that we should take our seats. "So, before this meal gets underway, would anyone like to say a few words?"

"I will if that's okay. That is, if no one minds." Sara's offer stilled the room, even the dancing candlelight. "I just learned this prayer from a Buddhist friend of mine at school. He says it at every meal, and I really like it. Maybe this would be a good time to try it out. It goes like this: 'We receive this food in gratitude to all beings who have helped to bring it to our table and vow to respond in turn to those in need with wisdom and compassion.'"

In the fullness of the silence that followed, Janey reached for her napkin and dabbed the corners of her eyes. Then, she leaned over to caress Sara's cheek and kiss the top of her head. "That was beautiful, honey. Thank you."

"Just a second, Mom. I'm not done yet." And here I watched my youngest child do something I had never seen her do before. With her left hand, she reached for her mother's hand and held it in her own. Then, with her right, she sought out her sister's hand and grasped it as well. The rest of us took our cue and held on to each other's hands while she continued.

"And to any deities that may be listening, I ask for something more so that others may find peace this holiday season. Grant the peace that comes from forgiveness to my mom and dad who are hurting so much right now even though they try not to show it, grant the peace that comes from wisdom to my sister so she may realize how good she's got it up in Madison, grant the peace that comes from loving oneself to Sophie who shares that love with everyone around her, grant the peace that comes from companionship to Mr. Lacy so he might openly receive love from others, and for my brother, Aaron, grant him the peace that comes from knowing that he will always be loved and never forgotten."

"And what about for you sweetheart," I said, reaching for my own napkin.

"Nah, I'm good. Let's eat." Pure grit, that kid!

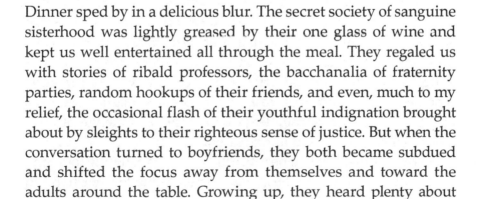

Dinner sped by in a delicious blur. The secret society of sanguine sisterhood was lightly greased by their one glass of wine and kept us well entertained all through the meal. They regaled us with stories of ribald professors, the bacchanalia of fraternity parties, random hookups of their friends, and even, much to my relief, the occasional flash of their youthful indignation brought about by sleights to their righteous sense of justice. But when the conversation turned to boyfriends, they both became subdued and shifted the focus away from themselves and toward the adults around the table. Growing up, they heard plenty about the courtship of their parents. That was an old and moldy story. Now they were eager to stock the shelves of their romantic larders with other, fresher exploits of college amour. And there were two people in the room who just might deliver.

Wilson volunteered to go first. He shared the story of finding his heart's desire in his very first year at Duke. To hear him tell it, he fell in love with a single glance. He claims she never even noticed. It took him all four years before he could muster up the courage to ask her out for a date. But then, in the final few weeks of their final semester, the pressure of the rapidly eroding calendar compelled him to action. So, he asked that girl to dinner and confided his feelings, recalling how simple love seemed after that. And he confessed that though he and his wife are no longer together, the memory of new love still endures. His story seethed with ardor and enthralled Hannah and Sara, who were no doubt left wondering if perhaps there was someone out there who loved them just as much and just as ardently.

Still, like wolves, they hungered for more. Now, it is true that the girls and I have invented an uncertain mythology about Sophie's love life, replete with heroes and heroines, conquests and surrenders, stormy passions and dire tragedies, and, of course, an occasional scandal or two. We sometimes indulge in sympathetic speculation about her past, but our constructions, like most myths, remain clouded by the lack of any verifiable truth. And Janey, who alludes to knowing all, only riles our mythologizing with her silences. So when Hannah asked Sophie about her experiences of love as a young woman, I, for one, anticipated a grand telling.

Alas, to my dismay, all she would say on *that* subject was that she had been quite a popular girl at the University of Florida, and that it's probably best left at that. Before leaving the subject entirely however, she did offer one piece of advice to the girls. And because of their great respect for Sophie's magnetic charms and glamorous ways, they leaned in close on the edge of their chairs, all ears and rabid anticipation.

"I think Wilson said it beautifully," she began, lightly touching his shoulder in a tender bestowal of credit. She left her hand to linger there while Wilson stared at his plate. "Love truly is the best thing this world has to offer. It is life's greatest gift, and I can't wait for the two of you to feel true love. Love will come. Rest assured, love most certainly will come, but maybe not where or when or how you expect. That is its mystique."

At first, the only sound left in the room was the quivering candlelight as it gorged on the air, more plentiful suddenly as we all held our breath. Then, taking her hand from Wilson, Sophie began twisting the bracelets she wore on her wrist. The sound of those bangles and the quivering flame excited our impatience for more. Her eyes were alight with the shivering jet as if to illuminate the unfolding thoughts in her mind. She shined that light directly on the faces of my daughters before shifting to a sterner, more serious tone.

"But whatever you do, don't ever let a man or his love define who you are. That, my dears, is a road that leads only to heartbreak. Knowing who *you* are, understanding what makes *you* special, figuring out what *you* want from life can only come from you—and no one else. Never, ever sacrifice that privilege or give it away to anyone. That belongs to you and you alone. You got that?"

Hannah and Sara nodded with spellbound looks. Their slack mouths and gaping eyes indicated that they did, in fact, most definitely get it. So, the mystery of Sophie's romantic past would endure for the time being, but I no longer mind. It's explanations for everything that we have in abundance these days. There are too few myths left in the world.

Nothing much remained of the meal. Wilson and I cleared the table, and we all moved to the living room for the tree trimming that followed next on the evening's agenda.

Janey suggested a fire, and Wilson offered his services. With his usual fastidiousness, he snapped up the kindling, and in no time at all, an elegant lattice of twigs sat on the fireplace grate. I watched with envy as it caught with a single match and then burst into a roaring, snapping exuberance of flame that would have put Ted and James Walker to shame.

As the years have gone by, the decorating of the Conway tree has taken on a comfortable shorthand that is blissfully free from pretense or facade. No longer do we feel compelled to hang *all* the decorations—one at a time, like Faberge eggs, in age-order rotation—or continually modify the tree's appearance to fit some Madison Avenue standard. Instead, there's a lovely casualness to the process now that we have all grown to relish. The ornaments come wrapped in stories that have ripened like legends. They have been retold so many times that only a word or two are needed to force them to blossom again. In short order, I was capping off the trimming with the crepe paper star. Hannah plugged in the lights, and we all stepped back to admire our magnificent seasonal handiwork.

With the tree decorated, Janey began setting up the tripod for the annual holiday photo, the last official item on the evening's order of business. Following her direction, the five of us arranged ourselves in front of the tree's most photogenic side while she peered through the camera to compose the shot.

"Okay, you guys look great. Everybody ready? Owen, I'm coming to stand right next to you after I hit the timer. Wilson, scrunch in a little to your left. There. That's splendid. Here we go."

The first take was perfect. No need for a do-over.

It was Sophie who then proposed that a Conway family photo should follow. So, Janey began realigning the camera, moving it in closer to tighten the frame. Wilson drifted out of the view and sat down on the sofa. And that's how we stood: Janey behind the viewfinder establishing the shot, Hannah, Sara, and me posing patiently in front of the tree.

As we waited, I noticed that the room felt warm, inexplicably so, and not just from the fire. It was like when you move from a chilly microclimate in a wood's hollow into more drowsy air just a few feet above. The change is sudden, startling, and occurs all at once. The source of that warmth soon became clear as I followed the arc of an extraordinary sequence of events.

It began as Sophie wiggled out of her shoes. She slipped across the room in black stockinged feet and headed straight toward the couch. Gathering the hem of her dress, she sat down beside Wilson, tucking one leg under the other. She handed him his wine and, with a dash of panache, offered her own for a soft, subdued click. Finally, she placed her free hand on the side of his thigh and murmured something into his ear. Gradually, a sublime smile overtook his face suggesting that a more narrow form of geometry might now be in play. *Two discrete points are plotted on a grid in Euclidean space. Each resides on a separate line segment. Assume the points are traveling independently along the line segments and that the lines are not parallel. Calculate the intersection point.*

"Hey, you guys—yoo-hoo, Owen, girls—over here, okay? Family photo remember? Everybody ready? I'm coming in right next to Dad again. Here we go."

It was somewhere between the snap of the shutter and the imprint of the image's impression, that Hannah twisted around on her pale painted toes and asked again in an expedient way, "Hey, Dad, Mike Flannigan is having some people over tonight. Is it okay if Sara and I walk over there for a while?" And for the second time that evening, the Conway girls displayed their remarkable powers of dissolution. Poof, evaporated, Fata Morgana, trailing their irrepressible élan and the scent of Ralph Lauren's *Romance* in their wake.

The house registered their departure by contracting around the four of us. It sealed us in with a quilt of velour that made everything feel snug, a bulwark against the falling snow and howling winds of a midwestern winter's night. But without the girls' sparkle to buoy us, we were left a little deflated and unsure about what to do next. Thankfully, Janey is well attuned to the rocky undulations of social gatherings that are sometimes occasioned by shifting geometries of one sort or another. She quickly picked up on the lull and asked, "Who would like more wine?"

"Oh yeah, right," I replied sprightly. "We have that cabernet to open." I started toward the kitchen to retrieve the bottle, but Janey had other plans. She often does—and they are usually too subtle for me to see.

"I'll get the wine, honey," she proposed with a wink. "Why don't you put on some music?"

Now that was a great idea. Music was just what we needed, and I knew just what to play. Years ago, I inherited a large collection of albums from my father including a selection of holiday LPs. Those records were the Con Man's single concession when it came to Christmas. The songs from those albums are permanently tattooed on my childhood memory. So when the needle touched down on side one of *A Jolly Christmas*, Sinatra's voice strafed me with a hailstorm of memories that sent me right back to that small, overheated two-flat on Kingston Boulevard. I guess music can fold time pretty well too.

Four fresh glasses of cabernet appeared, along with some cheese, apple slices, and plump red grapes. For the first time that evening, the four of us sat back with the quiet contentment of kittens after a warm saucer of milk. The wine, we agreed, was exquisite. We each basked in a moment of pleasure as it fragrantly bloomed in our mouths.

"I sure hope I didn't come across too harshly with the girls at dinner tonight," Sophie said apologetically as she reached for a grape. "I'm not sure where all that so-called advice came from. It wasn't my intention at all. It's just when I look at them, it's so easy to see myself as the young girl I used to be—the one who placed so much trust in the fairy tale of romance only to be disappointed time and again. You know I would never discourage them from their dreams, but it's a lot harder to be a young woman today than it was when we were their age. I hear that from the girls at the restaurant all the time. From what they tell me, Prince Charmings and Sir Galahads are pretty damn scarce these days, and the fact that two of them are sitting right here in this living room means there are even fewer to go around."

Janey laughed. "Well, boys, I think you both just received a compliment. But, Soph, are you nuts? That was great. That was the kind of advice they need to hear, and believe me when I say that it meant much more coming from you. Did you see the way they were watching you? You could have sold them on the return of acid-washed jeans."

"Yes," I enthusiastically agreed, touched a bit by the wine. "Speaking on behalf of the princes in the room *and* as the father of those two young ladies, I too appreciated the advice. We princes *are* as rare as unicorns, and we possess a unique combination of qualities that is to be considered the *minimum* standard expectation for *anyone* hoping to appear in the lead role in either of my daughters' fairy tale romances. Isn't that right, Galahad?"

"Well, I don't know much about fairy-tale romances, but I do know something about raising kids, and those two seem like absolutely terrific kids to me," Wilson said. "You both have done a wonderful job raising them. They do you great credit."

Sophie nodded with agreement. "They *are* strong young women, Owen. And Wilson is right. The two of you have done a remarkable job and should feel great about who they're becoming. They will do well in the world. They are smart, beautiful, kind, and tough. God knows they're tough. They've got their mother's fierceness and their father's compassion. That is a pretty terrific combination if you ask me, and they will need both of those qualities as they make their way."

The sigh that ensued could not be concealed, and she stared longingly into the fire. The next few words came more deliberately, intoned by a sorceress divining the future from the shape of the flames. "I just know that there are no fairy tales waiting for them at the end of some rainbow—life is too damn complicated for that—but there is an awful lot of magic out there just waiting to happen. And *that*, I am quite sure, they'll soon find out on their own. Cheers to that," she said, raising her wineglass and taking a drink, the rest of us following her lead.

Wilson went over to stir the sleepy logs, and Sophie watched him as he worked. Janey turned the lights down low, leaving the firelight on its own to suffuse the room with the charm of its chestnut glow. She snuggled in close, adding a few degrees more to the warmth I was already enjoying.

With his fireplace work completed, Wilson returned to the group, topped off the four glasses with what was left of the wine, and sat back down on the couch. The wine, the fire, the good food, and the friendship expunged from my mind anything more having to do with vertices and radii, preferring now to simply let the evening run its course along whatever tangents fate would allow.

Have yourself a merry little Christmas,
Let your heart be light.
From now on, our troubles will be out of sight.

Have yourself a merry little Christmas,
Make the Yuletide gay.
From now on, our troubles will be miles away.

The time passed in quiet conversation. Half-hearted suggestions of a game or a movie were vigorously rejected in favor of the lazy reposefulness that had overspread the room. We talked in low, hushed tones, not wanting to disturb the moment's delicate, soft texture. We talked about kids and parents, losses and loves, dreams and fears, and plans for the future. We talked about things we had experienced, those that we only wish we had, and those that we hope to experience before it's too late. We talked about ourselves and about each other and some of the others with whom our paths in life have crossed.

In time, the pauses began to lengthen as our energy slowly drained. Eventually, the fire consumed the last of its fuel, combusting itself into an iridescent mound of exhausted coals that looked like they were lit from within by tiny orange lights, cityscapes seen from space. In sympathy with the dwindling fire, the room began to shed its heat, and when the turntable shut off on the last of the holiday albums, it imposed a silent signal that the evening was coming to a close.

Wilson was the first to stand. "Well, all, if I stay any longer, I might have to start paying rent, so with your indulgence, I'll say my goodbyes."

Janey was next on her feet, stretching as always and letting loose a ripple of cracks that ran down the length of her back. She handed Wilson his coat and wrapped him in a parting embrace— no baking powder prints to mar his sweater this time. "It was lovely having you here, Wilson Lacy. I hope you had a good time. Thank you so much for the wine. Merry Christmas if I don't see you before the twenty-fifth. Oh, and happy 2016 to you too!"

"Thank you, Janey. It was very nice being here. Everything was delicious. And I hope you have a wonderful holiday as well."

I stood next. Our partings had begun to take on a simple, reliable pattern: a handshake, a square look in the eye, and then a verbal agreement to meet again soon. Obedience to the routine reigned once again, and we left with plans to see each other after the holidays. I told him I was looking forward to following his progress with the next phase of the experiment.

Sophie remained content on the couch, still gazing at the glimmering coals of the rapidly fading fire. The hours had done nothing to diminish her allure. She appeared painted in a palette of pastels that augmented the embers' soft glow. Finally breaking free from whatever thoughts had absorbed her, she turned to watch Wilson as he came over to say goodbye. But before he got near enough to offer his hand, she put down her wineglass and asked, "Did you drive here?"

Did ... you ... drive ... here? Just four simple words. Wilson seemed unduly confused by those four simple words, awkwardly spluttering a jumble of sounds and pointing uselessly in the general direction of his house. "Um, no, I walked, it's only a few blocks," he finally managed to say.

Sophie countered by getting to her feet. She swiftly gathered her things, slipped on her shoes, and firmly tendered in an adamant voice, the one obvious solution to the elliptical problem before them. "I'll take you home. It's full-blown nasty out there, you know." And just like that, Sophie and Wilson departed.

After they left, the house tightened some more, even more securely, and this time around just Janey and me. We pulled the curtains back to gain a bird's-eye view of the events unfolding outside: as Wilson and Sophie made their way to her car, as they shared a few words while snow fell like rhinestones around them, as they got inside, and as they drove down the street together, two points traveling along the same line of an endless ray that led away. Once they were out of view, we let the curtains fall and exchanged a silent grin that neither one of us chose to tarnish with words, at least just yet. It seemed better to let the moment breathe with its infusion of mystery.

"Well, that was a very nice evening," Janey said, offering an appraisal to which I heartily agreed. "So here's the deal, Conway," she then added. "I'll see what I can get done in the kitchen if you straighten up a little in here. We give it fifteen minutes, and then call it a night, waddya say?"

"I say that sounds about right to me, Conway. You got a deal."

A quick scan of the living room was enough to prioritize my chores, separating those that needed immediate attention from those that could wait until morning. The fire was spent so I closed the flue and began gathering the plates from the table. Once my hands were full, I started toward the kitchen when my eyes caught sight of the tree. It really was lovely. There's nothing like a fresh white pine that had been tended with so much care. *The Christmas season is really here,* I thought just as an unexpected tide of emotion rose up to capsize my composure. Ghosts of Christmas Past, I suppose. I had to put down the dishes to steady myself before I could safely reach for my phone.

"You guys having fun? Everything okay?"

I sent the text with an extensive selection of seasonal emojis. And when it chimed back a few seconds later, I knew they were out there, somewhere, my children, and they were okay.

"We're great. Home in about an hour. Mike's parents say hello. Mr. F. told me to tell you 'Badgers Suck!' :) Dinner was fun. Love you."

"Love you too," I said softly, just under a breath that suddenly felt shallow and squeezed.

I never did make it back to the kitchen that night. The glasses and plates remained where they were, right there on the coffee table, their final destination just out of reach, the washing forestalled until morning. I couldn't stop thinking about what Wilson had said in the tunnel.

Janey found me there a few minutes later, planted in the hallway, staring at the trio of photos that hang on the wall, listening for a hint of those silent disclosures. She came over and stood beside me, brushing up lightly against my body and discharging a shock that threatened to overwhelm me. It burned with too much current. But then she took my hand in hers, and that electricity flowed between us in a closed circuit of sympathy, the heat of its current diminished somewhat by her presence.

I have Janey. Janey has me. Our embrace welded our sorrows along with our joys while the jagged outline of our own peculiar geometry was in plain sight, there to be witnessed by the resplendent faces of our three beautiful children.

Chapter

9

Twice each year, the Chicago chapter of SOS opens its doors to residents who have expressed interest in the support services it offers. My own involvement with the group began just that way, with the summer open house that was held the previous year. Typically, these events attract a handful of new survivors desperately searching for aid or understanding or salvation. Like I was.

The setting for this last meeting of the year   is the same, ill-lit classroom in the basement of a local church. Though much about the room is unchanged, a few differences declare the season. A silver Christmas tree is perched on a table alongside a cardboard menorah, and the snacks reflect the holiday theme: red and green reindeer cookies wait on one side of the percolator, white and blue cupcakes on the other. Also, on this night, the room is full. Nearly forty attendees sit uncomfortably in plastic chairs, but no one seems to mind. It's not that kind of comfort we seek. Before the night is over, some of the newcomers will join the group. They will leave this suffocating room with a reminder of hope and a longing to return. The regular members remember.

Even for the veterans who have been coming for years, the holiday meeting always feels different. More perilous—if that's even possible. They wear the cologne of confidence hard won by their survival and openly extend their hands to the visitors. For more recent members, the event of a meeting—any meeting—still feels new as we struggle to find our way. And the guests move through the room like ghosts. But regardless of our status, the bond we share is tragic. We all know why we are there.

"Thank you, Stephen. Excellent suggestions. That was very helpful." Bill had already opened the meeting with an overview of the SOS philosophy and was now facilitating presentations by some current members. "So, this may be a good time to provide a little context for some of what we are hearing tonight. I'd like to take a moment to do that before we invite comments from another participant of our group.

"As you know, the approach we adopt is drawn from the SOS principles and foundations guidelines that we discussed earlier. You'll find those well outlined in the brochures I handed out at the start of the meeting. But, as you are hearing tonight, we also place tremendous value on the lived experiences of our participants, on the methods and tools that our members develop on their own. Now, I've been facilitating groups for more than twenty years, and I know that oftentimes the best coping mechanisms—the most impactful strategies for healing—arise naturally from the distinct way our members move through their own grief. We recognize the potential of these strategies and honor them by sharing them with others, here in group. In fact, we come to rely on those lived experiences to broaden the array of effective strategies we consider. We acknowledge that the broader our definition of what works, the more likely someone will find something that works for her or him.

"This is what we call 'emergent therapies,' and it is an integral part of the SOS approach. Tonight, you're hearing about those emergent therapies from some wonderful first-person accounts. Stephen just described the way meditation and yoga have helped him control his anxieties and deal with insomnia to feel more centered. Martha described the way her loss became a catalyst for dedicating herself to a new cause and how that has helped her find a renewed sense of hope. And Gideon talked about the way a new start—selling his house, moving, changing careers, and so on—has been so essential to his healing. These are powerful methods our members have used to cope with loss. They may not all be right for everyone, but perhaps someone here this evening will hear something that may be helpful. Good? Okay, we'll take a break in just a moment but I think we have time to hear from one more of our members. Anyone? Yes, Owen?"

Honestly, I'm not much of a volunteer. I tend to let others take that particular spotlight. So when Bill called my name, I looked at my raised and traitorous arm with a healthy scoop of suspicion. I had no notes to refer to, no script to rely on. Nothing at all had been planned. All I had was the fuzz of an idea that had been knocking around for a few days, something to do with Wilson's question from that night in early December, the one he asked as I was leaving his house, the one I didn't have much of an answer for. I guess the time had come to give that idea some air, to see how it sailed. And then too, there was the perilousness of the night and all those new, shaken faces. They all seemed terribly consequential as I found myself walking to the front of the room.

"Thanks, Bill. Hello, everybody. My name is Owen Conway, and I've been a member here for a little over a year. I just want to take a minute and add one more idea to the mix of great ideas we've already heard thus far. But I also want to preface this with an admission that my thoughts tonight are not particularly well developed. This idea is new. In fact, this is the first time I've talked about it with anyone, so please bear with me. I guess this is what Bill would call the most emergent of emerging therapies; here it is, emerging right before our eyes.

"I live in an area that is very neighborly. It's one of those areas where people are often out and about for a hundred different reasons. Since I'm an avid walker and a bit of a talker too, I make casual acquaintances with my neighbors all the time. Usually, as these things go, the acquaintances stay informal: a nod, a greeting, maybe a word or two, that's usually about it. And that's fine. It's nice. Uncomplicated. And then, every once in a while— I'm not exactly sure why—a stronger connection occasionally takes root. Something clicks. I assume it's due to a special kind of chemistry that sometimes exists between two people. There's an acknowledgment of things in common. It's hard to put a finger on it, but I bet you all know what I mean.

"Anyways, during the fall, I began to develop that stronger sort of connection with one particular neighbor of mine. His name is Wilson. Wilson and I had known each other by sight for years. He always struck me as an interesting guy, and we seemed to share a lot of similarities. We're about the same age, and we like many of the same things. I think we both sensed that good kind of chemistry in our interactions. I felt it, and I'm pretty sure he did too. It just seemed natural to want to get to know him better, to reach out and take that next step, and try to become friends with this curious neighbor of mine. I guess the timing was good for us both.

"Well, Wilson and I have been getting together pretty regularly the past few months. We quickly overcame the awkwardness that can sometimes arise when trying to get to know someone better, and we soon began talking about more serious things. It turns out that we do have a lot in common. More than just music and sports and beer, we share a similar outlook on things. And maybe most importantly—and I think this is what I'm trying to get to—we're both a little sad. Wilson is troubled by a kind of sadness that is different from mine. It comes from a different place, but I recognize the same familiar profile. His sadness is not the result of the loss of a loved one but rather, the loss of another kind, maybe the loss of his way in the world, which, I'm learning, can be just as devastating. And I've discovered that devastated people understand each other quite well. Just look around the room.

"Okay, so maybe you're wondering what's the point. I guess I'm trying to offer another idea in response to Bill's request for how we deal with loss. And no, I don't have any concrete evidence to support this idea, nothing more concrete than my own experience, and that experience has simply been this: reaching out to Wilson, being there for him in whatever way I can as he confronts his sadness—even while I deal with my own—is affecting me in a way that I never would have expected. I can't say that I've dedicated myself to a cause like Martha. It's not like that;

it's not as deliberate, nor am I as devout. I sometimes wish I were. I wish I could say that my motives are inspired by the selfless generosity of a saint or that I burned with a pious disposition to seek out others in their times of need and offer the consoling balm of friendship as a remedy for whatever ails them. I'm sure it's not quite as noble as that, but maybe it's in the same general neighborhood.

"I think what I'm saying is that up until recently, my natural instinct for dealing with my sorrow has been to withdraw into myself. For a long time, it seemed like that was all I could do. It sounds terrible, but it's true. But now, in a way, being with Wilson has taken me out of myself, and I think that's been a very good thing. For me as well as for him. It has made me realize that maybe I can use this tragedy and all my grief to help someone else navigate his own. And maybe that means something good can come from all this—from the worst thing imaginable—and just imagine that. Something good. I never thought I'd say that. I think Aaron would approve.

"So, I don't know, maybe there's an idea in there that makes sense to someone else. Find a person you can reach out to, someone in pain—god knows they're all around us—and see what happens when you do. See what happens when you introduce yourself to someone else's pain or sadness—the sadness I am beginning to suspect is in all of us—and maybe you'll find yourself better able to cope with your own. I think that may be what's happening with me. Now I'll bet there's a fancy term to describe what's going on, but I have no idea what it is. Nor am I sure that naming it really matters. All I know is how I feel. And lately how I feel is … kind of lucky, I guess. That's pretty much all I wanted to say."

Before turning back to my seat, I raised my eyes and glanced at the faces that had gathered so desperately in the room. Some, I noticed, were looking directly at me with varying degrees of interest. Others held their heads down low. A few shielded their eyes with their hands while they wept. But standing out from them all, nearly beaming with a look of unabashed delight, was the face of Bill right there in the front row. He was nodding his head with eyes nearly shut and the fattest Cheshire cat grin I had ever seen on another human being.

Outside the church after the meeting, a ferocious wind was blowing. Cyclones of newly fallen snow burned as they raked past my face. As old as it is, the Corolla still offered refuge on such an inclement night. I left the radio off as I drove toward home and thought about the comments I made before the group. It was hard not to admonish myself for all the things I wished I had said, but the idea was still so new. It hadn't yet coalesced around a reliable vocabulary, and I eased up by recalling the meaning of emergent therapies.

It was just past ten when I pulled up to the curb outside Wilson's house. An impulse I didn't recognize made itself known, and I sat in the car to let it incubate. Looking out the passenger window, I saw that the lights were all off. The house wore its familiar cloak of despondency. And then the impulse quickened. I tore a piece of paper from my SOS notebook and began to write:

Wilson,

I was just on my way home from a support group meeting and wanted to tell you something that's been on my mind. It's late and didn't want to ring the bell (remember last time I tried that?) so I hope you get this note. It'll do until we get together again.

Do you remember when I was at your house the other night and you asked me why all the concern? Why I would want to spend my time helping you think about heartbreaking things when I'm still suffering so much heartache of my own? Well, I've thought a lot about that and have realized something important. I wanted to be sure to tell you because I think you need to know it.

I've come to see that I *want* to do these things with you *because* of the heartache I'm going through. Maybe this will sound strange, but I have found that my own sorrow has become a little more bearable lately and though I'm not sure I can explain exactly why that is, I do believe it has something to do with our time together. What do you think about that?

From where I stand, it seems as if we both are shouldering our fair share of sadness right now—maybe for different reasons, but I sometimes think the reasons are not all that important—and maybe the weight of that sadness is lightened for us both by our friendship. I know it is for me. I just thought you should know that, especially now as we head into the heart of winter (the heart of darkness perhaps?). I hope you're well and making progress on the photographs. And I hope we will continue to bear each other's burdens.

Until next time … your friend,
Owen

I read the note a few more times. With each pass, I sensed the vocabulary beginning to cohere and felt more assured about what I volunteered in group and what I wrote in the letter. I folded the paper in half, addressed it to Wilson, and followed the path of the headlights' beam to the door. A spasm of dread greeted me as I reached for the mailbox. The bulk of several days' deliveries had accumulated inside. The box was filled to overflowing. It looked foreboding and darkly portentous, but I resisted the urge to knock. Instead, I wedged the note between the crowded stacks and hoped it wouldn't be lost among the clutter. Then, cinching my jacket tight against the gruesome bluster, I ran back to the car, hurriedly, as if chased by a demon.

Chapter

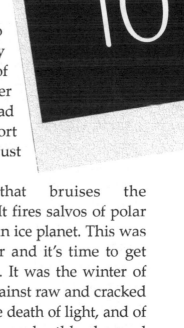

Winter was here. The cold, dead heart of winter had arrived at last. This was no longer the cheerful winter of the holiday season with its glittering blue frostings of newly fallen snow. Gone was the winter that lifts the spirit with merriment and glad tidings all wrapped in the plush comfort of cashmere and wool. That winter had just surrendered to a more sinister season.

This was the darker shade of winter that bruises the Midwest with a bitter battleship of gray. It fires salvos of polar explosives and leaves behind the ruin of an ice planet. This was the winter that screams playtime is over and it's time to get down to business: dirty, nasty, and grim. It was the winter of hostile winds that grate like sandpaper against raw and cracked skin, of unshakable fatigue induced by the death of light, and of arrogant temperatures that slash and gouge and ruthlessly expel any memory of a more clement time. This was the winter when the sun goes missing from the sky for weeks at a time, when the calendar stretches out toward infinity, demanding that we undertake the impossibly long march through January, through February, and then even through March driven on only by the faint insinuation that the earth may one day warm again. And for some, this was the winter that creeps inside the soul to deposit a blight that spreads like gloaming. Winter was here, and it just wasn't fooling around anymore.

By the first Saturday in January, our lives had resumed their normal, non-holiday rhythms. But without all the gingerbread, the ornaments, the calamitous Walker clan, or the heavy bulk of our anticipations to inspirit us, the house sagged with exhaustion. A tired funk had taken over as the excitements of the past couple of weeks fizzled away until nothing much more was left. Even walking by the living room window was enough to incite a bad case of the dark winter blues. For there on the curb, lying in plain view, indecently slumped on its once photogenic side, was the Conway family Christmas tree. Ripped from its fandangle and trailing stray strands of tinsel, it awaited its ignominious end in the jaws of the local chipper.

To the relief of her sister as well as her parents, Hannah decided to return to Madison and finish out her sophomore year at school. "Of course I'm going back. School is awesome," she bayed without betraying the slightest hint of irony. And just like that, the countdown began. The girls were suddenly anxious to get back to their "real lives," leaving Janey and me with nothing to do but mark the days as they dwindled away. In many ways, it was like they had already left—and the dislocation shoved us all a little out of sync.

All that morning, we kept getting into each other's way, scrapping over the coffee machine, the newspaper, the eggs. We were listless and bored and chafed with the itch of cabin fever. The prospect of watching the hours tick by on that sluggish Saturday made us glum. I guess it was the flagrancy of their imminent departure that weighed on our mood like a millstone. It's always like that at the end: the slow, painful pull of the Band-Aid. *Just get on with it for crying out loud!*

There had been talk of some last-minute returns at the mall. And I knew that the Cineplex had screenings of the new *Star Wars* movie scheduled that afternoon. So, in an effort to offset the doldrums, I proposed an outing. I offered to take the girls to the stores to exchange their gifts in return for joining me at *The Force Awakens*. Since Janey had taken on an afternoon shift, it would just be the three of us, and it sounded like a fine way to spend one of the last remaining days of the holiday vacation. "Join me, girls," I pleaded from the dark side of the kitchen. "I am your father." Though my impression was met with disparaging sighs, we were soon on our way, each silently grateful for the change of scenery.

The exchanges went smoothly, and the morning's gloom began to lift. And when we scored an extra seat at the theater to hold all the bags the girls had gathered, we became downright giddy with our good fortune. For the next couple of hours, those bags bore mute witness to my gasps of disbelief at the agedness of Han and Leia and Luke. They stoically tolerated my muzzled moans over the loss of innocence that made the first three movies so special. But it wasn't until we were stuck in a slow-moving line on our way out of theater that I could finally share my insights regarding the franchise's original installments. My pontifications on the zeitgeist of the seventies were soon interrupted, however, by a shout from somewhere up in the balcony.

"Hey, Hannah, Sara! Yo! Wait up." We turned around in line to watch as two young men in shorts, hoodies, and matching University of Iowa baseball caps zigzagged their way through the queue of exiting moviegoers and landed like Clydesdales behind us.

"Hey, guys," Hannah called out to the boys. She seemed not the least bit surprised to be ambushed by friends, as if finding people she knows wherever she goes would always be routine. She disappeared her bag of Sour Patch Kids with Houdini-like flair. Then she tucked in her hair, smoothed the back of her pants, and, inch by inch so that no one would notice, unzipped the front of her coat. "How's it going? What did you guys think of the movie?"

"It was pretty awesome, right? Killer special effects! Oh, hey there, Mr. C. Nice to see you." The taller of the two boys greeted me with an easy, cheerful grin. He bent his arm between the girls to offer his hand for a shake. The other retreated into the dark aisle.

"Hello, Mike. It's good to see you too. I was just explaining to the girls here that despite how good they make movies look these days, they'll never compare with the originals for pure adventure and fun. That's just not going to happen. But, yeah, that was still pretty great."

"Oh, and Dad," Hannah interrupted, cutting me off like the mortified child whose baby pictures had just been shared with a hopeful new suitor, "this is Reed Riskin."

Reed remained a step or two behind Mike, under the shade of the aisle light, slightly apart from the rest of the group. The hood of his sweatshirt was pulled over his head and masked the features of his face. The shadowy effect struck me as an unintended homage to Emperor Palpatine, the original phantom menace. But this was no cosplay. He kept one shoulder pressed against the wall as we crawled forward in line. He moved with the slither of a cold-blooded skink and could only muster a listless wave and what sounded like the mutter of a surly hello.

Over the years, there had been a lot of stories about Reed Riskin, or more precisely, about his parents. The innuendos spread like a contagion throughout the neighborhood. There was something to do with illicit financial schemes and Russian kingpins that drew all kinds of trouble down around them. An aggressive federal prosecution led to indictments that led to jail time for the father and probation for the mother. If I remember correctly, Reed was their only child and in middle school at the time. And as the sins of the parents often attach to their children, there were soon a slew of rumors about Reed as well: difficulties in school, brushes with police, rumblings of prior domestic abuse. He was thought to be a little wild, growing up more or less on his own in a house that was bereft of parental presence, supervision, or love; a "troubled" child. In our neighborhood's brief playlist of youthful dramas and indiscretions, Reed Riskin was the featured artist. His attitude in the theater that afternoon did nothing to dispel the rumors.

The line continued to plod. Slips of conversations floated around us in a cloud of hazy chatter. The closer we got to the exit, the more urgent the conversations became. Plans were being made. Propositions tendered. Hungers of various kinds assessed—even among our own little group. "So, ladies, Reed and I were heading out to get some pizza at Rosetti's and then maybe stop by the Nickel for a while. Foster's band is playing tonight. You guys wanna come along?"

"Sure! That sounds excellent!" Hannah exclaimed, bouncing deliriously on the tips of her toes as her face blazed with a smile. She slapped Mike a high five just as a random thought intruded on her bliss and the memory of the rest of us standing nearby boomeranged back. "Um, would that be okay, Dad?" she asked more soberly.

"Yeah, sure, of course. That sounds like fun." I started for my wallet to give her some cash, but a subtle headshake implied I could keep my money right where it was. Then she reached out her hands and began tucking strands of her sister's long hair behind those unadorned ears while tenderly appraising her eyes. "You coming, Boo?" Hannah asked, kindling the attention of Reed.

"I think I'll pass, but thanks, guys. Maybe next time." The invitation wasn't really considered. Instead, Sara tossed her head to free her hair before slipping both hands into her coat. The step she took away from her sister declared that her decision was final. The sideways glance she lobbed at Reed was more difficult to decipher. "I'll make sure the old man gets home. But you owe me, Hannah. Next time, you get to be the one to listen to his endless rants on the golden age of film."

The swimming crowds and shimmering lights of the busy mall were disorienting after the theater's black cauldron, but we recovered enough to say our goodbyes.

Hannah and the boys took off in one direction, trailing great gusts of laughter behind them while Sara and I went the other. "So, Mike sure looks good," I said as we snaked our way through the shoppers. "Looks like college agrees with him. You didn't want to go, huh?"

"Nah, not really. I have some stuff to do at home. I still need to find another English class before freshman registration closes.

And there's a prompt I have to respond to for my online psych class that already started. No big deal."

Maybe not, but the closer we got to the doors of the mall, the more distracted Sara became. Even the zesty chai smell and sounds of steaming milk from Starbucks passed by without comment. Impulsively, she began knotting her hair around her fingers, twisting it in tighter and tighter curls before letting go and starting over again. Ever since she had enough hair to twist, that gesture has been her tell. It usually implied there was something more to be said. After several more twists, she dropped her hands and groaned a rueful lament.

"All right, if you want to know the truth, Reed kind of creeps me out," she relented at last. "He's always been a little weird. I mean, pretty much forever. It drives me crazy. He's one of those people who just seem so uncomfortable in his own skin. Like he doesn't think he's good enough or something. And then, whenever anyone shows a little interest, he gets all close and clingy—too close, if you catch my drift—and it starts to feel skeevy." She hesitated before going any further and started to reach again for her hair. The rest of the thoughts that troubled her mind would not be admitted so easily. "And by the way, this is not something I feel particularly good talking about. I mean I'm sure he means well, and god knows he's had his own piles of shit to deal with. It's kind of sad, actually. Who knows? Maybe Reed Riskin just needs someone too."

"Huh. If so, he has a funny way of showing it. He seemed a little moody back there. I never really knew him, but I did hear the stories. Does Hannah ever say anything about him?"

"We've talked about it. She doesn't pick up on it though. Big surprise, right? And, besides, that girl is never going to turn down a chance to be with Mike Flannigan—no matter who he's hanging out with."

"What?" I heard myself shout like an absentminded father. You know the type: the clueless clod from black-and-white films who learns that the small steps his kid had been taking might really be giant leaps. My astonishment drew the attention of several mall walkers whose frowns conveyed their displeasure. "Hannah and Mike? Really?"

"You're kidding, right, Dad? You never noticed? The way she looks at him? Even just now? Really? You never knew she had a crush on him since like fourth grade? Sometimes I wonder about you, Dad. Mom sees it. She's known about Mike for years. But here's the latest scoop, and you didn't hear this from me. Apparently, he just broke up with his girlfriend from school. They were hot and heavy for over a year. She was a real bitch from what Hannah says. Totally possessive. And now big sister is turning on the Conway charm if you can follow that, Dad."

"Hannah and Mike Flannigan? No way."

"Way, Dad. Get used to it."

Getting used to it wasn't going to be easy. In fact, I was still working to adjust to this news when we finally left the mall. I shook my head to rack my brain but came up with nothing to suggest I had been delinquent in my paternal attentions. Honestly, I never suspected a thing. Hannah and Mike? Was I becoming blinded to the romantic entanglements of my children, unable to see them as grown people with their own longings and desires, their own swoons and heartaches and yearnings? The evidence was mounting. And though I knew that it would take some time to untangle these thoughts, the eruption of curiosity that followed could not be contained.

"Hey, have they ever ...?"

"Jesus, Dad. Come on. Let's get you to the car, and you can tell me all about Yoda and the swamps of Degobah again."

From the very outset, a quick stop at Waltons had been part of the day's bargain. Janey asked for some wine, and I was hoping for something stronger to offset the savagery of the season. I pulled into the parking lot and shut off the motor but made no move to get out of the car. Neither did Sara. Instead, I soaked up the silence and marveled again at the way time marches on, incessantly, relentlessly, dispassionately, and with an ever-increasing velocity that compels everything around me to change. Even, it appears, my own kids. Sara stared out her window.

"Hannah and Mike Flannigan," I said once more, hoping for some kind of reaction that might break her from her spell.

She refused to take the bait. Instead, she sat silently in her seat, looking off into the distance at something that lay beyond my capacity to see. Without Hannah there to balance the picture, she suddenly seemed older and more resolute, no longer the little sister. No longer just Boo. A body snatcher's trick had somehow replaced the girl I took to the movie with the unflinching young woman beside me. At that moment, I would have traded anything to know her thoughts, to listen to the silent disclosures that she persisted in hiding so well: my inscrutable child with the faraway eyes. How long had it been since it was just the two of us?

"Mike Flannigan. Go figure. I really never would have guessed."

Sara nodded slightly, her eyes still drawn to that thing outside the window that had so swept up her attention.

"And what about you, young Jedi? Is there a Rebel pilot somewhere out there traveling through the star system who has stolen *your* heart? Perhaps a brave and courageous defender of the Alliance that I know absolutely nothing about?"

"Christ, Dad, really?" she moaned, finally opening the door and stepping out of the car, the touch of a blush cheating her feints of anger.

"Scotty Richter maybe?" I needled back with a yell from my own open door and a clear memory of a middle school dance date that was all teeth, sharp elbows, and an unfortunate haircut. I watched with delight as she made her way to the front of the store, this striking woman out in the world who moved with an assurance I never really noticed before. And when she raised her hand in that same cool backward wave, it was for a moment the spring of 1980 all over again. But not for long. Nothing, it seemed, could slow time's arrow.

The clan of suburban drinkers was out in force that afternoon, laying in provisions as a stronghold against winter's trespass.

Waltons was doing a very brisk business. Generally, as a matter of principle, I refuse to take a cart into a liquor store. The sight of a guy schlepping down the aisles with all those bottles and cans—selecting a fifth of this booze here, a pint of that booze there, loading it up like a barge—stinks of despair. "Only buy what you can carry," the Con Man used to say. Seems like a pretty good rule of thumb to me. So when Sara offered to pick out the wine while I did some surveillance in the whisky aisle, I was grateful and relieved. Four hands are better than two.

I don't drink enough to know much of a difference between the endless varieties that stood for inspection. Scotch, Irish, bourbon, and rye—I'm sure they all have their charms, but my decision always comes down to more filmy criteria.

Sara found me a few minutes later, studying the labels for clues that might divulge a hint of their latent promises. A bottle of Janey's favorite red was in her left hand and a Chardonnay—the preferred choice of the younger Conway women and a treat for their farewell dinner planned for the following night—was in her right. She wilted against the wall of mixers with a cavernous yawn, making it clear that her reserve of patience was just about gone. So I pulled a random bottle from the budget-priced shelf, promising myself that I would be better prepared next time. And then I felt her tapping frantically on my shoulder.

"Hey, Dad," she whispered into my ear. "Isn't that Mr. Lacy over there in the checkout line?"

The way she whispered it—with a wince that bled concern—coaxed a shiver to surge down my spine. Instinctively, we skulked deeper into the aisle to steal a more camouflaged view. But she was right.

Wilson was there, waiting in the checkout line, a six-pack of beer and a bottle of gin in his hands. He was standing so still that he nearly vanished from sight, dissolving amidst the turbulence of the store like a cardboard cutout advertising Beefeater and Becks. As the customers in front of him completed their purchases, he would shuffle his feet to narrow the gap, and then that eerie stillness would resume. No one seemed to notice he was there.

"Yes, that's him," I confirmed with all the calm I could muster. We stayed burrowed among the bottles for a minute or two more, watching as Wilson languished in the scene. All that stillness was unnerving. I know it sounds strange, but the stillness was all I could see. That is, until he took another step. And then dissolved again. "Let's go say hello," I suggested to Sara, keeping my eyes glued to the tattered coat that hung on his back as we left the shelter of the aisle.

He never noticed our approach as we lined up several customers behind. Even from that distance, I could tell something was wrong. It wasn't like he was wearing pajamas or had left the house without his shoes or was mumbling to himself. He wasn't reaching for invisible objects or arguing with ghosts or weeping uncontrollably. It wasn't as undisguised as that. Instead, Wilson looked lost, like a bear awakening prematurely from a long hibernation. That anemic and bewildered bear crawls from his den and wobbles on rubbery legs. To find himself abruptly out in the world is surely perplexing to the bear, almost to the point of paralysis. He stands, wondering how he ever got there while the rest of the forest's business transacts around him. Eventually, there is only one thing left for that befuddled bear to do; he soon comes to see that the timing is all wrong and crawls back inside for the rest of the winter. Wilson looked a lot like that bear.

"Hey there, Mr. Lacy," Sara called out over the heads of the customers in front of us, a little sooner, I thought, than was necessary. She had to repeat the greeting a second time, and then a third more loudly and to the side, before Wilson finally turned around.

"Oh, Sara. Hello. Hi, Owen. How are you both?"

"We're good, Wilson," I replied. "Hey, we just got back from seeing the new *Star Wars* movie. Are you a fan?"

"Um, no, not really. I haven't kept up much with the sequels. Truthfully, I don't go in much for that kind of thing anymore."

He was next up in line. So as not to miss his turn at the checkout, he had to keep turning his head between the counter and us. That, along with the gilded ladies who stood between, their carts full of liquor and their faces full of impertinence, did not make it easy to carry on a conversation. He didn't notice the call of "Next."

"Oh, hey, you're up, my friend."

We watched as Wilson laid his items on the counter and then reached down for his wallet. He never once looked up. The peculiar way his eyes fastened on the credit card reader added to the pricklish mood of the moment. He completely missed the flutter of recognition that flashed across the cashier's face. Nor did he see the shy reserve with which the young man smiled as he prepared to say something more. Wilson was too far awry to notice. But we saw it. And then the moment sputtered as the next customer in line pushed her way forward. Wilson picked up his bags and shuffled to the door before recalling we were still there behind him.

"Hey, Wilson. Hang on a second," I called out as we moved up in line. "Wait for us, okay?" He nodded without looking up and sullenly stepped outside.

Gray as it was when we entered the store, it was several shades grayer when we left. The impression of steel that threatened overhead had thickened and lowered ominously. It felt like the sky had been plated with deadweights of pewter to compress the spirit. The wind died down, and it would soon be dark. The air smelled of sulfur and the likelihood of snow.

And then something even more foreboding appeared to fall from the sky. I watched nervously from the corner of my eyes as tiny particles of dark matter began to gather out of nowhere, summoned by some unaccountable force. They massed like locusts to cast a shadow that plummeted down hard upon my friend. That shadow shrouded him with an odious film that turned his face sour and pale.

"So, where's your car?" I asked as we all stood together in the parking lot. The specter of the dark matter had rattled me, and my voice let slip my concern. But I *was* concerned. I could tell that the avatar had him.

"I walked over. I needed some air." He put down his bags and quietly groaned as if the strain to stay upright under that dead-weighted sky was too much to bear. "I've been cooped up for a while. It's a mean time of year, don't you think?"

"I do indeed. In fact, our outing was motivated by much the same kind of thing. Hey, would you like a lift? Or, if you were thinking of walking back, how would you feel about some company? I could use the exercise. Mind if I join you?"

"No, that's fine. I don't mind at all," he answered inauspiciously with a shrug.

Sara offered to drive the car back, so I left her with a kiss and a promise to be home in time for dinner. By my count, there were just two nights left before the house would fall empty again. She wished Wilson a happy New Year but rejected his hand in favor of a hug that left him flat-footed and slightly flushed. "I'm sure I'll see you in the spring," she said before heading off toward the car. "You'll come for one of my dad's famous barbeques. Hannah and I are dying to hear more about those days at Duke you were telling us about."

His response fell well short of a promise before she fled like the sun, taking her radiance with her, whisking it away to shine elsewhere for a while but leaving behind enough incandescence to ease the chill of that otherwise bleak afternoon.

I picked up one of the bags, Wilson grabbed the other, and we started toward home. Despite the threatening sky, it was good walking weather—cold but calm—and I was glad to be wearing my sneakers. We didn't get very far.

"Dr. Lacy! Dr. Lacy!" It was the cashier from the store. He was shouting as he ran across the parking lot, signaling us with frantically waving arms.

"Oh good Christ, now what?" Wilson groused under his breath. He took out his wallet to check inside just as the young cashier caught up with us. "Something wrong?" Wilson asked.

"No, sir. No. Nothing's wrong at all. I just got someone to take my register for a minute. Dr. Lacy, I'm sure you don't remember me. My name is David Marder. I was in your class a few years ago. Over on the Lake Shore campus?"

Wilson finally looked up so he could scrutinize David's face. He seemed to be rifling through the mental archive of what must have been hundreds of past students. Remarkably, it only took a couple of seconds before a gleam of recognition softened his features. The correct file had been located.

"Yes, David, sure, I remember you. Spring of 2010 or 2011, wasn't it? Let's see—that was an outstanding group, and you … you were quite an exceptional student. You did that lesson on planetary motion if I remember correctly. We all went outside, and you had us simulate rotations and revolutions. That was outstanding. Very memorable. In fact, that was a lesson I often used as an exemplar in later classes. It was beautifully designed. Yes, sure, I remember that very clearly."

David's eyes widened, stunned by the praise. "Sheesh! Thank you, sir. That is quite a memory you have. But yeah, that was me. I actually still use that lesson. I'm at Middlebrook right now, middle school science in fact. I just take on some part-time work here during the holidays to help make ends meet. The life of a teacher, right?"

Though he ran from the store without a jacket, the shudder that made David tremble just then was not owed to the cold. Its origin was something quite different. He soon turned more timid, an apprehensive student standing before his professor. Whatever else he wanted to say had clearly not been scripted, and I think he was worried about how it would be received. Though it only took a second or two for him to arrange the words that followed, the expressiveness of that moment was exquisite. We clung to it with anticipation as David glanced back at the store. The ticking clock on his impromptu break was enough to compel him to continue.

"Actually, there was something else I wanted to say. I heard you left the university, and I would hate to think that I saw you today and never got around to mentioning it. I just wanted you to know that you were hands down the best teacher I ever had. I truly mean that. We all got so much from your class. For one thing, you taught us how to wonder. It turns out that was quite a gift. But you also inspired us to share that way of looking at the world with our own students. To this day, when I'm in my classroom, I think about what you taught us, and I remember the fun we had from discovering something new. I wanted you to know the impact it had on me and how those lessons continue to reach my own students. They hear about you all the time. I just thought you should know. Oh, and hey, if you ever want to come for a visit to see what I'm talking about, I would love to show you my classroom. In fact, we're starting a unit on force and motion in a few weeks that I know you would like to see. Think about it, will you?"

"Well, David," Wilson replied with a wan smile and vague, sodden tone, "it was very nice to see you. Thank you for your kind words and the invitation. I'll surely consider it. Good luck with the teaching. For whatever it's worth, I always suspected you would be great. And in case you don't remember, my suspicions are never wrong."

David laughed with the memory of a familiar refrain and then sprinted back to the store. His departure left a vacuum behind as the brunt of his praise eliminated the possibility of anything else—including air—from infringing upon our space.

Wilson and I stood breathless and still and waited for the equilibrium to return. Soon thereafter, the atmosphere revived.

"Whoa! That was amazing," I gasped while inspecting Wilson for any effect that David's words might have had. There wasn't much to see. "I'm not sure I have ever heard a nicer tribute. To anyone! About anything! You've changed lives. To have that much impact on someone is unbelievable, but to see how it pays forward to his own students—well, that's just incredible. That makes you immortal. Odysseus is in the house!"

Wilson was unmoved. His eyes were anchored to the storefront where David had just reentered. They were mashed into tight, tense slits as though he was peering inside to watch him at work or maybe—as I think about it now—peering farther back through time for any scrap of truth that would validate all that he just heard. I'm not sure he found it.

"Yeah, that was nice, but he really was a fine student. I imagine most any of my colleagues would have had the same impact. Maybe more. I doubt there really was all that much that I could have done to warrant such a nice eulogy. If it weren't me, it certainly would have been someone else. If that's immortality, then immortality comes cheap."

He shrugged again before turning away from the store. A knit hat was pulled from his coat while he checked my face, waiting pensively to see if I might have anything more to say. Satisfied that there was nothing on offer—I was simply too stunned by the agility of his deflection—he cinched the hat down tight, shook his head with a curmudgeonly grunt, and started walking toward home.

The streets of the neighborhood were deserted as night closed in around us. It felt like we were alone in an abandoned, forsaken world. White wisps curled from chimneys, and the air was filled with wood smoke. Every once in a while, we would spy through windows to see our neighbors sitting on sofas in front of their televisions—like cavemen around their fires—as they settled down into their own winter hibernations. I wondered how long it would be before they would emerge from their homes and the streets of our town would teem again. The derelict landscape through which we trudged made that day seem a long way off.

We passed the time talking of trivial things. The beer and gin swung between us like pendulums ticking off the steps, keeping time with the crunch of the snow beneath our shoes. And then we stopped talking, and the sound of the crunch was all there was left between us.

We turned down our street and walked up the path to Wilson's front door. I handed him the bag and was about to take my leave.

"You want to come in for a beer?" he half-heartedly offered while busying himself with the lock.

I knew Janey's shift was due to end in an hour, and I had promised to be home when she arrived. A glance at my watch assured me that I had time enough for the drink. "Sure, yeah, that sounds great," I answered just as his jaw muscles stiffened. He threw a shoulder at the door and entered the house, leaving it open for me to follow.

That's when I spotted the mailbox and felt the baleful dread return. The spectacle of that still overstuffed box made my skin crawl due to the accumulation of days and more days of disregarded deliveries. And there, wedged between the bills and flyers and soggy magazines, was the note I left after the SOS meeting. I could see its edges curled outward like the petals of a woebegone orchid, already weathering. The sight stung with a stew of anxiety and relief and the piercing realization that Wilson had never seen it. It took both hands and some considerable force to free the stubborn stack from its slot. Then I carried it into the house.

"Hey, I grabbed your mail," I shouted to Wilson who was already in the kitchen. "Is it okay if I just leave it here on the table in the hallway?"

"Yeah, sure. Anywhere is fine. The beer is in here."

Before turning to join him, I sneaked my note from the middle of the stack and left it in a more conspicuous place on top. A quick scan assured me that its message was still pertinent, and I briefly considered delivering it to him right then. But I rejected that idea in favor of letting fortuity run its course. I figured he would see it in time. On his own, alone, the way it was intended.

Heading to the kitchen, I remember thinking that nothing much had changed in Wilson's house. To be sure, it had only been a short while, but the odor of loneliness still pervaded, ripening in the stagnant air like a cellar full of old fruit. And the ghosts that patrolled the dusty rooms continued to make their presence felt at every turn.

Two beers were foaming in their glasses and waiting, oddly enough, in the basin of the kitchen sink. That was because the lovely pedestal table which otherwise might accommodate the drinks was all taken up with a litter of newspapers and the husk of a grimy old engine. A few tools and small pools of oil were scattered around, and a bin of tiny parts lay nearby. It appeared that everything had been readied for a midwinter teardown that was about to get underway. But when Wilson saw me admiring the motor, he explained that plans for the rebuild had been thwarted; "a sudden onset of an overwhelming lack of interest" was to blame. The engine had been sitting untouched for weeks.

He dropped his keys and phone next to the relic, and we took our beers with us into the den.

Grabbing the remote from the seat of the recliner, Wilson switched off the TV and tilted his head toward the wall, imploring my eyes to follow. What I saw as I glared at the wall was dispiriting. It was a dire, disheartening sight. The once rich tapestry that adorned his den had been defaced by the savage removal of countless photographs. It all looked bedraggled and so utterly vandalized, its surface befouled by pustulent lesions. Ragged holes and brown smears of tape were all that remained in places. Whole chapters of the story had been deleted, roles of major characters ruthlessly cut out. No longer did it read like the storyboard of an intriguing life. Instead, it served as a mirror to reflect the woeful condition of Wilson's current state of mind. I scanned the photos that had survived the purge but found nothing that would have foretold their persistence. And Wilson, sitting in his chair with his head hung in his hands, was in no hurry to offer an explanation.

"So what happened here?" I nervously asked.

He raised his heavy head and turned it toward the wall. Weariness retarded his movements as he slogged his way through a bog. His eyes were those of a lunatic who had lost all control and, in a kind of fit, cut his own hair with a butcher knife. It was that ghastly first look in the mirror. The relief of release always feels sweet until the reality of regret comes thundering down.

"Yeah, well, I'm not really sure. I guess I hit a bit of a bump in the experiment."

"A bump? What sort of a bump?" I asked.

"A bump like maybe this wasn't such a good idea. I'm not sure I like what I'm seeing."

He would not take his eyes from the wall. And the way his chest caved around shallow breaths made him look like an embattled old man; tired, weak, and deflated. Make no mistake; a wintertide darkness had taken possession and entangled him in a nest of malevolent, blood-sucking snakes.

I sat down beside him and rested my hand on his shoulder. "Well, these things *can* get a little bumpy, you know. We talked about that. I really do believe that if the road you're traveling down *doesn't* get a little bumpy now and then, you need to look for an alternative route that will. Those bumps are the journey's way of telling you that you're heading in the right direction. Believe me, they challenge you to keep going."

"Yeah, well, I don't know about all that," he replied. "I mean intellectually, I understand what you're suggesting. And I probably agree. I suppose the bumps are an indication of a rougher road where the meaning we spoke of before is pushing up from beneath the surface of the photos. But right now, that meaning seems impacted. All it brings is pain. I'm starting to think that maybe it's best not disturbed. Like it would be easier to avoid those roads entirely. I know you would argue that those are the roads that lead somewhere worth going, but the going is so damn hard sometimes. And it gets really bleak."

"Does the wall here have something to do with all this?"

"Yeah. Christ, it looks dreadful doesn't it? I'm just sick of what I'm seeing."

"Sick of what you're seeing in the photos?" I asked.

"Yeah, exactly. Sick of what I'm seeing … and thinking."

"Do you want to talk about it?"

He looked at me with a wretched face while deciding, I imagined, whether and how far to expound, how much to let go. When he started again, there were grim omens that dragged down his voice suggestive of some second-guessing as to the extent or degree of absolution. "I guess I've gotten stuck on the third photograph. But it could have just as easily been any of the others. You've seen the picture. My wife and I are in Cape Cod. It's the summer before we were married. We're sitting at a picnic table, looking out at the ocean. It is such a great photograph. Nothing but blue skies and calm seas. As I started writing, I got onto this idea about moments and how that picture captures a really wonderful moment in time, an instant, a snapshot, a heartbeat. And I began thinking about how many moments there were before that picture was taken, and how many moments there have been since it was taken, and then, naturally, how many moments are left. Have you ever thought about that, Owen? I warn against it; it's not good. There are only so many moments in a person's life. They all line up like dominoes and then carom off each other in a way that somehow lands us here, in *this* moment, for this heartbeat. But really, it's only a prelude to the next. And the next. And the next. A lifetime of moments, one after the other. I find the improbability of it all to be thoroughly exhausting.

"I know we've talked about this before, but here's where I've run into some trouble. I have come to realize that anyone's life— my life, your life—is made up of only a finite number of moments. I mean that's just the objective truth. That is simply the given: the independent variable. The allotment of moments we receive is certainly not limitless. Not for us mortals. And as I considered that, I began to see that most of the moments in my life—I mean like just about *all* of them—have come and gone without the slightest thought or conscious attention or any real appreciation on my part. They're just wasted, extinguished, lost forever to rot in the garbage heap of my rapidly fading memory, like compost to fertilize my regrets.

"So, I began looking at all the photos on my wall, and I now see that they are really just images representing a handful of my allotted moments, a fraction so small it can't even be calculated. Believe me—I tried. And yet because someone deemed those moments worthy of eternalizing on film, one could conclude that they must represent some of the *best* moments of my life, the ampoule of moments that describe the apogee of my time on this planet. And you know what? They're all gone too. Every single one of them. I mean, what a squandered life.

"What exactly do I have to show for it all? And, sorry, but here's where it gets a little dark. What does this say about me—about the six decades of my life that are reducible to the equivalent of less than two minutes of meaningful moments that I can barely remember or feel anymore? And again, you'll have to pardon me here, but what does it say about the future? What about the moments to come? I mean, for Christ's sake, look at me. Look at how I live. What's the nature of the moments that are left to me? What are the odds that any of those moments still to come will be worth sticking around for? Worth photographing and hanging on some stupid wall. And just how depressing is that?

"I don't see any silver lining here, Owen. I really don't. So I started taking down photographs of moments that I just don't consider especially significant anymore. I wanted to be left with only those that, for whatever reason, still resonate in some way, as a means of quantifying them, and as a reminder of just how few moments there are in one's life that actually mean anything. Their number continues to decline as you see in front of you. I keep taking more of them down. And I see no prospects to indicate that any new ones will ever be added. That's a bad calculus. That's a regressive trend. So what happens when the wall is bare? When there are no more photographs left? Then what? What happens then?"

To dredge: an excavation activity usually carried out with the purpose of gathering up bottom sediments and disposing of them at a different location; to clean out the bed by scooping out mud, weeds, and rubbish.

Dredge was the word that came to mind as I listened to Wilson's pain. He was engaged in the deepest kind of dredging imaginable, an archaeology of the soul, intended to excavate the gritty sediment of his life and then subject it to the coruscating glare of his reflection. Surely, some of what is uncovered would be difficult to confront, but dredging was precisely the point of this whole visual literacy process. Its value rests on the expectation that the excavated matter, whatever its size, shape, or composition, warrants examination. I firmly believed this. I knew this was true for me. I assumed that it would be that way for him. Still, there was an inescapable pang of uncertainty that rose in my gut when I heard the anguish in his voice. It made me question whether he may have been going too deep to unearth the rubble buried in those photos. Could he go too far? Was he strong enough to handle whatever he found? Have I been complicit in this? All I had was my own experience to go on and my conviction that the darkness he had just expressed was better for being out in the open, exposed to light and air, rather than festering inside.

"Look, I know that the stuff that comes up can sometimes be awful to look at. It sounds like you're getting a whiff of that right now. But I also know that this is one of those times that can be enlightening, in the truest sense of the word. Jesus, I can imagine how ridiculous that sounds. Sorry. But if you trust me on anything, trust me on this. See if you can give it a little more time, stick with it a little while longer. When you think you're ready, take another shot at that third photo and give yourself a chance to see what shakes free. I've been there. I really have. I know what it's like to stir up the shit at the bottom of the river, but I also know that is precisely the shit most worth looking at. Don't give up on the experiment just yet."

Even to my ears, those words sounded flimsy and lame, but the words were all I had.

It was time for me to go. Janey would soon be waiting, and I had the impression that Wilson wanted to be alone. So I left him in the den with his assurances that he was okay, that he would consider taking another run at that third photo, and that he would call me if he wanted to talk some more. That was good. That was good enough for now.

"Hey, and maybe you should go through your mail one of these days. It's kind of piling up out here," I teased as I picked up my coat from the kitchen but heard no reply.

After rinsing my glass in the sink I took another look at the magnificent engine that seemed so out of place sitting there on top of the table. Its complex intricacies and art deco design flooded my memory with images from that first afternoon in Wilson's garage. That deliciously sensory jambalaya felt like ages ago. By any reckoning, the ground we had covered since that day was vast. A reconsideration of the trajectory of neighborly engagements was probably in order. A little updating would be necessary to account for this new territory that Wilson and I had apparently entered, but that would have to come later.

As I was leaving, Wilson's cell phone started to ring. The sound struck me as strange, though at first, I couldn't place why. And then it dawned on me: the sound of his ringing phone was the first sign of contact between Wilson and the outside world I had ever detected in his home. Until that ring, there had been nothing to suggest he had any connection with another human being. I could recall no other phone calls, text messages, doorbells, or visitors. There had been no other voices, or stains, or remnants or footprints or fragments of anything that could be claimed by the presence of another. Other than the ghosts that roamed the halls and the phantoms portrayed in his pictures, nothing else was ever there. And then, suddenly, here was a ringing phone. I called into the den to see if he wanted me to answer it but again heard no reply. So I buttoned my coat and pulled on my gloves and left the phone where it was, ringing on the table beside the weeping motor and idle tools. In time, it stopped.

A few moments later, the phone chimed again—a second sound of contact—this time with the message that he had one missed call, from someone named Rachel.

PERTURBATION

Fall River, May 14, 2016

Chapter

11

Andrew Borden was not a popular man in the town of Fall River, Massachusetts. As a successful property developer, he had amassed impressive wealth but garnered little respect from his neighbors, his business partners, or the community. Even his own family held him in low regard as his miserly ways had indentured them to a frugal and drearisome life. He was churlish, odious, and mean, and he attracted the ire of the town's residents like flies to carrion. This ire even extended to the herds of youngsters in the area who often took special pleasure in japing the ornery old man.

In the spring of 1892, Borden was enraged after finding several dead pigeons on the floor of his barn. His suspicions fell directly on the heads of those troublesome kids. In an effort to quell their hijinks once and for all, he took a hatchet to dispatch the remaining birds. This action deeply upset his youngest daughter, Lizzie, who had loved those pigeons and tended to their care for years. Whether this contributed to the brutal murders of Abby and Andrew Borden three months later continues to be the topic of speculation more than a century after the crimes. Everyone in Fall River knows that Lizzie was tried under a cloud of deep suspicion but never convicted. And these days, the people of the town would rather not talk about the case.

It's only eighty miles from Eastham to Fall River, but they are worlds apart. The surreality of the Cape dissipates as you head south and cross Buzzards Bay, surrendering to the uncompromising urbanization of the unflinching city that sits at the mouth of the Taunton River. Today, Fall River shares the same struggles as other small towns. But with Boston to the north and Providence to the west, both within easy reach, residents can find plenty of promising employment opportunities. As such, young families of modest means can get a great start in Fall River. And thanks to low housing prices and the influx of rich, diverse cultures, many of the neighborhoods are experiencing an energetic renaissance of vitality and pride.

The house at 72 Bowler Street rests squarely in the Highlands neighborhood of Fall River, less than two miles from the legendary Borden home. Its Dutch Colonial design dates back to the 1930s and is typical of the construction in this residential area. The homes are neat and well maintained but lack the fussiness and ornament of the more prestigious enclaves around North End.

On this glorious Saturday in spring, the sky is pale blue and emblazoned with a pattern of die-cut clouds that looks like it was drawn from a children's book. The air drizzles with perfume; viburnum, lilac, and sweet mock orange offer up fragrant currents like dowries on which ride the profusion of small-winged creatures that seems to have spawned overnight. That heavy scent is everywhere, even reaching into the open garage that sits adjacent to the Bowler Street home.

The clutter of a young family fills the garage: bikes, strollers, toys, and games, all of it sharing the space with an old Volvo wagon. At the moment, the hood of the car is open. A shop light is suspended over the engine. A few tools and small parts rest along one of the sills. Springsteen's Born to Run is playing through a wireless speaker.

William stands on one side of the car in oil-stained overalls that are frayed at the knees. His son Trevor stands on a stool on the other side of the car, in a matching pair of blue overalls. Both are peering into the engine bay. A handwritten checklist is taped to the windshield.

William: All right, T. You can check off number 4. That one is done. How about we do one more before heading in for some lunch? Can you read number 5?

Trevor (grabs a purple crayon from the pocket of his overalls and places a check mark through the fourth box on the list): Check on number 4, Dad. And number 5 says, "Add oil."

William: Okay, great. So let's see—we drained the old oil out, right? And we replaced the oil filter. We checked to make sure everything was tightened up. Now we can add the new oil. Do you remember where the new oil goes?

Trevor (points proudly to the crankcase filler cap in the middle of the car's engine and begins to unscrew it): It goes right there.

William: You know something, pal? I think you're almost able to do this all by yourself. Maybe next year, I'll just sit inside eating pizza and playing video games while you handle working on the car. (William gathers up the quarts of oil and the gooseneck funnel, and they begin filling the crankcase.) So, little man, are you excited about your grandfather's visit?

Trevor: Papa's coming?

William: No, not Papa—your other grandfather. Papa is Mommy's father, remember? He is one of your grandfathers, but you have two, you know. My father—we'll call him Grandpa—he's the one who's coming to visit.

Trevor (a little confused): I have two grandfathers? Have I ever seen Grandpa before?

William: You did. When you were a baby, but you probably don't remember. He remembers you though. He talks about you a lot. He is very excited to see his big grandson and how he can fix cars.

Trevor: Did you and Grandpa used to fix cars?

William: We sure did! He taught me just like I'm teaching you. He was a very good teacher. I wish I were as good. In fact, I think

I have a picture of him and me fixing his car somewhere in this dirty old garage. You think you can put in this next quart of oil by yourself while I look for it? (He opens another quart and hands it to Trevor who begins pouring it into the mouth of the funnel, his face a portrait of childhood concentration. William then turns to the toolbox on the workbench and starts rummaging through the drawers.) Ha! I found it. Wow! It's a lot older than I remember. (The small photograph sits in a frame that is stained with grease, but the image beneath has been well preserved. He looks at it silently for what seems like an age before showing it to Trevor.) This is Grandpa and me back when I was probably about eighteen or so. We were living in Illinois. That's his car right there. It's called an MGA. Bet you've never seen one of those before. We used to work on it a lot. It needed a ton of work back then, but, boy, he really loved that car. It was awesome.

(Just as the last quart of oil flows into the car, William's wife, Amy, enters the garage. Her gingham apron is dusted with cornmeal and flour. She walks with the slow waddle of late pregnancy, arms crossed over and under her belly as if she is already cradling her baby. Her long black hair reaches down to her waist and is loosely pulled back with a narrow ribbon to reveal her flushed complexion. Nothing, not even the murky garage, can dim the glow from the force of the furnace inside.)

Trevor: Hey, Mom. Did you know Grandpa is coming to visit? I'm going to show him how I fix cars. And I'm going to show him my car collection too. Wish I had an MGA though.

Amy: I sure did know that. It's very exciting, isn't it? He hasn't seen you for a long time, and, boy, is he going to be proud of his big grandson who can fix cars all by himself. You can show him your car collection, and you can show him what a great soccer player you are, and maybe we'll even take him to Battleship Cove. I bet he'd like that. And who knows—maybe he'll even get a chance to meet his new baby granddaughter, who is just aching to get out and meet everybody. (As if on cue, she reels from a kick inside and softly smiles to herself.) It's really going to be nice to have him here, won't it? Hey, are you guys almost done? Lunch will be ready in a few minutes.

William: Just about. All we need to do is check to see if we put enough oil in the engine, and we can call this a job well done. T, you know how to check the level, right?

Trevor: The dipstick, you dipstick. (The small family shares a laugh while Trevor inspects the level and deems it to be spot-on. With his purple crayon, he then checks off the fifth item on the list. Father and son wipe their hands on some rags, collect the empty oil containers, and start putting away the tools.)

William: Hey, T, great work today. But you forgot one thing.

Trevor: Oops. Duh. I always forget to sign the check sheet. (He pulls the sheet from the windshield, prints his name in the box at the bottom, and then places the completed checklist next to the toolbox. He gives his father a high five and then grabs his mother's outstretched hand. The two of them walk back to the house together. While a few fragments of their conversation still flicker for William to hear, most are carried aloft by the wind and lost forever.)

William watches them leave: his wife and son bound by their love and the everlasting bond of flesh and blood. He gasps with the sudden onset of emotion. It sweeps over him like a gale, bludgeoning him with a cudgel of love and knocking him nearly breathless. And soon, a daughter. Where will he find room in his already overflowing heart for more love? He thinks about this as he watches Amy and Trevor disappear into the house.

In time, he collects himself and begins to close up the garage. His father taught him to never leave a project without ensuring that the work is properly squared away. He checks to make sure that the oil-filler cap is tight, that the filter is snug, and that there is no oil leaking under the car. The last of the tools are stored in their box, and he begins to secure the lock when he remembers the photograph.

He finds it where he left it, on the roof of the old Volvo and starts to return it to its drawer, but something abstruse brings a change of mind. Rather, he reaches for a shop cloth and some spray and gently cleans the surface of the frame. With each wipe of the cloth, more and more years are washed away until the memory of that moment captured on film so long ago returns in dazzling relief, uninvited but there just the same: that day when his heart first broke from the ruthless knowledge that his father was nothing more than an ordinary man, burdened by dreams, troubled by time, making his way through life. As it always does when he remembers that day, William's heart breaks some more, and he quietly weeps: an ordinary man, distracted by time, with burdensome dreams of his own.

A few minutes later, he locks the tool chest and heads inside, carrying the sparkling photograph in one hand and a hammer and nail in the other.

Chapter

By most accounts, 1975 was a very curious year. It was a strange, confusing, meandering time that was neither one thing nor another. It just sits on history's timeline, taking up space like the iceberg lettuce in a house salad. All year long, waves of momentum crashed together from opposite shores. The destructive interference caused by their collision left behind nothing but an innocuous trough filled with a Velveeta malaise.

It was a curious year in the Conway home as well as the normal flow of family things was temporarily—but dramatically— diverted. My father was away for much of that year, leaving my mom and my brothers and me to "hold down the fort" and "fend for ourselves." His absence created wide swaths of bewilderment for us all and confounded our lives with a combustible brew of loneliness, latitude, and mischief.

In 1975, Leland Conway was away on tour. During most of the summer and half of the fall, he worked with a team of recording engineers on what was rumored to be a major pop album project. Though he was gone for weeks at a time, he dutifully stayed in touch. In June and July and August, postcards arrived from California. The backs of these cards were packed with crazy schematics of the fancy equipment he was using at the Winterland Ballroom.

September and October brought more postcards, this time from New York, with reports of the acoustical hardships he faced in the airy architecture of the Long Island Arena. Every Sunday, his voice beamed across scratchy phone lines to tell us about the complicated live recordings that were sure to be the basis for a huge commercial hit. His excitement was boundless, and we soaked up every word. *This,* he declared, was why he became an audio engineer in the first place. *This* was the greatest privilege of his professional life. And, oh yeah, he hoped we were all doing okay without him.

And then, a few weeks before Thanksgiving, he triumphantly returned. The stories he told swelled with pride. "Groundbreaking!" he shouted. "Revolutionary!" he crowed. There was a glow about him during his retellings. It burned from a place we knew nothing about, yet we all basked in its blazes nevertheless. As he reclaimed his place at the head of the table, our lives slowly returned to normal. But our love for him was amplified by a fierce devotion that could only have come from being apart for so long and our undiluted dreams for his renown. We spent the holidays counting down the days until the record's release.

On January 16, 1976, *Frampton Comes Alive* made its heavily anticipated public debut. The album would go on to become one the biggest sellers of all time and validate my father's prophecies. The critics agreed. It captured the raw energy of a rock concert like no other record before, setting a standard for live recordings that still holds to this day. But that recognition would take time.

Nothing—no amount of future success—could erase the devastation we all witnessed as he sat in his La-Z Boy and unwrapped a release-day copy only to find no mention of his name anywhere in the credits. Only the lead engineers were acknowledged. The cadre of secondary engineers went unlisted. The signed copy of the album and handwritten note he received from Frampton a couple of weeks later did nothing to quell his outrage and the seeds of what would become a lifelong bitterness toward the recording industry were sown.

The record was banned from the house. That signed copy is long gone. But in an act of youthful malfeasance, I bought my own and proceeded to play the hell out of it for the next forty years, chasing after any trace of that one curious time and the Con Man's influence on the Winterland or Long Island tracks. So, for obvious reasons then, January 16 was long considered a dark day in Leland Conway's life. I like to think that changed somewhat when, on the same date eighteen years later, he welcomed his first grandson into the world.

And now, for different reasons, January 16 is again a very difficult day.

I planned to spend most of that Saturday up in the studio, occupying my mind with the distractions of work. Those design ideas I had promised to Dave and Tim for the updated Hennigan's label were just about ready. They needed only a light retouch and a final decision on the color gradient, neither of which would pose any problems. The boys had been anxious to review the proofs and approve a final concept to suit their rapidly expanding line of craft beers. They were moving fast on what everyone agreed was an ambitious production schedule and marketing campaign. Now they needed a label, and that was on me.

Janey too had chosen to blunt the concussion of the day with work, taking on a midday shift at the restaurant. Together, we placed our faith in the belief that the rigors of our jobs would be enough to deflect the sorrow that had been gathering for days. Truthfully though, neither one of us places much hope in faith. The day would have its way with us. It always would. We accepted that and hunkered down for the assault. And we found ourselves fused together by our grief as daybreak dawned.

Our morning was monasterial. Toast, tea, honey, and very few words. We hovered close, bound by the ligature of reciprocal needs and unwilling to cleave, returning to each other's side whenever our private orbits spun us too far apart. We drew strength from our routines, each watching carefully as the other brushed teeth, dressed, filled the coffee maker, or turned the newspaper's page, blinded by the astonishment of actually performing the most ordinary tasks on such an extraordinary day. When at last she had to leave, we clung like climbers suspended in the air, grasping frantically for any kind of handhold on the slickest, slipperiest, sheerest rock face. The absence that marked her leaving was absolute, and I considered staying fixed to that spot until she returned.

Her perfume endured a little while longer. It dappled the air with musk, and I breathed it in for as long as I could, deeply in selfish gulps, until it too steadily evaporated before winking out entirely. Slowly, as I knew it must, my self-consciousness returned, and with it came my resolve to make it through the day. Work would be my salvation.

Up in the studio, the designs were quickly completed. Three alternatives, each expanding on the label's original theme, were finalized and readied for printing. I sent the command to the sleeping machine a floor below and headed down to retrieve the proofs. The rest is best imagined like a Dali-esque dream.

To this day, I am still not sure how I found myself in Aaron's room, waking up from an accidental nap as the last of the sunlight was draining from the midwinter sky. I awoke like Dorothy in the poppy fields of Oz, dazed and displaced in both space and time. The afternoon slumber left a gluey stickiness that melted like toffee in my mouth, and my head felt filled with cotton. A pool of melancholy quicksand ensnared me. It promised impossible things and then doused the air with drowsy pollen to seduce my conceit.

As I started to rise, the room began spinning. My arms and legs felt pinned to the bed by vicious centripetal force, held fast with Velcro-like cuffs. Panic rose in waves of nausea, and sweat stung my eyes. To get out of that room was all I could think so I tore at the restraints that bound me. With every thrust, they slackened some more until at last they gave way, and I escaped to the hallway where sorrow's spell and the ogre of my burdens could not reach.

Once safely away from the room, the panic gradually subsided. In its place, a plan began to take shape, coalescing out of blind instinct to settle my soul. The distance between home and Hennigan's measures a little over four miles. If I left soon and maintained a reasonably good pace, I calculated that I could make it there before the end of Janey's shift. That would be perfect! I would explain my appearance by handing over the freshly finished proofs for the boys to review and thereby avert suspicions about the more desperate nature of my actions. Sure, Janey would see through that for the needful ploy that it was, but that was okay. We would be together. And right then, being together was the only thing that mattered. With her shift over, we could have a drink, maybe some dinner, regain our poise, and drive back home to face the darkest part of the night together. It was an excellent plan. So I shrugged off the slag of my delusion, grabbed the proofs from the printer, and prepared for the blustery walk ahead.

Saturday mail deliveries are always a little light. I sometimes wonder why they even bother. That's why it was so easy to spot the odd-looking note on my way out, strewn among the few pieces of junk lying on the floor of the front porch. The note had been elaborately folded into the shape of pyramid and was secured, not with tape, but intricate tabs. One face of the pyramid had been addressed to me with a thick black marker in precise block letters. Its origin was obvious, and I thought with a chuckle that this is how we would be communicating now, with messages back and forth like kids from a predigital age.

With the countdown on Janey's shift ticking away, I tucked Wilson's note into my pocket, still sealed, and, for the moment, unread.

Sixty-four minutes door-to-door—that had to be a personal best. I arrived at Hennigan's slightly winded but with plenty of time to spare. As expected, the place was lolling in the lull between the last of the lunch crowd and the first of the early-bird diners, a rare moment when a restaurant can catch its breath before bracing for the bustle to come. Happy hour.

Tim rushed by with a clipped hello, carrying coils of cables and microphone stands to the makeshift stage in the back. At a corner table, Sophie and Dave huddled with restaurant business: the lunchtime take, Alberto's plans for the dinner specials, or maybe the evening's staffing schedule. They both looked up and waved as I entered before resuming their deliberations.

I had just turned my attention back toward the bar when a pearlescent streak of silver-white light ricocheted around the room like a comet. My first thought was that the boys had gone retro and a mirror ball was being tested for later. But when I traced that streak back to its source, it turned out to have come from a more transparent location. It came, in fact, from that same corner table. Or more precisely, it came from Sophie's eyes. They glittered like moonbeams and surged with concern but left the impression that she had looked up too soon. It was not eye contact she was seeking. Rather, I think, she wished to regard me as I walked away, to see "how I was doing," on this of all days. Still, under the trance of her glance, the welter of the restaurant melted away, and it was just the two of us, sewn together by the keenness of her affection.

These spellcasts of hers never last long. They are as fragile as twilight. A blink, and they are easily broken. We resurfaced almost at once as the filaments of her eyes finally cooled. I smiled in acknowledgment of the moment, but it went unnoticed. She had already turned away.

I'm not much of a believer in holism, mysticism, or spiritualism of any kind. My own roots are in the deep permafrost of skepticism and are traceable to the unromantic pragmatism of my parents. So, I've never known what to make of Sophie's prodigious powers of healing. All I know is that as I made my way to the bar, I felt newly sanctified. I was visited by an indisputable sense of peace and calm for the first time on that very difficult day; no further explanation was necessary.

I wedged my way in amongst the regulars who were homesteading until closing. The TV in the corner was tuned to the playoff game between the Patriots and the Chiefs, but nobody was paying any attention. They were much more intent on the game to come.

"Cold one, coming down," was yodeled my way as I unbuttoned my coat. I looked up to see a mug of something dark bobsledding down the full length of the bar, courtesy of Jim in a signature move he only uses when the pace is slow. "You are going to love that one, partner. Guaranteed." The beer came to a stop directly in front of me, its foamy head layered like a proud soufflé. And, of course, he was right. Jim is always right when it comes to beer, and that brown ale was no exception. Unfortunately for him, his track record when it comes to football is far less impressive.

"Smart money is on the Packers tonight," he said in an opening gambit. His cockiness forced a wry smile to roll across the terrain of his tastefully unshaven face. The first volley had been fired, and he stood back, waiting to see if I would parry. The green and gold jersey he was wearing left little doubt about his intentions. Or his allegiances. Or his hardened dedication to the gym.

"Oh yeah?" I said, eagerly taking the bait. "Am I picking up the stirrings of a friendly wager? Tell you what, partner, though it breaks my heart to say it, I'll take the Cardinals to beat your Packers, and since they're playing in Glendale, I'll even toss in three and a half points just to sweeten the deal. You want a piece of that action?"

"Absolutely I want a piece of that action. Usual stakes?"

"Usual stakes, done!" Now I'm pretty sure neither one of us actually knew what the usual stakes were. Other than bragging rights, nothing ever changed hands even after all these years and the hundreds of bets we've waged. But we slapped hands anyway to cinch the terms, and I tried not to let him see me wince.

I grabbed a handful of peanuts to go with the beer and realized that I hadn't eaten anything since breakfast. So, I grabbed another handful and began explaining to my fellow bar mates why smart money always falls on the side of the home team to cover the spread during the playoffs. Statistics back that up.

"Hey, did you boys just make another one of your dumb bets?" Sophie asked, leaning an elbow on the bar and wagging an elegantly ornamented finger. Her meeting with Dave had just ended, but her shift had not yet begun. She arranged herself on the stool beside me in a complicated set of maneuvers that infused the air with jasmine and rose. Peeling a ribbon from her wrist, she twisted her hair into a champagne confection and then idly crossed her legs.

Several sets of eyes turned our way.

"Jim just made a dumb bet. Mine was brilliant."

"Oh yeah? We'll see, partner. We'll see," the barkeeper chided. Then, at a signal so subtle it might have gone unnoticed—it couldn't have been more than a wink—he poured a jigger of Bushmills into a glass. Like a showman, he raised the bottle over his head and missed not a drop before sliding the double shot over to Sophie.

She took the glass gladly and held it to the light sending prisms of gold to shimmer her face. And when she brought it to her lips and drank it down slowly, it seemed like the last liquor left on earth. "Good Christ, I needed that," she faintly confided. "It's gonna be a long night."

Jim signaled his agreement with a commiserating grin and left the bottle before heading down to tend the other end of the bar for a while.

The Hennigan's bar is shaped like a hockey stick: long and narrow and curved at one end. It's also chipped and splintered and deeply gouged with a sumptuous, noble patina. The stools are spaced in pairs that fall far enough apart so you can gain an illusion of privacy. When it's early, the bar can be a pleasant place for carrying on a conversation.

Sophie twisted my wrist to check my watch and then gently groaned. The whiskey set about its work. A claret bloom rouged her cheeks. Her hands felt like cool pillows. They lay light as feathers across my arm, tipped by ten red rubies. As she leaned in close, I could feel her breath on my neck and smell the wax of her lavender lipstick. She locked my eyes with hers.

"So, tell me, Owen, no bullshit now, are you doing okay?"

"Yeah, I'm okay. Thanks, Soph," I said, tracing a notch in the bar with my finger. "I will admit there were a few rough moments back at the house. It was a little touch-and-go there for a while, but I'm as good as I've been all day. The distractions are helpful. Thanks for asking. What about Janey? How does she seem to you?"

"It's hard to tell," Sophie conceded, letting go of my arm and arranging herself into a more temperate position on the stool. "She didn't want to talk much on her last break. She was too far gone into Iceland this time—must be the latest addition to the collection, huh? Oh, the places you'll go, right? But, yeah, I guess she seems okay. She's in the back just finishing up her shift. I'll let her know you're here." In the pause that followed, she shook her head sadly and held my hands in her own. Then she added more gravely, "I don't suppose this day will ever get any easier for you guys. I'm so sorry, Owen."

Before getting up, she grabbed her glass and tipped the last of the dregs into her mouth. For a moment, it looked as if she were about to pour another but then, with the smallest of shrugs, decided against it. "I'll go get her," she said.

"Yeah, thanks, but tell her not to rush. I never mentioned that I was coming. Oh, and hey, if you see Dave or Tim back there, could you give this to them?" I slid the portfolio in front of her. "Those are the proofs for the new label. Tell them if they don't see anything they like, they can get themselves a new designer. Nah, just tell them to let me know either way. I'd be happy to work up something else."

After helping herself to a sip of my beer, she bundled me up in the tenderest of hugs that maybe lasted a little too long. But given the cruel circumstances that fall on that particular day, probably not. "Will do," she called back over her shoulder before heading off to the kitchen. I watched as she walked away, arresting attention with every step in her elegant black dress and sharp red heels, still afloat on the crests of peace and calm that continued to course through me. Her prodigious powers. And maybe I was watching a little too closely only to be caught off guard a moment later when she turned around on those very same heels and asked with the voice of a vixen or maybe it was in a temptress' tone, "Oh, and, Owen, how's that fine-looking friend of yours? Nice guy that Wilson Lacy. Tell him I said hello. And to get his ass in here again, will you please?" A smile spread slowly like sweet molasses along the arch of her mulberry lips. And then she was gone, dissipating like a dream at the first break of dawn.

The restaurant was filling up. The crescendo that would soon reach its peak was beginning to build. It rumbled in moderate tremors underfoot. It *was* going to be a long night.

The evening crew appeared on the floor, looking freshly rinsed and well pressed. Their afternoon counterparts straggled out like zombies from *The Walking Dead*. The whole place had begun to hum with an insurgence of noise. The room was coming alive, vivified by an excess of zing as more and more current flowed through the narrow spaces between the tables and under the chairs. Janey was still nowhere in sight, so I called down to Jim for a top off on the ale.

"It's good, right? Maybe not for everybody, but I had a feeling you'd like it." He filled the glass but had no time for a flourish as orders were flying from every direction. I envied his composure and his cool under fire. He was like a danseur back there behind the bar; always en pointe, effortlessly gliding across his hockey stick stage and thrilling the patrons with his bartending craft, his broad shoulders, and the tint of his amethyst eyes. The overturned Bears helmet that doubles as a tip jar looked mostly empty, and even though it was early, that just didn't seem right. I reached for my wallet to make a donation and felt Wilson's note at the bottom of my pocket. My curiosity about its contents grew unquenchable as I turned it over in my hands. So, I put ten bucks in the helmet, grabbed another handful of nuts and a glance at the game, unfolded the tabs of the pyramid, and started to read:

Owen,

Thank you for your note. I'm sorry that it has taken me so long to respond. I think I told you last fall that I'm really not very good at this kind of thing, though it's not from a lack of caring. I can figure out the orbit of distant planets as they hurtle around invisible suns, but I don't think I ever figured out how to be a good friend. Still, it was heartening to read that this relationship of ours (this friendship?) that appears to have manifest by chance is working both ways. That seems just as it should.

As I'm sure you noticed, I was not at my best last time we were together, and I apologize for that too. I still question if all this introspection around my photographs is the best thing right now. Might it be exacerbating my mood in some way? Forcing an examination of aspects of my life I'm not ready to undertake? Or is this the dark hour that precedes the dawn? I realize there is no way of knowing the answers to these questions. I don't have the necessary perspective yet. I also realize that I made a commitment to myself (and to you?) to see this through, and that is exactly what I intend to do—darkness be damned.

I wanted to let you know that I took your advice and tried again to work through that third photograph. For reasons I still don't understand, that one was particularly difficult ... but it's done now, and I'm ready to move on. For the record, my experience thus far with this experiment supports your contention that unmasking the meaning in visual images can be an enlightening process, exposing otherwise latent themes of one's life, but I hasten to add that it can also be deeply challenging. I know that I am suffering through those challenges now as I was the last time you were here. To borrow your metaphor, the sludge I am stirring up stinks like shit. There is, I believe, an inherent danger of things collapsing, of an implosion where the weight of all this reflection causes a disintegration (e.g., dis-integration) of the psyche into a singularity of sadness, its pull like that of a black hole and thus inescapable. That, I contend, may well be the heart of darkness you referenced in your note. I would like to believe that I'm strong enough to face that darkness wherever it might lead, though sometimes I'm not so sure. And I would also like to believe that the light of day may someday shine even on me to curtail this insufferable darkness, at least a little bit and maybe for a little while, though, again, I'm not so sure. It is winter after all, and light is in very short supply. Know that I know that I'm not alone. And that I will see this through.

Wilson

"Hey there, handsome. What's that you're reading?"

I didn't even notice Janey's arrival. She came up behind me, on slippers it seemed, and rested her head on my shoulder. Having her so close again—to feel the flush of her body along the length of my own—was soul-soothing salvation, and I took great comfort in knowing that we would never be apart for the rest of that monstrous day. Her lips tasted of thyme.

"It's a note from Wilson," I answered, holding up the letter for her to see. "He must have left it with the mail this morning. You know, for a scientist, the guy really has a way with words."

Though there was more I wanted to tell her, I never had a chance. Without even looking, she bluntly forced her arm through mine and wrenched me away from the bar. I knew from the way she pulled—frantic and sharp—that the day's convulsions had left a mark on her too. Rue contused her eyes, leaving them marked with striations of grief. And her face showed the fatigue that comes from smiling at strangers all day. My fingers grew numb under the strain of her grip, and when I tried to steer her back to the bar, she felt mulish, no longer so lithe.

But the longer we adhered, the more her grip began to relax. I like to think it was my nearness—and *her* knowing that we would never be apart again for the rest of that day—that worked like an opiate to dulcify her senses. Her hold on my arm gradually loosened as she stood beside me while I finished my drink. And when I put my mug down on the counter, her fingers were whispers. Some of the rue had rinsed away too. It turns out that being together *was* all that mattered. "Sophie saved us a table over there," she said, looking into my eyes for the first time that day. "How about I let you buy me a glass of wine and a nice dinner, and you can tell me all about that note from Wilson Lacy? What do you say, Conway?" A second taste of thyme sealed the deal.

Dining with Janey at Hennigan's is always entertaining, and even that night was no exception. She is treated like royalty by the adoring staff, and that treatment gets extended to me by association. Waitresses stopped by with the salt of kitchen capers and odd behaviors at the bar. Busboys spread rumors of secret affairs and risqué goings-on under the tables, of a burgeoning drama among the waiters and brewing tensions among the cooks. And Sophie supplied shots of tequila and the inside jokes that I never quite got but laughed along with anyway. It all lent some lightness to the dinner that helped steer us away from the more treacherous terrain that constantly threatened to intrude.

But after the meal, our conversation began to drag behind the troublesome weight of the day. An excruciating silence ensued. When at last she remembered to ask about Wilson's note, we both exhaled with relief.

I put down my napkin, pushed away my plate, and began recounting the events leading up to his letter. I described the strange occurrences at Waltons and the deep despair I saw in him later that afternoon. I went back further to tell her about the avatar of sadness, and his photograph wall, and the loneliness that haunts his house. And I told her about the darkness that rains from the skies, the kind that leaves him drowning on dragonfly wings. But despite all the details, Janey seemed unconvinced. She just couldn't reconcile my depiction of Wilson with her own recollection of his time in our house before Christmas.

"I don't know. He didn't seem all that sad to me that night. Maybe a little shy or nervous, but I wouldn't have described him as sad or depressed."

"Well, it sort of comes and goes. You know, some days are better than others, that kind of thing. To be honest, that evening at the house was about as good as it gets. Unfortunately, that's not really the norm though, especially lately. He's having a pretty hard time right now."

"Hmm."

Janey sometimes hums to herself. That's when I know her mind is at work, when she's figuring things out in her head, calculating the different angles, teasing out various notions in all their endless variations, assessing their fit, aligning one thought with another, bending, shaping, forming an idea so that it can blend with the others. That's when she is in her element, the Janey Conway zone: planning, plotting, devising. It's the humming that gives it away. And I can tell too when her mind touches down on a theory that calibrates neatly with her intuition. Then it's the knees: the way they bounce. Just like they did in that moment.

"So, then, that's kind of interesting, right?" Before going any further, she swept the room with her eyes. It was a long and deliberate look, nothing that resembled an idle search: a lighthouse lantern or maybe more like a searchlight now that I think about it. It was confirmation of some sort that I assumed she was after.

"What do you suppose it was about that night that made him seem better to you? You know him a lot more than I do. Hey, maybe it was the marsala! Sure, that's probably too simple, and I'm not suggesting any great insights here. But sometimes aren't the simplest explanations the best explanations? Look, all I'm saying is that if what you said is true, if he really was better that night, then maybe he was able to forget about being sad for a while. It's possible, right? If you could figure out why, maybe you'd be on to something. You should think about it, Owen. You really should."

By now, you could probably guess that I already was. Thinking about it that is, about why Wilson seemed different that night, maybe even a little less sad. And, honestly, I never stopped thinking about it. Neither, apparently, did Janey.

It was full-blown Saturday-night mayhem by then. The line for a table was already to the door, and a sound check was underway on stage. Fiona Bloom, the locally famous lead singer of The Tillerson Blues Band, was colluding at the bar and readying herself for the first set of the night. Her entourage was keeping her stoked with Jack Daniels. Jim was keeping her well charmed. Dinnertime was over, and it was time to put the old folks to bed. Youth had ascended in their ripped jeans, Janis Joplin sunglasses, and Buddy Guy T-shirts. The room crackled with their needle-sharp devotions. Janey and I took our cue and decided to pass on coffee, preferring to turn the table over to the next group of fans waiting in line. So, we signaled to our waiter for the check.

A sharp-eyed busboy intercepted that signal, grabbing it out of thin air and appearing like a genie at the table. I had to look twice as he set about his work. There was something about him that was definitely familiar, but the context was all wrong. The cues were too confusing. It's like when you see your doctor in a bathing suit at the beach. Recognition, if it comes at all, is glacial in dawning and then sorely suspect. Nothing about the situation made any sense until the busboy started talking.

"Hi, Mrs. Conway, Mr. Conway."

"Oh, hey there, Reed. So you're on tonight, huh?"

He nodded to Janey while piling our plates. "Owen, this is Reed Riskin, the newest member of the Hennigan's team. Reed, this is my husband, Owen. And, Reed, drop the 'Mrs.' already, will you? I'm Janey, okay?"

"Yeah, right. Sorry … Janey. Hello, Mr. Conway." He wiped his free hand on the towel that hung from his shoulder and then held it across the table. Without the dark hoodie to cover his head, he looked much younger, just a kid really, wearing a rather sweet and unpretentious smile. An intricate set of angles incised the lower half of his face—*chiseled* we used to call it. That, along with the rough shag of jet-black hair that nearly hid the studs in his ears, gave him the rugged aspect of a rebel. It was a look I once tried to cultivate myself—without much success. Even under his apron, I could tell that his busboy uniform hung a little too loosely on his frame. Either it was a size too large or he could have used a few good meals, but his watery eyes held onto mine with a steady intensity while we shook hands. That's when I noticed the full sleeve of botanical tattoos that covered his arm. A profusion of color sent tendrils of vines toward his neck. I tried not to stare, but it was really quite beautiful.

"Hello, Reed. It's nice to see you again. I didn't know you worked here. How are you?"

"I'm pretty good, sir. Thanks. Good to see you too. And, yeah, I just started." The tower of plates he held in his hands continued to grow as we spoke. Never once did they threaten to topple. He handled the strain with surprising aplomb. "So, I guess Hannah and Sara must be back at school, yeah? If you get a chance, will you tell them I said hello?"

"I sure will, Reed. I promise. And, hey, that's a hell of a nice job with those plates, son. You're a natural."

He paused for a second to inspect his work. My compliment seemed to confound him. The way his eyes darted from the nearly cleared table to the high stack of plates in his hands made it seem that he never considered the job worthy of praise. It's just bussing a table after all. Who would ever take note? Let alone comment. Janey and I watched as a bashful half grin flitted across his ruddy young face and the vines along his neck sharply reddened. Then he resumed his work, and when the table was cleared, he wished us good night and hustled back to the kitchen.

"*Again*? What do you mean 'nice to see you *again*'?" Janey asked, staring at me wide-eyed and plainly confused.

"Yeah, I met him at the theater with Hannah and Sara over break. He was there with Mike Flannigan, and we bumped into them on the way out." Along with the explanation came a humble concession for what suddenly seemed like an ungenerous first impression. *Cold-blooded skink? Really?* In retrospect, that might have been unfair. I tried to remember what Sara said about him at the mall.

"Yeah? Well, that's a coincidence, huh? He came in a couple of weeks ago, just after Bobby Savino quit. His timing couldn't have been better. Dave hired him right on the spot. He's a nice kid. A little lost at the moment, but there is a genuine kindness there. Everybody sees it. We've all kind of taken him under our wing. And the boys are thrilled with his work. The kid never complains. He's always the first one in and the last one out. He can fix anything that breaks anywhere in the place, and he's happy to take on the dirtiest jobs. And there are some pretty ugly jobs back there, take it from me."

"Huh," I grumbled, still a little wounded for having judged him so harshly before. "Isn't he supposed to be in school?"

"All I know is what Sophie told me. Apparently, school wasn't working out so well. I hear he's living at home, but I get the feeling that things aren't so great there either. It's hard to know what to believe. How a kid can survive in an environment like that—if all the stories are true—is really beyond me. And keep this under your hat, but Dave set up a cot for him in the back. He can use it whenever he wants. I think maybe he's one of those kids who could just use a break, you know, a chance to get his bearings and find his way, and maybe this is it. It really is a pretty good gig, all things considered."

The stage lights flashed a succession of sunbursts, and the crowd responded with cheers. The crescendo had arrived. Time to ride the wave. We paid the tab, gathered our coats, and began the procession of goodbyes. As we carved our way through the throng, I yelled over to Jim, but he never heard me. Nor could I get a score on the game. The line at the bar was three deep, and everyone was clamoring for another round. We found Dave and Sophie waiting for us by the door just as the first few bars of "Statesboro Blues" howled through the speakers.

The Tillerson faithful erupted.

"I woke up this morning, I had them Statesboro Blues."

"Owen," Dave shouted over the roaring guitars and Fiona's brass. The portfolio of design proofs was in his hand. He kept waving it around like he was fanning a flame. "These proofs! Man, they're fantastic. I just went over them with Tim, and we love them all. We want to purchase the rights to the set and introduce them slowly over the next couple of years. Keep the look fresh for a while, you know? They're perfect for that. How about we call you next week to go over a purchase agreement?"

"Well, I looked over in the corner, and Grandpa seemed to have them too."

"What? What did you say? Say that again, Dave." I asked him to repeat it some more, right into my ear and then again on the other side just to make sure I heard him correctly. I couldn't really trust the situation. Sure, I knew the proofs were good, but rounds of revisions are routinely required. I fully expected to be asked for some changes. This was not the way these things typically go, and Dave's reaction left me dumbstruck. It felt like rocket fuel for lighting my ambitions of shooting off on my own, full-time, as a real independent design artist, and I greedily sucked it in.

Janey squeezed my hand to keep me grounded. She didn't need me drifting away just then.

"I'm goin' to the country, baby, do you want to go?"

"Of course," I shouted back, realizing that he was still standing there and waiting for a response. "That's great, Dave. Thanks. Yeah, sure, call me whenever you guys want to move ahead."

He screamed something back that was lost in the din and swatted me on the arm with the folder. A moment later, he was gone, swallowed up by the crowd and their wild Saturday-night fevers.

"Wake up, Momma. Turn your lamp down low."

Sophie hung back a little longer. She started to say something, but her words too were squelched by the noise. So she motioned to the door with her hand, and we began to squeeze our way out.

As I trailed along behind, I noticed that Sophie's other hand held onto a small package. The sight of that package caused my stomach to clench. And though her eyes were lowered beneath tired lids, I knew that Janey's dark contusions had returned. The trauma of the day had caught up with us again.

After the swelter of the bar, winter's sudden earnestness was shocking. It came at us swiftly and surely, and the quiet fell like eiderdown. The night was cold, and the sky glittered with stars. They kaleidoscoped above us in a silver net. The three of us stood on the sidewalk, shivering with the uncertainty of what was supposed to happen next. I kicked snow off my shoes leaving flakes of white waffles on the ground while we looked at each other for a sign to tell us what to do. That sign came at last from Sophie.

"They really are impressed with your designs," she began. "That ought to keep you swimming in Hennigan's for a while."

But that wasn't why she led us outside. Something more pressing was weighing on her mind. Anybody could see it, clear as the wolf moon rising above. When she saw us glance again at the package, she lowered her head. Her heels began tapping, and I had the impression that the snap of a twig or the crunch of a boot would have been enough to send her scurrying back inside. Perhaps there was too much exposure for her, out there beneath all those silver sparkling stars, with whatever precious thing was in her hands and the strange trepidation that caused her to tremble.

"So, here, I wanted to give this to you both tonight. I've held onto it for too long." She placed the package in Janey's hands before blanketing them with her own. A tiny tear began to glisten in the corner of those luminescent eyes. It reflected the starlight that fell in facets all around us. The tear filled with love and nearly overflowed but never had time to fall. Instead, she wiped it away with the back of her hand just as others arose to take its place.

Janey handed the gift to me and then enfolded her with a hug. They stood that way and wept as stars streaked by overhead. All I could do in that melancholy moment was let my eyes fall to the gift. It was wrapped in thick, textured paper decorated with red and green wreaths, a leftover scrap from the holidays. A pale blue ribbon embroidered its length, and a small card was taped on top. I started to pull the card from the wrapping when Sophie suddenly looked up.

"No! Stop! Don't open it here," she pleaded as she stepped away from Janey's embrace. The soreness in her voice implored us to wait, and my stomach clenched even tighter. When she saw me tape the card back to the paper, her tone grew more composed. "Take it home and open it there. Please. It'll be better that way. It really will. And, listen, I love you guys. Remember that when you open it, okay?" She cried through the clasp of one last hug before rushing back to the refuge of the raucous crowd inside.

The day had left us spent. Janey and I were silent on the car ride home. We were each consumed with muddles of thoughts that sprouted like weeds after such a long and difficult day.

Janey held the gift on her lap while the winter landscape shuffled by her window. The snowy panorama had become so commonplace now; the season seemed stuck. It was as if the world had always been frozen and powdered with white and would remain that way forever. We were hostages held inside a cheap, plastic snow globe and the thaw would never come.

Once, during the short drive, she placed her hand on my arm but quickly moved it away, satisfied with the certainty that I was there, wedded still by ties of heartbreak and sorrow.

Arriving home was hard. We both knew it would be. The house had been abandoned for long hours on this of all days. It had time enough to work up a fury at our absence and then maul us as we entered with pent-up squalls of rage.

We hung our coats and put away our shoes, and then I broke the silence. "I don't know about you, Conway, but I am beat. I need sleep."

"Not just yet, Conway. Stay with me a little longer. Please." She reached for my hand and led me to the kitchen, by the skim of our fingertips only. The light from the tunnel that lit the three portraits was all that stood between the darkness and us.

We sat down at the table with Sophie's present between us. My heart felt like mud in my chest.

"You want to open it?" Janey asked.

I wasn't so sure. I think I was afraid of what might be inside, of what it might reveal and whether I was ready for whatever would be exposed. I pulled the box toward me and held it for a moment while my mind shut down. Then I took the card from its envelope and read aloud in a voice that I no longer recognized as my own:

Dear J and O,

I thought you might want to have this.

It was taken a few years ago during one of our afternoons at the beach. He asked me to never tell you about those afternoons, but I can no longer keep them secret. There are stories to tell. Good stories. Stories you will love to hear. Whenever you are ready. His heart was so big, and he loved you all very much. Always. Through everything. As do I.

Happy birthday,
Dear Aaron,
Happy birthday to you.
S

A vacant mind. Those elusive threads. Tangled somewhere deep below. A photo whispers. Silent disclosures. It's my son as a young man. Grown tall and willowy, like his mother. Smooth and nimble limbs. Bare feet planted like taproots in the sand. Throwing stones that skip for miles. Carrying dreams along the waves. A cobalt sky at sunset. Buttery clouds. Turquoise water ruffled by wind, set afire by the setting sun. His fading smile. Rhapsodic. Radiant. Reticent. Always reticent. My unassuming son. Here he is now … walking through the door like always …

hugging me good night one last time, and we sleep like warriors under the same roof forever.

I leaned the photograph against the counter so Janey and I could look at it together while we wept. Come what will. Tears. And misery. And woe.

After a while, Janey stood and softly sighed. It was the sound of a mother's despair, embittered by storms of anguish and pain, and it wore the weariness of ages. From a cupboard in the pantry, she removed the special plate, the one reserved for birthdays. It held five of his favorite cupcakes, chocolate with yellow buttercream frosting.

"I baked these yesterday while you were at work," she said. Her voice ruptured with the memory of other birthdays when the kitchen was filled with so many cupcakes. And so much love.

I watched through my tears as she placed a thin white candle in the middle of each little cake and lit them one at a time so we could sing him his birthday song. Of course, we never made it through to the end. The quicksand was still too deep. But we would try again next year.

Chapter

A paper banner stretched across the full length of the wall. Huge pink letters. Purple glitter outlines. Red hearts dotted all the i's:

Middlebrook Middle School
Sadie Hawkins Valentine's Dance
Saturday, February 13, 7:30 p.m.

"So who was Sadie Hawkins anyway?" I asked as we admired the banner's florid design.

"You know, I have no idea how I know this," Wilson began, "but I think she was a character in the Li'l Abner comic strip. They called her the 'homeliest gal in all them hills.' Apparently, if I remember this right, she was too ugly to catch a husband on her own. So her father came up with the idea of a race between all the eligible men in town. The first one Sadie caught would be obliged to marry her. Somehow that appalling premise from the 1930s got turned into Sadie Hawkins Day when girls invited boys out for a date or to a dance. We used to call them turnabouts, but it was all the same thing."

"Yeah, sure, we had those too," I recalled. "And if things are still the same, I'm betting there are a lot of anxious boys roaming these halls just waiting for that text message to ping. Man, middle school was rough, wasn't it? So much pressure to fit in all the time. Do you think these kids would believe us if we told them that it won't always be like this? That life really does get better?"

"I doubt it," Wilson answered. "Would you have believed it if some old guys told that to you back then? I imagine you would have thought they were crazy."

We were sitting in the reception area outside the office of Dr. Jennifer Rabin, EdD, principal of Middlebrook Middle School. We had front-row seats for observing the menagerie of preadolescents who paraded in and out in a never-ending flow. Some were delivering notes to the assistant behind her desk, others whisked messages to the farthest reaches of the school, while still others sat morosely, waiting to have their fate adjudicated beyond the paneled doors just a few feet away.

We had just handed over our driver's licenses to Dr. Rabin's assistant and were waiting for the school computer to pore over our backgrounds before printing our badges. While we waited, I took out my note cards to go over the key points of my talk. Admittedly, I was a little nervous at the prospect of speaking in front of a classroom full of kids. Wilson didn't seem anxious at all. He craned his neck to peek at my notes, and I swear there was a smidge of smugness in his smile. I was just about to ask him about his own preparations when the doors to the reception area were flung open.

An impeccably suited middle-aged woman with a hive of bright silver hair marched in and immediately seized the attention of everyone inside. Even on her heels, she couldn't have been more than five feet tall. But sparks of self-assuredness and dense, magnetic energy surrounded her like a force field. Those sparks beamed to every corner of the room as if by command from her incendiary glare. She breezed through the outer office like a cyclone, appraising the scene with a single glance, and then pointed her assertive stride directly toward our chairs while Wilson and I held our breath.

"You must be Dr. Lacy and Mr. Conway, yes?" she said, with the lilt of a southern accent and sudden heaps of disarming charm. The smile she bestowed began in her shamrock eyes. They crinkled like cellophane and pranced with a playfulness that invited us to tag along in her charade. "I'm Dr. Rabin, the warden here, and I wanted to welcome you both to our school. I can't tell you how much we appreciate your time today in support of our kids."

Wilson and I introduced ourselves, still a little unnerved by her bluffs and suffering from the same complicity that attaches to the principal's proximity no matter how old you are. Or how charming she might be. She handed a set of folders to her assistant and then turned to face Wilson. And just like that, the playfulness was gone. All business now.

"David speaks very highly of you, Dr. Lacy. I understand you were one of his professors in his teacher-education program. Is that correct?"

"Yes, that's right," Wilson replied. "He was a student in my science methods class a few years ago. He was a terrific student back then, and I'm not at all surprised to find him doing so well here."

"Well, I have to tell you, Professor, I've seen a lot of science teachers come and go over the years. And I've interviewed many more. Whatever you do in that class must be pretty remarkable. You ought to find a way to bottle it and distribute it nationwide. He is among the best science teachers I have ever seen. Anywhere. His students adore him. The faculty admire him. We're lucky to have him on our staff. On behalf of the public schools, thank you for the important work you do. But now, gentlemen, you'll have to excuse me. I hope you both enjoy your time in his classroom today. I'm sure you'll see something wonderful."

She shook our hands with an emphatic grip, the kind that lets you know you've been seen and now it's time to move on. And then she trooped away, stridently on sturdy legs, wearing her silver hive like a fez to her office just past the main desk. She laid a hand upon the knob but did not immediately enter. Instead, she turned her head over a shoulder, and all the frivolous noise just withered and died. Those fiery eyes scoured the room until she landed a flare that blistered the face of a mournful and forlorn-looking student. If this were a graphic novel, a word balloon would have appeared above his head with a single, onomatopoeic syllable: "Gulp."

"Okay, Michael, you're up. Let's go, young man."

The ruined detainee known as Michael, though he stood a head taller than the warden, rose from his chair in obvious fear and reluctantly followed her inside. His face was the color of ash.

"Dead man walking," I whispered to Wilson as the door shut sternly behind them. But he never acknowledged my joke. His thoughts, as they often do when he's thinking about things he just heard declared, had drifted off elsewhere.

The bitter smell of freshly laminated plastic announced that our ID badges were ready. They were warm and soft like fresh-baked cookies when we clipped them to the Middlebrook lanyards we wore on our necks.

"Which room is David's again?" Wilson asked while we gathered our things.

"He's in room 213," the assistant replied. "Take the first flight of stairs up, make a left, and then all the way down the hall. You can't miss it. Believe me. You can't."

It was the middle of second period, and the hallways were empty. As we walked past homemade banners and laser-printed signs for the Valentine's Day dance, I noted that not much had changed over the years. It still felt safe and timeless. Schools can be like that, connecting children to parents to lost generations while remaining immune to the upheavals that impinge upon the rest of the world. But despite all the constancy, my reason for being in Middlebrook that day was highly unusual. Let me explain.

I learned just a few days before that Wilson and David had been trading emails ever since their encounter at Waltons. The focus of their discussions was the force and motion unit that David had mentioned. They were brainstorming. It seems that every year, David's students plan, design, and build marble roller coasters as a way of investigating concepts from the physics curriculum. Those lessons were always a big hit with the kids. This year, he was hoping to update the unit to highlight the district's emphasis on STEM education, and he turned to Wilson for advice.

Now, according to Wilson, STEM stands for Science, Technology, Engineering and Mathematics. It's is a new way of thinking about teaching that gives kids a real-world problem to solve and then turns them loose as investigators. In order to work the problem, the students carry out projects just like scientists and engineers do in real life. Wilson claims that STEM not only teaches kids what they need to know but also inspires their creativity and imagination and prepares them to manage a world dominated by science and technology. He calls it "the science literacy imperative." The roller coaster unit was a perfect test bed for trying out some STEM ideas, and the professor and his protégé had been planning for weeks.

Apparently, one of David's goals is to enlighten his students about the nature of science and the exciting work that scientists do. What better way to do that than to bring a real scientist into the classroom—and what better scientist than his old mentor, Wilson Lacy? But that wasn't all. In progressive schools like Middlebrook, STEM often expands to STEAM, the "A" representing the additional integration of art. In the course of their planning, Wilson suggested that he just might know someone who could be convinced to take a day off to discuss the work of an artist as well. It didn't take as much convincing as Wilson imagined. I was intrigued by the idea from the start. But as we made our way toward room 213, past closed doors that leaked a monotonous drone, I was no longer quite so sure. My note cards suddenly seemed ridiculous.

And there is one thing more that needs to be said before we can go any further. It has to do with how we wound up at Middlebrook that day. Wilson showed up at my door the weekend before and invited me out for a walk. "Owen," he began as we strolled down the block, "do you ever think about trying to change the world?" On we walked, and on he talked about STEM and kids and his plans with David. He spoke for a good mile or more, and that same familiar insistence was back, his own peculiar brand of edginess that betrays a need to get on with a thing. That compulsion I always admired. His words and ideas were locked in a race, each trying to outrun the other. His hands could barely keep up. They flittered like bees with bellyfuls of nectar drawn from sweet blossoms. He buzzed with the vim of that heavy ambrosia, heaving with desire to pass it to another so it could be churned into honey. But this wasn't the drive of some biological need. It was more susceptible than that. This was exuberance he spoke with that day. Pure and simple and lately quite scarce. It came from the wish to tell me something he loved so I may find a thing that was in it to be loved by me as well. And in the end, isn't that what friends do?

The assistant was right; we really couldn't miss it. All we had to do was follow our ears. It started the moment we reached the second-floor landing: a low hum of white noise. At first, it mingled with sounds that seeped from the rows of classrooms we passed by. But as we continued walking, the hum grew louder. It soon separated from the clutter and turned more distinct until it became a turbulent rainbow. And by the time we arrived, the rumble from the room at the end of the hall had fractured the sobriety of the school. We stood outside and listened to the riotous commotion. My hands grew sweaty as I pictured the maelstrom we were about to enter—think more *Lord of the Flies*, less *Dead Poet's Society.*

Wilson noticed my panic and steadied me with a look of subzero cool. "No worries, Owen," he said, his eyes all suddenly aglow. "That, my friend, is the sound of science."

No one noticed our entrance. Not a single student looked up. Instead, we were carelessly consumed into the pandemonium. Thirty or so students sprawled around the room, working in groups that clustered around tables. On top of each table sat a structure composed of a bewildering array of materials. These were the roller coasters, but they were unlike anything I had expected. They were working sculptures of intricate designs, beautiful, complex, and Rube Goldberg-ian in construction. Each one was unique. They were built around chutes down which a marble could roll, but they also featured jumps, loops, twists, drops, lifts, cutoffs that led to dead ends, and bifurcating routes that multiplied before converging again into single-lane thoroughfares. Everyday objects had been ingeniously incorporated to accomplish astounding effects. And they were works in progress. Everywhere I looked, students were immersed in testing, observing, recording, modifying, debating, thinking, and analyzing, but they were also playing, laughing, and screaming with glee as some kernel of idea went from concept to paper to trial to fruition.

At the first table we came to, a group of girls was preparing for a test—and we eagerly accepted their invitation to watch. They began by describing their coaster's design, taking turns to point out each of the variously engineered sections. Then, a shiny blue marble was pulled from a box. Each of the girls kissed it for luck until the last in line placed it in position and raised a Popsicle stick gate. Three seconds later, the ball jumped over the pipe cleaner rails and went skidding across the floor. Two of the girls howled with laughter and chased after it.

"I knew it," one of the chasers shouted back to the rest of her team as she looked around for the marble. "That first run is too steep. The marble gets too much velocity. We need to *slow* it *down.*"

The second chaser found the marble and brought it back to the table. "Hey, what about that sandpaper?" she proposed as she hunted through a shoebox full of supplies. "Maybe we could glue some pieces to the floor of that first chute and try to build up some friction. That should slow it down. You think that would work?"

I shook with amazement as they debated the problem of the too-fast marble. Wilson stared with delight. He acknowledged their good thinking with a comment or two as they took out their rulers and started measuring sandpaper strips.

Shouts and screams were coming from every direction, and there was so much we wanted to see. So we left them to their work and walked away just as one of the marble chasers called after us.

"Hey, so which one of you was Mr. Marder's teacher?" she asked in a way that seemed to convey that this lab was her turf. And while she bided her time awaiting a reply, a purple ruler swatted her thigh keeping beat with some furious rhythm.

"That would be me," Wilson acknowledged.

"That's cool. You look like a teacher. So, tell us, Professor, what kind of a student was Mr. M?"

Wilson smiled widely and brought a hand to his chin while he considered his response. He allowed his eyes to scan the room, and his head began to nod. Somehow, the girl never flinched or even much blinked as he bent his large frame down beside her. But the rhythm of the ruler most definitely slowed. "Actually, he was one of the best students I ever had," Wilson remarked while peering into her eyes. "And this … this is exactly how I suspected his classroom would look. And you … you are doing exactly the kind of wonderful work I imagined as well."

"Yeah, that figures," the young scientist groaned as the ruler's rhythm resumed its pace. "And lemme guess. You're the guy whose suspicions are never wrong, right?" She held out her hand for a high five, but it took Wilson a second or two to respond. He stood back up in slow, incremental steps as the confusion on his face grew, then peaked, and gradually ebbed. For a moment, it looked like he had seen a mirage or stolen a glimpse of some hidden, underground grandeur. "Well, don't leave me hanging here, Doc," she earnestly pleaded before Wilson tapped her hand, and she bolted back to her group.

We resumed our rotations around the room to inspect more designs. But even as we admired the other creations, Wilson's attention kept skipping back to that first table and that group of young girls. It was their progress that he followed most closely. That we had seen no signs of David was no matter of concern. The entire class was running on its own power. It was not unlike a finely designed piece of clockwork that operates perpetually, flawlessly, with zero awareness of its mechanism. It could have gone on for hours. This wasn't the drudgery of science class like I remembered. This was play—joyful, productive, purposeful play to be sure, but play nonetheless.

We were halfway around the lab when a door in the partition opened.

David strode toward us and expressed his apologies. The squeak of his black canvas sneakers was audible above the ruckus. His jeans, though scrupulously clean, were frayed along the cuffs. Cartoon telescopes brightened a tie that hung around the neck of his Grateful Dead T-shirt, and a mechanical pencil sat behind an ear that was pierced with an ingot of the space shuttle. And just as it was in Waltons, his thin blond hair was pulled back in a bun. But the quiet deference he showed the customers from behind his register was gone. *This* was his natural habitat.

"Sorry, I was just setting up the other part of the room for your talk. I am so glad you both agreed to do this." He took a quick inventory of the room and then glanced at his watch. "So, the kids have about ten more minutes of lab time, and then we take a five-minute break to transition next door. Let me show you around."

As we roamed from table to table, David invited the students to explain a bit about their creations. With each presentation, Wilson engaged them with questions. The bona fide pride they had for their designs was matched by their deep knowledge of physics. I learned about gravitational potential energy, critical velocity, and frictional loss. And when the students used their roller coasters to demonstrate these concepts, it was like no textbook I had ever seen.

It was only when David announced that it was time to clean up that this group resembled a class full of eighth graders. They milled about in packs according to strict social codes and gobbled down snacks pulled from their backpacks. With a little more urging, they began filing through the partition to take their seats in the classroom next door.

David showed us to our chairs in the front of the room and waited for the class to settle.

"All right, it looks like the groups made some good progress today. We'll hold off on our daily debriefing, but rest assured that we will pick up with that first thing tomorrow. And that's because, as promised, we have a couple of special guests joining the work today. This is Dr. Wilson Lacy. He is an accomplished physicist who worked at Argonne National Laboratory and has even logged time at the CERN cyclotron. And he is also a science educator who teaches teachers. In fact, as many of you know, he was my science teacher when I was in college. And this is his friend, Owen Conway. Mr. Conway is professional artist and graphic designer who works for an advertising firm in the Chicago area. So, a scientist and an artist are in the house today. Any idea why?"

Almost immediately, several hands went up.

David scouted the room for volunteers and called on one of the marble chasers sitting in the back row.

"Well, for one thing," she began, "you're always telling us to think about the ways that science and art are similar, right? Maybe they can help us with that. And I think it's a pretty good bet that you're about to put our three pictures up on the Smartboard again. But I'm also thinking you're trying to get us to think about our roller coasters as both science *and* art, and maybe these two guys are going to help us with that too."

"That's excellent, Maria. Well done. Yes, we *have* been studying the overlap of science and art all year, and we will continue to do so until the end of time. And, yes, again, our roller-coaster project *is* a great example of how science and art can be applied together in the real world. So, I invited 'these two guys,' Dr. Lacy and Mr. Conway, to describe for us the work they do as a scientist and as an artist and how they view the world. I've asked each of them to share their perspectives with us, and then we'll talk about the things we heard that might be in common. And maybe we'll think some more about how we are using both the scientific lens *and* the artistic lens in developing our roller coasters. But first, as Maria indicated, I will indeed put up our three images. Our guests know that we've been using these as examples of the intersection of science and art, and they may refer to them in their comments."

He pushed a button on his computer, and the board at the front of the room lit up with these images:

"Gentlemen, the floor is yours."

Wilson went first. He rose from his chair and walked to the back of the room. Every eye trailed his every move. Now, the only sound in room 213 was the whir of the projector's fan. He leaned a shoulder against the partition and folded his arms in front of him. He stood that way and stared at the images displayed on the board.

One by one, the students shifted their eyes to look more closely at the Smartboard. Then they resumed their watch on the strange scientist in the back of the classroom who was saying nothing at all. They ping-ponged around for a minute or two more until, at last, when it could grow no quieter, Wilson began, "What do you see when you look at those pictures?"

"I see a glider, a windmill, and a galaxy," a student called out.

"I see an invention, a way of saving the planet, and stars," called out another.

"I see three things that all have something to do with motion," offered a third.

"That's good! That's very good. And how do those three images make you feel?"

"Confused."

"Light."

"Curious."

"Small."

"Hungry."

"Yes! Those are all great answers. But now I'm hungry too." Wilson paused while the laughter passed and to allow the tension to gradually rebuild. Make no mistake; he was in total control, like a maestro tapping his baton on the podium, preparing to make glorious music from an aspiring ensemble. With the full attention of the class turned again toward him, he resumed.

"Well, when I look at those pictures, what I see is wonder. In fact, if someone were to ask me what wonder looks like, maybe I'd show him those three images. And sure, I see all those other things too—the windmill, the nebula, and so on—but first and foremost, to my eye, they each resemble wonder. There is so much in those pictures to wonder about. If you look carefully, you just can't miss it. I wonder why, or I wonder if, or I wonder how." He glanced over at David whose eyes, like those of his students, were transfixed by the images on the board and whose face, also like those of his students, was lit with interest. As was mine.

"I look at those pictures, and I feel my pulse quicken. I feel my heart start to race. I get excited. Restless. I even get hungry, but—and I know this is going to sound corny—I'm hungry not so much for lunch, but I'm hungry to know more. When I look at those images, a thousand questions arise. Where did the Wright brothers get the idea for flight? How does a windmill turn wind into electricity? How do nebulae form? And each question I ask represents something I want to learn more about. I want to read about those things. I want to explore them, to investigate them for myself and talk about them with others. I want to do experiments, build things like your roller coasters to test out my ideas, and I want to hear what experts have to say about them. I want to sit alone and think about those things and astound myself with my own ideas. I want to do all these things because I know that when I do, the chances are good that I will discover something truly amazing. Does anybody know what that is?"

"Answers?" called out a student from the front row.

"Maybe," Wilson replied. "But more than just answers—I'll discover *truth*. Truth is a by-product of science. It is the sum of our greatest ambitions. And I know too that that with each truth I uncover, there will be more and more questions to keep me hungry and knowing all this—knowing that there is a universe full of things to wonder about, from way out into the farthest reaches of space, to your schoolyard out back, and even inside our own bodies, all patiently waiting to be discovered—well, that makes me feel alive. That makes me feel happy."

And this is where he paused. Full stop. Dead silent. Just the tedious whir of the fan. He stopped long enough for those of us in the room to notice that something unscripted was occurring. It wasn't because of some pacing demands of his presentation. He hadn't lost his place. And it wasn't due to some unexpected reaction from the students. I know I will never know for sure, but to this day, I truly believe the reason why Wilson stopped at that precise moment had to do with those last few words. It was as if hearing them out loud ("makes me feel alive … makes me feel happy") had disrupted his flow. They snagged his attention on a thorn of barbed wire, and before he could free himself, he was compelled to repeat them—over and over again—to verify that he really had said them, that the words had come from him, that such a thing could even be uttered by him and then might even be possible.

As the pause stretched on, he turned his face and smiled at me—wryly, knowingly, almost slyly, arched eyebrows and all—as if he had just uncovered a new, significant truth. I thought for a second that he was about to say something more, just to me, to ask perhaps if I had recognized the truth in those words as well. Just to be sure. But he soon recovered his poise, turned back to the class, and continued along as if nothing much had happened.

"From my perspective, that is precisely what science is. It's the adventure of discovery, of finding the wonder—of designing, building, and testing roller coasters—and to me, it's the most exciting thing—the most perfect thing—in the universe. Do you all know who Albert Einstein was? He once said, 'The most beautiful thing we can experience is the mysterious. It is the source of all art and science. He to whom this emotion is a stranger, who can no longer pause to wonder and stand rapt in awe, is as good as dead; his eyes are closed.' Now, just think about that for a moment. The source of all art and all science is the mysterious. How wonderful is that?"

If the looks on their faces were any indication, the students thought it was very wonderful indeed. They wanted to know more.

Wilson went on to describe the research he did in Switzerland and some of the particle experiments he conducted here at home. I listened along with everyone else, enraptured by his passion for finding wonder in everything around him. But he wasn't just talking about his experiences as scientist or how he views the world; he wasn't simply lecturing or demonstrating. He was weaving together an intricate pattern of ideas while—at the same time—guiding the students to formulate their own ideas about the nature of science. He was *teaching*, and it was masterful. And I was supposed to follow this?

I don't think he intended to blaze any trails for me to follow. We never tried to coordinate our ideas at all, but an unobstructed trail was exactly what I saw in front of me, and that was thanks to Wilson's genius. When it was my turn, I left the note cards on my chair, all except one, and began to make my own way to the back of the room. Again, I felt the tension build, but this time, it was because of me. All those eyes were watching, following, expectantly waiting. The pressure imposed by those silent glances ratcheted up quickly, and I gave in too soon, jumping in before I could make it all the way to the back of the room. Ugh. Rookie mistake.

"Well, when I look at those pictures, what I see is beauty. I see the way light and shadow mix with line and form to create a visual impression that I perceive as something beautiful. The way I look at it, beauty is everywhere in nature. Therefore, beauty is in us. In fact, after nature, we alone can create beauty, and that's what I would call our highest achievement, the ability to set out and create something beautiful. Beauty is all around us, all the time, it's even in your roller coasters. I saw that the minute I walked into your classroom. That's not to say there is beauty in everything; I'm not sure I'd go that far, though I know some people do believe that is true. It's a good question. But beauty surrounds us, and it is the heart and soul of all art.

"Now, Dr. Lacy talked about how those images make him feel. Okay, so my reaction is pretty similar, but I'll use different words. When I see beauty like in those images or in a flower or a skyscraper or the way a leaf falls from a tree, it makes me feel lots of things, but most of all, beauty make me feel *awe*. Interesting that Einstein used that word. If I were alone, I would stare at those three images, and their beauty would flow through me and—I know that this too probably sounds corny—I would be shaken by them. I would stand 'rapt in awe' just like Einstein said. I'd be discombobulated by their beauty. And it would even be hard for me to breathe.

"That's why I always try to go to art museums alone. It's not a pretty sight. But the truth is that I'm not alone in the world, and I can't go through life always gasping for air and discombobulated by everything I see. So that forces me to do something with all this beauty and awe, and for me, that means finding ways to think about it, to understand it, to share it with others, to interpret it, and even try to create it for myself so that maybe I will understand it a little better, but maybe too I'll even inspire someone else to look at something in the world and feel a similar sense of awe. That's why I'm an artist. Did you know Einstein was an artist too? And funny enough, I also have a quote from him that I wanted to share. Get this, he once said, 'The pursuit of truth and beauty is a sphere of activity in which we are permitted to remain children all our lives.' I wonder what he meant by that."

At first, I didn't hear the student in the back ask me about what I do all day as an artist. Or the one who asked if I ever saw something in nature that wasn't beautiful. Or the one who wanted to know what I thought about that Einstein quote. I was too far inside my own head to notice as I made the long walk back to my seat.

But when Wilson repeated the questions for me, I began to describe the way I go about making art. I relied on some examples from work to highlight the steps I take from concept to final design, and I offered a bit of the lore behind some of the more famous advertising campaigns I was sure the students would recognize. I even drew comparisons to the conceptual designs of their roller coasters as legitimate examples of functional beauty. They seemed to like that a lot.

David followed up our presentations with a short discussion by posing two questions for the students to consider. He asked his class, "What is the relationship between beauty and wonder? And, can you have one without the other?" The conversation that ensued was more like a college seminar on science and aesthetics than the last few minutes of an eighth grade physics lab.

As the bell rang, David asked each student to come back the next day with a list of three things they observed on their way home that caused them to wonder and three things they saw that fit their own definition of beauty. The students recorded the assignment in their notebooks and then started filing out. A few stopped by to thank us for coming or to share an idea of their own, but it was Maria's comment that still stands as the most memorable moment of our morning at Middlebrook.

"I don't see why I would ever have to choose between art and science," she began while adjusting an overstuffed backpack across her butterfly shoulders. "To me, they're pretty close to the same thing. I think that's what I just heard you guys saying. I'm pretty sure that the only jobs I'll ever take will be ones that let me be an artist *and* a scientist—so I can do both all the time. That would be awesome." She slapped us each a high five, one for science and one for art, and then fist-bumped David for teaching before fluttering out the door to catch up with her swarm as they made their way to lunch.

Since David was on a free period, he offered to escort us back to the office. We retraced our steps down to the first floor, threading our way through the now crowded halls and the avalanche of fist bumps that the star science teacher received. "Well, that really went well," he shouted as we scuttled down the stairs. "I can't thank you both enough for coming." We assured him that it was our pleasure and that the morning had been fun.

"Well, I'm glad to hear you say that," he insisted as we entered the relative calm of the office. We stood to the side to get out of the way of the trickle of teachers that flowed back and forth from lunch. After handing a note to the assistant, David reached into a cubby marked "Science" and pulled out a clipboard piled with papers. As soon as he located the sheet that he wanted, he continued in a more solicitous voice. "So, I'm not sure this is the best time to bring this up, but I just can't resist. If it's too much, please tell me, but I wanted to run one more idea past you."

"Not at all, David," Wilson replied as the loose sketch of smile tinged the slope of his face.

"Yeah, sure. Fire away," I added.

"Well, we just received a small grant to start a residency program at the school. Our plan is to partner with community professionals to create in-school positions in several content areas; a scientist in residence, an artist in residence, a writer, a historian, and so on. I'm wondering if the two of you would consider joining us. There would be a pretty generous stipend for your time, and I think you would find the work to be very rewarding. You are both so great with the kids. Would it be okay if I sent you some details about the project?"

Wilson must have known this was coming. The look on his face told me that much. That sketchy, nebulous smile spoiled his efforts at a deadpan reaction, and his eyes kept fidgeting away. I figured that he and David must have discussed the project in one of their email exchanges, a wrinkle that Wilson chose to leave out the other day. But artist in residence? It had a nice ring to it. I admit I was intrigued once again. We added our contact information to the roster on David's clipboard, and he left us with the assurance that an outline would be in our inboxes before the end of the day.

Dr. Rabin's assistant had to be lured from her Xeroxing so we could reclaim our driver's licenses, but she happily obliged. We turned over our lanyards and were signing the log just as the door to the principal's office opened and another downtrodden student walked out.

"Don't you dare say a thing," Wilson begged under his breath as I offered a conspiratorial wink and understanding smile to the warden's latest parolee. I hoped it would be enough to ease the pain. And for our five-dollar donations to the Sadie Hawkins fundraising campaign, we left Middlebrook sporting bright white carnations to spruce up the buttonholes of our warm winter coats.

————◦◦◦————

Ernie's Deli sits at the corner of Kedzie and Main, two short blocks from the school. For years, it has been a regular hangout for the Middlebrook crowd as they meet up for a snack on the way home from class. But lunchtime is Ernie's busiest hour. By noon, the booths that line the front window overflow with childcare gear as young moms congregate with their toddlers in tow. The faded yellow counter that skirts the kitchen is where the working class comes to perch. They alight on stools to peck at a morsel before darting back to the office. And the tables in the back are a flotilla for the more elderly folk who always seem to have a standing reservation. They come for the coffee and to nosh on the rolls, but linger for the comfort of others while they whittle the day away.

"Two for lunch?" Denise asked, more like an accusation than anything else while mercilessly torturing her gum. Juicy Fruit, as always, a spare piece tucked safely behind her ear. Denise has been working the floor at Ernie's for as long as I can remember. The vapors of the place cling to her like drugstore perfume. Her green and white uniform has proven impervious to fashionable trends. But her broad, open face has been a fluid barometer by which the regulars have gauged the passage of time.

We followed her to a round table in the back, right in the midst of the venerable flotilla, the irony as thick as Ernie's split pea soup. "You boys celebrating?" she asked as we took off our coats. "Y'all seem charged up about somethin'. How 'bout a cuppa to start?" We turned over our mugs, and she began pouring from the pot that seems permanently attached to her hand. "You boys start with that, and I'll be backatcha for your order."

The replaying of the morning's events left my head swollen with exhilaration and adrenaline. Now add to that the caffeine. My enthusiasm, I realized with a stab of self-awareness, was running amok. I caught myself still raving as Wilson and I skimmed over the menus.

"I just want to say it again. You, my friend, were awesome back there. That was like witnessing a master class in teaching. It all looked so easy for you, so natural. It was like you were laying out crumbs for the kids to follow but guiding them along the way to think for themselves about some pretty complicated ideas. Damn, you were good."

"Well, thanks, Owen. I appreciate that. You were pretty good yourself, by the way. Beauty and awe, huh? That was incisive and well conceived, but I don't believe I saw that in your notes. In any case, I thought our two parts fit together quite well. Especially the Einstein. Magic in a bottle perhaps." He waited while Denise took our orders and refilled my coffee. She rested a hand on the back of my chair and popped her gum while she poured. Once my mug was filled, she hung around like a stray, looking for some scrap of conversation to chew, but we really didn't have anything for her. So, she crisply tore the check from her pad, placed it under the pepper and walked away shaking her head thinking, I supposed, *Don't those boys have anything better to do?*

Wilson cradled the cup with his hands and blew away the steam. He was just about to bring it to his lips but put it back down instead. The exhilaration and adrenaline must have gotten to him too. "To tell you the truth, it was wonderful to be in a classroom again. I keep underestimating how much I miss it. I suppose it's a part of me that has been lost for a while, and I haven't found anything else to replace it with. And that's not good. Today was different though. It felt like that void was filled, at least temporarily. What did you think of David's offer by the way?"

"Artist in residence? Artist in residence?" I crossed my arms and stretched out my legs, repeating the phrase a couple more times. The words rolled around on my tongue like smooth, buttery caramel. "Honestly, I have no idea what an artist in residence does, but I do like the sound of it. Would you ever consider taking him up on it?"

Wilson still could not find time for his coffee. Whenever he went for a sip, there was something more he wanted to say. And he so intently hung onto my words that he forgot about the coffee entirely. "I like the idea. I really do. I want to read more about the project, but if I know David half as well as I think I do, I'm sure it's well thought out. I imagine there would be opportunities to consult with the kids on projects, model professional behaviors, offer instruction, and maybe contribute to some larger planning and development. I'd like to think that I *could* do something like that again. Lord knows I have the time. What about you?"

"Yeah, well the timing is pretty interesting for me too. I'm still toying with the idea of leaving the firm and trying to make it on my own as a freelance designer. It looks like Janey and I have saved up enough of a nest egg to actually give it a shot. So, maybe by the fall, I'll have some control over my schedule. And now something like this gets added in to the mix? That seems like a pretty terrific coincidence if you ask me. I gotta say, that really was a fun way to spend a morning."

Our sandwiches arrived, and in the time it took for Denise to remember who ordered the Reuben and who ordered the BLT, we had formulated a plan. Wilson and I agreed to regroup after reviewing David's proposal and then make a final decision. But I could tell that the words, "scientist in residence" were making his mouth tingle too.

Then we set that aside to enjoy our lunch, and our conversation was free to roam. We talked about the politics of the primary season and the prospects for baseball as pitchers and catchers were about to report to spring training. I got him up to date with the girls, and he told me about some new planets that had just been discovered at the outermost reach of the universe. One topic that we still never discussed was the notes we had recently exchanged. I'm not exactly sure why we avoided the subject. It may have been territory that was still too raw to tolerate much probing. There were admissions in those letters that maybe we weren't quite ready to concede: silent disclosures of our own that were better off left in writing than spoken out loud, perhaps for a little bit longer. That brief period of time bookended by our notes still felt perilous, at least to me. I could imagine it remaining partitioned from the rest of the ground that Wilson and I were covering as we made our way through stage 3: separate, isolated, and inviolate.

And then we turned our talk to his experiment.

"Well, on one hand," he started to report as he finished the last of his sandwich, "it isn't getting any easier as I move through the photos. Not that I thought it would. There is so much to examine and think about. On the other hand, when I look at the pictures now, I find that I'm more facile. I don't have to sit and ruminate for as long anymore. I'm able to identify a theme and frame the writing more quickly. It's almost as if the more I do this, the better at it I get. There's a process developing. And the pages continue to add up."

Then he took a deep breath and began arranging his silverware and plates. Once everything had been neatly arrayed, he slid them aside and whisked the loose crumbs to the floor. He folded his hands on the newly cleared space, working his knuckles like gunshots. All these machinations imparted to me a feeling of mounting import—a sense of impending gravitas. And after a throat-clearing cough and a second deep breath, he was finally ready to add this little bit more. "And perhaps this is related, but I'm also finding that something more than meaning is beginning to emerge. I'm starting to see that there may be implications for action behind all this reflection. Like there may be things I can *do* as a result of this process—*actionable outcomes* you might call them—that could be significant in dealing with my—you know—my problems. Don't ask for examples. I'm not ready to get into specifics just yet, but I find that sort of encouraging. Another result I hadn't anticipated."

If Wilson was expecting a reaction from me, he must have been sorely disappointed. Now it was my turn to flash my own brand of subzero cool. You see, I knew exactly what he was talking about. The same thing happened to me. In fact, joining the SOS group was precisely the same sort of "actionable outcome" that resulted from my own experiment with visual literacy. I've come to believe that actions are a natural step in the process. Looking leads to seeing. Seeing leads to meaning. Meaning leads to understanding. And understanding paves the way for doing. Though I was dying to know what sorts of actions might be arising for him, I knew better than to ask. *Whenever he's ready.*

Instead, I simply smiled and riffed, "No worries, Wilson. That, my friend, is the sound of hope."

I signaled to Denise for another refill while Wilson pulled out his phone. He was anxious to show me the next photograph for review. This one was a family selfie taken, he said, at his son's grad school graduation a few years ago. A print he made of the photo still hung in his den.

"That was about a year before my wife and I separated. Things were okay then—but not for much longer. I was heading into a much darker place. What I find so captivating about this picture is the chaos. It's so conspicuous, isn't it? We're all jammed together, barely fit within the margins of the frame. At the same time, we were all spiraling away from each other along our own separate paths. That's a little harder to see. I think of this as the moment of a seismic big bang. Our time as an organized family system had just about run its course. There we are, held together for one last moment before spinning off along much different orbits. I find that whole notion to be very bittersweet."

As I looked at the picture, I could see what he meant about the chaos. It was right there, plainly ingrained on the screen. All those heads jumbled together, squeezed like sardines into the tightly packed frame. It looked like the slightest of jolts would have been all that was needed to spring them out into space. And then, after the jolt, who knows what might happen? It really was a beautifully bittersweet photo. I handed him back the phone, suggesting that it sounded like he already had a pretty good theme for his next entry. He clicked it off and returned it to his pocket without even giving it another glance.

⸺◈◈◈⸺

Outside Ernie's, the afternoon was dark and overcast. The sky sagged with yet another glut of gray. Had it ever been anything other than gray? The run of uninterrupted bleakness had grown tedious as it always does in February: the perfect predictability of it. Old man winter was exhausted, still hanging around not out of some meteorological necessity but simply because he was cranky and bored. Walking home, we had to dodge our way around puddles of melting snow that had sprung up everywhere. Those puddles would soon freeze over, and the walking would be treacherous for weeks to come. It was still a wet and sunless world.

And yet something *was* changing. It was undeniable even though the evidence remained elusive. It was more easily glimpsed out of the corner of the eyes rather than seen head-on, but an astronomical reality was at work, and it brushed against the senses like a butterfly kiss. Maybe we hadn't quite yet turned the corner on the season, but we were surely approaching the apex. The home stretch was in sight. Day by day, we were inching our way closer to the end of winter, and even if we couldn't feel it just yet, we knew it to be true—and that was something.

"I don't know, pal. Wonder and beauty in February? In Chicago? What was David thinking?" At first, the homework assignment seemed like an impossible task. I couldn't imagine what an eighth grader could find that would cause her to wonder or impress him as beautiful on such a frigid February day. But the more we walked, the more I could see that with the right perspective, the extraordinariness of the world is always on display. You just have to know how to look.

Over on Kincaid, thick rows of maple trees line the street. In just a few months, those trees would lavish the neighborhood with an arboreal roof of the coolest shade. Broad leaves will spread overhead like layered shingles to mottle the sun. But that marvel was still a long way off. The desiccated husks we passed seemed as far from a source of wonder or beauty as I could conceive. And yet, at Wilson's insistence, I looked more closely. When he held out a branch for my inspection, I bent my head to see. The professor was right. There *was* something miraculous about those trees. Something *was* occurring even then, at the end of a dreary afternoon. It was right there in front of my eyes, and it was breathtaking. Scarlet buds, no more than half an inch long and glowing with a fiery band of gold, screamed in violent contrast with the bleak surroundings to entice our attention. I reached out my hand to touch them. Their density was shocking. It was as if they were packed with something wonderful, just waiting for the right moment to burst, and all at once, by some small degree, the Chicago winter shed a bit of its gloom.

"It's for science," I said unconvincingly in response to Wilson's horror as I tore a branch from a tree. "I wonder ... do you think anything will happen if I put it in water? Will it leaf out? Will it root? And why are the buds so incorrigibly red when I know the leaves will be green? I hunger for the answers, Dr. Lacy!"

"Well, that will do quite nicely for wonder," Wilson said. "How about beauty? What do you think? Can you have one without the other?"

"Hmmm ... I'll have to get back to you on that one," I replied. "Janey and the girls got me a new set of watercolors for Christmas, and I've been dying to try them out. I do believe I have an idea for my first still life." I secured the branch inside my jacket, and we continued to make our way home.

From the direction of Ernie's, my house comes up first, and we soon arrived at my door. We picked a date to meet again to finalize our decision about David's offer. And when I entered that date into the calendar on my phone, I noticed that the residency outline was already there.

He was just about ready to turn down the street and make his way toward home when I reached out and grabbed hold of Wilson's elbow. I couldn't let him go just yet, not before delivering the clincher. Keep in mind that these next few words were supposed to sound casual and off the cuff rather than something that had been etched into the plan all along. But the simple truth is that I've never been good at subterfuge and doubted I was up to the task. All I could do was try.

"Hey, so, Janey and I got some tickets to the opening of a new exhibit at the Art Institute. It's called 'The New Contemporary.' It features some of my favorite artists: Warhol, Lichtenstein, Jasper Johns. It's at the end of March, the twenty-fourth, I think. Because we're such high-rolling donors, we got four free tickets. There's a champagne reception with hors d'oeuvres, a short talk from one of the curators, and then a tour through the exhibit. It should be pretty great. We were wondering if you wanted to join us."

How many times had I stood by as Wilson deliberated over one sort of invitation or another? I tried to remember them all. More often than not, those deliberations revealed a semblance of strife as he assiduously calculated the assets and liabilities attached to accepting or rejecting a particular offer. I didn't expect the current deliberation to be any different. I was even ready with several persuasions if necessary. But all Wilson did on that late winter day, as he considered this most recent proposal, was reset his feet, adjust the flaps of his hat, hitch up his pants, and respond with no apparent agitation at all.

"Yeah? Well, that does sound interesting," he said. "Actually, I do like modern art. And I appreciate the offer. Can I check a couple of things and let you know tomorrow?"

"Of course," I replied, still fabricating a nonchalant air. The tough part was coming, and I hesitated while debating which of my hole cards to play. *Might as well go all in,* I thought. *No sense holding anything back. At least I can tell them I gave it my best shot.* To avoid the scrutiny of his curious eyes, I stared at the carnation on his coat.

"Oh, and this time, I should tell you up front. I don't know if it affects your decision one way or the other, but Sophie would be the fourth. That girl is never one to miss a champagne reception. In fact, you should probably know, asking you was her idea. The ghost of Sadie Hawkins strikes again, I guess."

And for the first time ever—and I really do mean *ever*—I heard the sound of Wilson Lacy's laugh.

PERTURBATION

Boston, May 16, 2016

Chapter

Boston is New England's largest and most historic city. It sits at the apex of a nearly equilateral triangle that connects the towns of Eastham and Fall River at its base. All three cities fall within a shallow orbit; the distance between any two points in the triangle is never more than ninety miles. The universe on the East Coast is neatly prescribed. So it's simply a matter of physics that, in such a tightly configured system, flyby encounters among related objects would not be uncommon. And so it was with Rachel and William and Nora.

In 1858, Oliver Wendell Holmes published a series of articles in the Atlantic Monthly under the title, "The Autocrat at the Breakfast Table." The wide-ranging essays portrayed the fictionalized conversations of residents at a New England boardinghouse. Holmes used these essays to convey the idea that Boston was the center of everything—the economic, political, social, and commercial enterprises that kept the world spinning— and the city soon became known as the "Hub of the Solar System." In truth, Holmes's essays were only referring to the Massachusetts State House, but the proud residents took to the nickname—and Boston has been known as the Hub ever since.

Nora has lived in Boston since graduating from Tufts in 2008. She never went back home, never even considered it. Instead, she parlayed her degrees in English and Business into a lucrative career in the tech industry. In 2014, she launched her first start-up, Connect Up, that links urban schools with community-based nonprofits across the country. Her success has required the kinds of sacrifices that one would expect and that most of her peers are unwilling to make. To say that her work is her life might be an exaggeration, but only slightly. In most of the ways that matter, she is alone and has unwittingly become the hub of her family; it is to her that her mother in Eastham and her brother in Fall River come for the occasional gathering.

Along Massachusetts Avenue in the South End neighborhood are magnificent rows of redbrick buildings that date from the time of Oliver Wendell Holmes. The real estate listings for the area will often boast that these "Renaissance revival bowfronts offer spacious and stylish accommodations for residential and commercial purposes." And every word of that is true. Nora leases a second-floor walk-up in a stately old building midway in the 500 block.

At the moment, the apartment is too much space for Nora and her cat, Austin, but she imagines that one day, it won't be. In the meantime, she loves the location with its hipster bars and trendy shops, and though she rarely ever visits these, she likes knowing they are there, waiting for her life to unfold. The proximity to work makes for an efficient commute, and two doors down is the home office of Sylvia Bern, her therapist, which is convenient as well.

The window in Sylvia's office is open, and Nora leans by the sill, letting the soft spring breeze run across her face. A storm has just chased away the muggy air and replaced it with peppermint that gambols into the room. Slivers of sun peek from behind quickly fleeing clouds while slats of blue spread like laminate across the western horizon. The warm rain has left a sheen that glistens everything in sight, and the world looks wrapped in cellophane. Across the way, orange and yellow lilies stretch slender stalks upward to the sky. How a city as dense as Boston can be so quiet in the late afternoon has always amazed her, and she shuts her eyes to invite the quiet inside.

Sylvia: You there, Nora?

Nora (opening her eyes and shaking her head): Sorry.

Sylvia: Yeah, you sort of checked out again. I asked you why you think this news has caused so much distress. Do you want to say anything more about that?

Nora (moving across the office and sitting back down in her chair): Well, it's pretty obvious, don't you think? I mean, what the hell, Syl? I haven't heard from him in months—I mean not a word all winter long—and then all the sudden, he calls out of nowhere to tell me he's coming out here? Just like that? What does he think is going to happen? We're all going to be a happy family again? Yeah, I don't think so.

Sylvia: Have you asked him to explain his reasons for the trip?

Nora: Nope. All I have is a voice mail. I haven't called him back.

Sylvia: Well, you know, you always have that option. In fact, when you call him back, you can just ask him those very same questions: why and why now?

Nora: Of course, that suggestion builds on the assumption that I will call him back.

Sylvia: Yes, I recognize that. It was an assumption I thought was reasonable to make.

Nora: I'm not so sure, Syl.

Neither therapist nor patient says anything after this. The office is hushed. Nora lowers her head and silently broods, refusing to look up. Sylvia waits, knowing from her years of practice that these are the moments that can lead anywhere and should not be interfered with.

Nora (tracing the geometry of the carpet's pattern on the floor): Who knows. Maybe he's thinking that time is passing him by, that the years are fleeting, and maybe that scares him a little. I know it would scare the hell out of me. Probably you get to a certain age, and you begin to see the finitude of things, and to be facing that all alone in that big old house must be pretty terrible. I can't even imagine that: to be alone in the world and have the clock ticking down all the time. And he is awfully alone. Part of me thinks that's always how he wanted it though. It was like he just let his sadness take over until it forced everyone away. It still pisses me off.

Sylvia: What do you mean that he just let his sadness take over?

Nora: Well, for as long as I can remember, he was always so busy: building stuff, fixing things, working on his experiments. It was like there was nothing he couldn't do. And he knew everything too. He just seemed happy. We all loved to be around him. But looking back on those days now, I know that there were times when he'd go missing. It's like he would shut down for a while. We used to call it 'Dad's moods.' We'd wait it out, and a couple of days would pass when we'd keep our distance, and then somehow, he'd just come back to us and things would be like they were. And then toward the end of high school, just before I left for college, it seemed that those moods became more frequent … and more severe. They'd be darker and last longer. And then he stopped working, and that's when things got bad—so bad in fact that my mom had to get out, to 'save herself' as she puts it. It felt like he gave up on the rest of us and let himself get old. (She stops here and chokes back the rising gorge of her grief.)

Sylvia: Does it seem fair to hold that against him? Getting old happens to us all, you know. If we're lucky, that is.

Nora: Hey, whatever happened to therapist impartiality? Of course, that doesn't seem fair. I'm not particularly proud of myself for saying these things, but that's how it feels. And it's just so sad, watching that happen to someone you love and not being able to do anything about it. I feel so bad for him. He used to be so strong and fearless. And now … (The sorrow overwhelms her, and she breaks down and cries.)

Sylvia: I am so sorry, Nora. Does he know how you feel about all this?

Nora: I don't know. How could he? I don't even know how *I* feel about it. It's not like we ever really talked about it. And that seems so damn stupid now.

Sylvia: What seems stupid?

Nora: That we never talked about it, that we just let the whole thing get away from us without really doing anything about it. Why the hell would we do that? That's what seems so goddamn stupid.

Sylvia: Well, we've talked before about the complexity of family dynamics. I'm sure it does nothing to lessen your own sadness, but maybe it's worth knowing that such unexpressed—or repressed—understandings within a family structure are nearly universal. The question that arises from my frame of reference has less to do with the origins of those understandings and more to do with how you choose to address them now. Is that something you'd like to look at in here?

Nora (thinking about the question and letting her mind wander over the ramifications): Yes.

Sylvia: That's fine. That's good. So, it looks like our time is just about up for today. You said his message indicated that he'd be in Boston toward the end of the month, yes?

Nora: He said around the twenty-eighth.

Sylvia: That would give us a couple more sessions to explore some of this more deeply before he arrives. I think that would be a wonderful way to spend our time, but I'll leave that to you to decide. Okay?

Nora: Yeah, Syl, okay.

They both stand and make their way to the door. Just before separating, Sylvia places her hand on Nora's back, and they pause for a moment in the hallway. No words are exchanged, but communication between the two is clear; enough has transpired to ease the transit until next time they meet. Nora dabs her eyes with tissue, fills her lungs with a reassuring breath, and heads out into the dusk of a supple May evening.

The lights in the apartment can wait a little longer. The lazy sun has seen to that. The folder of work she brought home is left on the kitchen table for later. Austin whines with hunger, but Nora is still out of cat food. So she reaches into the cupboard for another can of tuna and places half the tin into his bowl. She scoops the last of the tuna onto a spoon for her own dinner and then rinses the can in the sink. The answering machine on the counter shows only the one old message, and she presses the button to listen to it again. It's not so much the details she's interested in; those have been recorded on a Post-it note and hang on the refrigerator door. It's the last few lines she wants to hear once more: "I hope you're well, Nora. I miss you, and I think about you all the time. I love you, sweetheart." And before she can stop herself, she hears the faint whisper: "I love you, Dad."

Nora tosses the empty can into the trash and notices the torn pieces of the photo she left there last night. It's a picture that has followed her around for years. The two of them are standing at the summit of Lassen Peak in California. They were on a driving trip out west the summer after her sixteenth birthday—just the two of them, alone, together, for three whole weeks. She remembers the imposing view as they approached the mountain, and she can still taste the fear when they arrived at the trailhead. But she refused to let on or give in. Instead, they climbed, and the closer they got to the summit, the more confident she became, the stronger and more alive she felt. At the top, her father asked her to look east and see all the way back home. He assured her that the distance they covered that trip was nothing compared to the distance she would travel in her life and that this would only be the first of many peaks she would surely ascend. And he promised that he'd be by her side for every one. On the long drive home that long hot summer, her head was filled with dreams.

She wonders whatever happened to all those dreams. They still stand out in sharp resolution like the rock crags and rainbow water that encircles Lassen Peak. But somehow, she has lost her way. A faint sigh flutters in her chest that only Austin hears while the last ray of light casts cloudy shafts of dust that rise and fall like tides. Before the darkness comes, she rescues the fragments of the photograph from the trash. A paper towel wipes them clean. She spreads them on the kitchen table like a child's jigsaw puzzle just as the light above switches on. At last, she pours herself a glass of wine, grabs a roll of tape, and starts putting the pieces back together again.

INTERLUDE

The sun was warm but the wind was chill.
You know how it is with an April day
When the sun is out and the wind is still,
You're one month on in the middle of May.
But if you so much as dare to speak,
A cloud comes over the sunlit arch,
A wind comes off a frozen peak,
And you're two months back in the middle of March.

—Robert Frost, "Two Tramps in Mud Time"

EQUINOX

And now the world was on fire.

Chapter

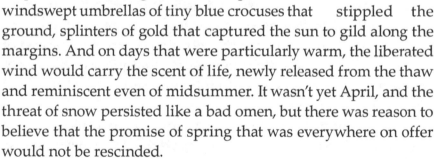

15

The calendar said spring, and there were days when the world responded in kind, days when the cold clench of winter that had held for so long was briefly forgotten and the air would tender its softest embrace. These were the days when a presumption of color began to poke through the lackluster landscape, each new appearance a thrilling surprise: a swatch of green to laze upon a field, windswept umbrellas of tiny blue crocuses that stippled the ground, splinters of gold that captured the sun to gild along the margins. And on days that were particularly warm, the liberated wind would carry the scent of life, newly released from the thaw and reminiscent even of midsummer. It wasn't yet April, and the threat of snow persisted like a bad omen, but there was reason to believe that the promise of spring that was everywhere on offer would not be rescinded.

I'm sure I used to know why the seasons change. I must have learned it in school. But those lessons had been lost long ago. So, I looked it up in my old physics notebook, exhumed from its tomb of an ancient cedar chest and kept all these years as a talisman of the past. And sure enough, there it was, just as Mr. Mitchell taught us in eleventh grade. If you take the flat edge of a protractor and hold it straight to the horizon and use the graduated side to measure the center of the sun at its highest point, you can determine what he called the *solar elevation angle*. Our measurements were messy and lacked the fidelity of his more decisive calculations, but the activity confirmed our suspicions that the sun rises in the sky as the new year unfolds. As a hedge against our imprecision, he made us copy down the angle for every day of the year in a data table that had somehow survived intact on a neatly constructed foldout page tucked inside the notebook.

My notes show that on December 21, the angle is the lowest of the year at 24.6 degrees and that, Mr. Mitchell explained, limited the amount of solar radiation that reaches the earth. By the first days of spring, the angle is 26.7 degrees, an increase of a measly two degrees. I can still feel the insignificance of those two degrees sloughing off the shoulders of my teenage indifference. For despite all the lectures and labs and films and tests, Mr. Mitchell never taught us the meaning of two degrees. He never let us feel how those two extra degrees could warm your face and rile your heart or loosen the rust that ravaged your joints all winter long. He never tilted our imagination to the ripening that was happening all around us, as swelling buds grew fat under the power of those two additional degrees and a groundswell brewed beneath our feet. He failed to fan our wonder at how differently our world looked with the softening shadows and growing incandescence that suddenly stretched from the morning bus ride to the end of soccer practice. Or stoke our curiosity about what magic might be loosed by the two degrees to follow. That was a lesson I was left to learn on my own.

I was relating that story to Wilson as we walked to the museum in the silken spring twilight. At that hour, heading east from the train on Monroe was like swimming upstream, and we fought our way against the current of the city's daily exodus. Every so often, a glimpse of the lake appeared through a crack in the canyons, and the sky unfurled before us. Countless shades of dusk clung to the horizon like a stubborn stain, reluctant to call it a day.

Janey and Sophie straggled behind, slowed by the indulgence of their window-shopping. I turned around to watch as they strolled the busy street, whispering and laughing and jabbing each other with elbows. From that distance, they could have been teenagers.

"He probably meant well, but it didn't do much good," I continued with the story as Wilson and I crossed Dearborn. The roar from the overhead trains nearly drowned out my words. "I know nothing about things that I should have learned cold when I was a kid. David's students are lucky to have him."

"They are indeed," Wilson agreed before sneaking his own look back at the girls. "But you shouldn't be too harsh with old Mr. Mitchell. Sometimes I think we have to be ready before we can appreciate the things our teachers try to teach us. I suspect that, back in eleventh grade, you probably weren't ready to be impressed by the change of seasons. The science may not have interested you back then. I'm sure you did well enough on the test, that would be easy, but this deeper level of appreciation that you allude to would require a readiness on your part that perhaps wasn't quite there. Sure, maybe he could have done more to encourage it, but without that readiness, no amount of persuasion will work. I think it's true that some of the things we need to learn come to us on our own terms, in our own time, when we're ready."

My eyes were glued to the skyscraper tops as he spoke. The light from the lowering sun reflected off the shiny surfaces, sending chips of colored mica to fall from the sky. But only for a moment until the dusk deepened some more. We walked along with the lengthening shadows while I thought about Wilson's idea. Honestly, I didn't have to travel all the way back to high school to find plenty of examples that proved his point. And I supposed that neither did he. They cascaded freely from memory, each one lending another layer of support to his premise. But the more I thought about it, the more I began to wonder if readiness might only be part of the equation, a necessary—but not sufficient—factor in nurturing learning. *Maybe,* I thought, *the most important discoveries we make occur at the intersection of readiness* and *opportunity.*

At State, the light turned red. I was just about to ask Wilson for his thoughts when I noticed he was no longer beside me. I canvassed the block ahead to see if he had already crossed the street but saw no sign. And when I turned back around, there was only the crush of pedestrians pressing in close, waiting for the walking green. So I lowered my head and broke through the pack to retrace my steps back the way we had come. He was standing quite still when I found him, just a few doors down in front of a store with a tumbledown awning embroidered with green-stenciled letters that read, *Vintage Framing.* Something in the window had caught his eye, and he stayed standing and staring as I stepped alongside. His right hand was raised. A finger pointed toward the glass.

"One. Two. Three. Four. Five. Six. Seven," he counted aloud, each number accompanied by a bob of the finger.

"What's going on?" I asked.

The counting had stopped, but the pointing continued.

I tried to follow the line from his finger, but there were too many items on display. It was impossible to tell what he found so riveting.

And then, in an instant, the trance was snapped. Wilson's eyes flashed brightly as he peeled them from the window and turned them toward me. He hastily patted his pockets the way a cop might frisk a felon until he found whatever it was that he needed. "Hey, hold on a second. I just had an idea," he nearly shouted. "Give me a minute, will you, Owen? I'll be right back." And he swiftly ran inside.

Rather than follow him in, I stayed on the sidewalk to flag down the girls before they passed by. Even with my nose to the window, I could see nothing of what was transpiring inside. The dimly lit interior and thin skin of grit that was glued to the glass made it impossible to see beyond the storefront's display. So I kept up my lookout for Janey and Sophie by pacing the sidewalk while the unending flow of commuters rushed past. I tried not to look at my watch, but the twilight continued to dim.

The girls arrived a few minutes later, arm in arm with twin looks of confusion, never expecting to find me alone on the street and Wilson nowhere in sight.

"He went inside for something," I explained waving a hitchhiker's thumb toward to door. Skeptically, they both stepped back to the curb to appraise the front of the shop. But they found nothing that would explain Wilson's interest in a store that specialized in old vintage frames.

As we resumed our vigil in front of the window, a pale white hand slunk from behind the display. We watched that disembodied hand worm around blindly until it snatched one of the frames. It reminded me of those old toy banks, the mechanical ones with a skeletal arm that lunges from a grave to pluck up a coin.

We looked at each other with grunts of bewilderment just as the door jingled open.

Wearing a sheepish smile on his face and a forest green bag on his arm, Wilson blithely walked out. He turned east toward Michigan Avenue and went half a block before mentioning anything at all. "Sorry for the delay," he apologized as we tried to keep pace. "I saw something in there I didn't even know I was looking for. I guess I couldn't pass it up."

"Oh! A shopper!" Sophie exclaimed with delight. "This just keeps getting better and better."

Wilson kept the bag pinned to his side making a peek at its contents unlikely. No one ventured to ask. Instead, Sophie slid her hand through the crook of his arm. Janey did the same with mine. And with no further delay, our party of four made our way to the museum beneath a sky that had been touched by an Impressionist's brush.

I've always maintained that members' events deliver a special kind of intimacy. The experience becomes immersive as the drama is magnified and made more personal. It's like the difference between viewing an event as a spectator and more nearly participating in it. A basketball game from the floor seats or a small house play from the middle of row A heightens the illusion of engagement, of being in the fray. Or so I'm told. The closest I ever get to the fray are members' events hosted by the different art museums in town. The premium prices for the premium memberships don't seem so outrageous when, for an evening, you can lose yourself in a Warhol silkscreen for however long you choose. Or when you can reacquaint yourself with an old love that once enchanted your dreams.

"I don't get it. Why this one, Owen? Out of everything in this whole exhibit, what's so special about this painting?" I was standing with Sophie and Wilson in front Lichtenstein's masterpiece, *Drowning Girl*, on display in a soaring new wing of the modern gallery. It was on loan to the Art Institute as part of The New Contemporary exhibit we had come to see. The lecture from the chair of modern art had just ended, and we were exploring the exhibit on our own. Sophie's question woke me from a spell.

"Well, there's a bit of a backstory about this painting," I quietly admitted. "You could say we have sort of a special relationship. It goes back years." The two of them stood in identical poses, staring at me with the same inquisitive face. Their pinwheeling hands and saucer-wide eyes beseeched me to continue.

"Okay, so, in the fall of my junior year, I had a visual arts professor who thought she saw something in my work that had eluded most everyone else; a 'mechanical abstractness' she called it. I never really knew what that meant, but it sounded nice, and it seemed like a good idea to align myself with a genuine professional identity. 'I'm from the school of mechanical abstractness,' I used to tell people.

"Anyways, at her urging, I applied to a summer program at MoMA in New York. I really didn't know a lot about it and didn't think I had much of a chance. In fact, my selection came as a surprise to everyone—even that kind professor—and three months later, I was sharing a walk-up in Brooklyn with four other wannabes from around the country. That was probably the best summer of my life. By day, we got to mess around with all kinds of styles to find a persona that we could live with for a while.

And at night, we gorged on punk, parading our artistic chic for everyone to admire at the clubs.

"But the most impressionable moment of that entire summer happened the very last week of the program. I happened to walk by as two curators were reinstalling this very same painting after some light restoration. I took one look at it and felt my artistic vision harden like plaster. I had never seen anything like it before. It made perfect sense to me. I instantly understood the vocabulary. I stood in front of this painting as much as I could during those last few days, trying to memorize every detail. It was the storytelling that got to me most: the way an artist's image can convey a story and how that story can mean different things depending on who is doing the looking. That seemed like a great aspiration at the time. Kind of like my calling, I guess. I knew that was what I wanted to do. So, I just had to see it again."

I listened as the thin echoes of my words faded out. The silence left behind fatigued me. Like so many of my stories, it had become a little frowzy over time, trotted out too often with an ever-dwindling capacity to sway. Maybe Janey was right. Those miraculous collisions that once seemed so auspicious no longer sparkled as brightly, and I found myself blushing when the story came to an end. Perhaps, I thought, one's raptures are best kept to oneself.

But Sophie and Wilson didn't seem to mind. The depths of my self-reproach went unnoticed. They were too busy staring at the painting. At first, their eyes kept sweeping across the large canvas, absorbed by the pop art technique and Ben-Day dots. There was a lot to take in. Only when they stepped back from the wall, and their glance could finally relax, did the lovers' tale begin to emerge.

"What do you suppose Brad must have done to make that girl feel so helpless?" Sophie pondered aloud. "I mean, she looks like she'd rather die than ask him for help. Can you imagine being that pissed off at someone to sink that far down, to drown in a sea of your own tears? It's so operatic!"

Wilson continued to gaze at the painting before adding a note of his own. "Yeah, can you imagine? That's some grudge. But I worry about a misunderstanding. How tragic would it be if she let herself drown because of something that was misconstrued? Or something that, in retrospect, seems so trivial but still set off a catastrophic chain of events. It's the way she's holding her hand that make me question if it was all a big mistake. Hey, do you think that might have been Lichtenstein's intent ... to get *us* drowning in all this glorious melodrama? That would be genius!"

And thus I began to wonder, as we stood before the painting, talking in such passionate tones about all the things it allowed us to see, whether they might have found a thing that was in it to be loved by them as well.

"Let me guess, the Lichtenstein prophecy, right?" Janey quipped as she returned from the bar. Four glasses of champagne were in her hands, and a member of the catering staff was in tow. "Everyone, this is Mario. Mario, this is everyone." Mario smiled in his ill-fitting suit and uncommonly white teeth. He offered small squares of cheese and pink prosciutto before putting down his tray on a gallery bench.

"Mario has agreed to take our picture," Janey gaily announced. She handed over her phone and shepherded us into an organized foursome in front of the Lichtenstein. We stood close, not just to accommodate the camera's field of view, but also because the ties of affinity had lately laced us together. It was comfortable standing together that way. We raised our champagne in a jubilant toast and waited for Mario's cue. And that was when I detected the notes of a new perfume. Spices, I thought. Cinnamon for sure. Traces of clove and vanilla too. It was lovely and exotic and suggestive of faraway places. I tracked it with my nose before locating its source along the hollows of Sophie's neck.

She turned her head and caught me sniffing only to send a still stronger sliver of scent to frisk in the museum's perfectly clean air. The flush of a smile enveloped her face, and she nearly laughed out loud. I knew it would make for a sensational photograph.

Mario snapped off several shots, calling out directions like an auteur. "Good-looking group," he said as he returned the phone to Janey. "A couple of beautiful couples." And then he reached into his jacket and pulled out a card. "Should you ever need the services of a photographer," he offered as he handed the card to me.

Mario Rivola
Professional Photographer

A photograph is a secret about a secret.
The more it tells you, the less you know.
—D. Arbus

He watched my face as I read the card and we both nodded knowingly as I put it away. "Who knows, years from now, when you look at those pictures again, maybe you'll remember the nice waiter who snapped an instant out of time and then held it still for you all to see. In any case, I hope you enjoy the show." Bowing as far as his suit would allow, he departed to circulate his snacks and his considerable charm to the rest of the guests in the room.

The champagne was delicious, and we murmured our approval while deciding what to see next. Wilson wandered off to inspect a collection of Man Ray photographs he spotted when we entered the gallery. Janey and Sophie scrolled through Mario's handiwork on her phone. I turned my attention back to the Lichtenstein to recapture the rapture of that distant summer day, but only vestiges remained. So be it. Time, perhaps, to let go.

"Hey, if it's okay with you guys, Wilson and I are thinking of checking out the Monets." The girls were just finishing their champagne along with the last of the photos when Sophie made the suggestion. By my estimate, we had about an hour left in the museum, plenty of time to take in another gallery or two. The Monets would be perfect. "He's never seen them," she went on to explain. "Can you believe that? I can't imagine being here without showing them to him. How about we just meet you guys at Viaggios at seven thirty? Would you mind?"

"Oh. Yeah. Sure," I replied, the intent of her proposal gradually dawning. "You guys go and have fun. But, Soph, take notes. I'm dying to know how he reacts to the paintings. I'm worried that you and the Monets may be too much for the poor guy. We'll see you at the restaurant—seven thirty sharp."

She left us with hugs and a promise to be prompt before turning to join Wilson at the far end of the hall. The strike of her heels as she strode the parquet reverberated with an extravagant drumbeat: a spicy tarantella in 6/8 time. With the flick of a wrist, she unclipped a barrette, and her hair spilled lazily over her shoulders. As if by instinct, Wilson looked up to catch her display, his study of the Man Ray photographs interrupted now for good. At last beside him, she stood on her toes and whispered into his ear. Then she took his hand, and off they went, the two of them together, alone, in search of the famous Monets.

"You know, we really do make a good-looking group," Janey said, draping an arm around my waist and pulling me in close so we could swipe through the photos together.

Mario's eye was excellent. There were several good shots that captured the moment, but Janey and I kept coming back to one particular picture. It was a remarkable image. Its unrehearsed quality made it hard to resist. It wasn't postured or staged. It simply caught us unawares—in between poses—plucked out of a natural, casual moment to leave behind an indelible impression of a single sweet instant in time.

The more I looked, the more I could see that the improvisation revealed something else in the moment as well. And I could tell that Janey saw it too. The four of us had peeled into pairs, each bearing an uncanny resemblance to the sensual sculptures of modernists like Arp and Hepworth and Moore: soft, surreal curves of one form melding organically into the cavity of another as if they belonged together forever in the curving language of love. That blending was evident as I stood close to Janey. The lines of our sides were welded together and followed a smooth, unbroken, undulating edge that exposed a bimorphic beauty: forms alluding to a natural order.

But I also saw it in the blending of edges along the length of Sophie and Wilson as well. That photograph declared that they were paired, held together by bonds made up of private forces that follow laws of attraction, bonds that no one else can see, secured by shared secrets and the metallurgy of time to cement a strong amalgamation. It portrayed the unmistakable dissolution of two into one: a fusion of parts along an unbroken bow that blurs the boundaries between one and another. I followed that bow through a procession of moments that flowed like the pages of a flip-book: from the first night at Hennigan's, to the holiday dinner at home, to the way she asked about him on the night of Aaron's birthday, to the look in their eyes a moment ago, and to the photograph I now held in my hands. I traced those memories along the sweep of a delicate story until I laughed to myself in delight.

Janey was watching as I looked up from the picture. Her eyes were alight, and I could tell she knew my thoughts.

"Hey—"

"I know," she said.

"Are they?"

"I think so," she replied.

We looked at the photograph a little longer while I imagined them there, a few galleries away, standing together, still in hand, quietly sharing the incomparable Monets. But it was no longer the past that left the strongest impression. What, I wondered for the very first time, would be the story to come?

Janey shut off the phone, and we both let out a sigh. Sophie and Wilson's departure left us feeling slightly vagrant, and we looked around the room without much devotion. Flocks of patrons kept blowing by like wraiths on an aimless search. We needed something to rally us from our languor.

"Damn," Janey playfully groused, suffering a touch of melodrama of her own. "I wanted to see the Monets too, but no way am I going to get in the way of that."

"Agreed. No way. How about *Nighthawks* then," I proposed. "Have you ever looked at Hopper with a champagne buzz?"

"Sure, I guess that'll do. *Nighthawks* but then Motley's *Nightlife* too. I love looking at those two side by side. And if you play your cards right, Conway, maybe I'll even let you tell me about the Hemingway connection again. But I need a refill first."

"Will you hold my hand, Mrs. Conway?" I asked as we waved our goodbyes to a smiling Mario and made our way to the bar at the mouth of the gallery entrance.

"I will, Mr. Conway, but you should know, that's as far as I ever go on a first date."

———— ✻ ————

Ten days later was the first Sunday of April, and even though April Fool's Day had passed, shreds of its strange sorcery still persisted. The studio was gradually filling with daylight as I sat at the open window thinking about work. Springtime breezes swirled the lacy curtains into ornate kites. The coffee smelled like comfort. Thankfully, it kicked like a mule.

I was just about to turn on my computer when the telephone began to ring. That alone would have been strange enough so early on a Sunday morning, but when I saw that the call was from Wilson, the strangeness was doubly compounded. This was unprecedented. Until then, our communications had been restricted to texts, the occasional handwritten note, and email. Odd as it may seem, we had never spoken on the phone.

"Hey, Wilson. Everything all right?" I asked, startled by the ruffle of concern in my voice.

"Yeah, sure, why wouldn't it be? Hey, sorry to be calling you so early, but I was wondering if you had any free time today. I've got a project underway and could really use an extra pair of hands. *Your* hands actually. If you're free."

A quick scan of my plans for the day turned up nothing more than a few routine chores. Nothing that couldn't be put off a little longer. So I wiped the slate clean. "You're in luck. My day is yours.

What's on the docket? Anything I need to know about this project ahead of time?"

"Nope. It's pretty straightforward. I'll explain when you get here. Oh, yeah, one thing. It may get a little messy, so watch what you wear. Other than that, we're good to go. Can we say around ten?"

I told him that ten would be perfect.

"And thanks, Owen," he said before clicking off.

"Your hands actually?" Now that was a curious phrase. There were several possibilities, and my imagination prodded each one. Was it time to awaken the car? Would we finally go for that ride and blow out the cobwebs of winter? Did he need some help with a motorcycle project? Or was this something else entirely, something unrelated to anything in the garage? And why *my* hands especially? Whatever the reasons, the prospect of a day's endeavor with my friend on an otherwise ordinary Sunday was cheering.

"Owen. Owen. Hey, Owen!"

I first thought I'd find him in the garage, looking after whatever preparations were required for the project. But the door was down, and my knocks went unanswered though the padlock from last fall was gone. The tomb, it appeared, was unsealed. Instead, the shouts came from the back of the house, and it was there again that I found him: a cup of coffee in one hand and a half-eaten bagel in the other. His paint spattered jeans and Blue Devils sweatshirt offered the first hints of what was in store.

"Hey, Owen. Thanks for coming." He held the screen open and followed me inside. "But our work is indoors today. The garage will have to wait for another day, though that day is fast approaching. Things are afoot in there, I assure you. There's fresh coffee in the kitchen and some bagels too. Help yourself. I just need to grab a few things from the basement." He left his breakfast on a corner table and disappeared down the back stairs.

The strangeness was there the moment I walked in. It intruded upon my senses like a revenant. But whatever it was that appeared so peculiar eluded me at first. It wasn't as if there had been any major renovations to the house. The small rooms stood exactly where they stood before. All the walls were in their usual places. There could be no confusion about whose house I was in. Nevertheless, there was something very different about being inside Wilson's home that day.

It smelled different for one thing. Sure, the windows were open. Currents of fresh air skipped about with a springtime license, but it was more than that. Maybe it was the vases of fresh flowers—*vases of fresh flowers?*—hyacinths, honeysuckle, and daffodils—that had sprung up to sweeten the air. But it was more than that too. There was another fragrance tiptoeing just below, gliding capriciously through the house. Whenever I tried to identify its source, it would scatter like a flock of starlings chased by a hawk.

As I waited for Wilson, I tracked that lovely fragrance around the main floor. I drifted past rooms that remained precisely *where* they had been before. Yet they were conspicuously not *as* they had been before. There was, for example, a sad-looking mattress on the floor of the first of these rooms. The duffel that sat on top looked like it had been battered by a troop of mad apes.

Not perplexing enough? In the room next door, an artist's easel was set adjacent to a large picture window that overlooked the backyard. Oils in foil tubes, a selection of brushes still in their store packaging, and a tall glass vase with one red tulip rested on a makeshift table. None of that was there before. On their own, any one of these changes would have been strange enough to attract my attention. But the cumulative impression of the collection of changes added up to one unassailable conclusion: the ghosts that had previously laid claim to these rooms were gone. They had been exorcised by other, more powerful forces that I neither anticipated nor knew anything about.

The sounds of rummaging coming from the basement soon put an end to my snooping, and I retreated to the kitchen to see about that coffee. Wilson emerged from the back stairway carrying two gallons of paint, some rollers, and a Home Depot bag bulging with tools and supplies. "How do you feel about painting?" he asked.

"I'm good with painting," I mumbled through a mouthful of bagel. "But what will we be painting today?"

"I'll show you in a minute. Just let me drop this stuff in the den. There's cream cheese, onion, and tomato if you want. Help yourself. And juice in the fridge too."

I added a shmear to what was left of my bagel, poured another cup of coffee, and waited for Wilson to return. Sure enough, the strangeness extended to the kitchen as well. Hanging by magnets on his refrigerator door was a drawing of a soccer match skillfully rendered in crayon. Apparently, the Sharks had defeated the Cougars by the score of 6–4, but the home team had a distinct advantage: a purple fire-breathing dragon made a formidable goalie.

I was admiring the new artwork when Wilson returned for a refill of his own. He topped off his cup, leaned against the sink, and slowly sipped his coffee. He looked restless standing there in an angular kind of way, everything akimbo and pulling him in different directions. His fingers kept drumming the porcelain. And the odd slant to his head made it seem like a surprise was in store, nearly ready to be unveiled, and the onus of its secret was too much to bear. His urge to get going was in overdrive, and it felt like he was waiting for me or silently inviting me—or maybe even daring me—to say something about all that I had seen.

"So, I'm not sure about this, but things seem a little different around here. Am I crazy? Please tell me I'm not crazy," I said as we both sat down at the table.

Two chairs?

"Yeah, well, let's see—last time you were here, I think there was a motorcycle engine on this table, right? That's back in the garage for now. I never did get around to the rebuild. Maybe this summer. We'll see."

"Sure, yeah, but no," I sputtered. "I forgot about the engine. You're right. But it's more than that. There's something different about the house. I did a little nosing around while you were downstairs. What's with all the flowers? Or the easel and paints? And there's a horrible-looking mattress on the floor of the first bedroom. What's going on? Am I just imagining all this?"

"Huh," he grunted, apparently unflustered by my index of observations. But he proffered no reply. Instead, I was left on my own to puzzle over the conclusions that could conceivably be drawn from the confluence of strange evidence I had seen. And it was no help at all when he got up from the table, left his dishes in the sink, turned toward me with a roguish little grin, and replied, "No, Owen, I don't suppose you're imagining anything at all."

I finished my coffee and followed him into the den, hoping for a more satisfying explanation of things. That hope, however, was soon washed away. Chalk marks in the rain. Even before entering, I could tell that this was the room we'd be painting. The furniture had been stacked in the center and loosely covered with drop cloths. Blue tape masked molding and the edges of the ceiling. But once again, as it seems it always must be, it was the sight of the den's south-facing wall that tore the breath from my chest.

This time, the wall was completely bare. Not a single photograph remained. The vast collection of photos that recited the saga of Wilson's life was gone. Totally, utterly, perfectly gone. Every moment that had been captured on film to document his journey and then lovingly hung to be read and remembered and told again had been expunged. In their place was only a constellation of tiny pinholes waiting for some spackle and a new coat of paint. I stared at the blankness before me, searching for words to convey my disbelief.

"What the …" I uttered incredulously. "What the hell is going on, Wilson?"

"It was time, Owen," he quietly replied, looking down at his palms. The twitchiness I saw in the kitchen had been punctured at last to release whatever had been churning inside. We were now, most definitely, getting on with things, and a calm assurance had claimed him.

"What do you mean?"

"It was time to take them down. I think I'm ready to move on. Here, take a look at this."

He reached a hand under a cloth and removed a very old frame. Up close, it looked to be made of ash, beveled and deeply grained, beautifully distressed by time. Seamless rabbet joints held it together with an astonishing level of craftsmanship. It smelled tartly of linseed oil. A light gray matte was cut to expose seven windows. In six of those windows, familiar photographs showed through. These were the photographs that Wilson had selected on that night many months ago, captured moments that he wished to explore in search of the meaning of his life's story. The seventh window stood empty.

"When we're done painting, I'll hang this up on the wall. These are the only ones I really need to see anymore. They represent most everything. I guess I'll just store the others in case I ever need them again. Who knows, maybe my kids would like them someday."

I sat on the arm of the love seat trying to make sense of what I was seeing. No reliable inventory of emotions seemed to be available just then, so I continued to glare at the wall. They were all tangled up in a hodgepodge of feelings that made it difficult to sort out one from another. There was a ripple of fear that mingled with concern that gave rise to a tinge of sadness (*Was he throwing his past away? Has he had enough? What about the story?*). But there was also a swell of excitement that alloyed with happiness that exacted a sense of relief (*Maybe this is one of those outcomes he was talking about. Maybe he is seeing things a little differently. Maybe this is a good thing.*) In order to know what to think, I knew there was more I needed to know.

"What inspired all this? Have you really thought this through?" I asked.

"I have, Owen. I've come to realize that I could never move on with all that past hanging over me, constantly looming down from this wall. It started to feel a little suffocating. Regrets were all I could see. And I have grown tired of shouldering so many regrets. If there's one thing I'm learning from this experiment, it's that there's nothing wrong with the past—it can be a reassuring reminder of a lived life, a way of taking stock—but if that's all there is—and for a while that's all there was—the possibility of any kind of future is obstructed. Maybe it's the springtime talking, but I think I'm ready to see about my future. It's about time, don't you think? Time to get cracking. And you know what else I've come to understand?"

"I can't even begin to imagine," I responded, still staring in shock at the wall.

"*This* is what happens when the wall is bare. When there's nothing left anymore. Can you believe it? That's just one more thing I didn't see coming."

There was a time, not so long ago, when I stood in that room and imagined a beam resting on a fulcrum. Two possible futures were hung in the balance. They were poised on the pivot of the present. At first, when I looked upon Wilson's wall, the weight of what I saw tilted the beam to favor one of those futures, though I was unsure which one it would be. Now, standing there again, gobsmacked with astonishment while looking at nothing at all, I was no longer unsure. The pictures it seemed, had spoken to him at a time when he was ready to listen. And the future, I supposed, had arrived.

"Initially, I thought maybe I could get by with painting only the one wall, but a full, fresh coat would be awfully nice in here, don't you think? And I hate to drag you into this, but it seemed properly symbolic to invite you to help. The metaphors abound. Are you okay with this, Owen?"

"Are you kidding?" I shouted while rolling up the sleeves of my sweatshirt. "I'm great with this. Hand me a roller. Let's do this! You got any tunes?"

"Ah … I thought you'd never ask … voilà!" he shouted while pulling a small set of speakers from under another cover. And in no time at all, the paint was poured, the rollers were flying, and we were rocking to side one of the best Doors album ever. I'm not even making that up. *Strange Days* indeed.

Hours passed. The afternoon sun took its sweet time to stretch across the sky as it tends to do in spring. We were grateful that it had decided to stick around and light our way as we put the finishing touches on the den's new look. When at last we were done, we picked up the trash, folded the cloths, and replaced the furniture, taking great pains not to scuff the soft paint. Wilson carried the supplies back down to the basement while I stood back to admire the results. There really is nothing like a clean coat of fresh paint to stir the soul's gratitude for a new beginning. As sad as I was to see the pictures gone, I knew what he meant about moving on. About getting on with his life. I guess there comes a time when it's time for each of us to let go. With a little hard work, the room had been liberated from the sticky encroachments of the past. A heavy curtain had been raised on the promise of a new act. Tabula rasa. Or maybe that curtain had been pulled back to allow a runnel of light to shine on a future waiting to have its own story inscribed on these very same walls, or maybe in a book, or in another photograph. Wilson was right; the metaphors abound.

He returned to the den in a fresh change of clothes. His face and hands were well scrubbed. In one of those hands were two bottles of beer. A cordless drill was in the other. "One last thing to do." He took a tape measure from his pocket, and we marked off a spot on that same south-facing wall: the first mark upon its unblemished surface. There were sure to be more. He then drilled a perfect hole, pressed in an anchor, added a screw, and hung the frame that held his handful of photographs. He leveled it with a touch, and we stood back once more. The story, I thought, had just taken a turn.

"So, let's see," he said as his eyes ran over the pictures. "Where are we? I think you're pretty much all caught up, right? On my progress? Yes?"

I went through them all, one at a time. A teenager leaning beside his car about to go out on a summer night and into a time of transcendence, a professor thrilling his students with the grand adventure of discovery, young lovers gazing upon an unbounded ocean and the promise of a luminous future, a son cradled in the arms of his father (a moment about which, I just then recalled, Wilson never said a thing), a family held together while facing the unpredictability of uncertain changes: a small selection of life's moments captured on film, chapters in a story that was still being written, way stations on a temperamental, unpredictable, and wholly remarkable journey.

I knew them all until I came to a picture of an old, derelict motorcycle resting outside against a white wall.

"Yes!" Wilson exclaimed. "That one is next. That's the BSA that came from my uncle, the one with the engine that was on the kitchen table. It arrived in precisely that state, and it still looks pretty much like that now. Like most everything else out in the garage, I think of that old bike as a time machine too. Even in that condition, it is capable of whisking me back to the past, to the way the world was a long time ago. That's what I love about it. And that's why I originally chose that photo: to journey back again."

He hesitated while his hand ran over the frame. But rather than slip away as he often did when ruminating about his past, Wilson simply stood his ground and continued. "But here's the thing, Owen. I'm just now starting to see that a time machine can travel in *two* directions. It can also propel me ahead, toward the future. Who knows how long it will take to complete the restoration. Or what the world will be like when I'm finished. Or better yet, who knows what my life will be like when I finally get to ride it—or who I might be? When I try to envision all that, I feel myself being pushed along toward the future. That's something I haven't felt in a very long while. And that's what I want to write about when I sit down with this picture. Those two ways of looking at that lovely old bike. And what they might mean going forward."

"And what about this one here?" I asked, pointing to the empty window in the frame.

"Well, I've given that some consideration too. You may remember that I had seven photos originally selected. But as this experiment got underway, one picture kept getting snubbed. It soon began to feel a little redundant, like the meaning I could have expected to extract from it had already been uncovered. So, I rejected it in favor of another idea. I'm curious to see if there is another moment out there, still to be photographed, that could draw my attention as convincingly as these others. So I left that space blank. You see, I think that space represents the future and the possibility that there may be more moments to come that are worth exploring."

"Of course," I said, "the implication of that kind of thinking is that there may be something to look forward to. Christ, that sounds hopeful."

We both laughed for a while at the irony of that—at the promise of hope that ripens in the fullness of spring. And after the laughter subsided, Wilson picked up the beers and the screwdriver he used to hang the frame. With a well-placed blade and the slap of his hand, the caps went soaring, and he passed a bottle to me.

"You have *got* to teach me how to do that someday." I held the bottle in my hand and let my eyes fall around the darkening room. The litany of all the strange things I had seen in Wilson's home streamed through me just as a new thought began to take shape. Maybe all the changes I noticed that day weren't so strange after all. Maybe there was a more straightforward explanation. Seen from a different angle, say from Wilson's perspective, those changes may simply have been the net result of gradual forces that had been at work for a very long time. I suppose a particularly good chaos theory might even have predicted them. Maybe the changes were just the tangible inevitabilities that come with the turn of the seasons after a long and difficult winter, the offspring of hope. Maybe opportunity had come knocking. And he was ready to answer. Not so strange when you think about it like that.

It was time to christen the den. A toast was most assuredly in order. "Here's to the future, my friend," I proclaimed as we lofted our beers. "Let's never forget the lessons we learn from the important moments of the past while we look forward to the ones that await. Let's use those lessons to seize the promise of tomorrow."

"Well said, Owen. Well said, as always. I'll drink to that."

We clinked our bottles as the last of the sunlight filtered through the panes of those old, mullioned windows. Nightfall. But even in the dwindling light, I could tell from the label; those were the brand-new Hennigan's beers we were drinking.

Chapter

16

On days when the weather is mild, the group will often meet outside. Just beyond the rectory sits an aged courtyard that is lovingly tended by the Saint Jude parishioners. Branches of old willow trees cast pools of shade that dapple the grounds while candy-colored tulips dot beds of rich, loamy soil. Stone benches weathered by the decades encircle an overgrown pavilion. Tufts of emerald moss fill every crack between the brick red pavers.   The air in that courtyard is sometimes so still that even the most reluctant voice carries freely, unimpeded by wind or the rustle of leaves or the chaos of the world beyond the willow trees.

It was Nina and Jason's third SOS meeting and their first time sharing. First stories of new members are always impossible to bear and theirs was no exception. The anguish was raw. It tore at the scabs of the gathered, exposing wounds that never seem to heal. Never fully. In the quiet that followed their share, the song of passing birds drew the sorrow skyward. The weeping gradually lessened and lightened and finally faded.

Bill waited as the faces of the group lifted back up. One at a time, we turned our eyes toward him, entreating deliverance or at least consolation. He offered his encouragement and invited others to do the same. Then he began to bring the meeting to a close.

"Okay, I have one quick announcement, and then we can wrap up our work for today. Back by popular demand, Anagret and I will again be hosting our annual Memorial Day barbecue at the house. More details will be forthcoming to your emails. As always, a spouse, a significant other, your children, parents, and so on are all most welcome. We'd love to have you, so watch for the invitation over the next couple of weeks. And let us know you'll be coming. All right, so it looks like we still have a few minutes before we break. Anyone want to share something? Yes… Owen?"

This time, my words had been carefully planned. I knew exactly what I needed to say.

"Thanks, Bill. I'll try to keep this brief. But first let me personally vouch for the great time that is had by all at the Memorial Day event. It's an excellent opportunity to get to know each other outside of the group meetings. And that helps make the work we do here that much easier. But that's not why I raised my hand. I raised my hand because I do have something I'd like to say, but I'm suddenly finding it a lot harder than I imagined.

"So … well … I guess I'm saying farewell. This will be my last SOS meeting, or at least my last meeting for a while. I hereby reserve my chair in the back row in case I'm not as ready as I think I am. I want you all to know that this has not been an easy decision. It has raised a good deal of turmoil for me, but I think I'm ready to move on. I think it's for the best. I think it's time.

"Now, as most of you know, I'm never one to let go of a moment without a comment or two, or in this case, three. There are three things I want to say before I go. The first goes out to those of you who recently joined the group and who I have only just started to get to know … to Jason and Nina and Robert, and Taylor, and Ivan, and Denise … you are in a very good place here, a very good place indeed. There is safety here. And comfort. You may even discover that there is hope. Finding it will take time, but the group is here to help. I expect that you'll find some measure of peace through your work here, as I have, and I encourage you to allow Bill and the others the opportunity to earn your trust.

"And to the rest of you, what can I say? If ever there were a time when words are insufficient, this may be it. So I'll just leave it at this: thank you. Thanks for the support, the kindness, and the patience you have shown me over the past eighteen months. I know I have come a long way, a very long way indeed. Of course, there are still days when the comforts of sleep end too soon and the prospect of getting out of bed seems as unlikely as a trip to the moon. But the truth is that those days are less frequent now. I know that is due, in large part, to being here with all of you. I get to walk through those doors and spend some time in the company of others who truly understand. And that has been my salvation.

"Now I know that when someone prepares to leave, Bill asks that member to offer up a lesson learned during his or her time in the group. I think he's secretly compiling these pearls for his next book. And even though I did give this some thought, I have to admit I struggled to come up with something that didn't sound too cliché. It wasn't so easy. But just the other night, I came across a wonderful quote from an old English novelist by the name of Eden Phillpotts. I had never heard of him before, but I really do like this quote. It captures the essence of something I've been thinking about lately. And like so many lessons in my life, it has taken me a while to fully grasp its meaning, but I think I may be getting close. In any case, I thought it would work well for this assignment. So here goes.

"It comes from a book of lovely observations called *A Shadow Passes*. In it, Phillpotts writes, 'The universe is full of magical things patiently waiting for our wits to grow sharper.' Isn't that beautiful? I think so. And I really do believe that to be true. Or at least I do right now. Now I'm pretty sure that the magical things he is referring to has nothing to do with unicorns or leprechauns or pots of gold at the end of rainbows. In my mind, what Phillpotts is alluding to has more to do with the extraordinary qualities that reside in the simple, everyday things all around us, a quality we often overlook or can't even see because we're too busy or distracted or blinded by numbness and pain. Like I was. And often still am. But I think I've come to believe that in order to recognize the presence of those magical things, we just need to sharpen our wits and look.

"Okay, maybe that *does* sound a little clichéd, especially coming from a skeptic like me. *Magic* is not a word I normally use, but that doesn't mean it's not true—or that the idea is not worth considering. I know that my wits *have* grown sharper lately, and my time in this group has certainly had a lot to do with that. I find that I look at things a little differently now. Almost like a fog is lifting. I can see more than I did before. And what I'm seeing sometimes has a magical quality to it that I'm not sure I ever really noticed or fully appreciated.

"What is amazing to me is how that sharper way of looking can reveal the utter preciousness of things—the magic of things, I guess—like a bud on a maple tree, the colors of the sky at dusk, or a wave from my daughter's hand. I know I couldn't see things like that before. My wits were too dull, and I was too ruined by pain. But here's the important part, the part I've just recently discovered ... the part I really wanted to share. I've also seen how that preciousness—*that magic*—can make the world a more tolerable place to be. And that's my point. Just think about that for a moment. Because it's only in a more tolerable world that a crushed and broken middle-aged man, a man who lost his only son as well as his will to live, can begin to heal. To really start to heal and move on again with his life. That's pretty magical if you ask me. And it's only in a more tolerable world where that same middle-aged man can find the will to reach out to others and help lighten the burden of their sadness.

"For a long time, the world was way too intolerable for anything like that. In fact, not so long ago, I probably would have told you that this kind of talk was pure bullshit. And maybe you're thinking that right now. Fair enough. But the only way I can explain the simple fact that I am now ready to leave this wonderful group is that Phillpotts was right. And as we start to recover from the devastation of loss, we gain the perspective— and the opportunity—to find that sense of magic again. I think

I get that now, and I hope that each of you continues to look ... hard as I know that can be.

"Okay, that's it, I'm done. I know I'll think about this group all the time, and I expect I'll check in every once in a while. Thanks again for listening and for everything else you've given me here. It has truly meant the world to me."

The drive from the church to Greenbriar follows a northward curve along the sandy shores of the lake. With each passing mile, the density of the city diminishes a little more until the land opens up and breathes. The border's crossing augurs a vanishing point. Farmlands stamped by the fruitful smell of manure stretch on for miles. Battered silos and dilapidated barns dominate the landscape until the hilly road joins the moraines of the Kettle Region. Here, receding glaciers and the topographical depressions they left behind have created woodlands of timeless beauty that seem a world apart from where my journey began. From the very first time I saw it, I knew it would be a good place to rest.

I knelt down at the gravesite beneath the pall of a chiffon mist and felt the damp, spongy earth give way. As always, the stones from last time had been scattered around the spot. Wind, animals, or other forces I wish not to think about are at work when I am not around. So I gathered them up again and added the handful I brought with me from home.

At last, I began arranging them on the headstone. First, the five points of the star. "This is Mom. This is me. This is Hannah. This is Sara. And this is you." Then, using the smallest of the stones—pebbles really—I formed the lines that joined the points together. "As it was. As it is. And as it always will be." Finally, I reached into my pocket and removed the photograph I had carried with me all day. I knew that it would never last. I knew that this picture—the two of us peeking out from a glistening snow fort on a brilliant winter day—would not be there when I next returned, but it really didn't matter. *As long as it lasts the night.*

I placed the photo on top of the headstone, securing it for the moment with rocks. I then sat alone with my thoughts, the star, and the photograph while the late afternoon sun set the woods aflame.

As dusk descended, I stood and looked at my watch, figuring that there was just enough time to say hello to the Con Man before the cemetery closed.

Chapter

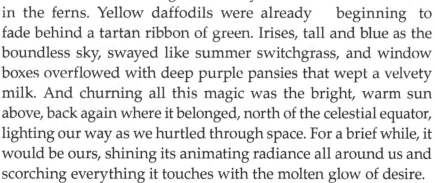

And now the world was on fire. It burned with the delirium of spring and set everything ablaze with a conflagration of color. After another long winter, the luridness of nature's spectacle was astonishing, and we walked amongst the rainbows. Bloodred tulips, painted like a harlot's lips, flaunted their tawdry flamboyance. Orange buttons crowned miniature marigolds that lay hidden in the ferns. Yellow daffodils were already beginning to fade behind a tartan ribbon of green. Irises, tall and blue as the boundless sky, swayed like summer switchgrass, and window boxes overflowed with deep purple pansies that wept a velvety milk. And churning all this magic was the bright, warm sun above, back again where it belonged, north of the celestial equator, lighting our way as we hurtled through space. For a brief while, it would be ours, shining its animating radiance all around us and scorching everything it touches with the molten glow of desire.

The neighborhood awakened in the fires of spring. The resurrection came in waves. First, the warm days siphoned vulnerable young children from their rooms, enticing them with mud-spattered bikes, deflated soccer balls, and the frenzied joys of being outside with friends. Parents followed a bit more cautiously, still in sweaters and long pants and clutching mugs of hot coffee. Some carried new babies out into the fledgling spring for their first forays among the bustle and to receive their benediction.

They were welcomed into the fold like celebrities. Last to come were the empty nesters. Assured that the days of snow and ice were past, they emerged from their homes, squinting in the bright light and cowed by memories of the bullying cold. Wave upon wave tumbled out to gather and greet. They came together like blobs of quicksilver and renewed ties that had slumbered for months. A little coolly at first, they wondered at all the lost time and then, warming to each other like reunited friends, they talked of the summer to come. Soon, chores were begun, and the hum of activity returned. The air filled with the sounds of laughter and the shouts of play and then thickened with the smell of charcoal and hickory and oak. At last, the season of rebirth was underway.

The fever of spring burned in me too. I bristled with restiveness that lengthened with the days as a procession of marvels unfurled under my window. I seethed at the confinement imposed by my work, and when it all became too much, I put down my pens and laced up my cross-trainers so I could go outside and be a part of it all. A sharp astringency had been imposed upon my senses, and I was galvanized by a newfound call to wonder. There was so much to see as the world immodestly changed before me.

And I photographed everything. Pictures accumulated on my Nikon like so many passport stamps, testifying to my travels. Back inside, those photos were carefully reviewed and then filed into albums with titles like "color" and "light" and "form" and "texture." These were not photographs to be mined for any deeper meaning but rather touchstones to serve as a gateway to the wonders of the seasons. I justified this activity as "work," and even Janey began to notice the influence of these natural forms on my designs. It was as if the last remnants of my old mechanical abstractness were played out and a new aesthetic had taken its place with roots firmly entrenched in nature. The origin of this new sensitivity no longer mystified me. I had a pretty good idea of its source.

On weekend mornings when the weather is fine, the Harvest Rose Cafe at the corner of Oak and Woodlawn is the place to be. It is there that local musicians come and congregate to perform a casual couple of sets for nothing more than the joy of making music with others. Janey and I like to get there early, just as the band members arrive. Unhurried and with no schedule to obey, they emerge from cars into the sunshine and unpack their instrument cases. They tune up over the chatter, tossing out notes and ethereal trills like pennies from heaven. And then on cue, everything stills with an abiding hush until a rousing fog of song diffuses through the neighborhood. It rides an updraft into the atmosphere and swirls around the faithful like sweet cream as another harbinger of the long lazy days arrives. Parents watch with ecstatic faces. Children dance with muffin hands. Whatever else may come for the rest of the day, it is that moment they remember as night descends.

It was on just such a perfect morning in early May that Janey and I were sitting close, enjoying the music, feeling the cool grass between our fingers, and making quiet plans for the summer. We came alone after agreeing to let Hannah and Sara sleep in. Another school year was over.

The girls arrived home the night before, and though they both loved the idea of Rose's coffee in the park, we all conceded that a little extra sleep was a fine idea. After all, we had a whole summer of sunny mornings ahead of us as plentiful as the maple seeds that helicoptered above.

The first set opened with a series of covers that featured a west coast theme: "California Dreaming," "Going to California," "Hotel California," and "Californication." That was followed by a few original compositions, and then the group brought the set to a close—and most of the crowd to their feet—with a spirited rendition of "Tangled Up in Blue." It was nice lying there in the park, serene under the warm sun, feeling the surety of Janey's weight on my chest and the combined rhythm of our breathing. An orange halo seared beneath my eyelids and made the sun seem miles closer. The brush of Janey's lips was like a fuzzy caterpillar as she sang in my ear, "We always did feel the same, we just started from a different point of view..."

She must have caught me as I was dozing off. I never miss the refrain. But that time, when the cradle of the earth had just about lulled me to sleep, Dylan's line was left hanging in the wind. "Hey, Owen, don't drift away just yet," she pleaded while shaking my head and lurching me back to consciousness. The hole she left on my chest when she started to get up felt cold. And the chill of her separation grew colder still as she stood and loomed over me. "Maybe I'll run in and get the girls some coffee to go. You okay if we head back home—or would you rather just nap the day away like an old park letch?"

"Yeah, no, sure." I yawned, pulling myself up into a sitting position. "Whenever you want to go is good with me. I'm ready. You go ahead and get the coffee. I'll be right here waiting for you."

In the quiet that fell between sets, it was easy to hear the unease that sullied her voice. It was the same unease that appears from time to time whenever—despite her best defenses—the memory of other spring days gets the better of her. I watched with heed as she brushed the thatch from her jeans, started toward the café, and then suddenly stopped. The length of her form eclipsed the still-rising sun so that all I could see in the dark penumbra were the hazy outlines of her body. They shimmered with yellow licks of light, and she glowed like an angel.

For that one brief moment, standing there in the shadows, she looked like the girl I once met on a blind date. The weight of the years was smoothed away by the softening effects of the light, and the memory of her lissomeness burned with a hot flash of love. Then the toe of her sneaker kicked the heel of my foot, and I heard her proclaim, "I love you, Owen. You know that, don't you? I love you very much."

Her sideways step away from the sun was blinding, and by the time my eyes adjusted to the glare, Janey had disappeared.

I love you very much. How long had it been since we shared those words? It must have been years. It sounded as though she were staking a claim, loudly asserting a thing we both tacitly accepted as a simple matter of fact, perfunctory, as steady and uninteresting as a rock. But now, by resurrecting those words and uttering them aloud—in the park of all places under that furious fountain of sunlight—the rock had been laid bare, stripped of its ordinariness to reveal a sparkling geode inside. With nothing more than a few brief words, my vulnerable wife had exposed a hidden place in her heart and asked for nothing in return. I tried not to think about why.

I was still swooning when she came out a few minutes later, carrying a cardboard caddy with two large coffees. At some point inside, she had taken off her jacket. The T-shirt she was wearing was another old one of Aaron's. Its Escher print was badly faded. All that remained was the ghostly illusion of fish as they steadily morphed into birds. But the illusion was there all the same. She stalled once or twice as she made her way back and ransacked the park with her eyes. I held my arm high, waving it around like a beacon.

"I asked for double shots of Devil's Brew," she said when she drew up beside me. "This coffee is not fooling around. If this doesn't get them out of bed, nothing will." There was no further mention of her earlier vow.

The farther we got from the park, the more Janey's spirit seemed to sag. Though our pace was slow, she lagged behind, and I had to stop every so often to let her catch up. But I didn't mind. Beneath all that splendid blue sky, it felt as if time had been rendered inert and that moment, that day, and the entire summer stretched out luxuriantly before us. It was only early May. There was no hurry at all. Nothing to feel so urgent about. The sounds of the second set continued to recede until the notes that traveled so far finally dissolved as we arrived at the door.

The morning had grown warm, and the tender humidity turned the lake breezes into flannel. Prospects were good for the first hot day of the season. We lingered outside to let the newly sprung warmth soak in. Robins, cardinals, and blackbirds twittered arias that swelled above us while Janey pulled at some weeds already sprouting between the pavers.

"Hey, Owen, can I ask you something?" Her back was to me as she feverishly tore at the weeds. A small mound of dandelions had formed at her feet, and that tinge of unease was still in her voice, just as it had been in the park. And when she finally turned away from the pavers to say something more, there was a mascara of worry that tarred her eyes. She no longer looked so young. Or so lissome. "So, I've noticed that you've seemed pretty good lately, you know? Kind of centered. And more relaxed. Happy even. I'm just curious. What's going on, Conway? Are you having an affair or something? Anything I need to know about?"

"Ah, so you've noticed, huh? No, no affair alas." I took the last of the weeds that were clenched in her fists and scattered them onto the driveway. Then I reached for her hands and swept the dirt from her palms. One at a time, I held them to my lips. Her knuckles were red and tasted of earth. Streaks of tears lined her cheeks, and the moment was made more grievous by the terrified look in her eyes.

"I don't know," I continued more prudently, sobered by her distress. "I guess the truth is I *have* been feeling a little better lately. I don't want to overthink it right now, but it feels like I'm becoming more a part of things again, more connected maybe, or a little less marooned. I'm excited to have the girls home, and the prospect of a whole summer in front of us is nice. It makes me feel that things are possible. Good things, even. For all of us. And on a day like this, with things to look forward to, how can anyone not feel a little happy? I guess I just feel like we're going to be okay, Janey. I really do. For the first time, I feel like we're going to make it. What about you?"

She rubbed her eyes with the sleeve of her shirt and tried her best to smile. Her breath came sharply in gusts while the tendons in her neck were stretched like a halyard. She looked like she might shatter. "Yeah, well, I'm not quite there yet. I see you doing better, and that's great, really it is, but sometimes it scares me because I just can't seem to catch up—and I'm afraid you may be leaving me behind. It hit me back in the park. You seemed so at peace. Like before. I could almost feel you pulling away. Don't pull away, Owen. Wait for me. Give me a little more time. Please. I was thinking how much I need you, how much I love you. I *do* love you, you know. I have always loved you, and I guess I always will. Do you love me still?"

Do you love me still? For the second time that morning, my chest was scorched by love. This time, its heat burned like wildfire and turned my negligence to ash. I held Janey's face in my hands and drew her toward me so I could kiss the corners of her eyes. It did nothing to stanch her tears. Then I pulled her closer and let her shivers tremble my chest. I just held on and let the time flow. And when her sobbing slowly eased and her breath returned, I whispered in her ear, in that place she always likes, "I have Janey. Janey has me. We face our lives together. Always together. Forever."

Why is it that the things we should say the most and proclaim the loudest are things so rarely heard? How can we be so neglectful? So stingy with our words? When the cost is so small. What are we saving them for when their value is only redeemable in the heart of another? Even now, I can find no reasonable explanation for this failing. I suspect I never will. All I could do in that moment, with Janey so brittle in my arms, was promise myself to do what I must so she would never again have to ask. Or be so fearful. And when she was ready—when her eyes were dried, and she *knew* I would always be by her side—we walked into the expectant house together, on a day that brought with it the incorruptible tidings of summer.

The girls were up and greeted us in matching pajamas. They slobbered like bloodhounds when they smelled the coffee, and slowly, sip by sip, they came back to us with all their mirth and grit intact. The four of us sat around the kitchen then, getting caught up on finals and friends and plans. The house responded by enlarging again to accommodate the increased volume of life that now surged beneath its roof. Our elastic lives. When a request was made for my southwestern omelets, I happily gathered the ingredients that had been stowed away the previous day in hope that just such a contingency would arise. As the omelets cooked, we talked of small things, and the house felt full—more or less— while a rumor of gladness sustained us all.

With breakfast done and the table cleared, the girls vanished into the day. The sun, the season, and their friends were calling. Janey also vanished only to emerge a short time later in a clean white blouse and a mop of freshly washed hair. With deck chair in hand, she proceeded to encamp herself on the patio. Her travel guide to Greece and pitcher of iced tea made it clear she would be there for hours. And it was only ten thirty. The rest of the morning and the whole afternoon were wide open and waiting, inviting me to do something grand and commensurate with the day. I had no interest in squandering any of it. That was for August. I only had to choose.

"Hey, Jane," I called out through the sliding back door. "Do you mind if I go out for a bit? I think I'll take a walk, okay?" She had arranged her chair to take full advantage of the sun, leaving the impression of her back in the bright plastic webbing as the only thing I could see. For a moment, I thought she might be asleep. But then an arm dropped down to reach for the tea, and I heard her singsong reply, "Sure, go ahead. And, Owen, tell him I said hello."

Even from several doors down, I could tell Wilson was home. The rattle of his asthmatic air compressor pierced the otherwise sleepy street like a murder of angry crows. The racket grew vicious as I turned up his driveway and then, unexpectedly, it quit and the neighborhood was buffeted by a Sunday morning quiet.

The blaze of his halogen floodlights was visible from the street, and I could see him rooting around as I walked up the steps. An enormous pair of shiny red noise protectors sat on his head, the kind you see at gun ranges or on construction sites, and he was shuttling between the workbench and the front of the car. And the car? Oh my—what a lovely sight! The old MGA had been stripped of its shroud and looked spectacular. Its coat of black paint gleamed in the artificial sunlight, obsidian waxed with ravens' tears. It sat poised and anxious, grown tired of its long confinement, and hungry for a blast down a winding road.

I stood unnoticed in the doorway while my eyes drifted over the scene. As I watched, I couldn't help but be reminded of the other times I stood there and gaped at the magnificence of Wilson's garage. More than ever, it seemed that the events of the past seven months *had* played like the quest in a heroic saga after all. Okay, sure, the Homeric comparison may have been a little much, but the journey Wilson and I had been on—the one that stretched from a golden afternoon in October to an opulent day in May as we trekked our way across the trajectory and entrenched ourselves into each other's lives—had been as arduous and unpredictable as any great odyssey must be. And if my instincts were right, there was still more questing to be done. But as I watched him at work, with his pockets crammed with screwdrivers and his overalls smudged with grease, he simply looked ecstatic, and I knew that we had survived the cataract of winter. Maybe more than that too.

And was that Adele playing on the stereo? Adele?

The compressor was off, but the silencers were still on his head, and he remained wholly oblivious to my presence. I grew curious as he pulled out a pen to mark on the windshield and then began digging beneath his workbench. As he turned his attention back to the car, a streak of malachite green swooped from under the hood and darted wildly around the garage. Four transparent wings beat with a furious tempo to power staccato-like movements. Wilson watched the insect fly with a rapturous look that illuminated the moon of his face. He followed its path with fervent eyes until it escaped into the sunshine. That was when he finally noticed me, leaning on the jamb, arms folded across my chest and beaming, no doubt, like a fool.

"Ohmgffn, thigssat. Purffft." The muffled sound of his voice confused him at first until I pointed to his ears. He shook his head and smiled with embarrassment before taking off the headphones and trying again.

"Oh my god, Owen. This is great. Perfect timing. How did you know?"

Classic Wilson. Never one for chitchat. There was no "Hello" or "How's it going" or "Sorry, I didn't see you there," just that same reliable insistence to get to the matter at hand, to get on with things. After all, there was work to be done, and there was no time for nonsense. Small talk was for strangers and stage 1 greetings. I liked that. I liked that about him when we met, and I like it about him now.

"How did I know what?" I replied, still feeling the stretch of the grin on my face. "And what the hell, Wilson? Is that Adele playing? Since when do you listen to music from this century? Are you kidding me? And Adele no less?" Deeply suspicious, I planted my feet to stake my ground and waited for his reply.

"Yeah. Don't ask. Some new influences are in play. I'll fill you in later. But more importantly, I can't believe you're actually here. I was just getting ready to fire her up, and if she cooperates—and I'm betting she will—I was going to take her out for a spin. You want to join me?"

Now I've been asked to do some pretty great things over the years. I guess that if you live long enough and are fortunate enough to make acquaintances along the way, the chances are good that you get asked to do all sorts of wonderful things. But this was of an entirely different grade. Wilson asked me to go for a ride that day, not out of some pretense about the kinds of things that friends do—pretense was never Wilson's way—but because the story demanded it. It was something that needed to be done: a piece of unfinished business.

The ride had remained an unrequited promise since October. It hung in the air between us like an obstinate odor, our own sword of Damocles, an unrelenting reminder of the troubles we faced as the gloom of winter descended and then persisted. Only by taking that ride would we finally lay those troubles to rest—at least for a while—at least while the sun was still so high in the sky. Then we could both look back and marvel at the terrain we had covered during the quest and scan the horizon for signs of whatever was next to come.

"Holy crap, yes, Wilson. I would love to join you," I said as I held my hand up for a friendly high five that left streaks of black grease on my palm. "And it's about goddamn time too!"

Together, we made a few last adjustments to the car. The tires were checked and inflated to the correct pressure. Leaves from last fall were cleared from the radiator with a blast of air from the compressor. Battery poles were greased and secured. The glass bowl beneath the fuel pump was cleaned of sediment and then primed to ensure that a full shot of fresh gas was available on demand to the carburetors. After each task was completed, Wilson had me place a check mark on the appropriate line of the 2016 to-do list that was taped to the car's windshield. The column of tasks we were working on was labeled "Start Up," but a second column of tasks—all suspiciously unchecked—was labeled "Prep." I started to ask about the items in that column when Wilson began explaining some important sounding procedures.

"Okay, I think that's it," he said as he peeled the checklist from the window and reviewed it with an approving nod. He then introduced me to the engine's throttle linkage under the hood. This was an impossibly complex-looking assembly made up of countless intricate parts that somehow had functioned exactly as designed by the engineers at Morris Garages for nearly sixty years. My job, he explained, was to lift the assembly "just so" when he flashed me a sign from the cockpit. He called this "giving it the beans" and promised that it would be all the inducement the old gal needed to start.

"But cross your fingers anyway," he said apprehensively as he shoehorned himself into the driver's seat, the sumptuous leather scrunching gravelly under his weight. Then quiet. Tense suspense filled the garage as he sat motionless in the seat.

From my post on the opposite side, I could hear the key slide into the ignition. Tumblers clicked into place.

"Full choke," he called out, and I watched a wire pull under tension beneath my hand. "Contact," he barked almost like a prayer as he turned the key. And when he pulled out the starter knob, the car growled with grumpy indignation, irate at being woken from its slumber. The terrible grumbling continued for a couple of seconds before he shut it off and crawled back out of the car. "Needs more gas," he diagnosed, showing no signs of worry at its unwillingness to fire. He primed the fuel pump a few more times and sprayed a couple shots of starting fluid into the carbs before getting back in and repeating the procedure. This time, when he pulled the starter, he yelled, "Lift, Owen."

I raised the linkage just as he showed me, and the car suddenly burst into song. Running on full choke, it sounded like a banshee. I feared that the whole thing would rattle to pieces, but Wilson calmly walked back to the front of the car, listening for sounds within sounds within sounds that I imagined only he could hear. He blipped the linkage a few times, causing the car to rev even higher, tilted his ear to listen some more, made a small adjustment with a screwdriver, and then went back to shut off the choke. We both stood back to watch as his car settled down to a sweet, mellow idle.

The MGA was alive.

We headed north. He drove cautiously at first, getting a feel for how the car was responding and not asking too much of it at the outset. "We'll take it easy for a bit, get some heat back into the motor, then we'll see how she goes." So we snaked along Sheridan, following sweeping curves that served up generous glimpses of the lake on our right and the manicured mansions that hugged both sides of the road.

The wind blew freely through the open car, unchecked by any obstruction. It carried the scent of flowering trees, sunbaked leather, and warm motor oil. Shorebirds, maybe heron, rode the thermals above us, their long necks and pointed beaks imploring us to follow. We glided along effortlessly, and a quick check of the dashboard instruments indicated that the car was performing exactly as it should. A symphony of tiny explosions rumbled through the exhaust and blared behind us like a troubadour's cry. It let loose a low, throaty note that tolled in my chest to harmonize with my heart—until he put his foot into it, and then it wailed an octave or two higher. It was thrilling music, and for the briefest instant, I longed for the Con Man to hear it.

We rode the lakeshore all the way up to 173 and then headed west. By then, the traffic had thinned. The sprawling metropolis was safely in the rearview, and the road reached out before us with an end that was nowhere in sight. We drove along for several more miles, past freshly tilled farmlands and just-planted cornfields that seemed to go on forever.

Finally, just past Richmond, we came upon a wide-open stretch of freeway. No other car was in sight. Wilson pulled a set of leather goggles from a pocket in the door and strapped them onto his head: an aviator of old on a transatlantic flight. He looked over at me and grinned the grin of a madman. His eyes bulged wildly through the lenses. Fingerless gloves slid onto his hands, and I'm sure I heard him start to hum. Leaning forward just a bit, he lightly cradled the wheel. He couldn't stop grinning. "Time to hold on, Owen," he said with a touch of menace in his voice. Then he really started flogging it. I mean, real *Fast and Furious* stuff.

The car took everything he threw at it and held nothing back. Torque from the rear wheels ground the pavement into dust. It propelled us forward with steady acceleration, and the back end loosed a tremulous shimmy that made me gasp. We drifted into turns with ease and exited with a thundering roar, and when we hit a long, empty straightaway, I watched the speedometer climb: sixty, seventy, seventy-five, eighty. At those speeds, modern cars feel numb by comparison. But in that old MGA, mere inches off the ground with nothing between our heads and the heavens, approaching eighty is like dancing with the devil at the speed of sound. And when we finally hit that mark, Wilson let out a scream that was all but lost behind the raucous din of the engine. The force of that scream shattered the shell of the event horizon, and we sailed on tides of calm. We were weightless scintillas skipping through time. The world blew by, and we just let it go, without thought, care, concern, or worry. In that moment, I felt free—and I suspect he did too. We were free from the earthly constraints that always seek to bog us down, to encumber us with the utter gravity of things, the kinds of things that can only be sundered at escape velocity. Nothing could catch us now. We had slipped away at last.

Near Rockford, the traffic picked up, and Wilson feathered it down to a comfortable cruise. We followed a series of side roads that eventually led back to 94, and we drove home among the masses. Along the way, he pulled a notebook from the glove box, and asked me to record his observations of things that needed sorting once the car was back in the garage.

By the time we got back to Sheridan, he had run out of ideas, and the last few miles sped by in silence as we both privately lamented the end of the ride. A little over three hours after we started, he pulled up to my curb and shut off the engine. The venerable old car panted as it cooled like a greyhound after a race.

"Well, that was pretty fantastic," I exclaimed while shaking bits of road grit out of my hair. "What a ride. You really have this thing dialed in. You just don't find soul like that in cars anymore."

Wilson nodded. His hands glided over the steering wheel before he took off his gloves. The combined effects of the sun, the wind, and the slag from the road had pasted his face with charcoal, everywhere except the eyes. "Yeah, she ran pretty good. There are a few things that need looking after, but all in all, I'm pleased with the way she performed, especially for the first time out. The old girl's still got it." He replaced the notebook, goggles, and gloves and then gazed over the windshield and out into the distance.

It was impossible to tell if, at that moment, he was glancing back over the roads we just traveled or was looking forward to the road ahead, but I felt certain it was one or the other.

"And hey," he began again as if he had just remembered something important, "I'm really glad this worked out. Sorry again that it took so long."

"I'm glad it worked out too. It was worth the wait. Somehow, this timing feels right."

We both sat quietly while the fury of all that combustion continued to whir inside us. I wondered if Wilson could tell that

I too was slipping away just then, peering out over the low-slung windshield and toward that far horizon where every journey ends.

By then, the heat of the day had begun to wane, and the sun had turned to butterscotch. Shadows spread over lawns and extended dark tentacles, a prelude to dusk. Here and there, trash cans were rolled out to await the Monday-morning pickup. Up and down the block, they stood like soldiers on sentry duty. Everywhere else, the neighborhood exhaled after the hustle of such a splendid day.

"So, Wilson, can I invite you in for a beer?" Though I assumed he'd rather just get on with his day, I thought I'd make the offer. I still had not forgotten about his promise to fill me in on those "new influences" and was anxious to hear more. After such an exhilarating ride, a cold beer might be just the right tool to pry something loose. "I'll bet Janey has something cooking if you want to stay for dinner. Hannah and Sara just got home too, and I'm sure they'd love to see you," I added in an effort to sweeten the deal.

"Nah, thanks. I really should be getting back, and besides, I've taken up too much of your time for one day already. Go be with that beautiful family of yours, Owen. Next time though, I promise."

"No problem," I replied. "Next time it is. But, hey, just one thing before I go. I'm curious what you meant back in the garage when you said that there were some new influences in play? You never did tell me. Or what the hell Adele was doing on your stereo. What exactly are these new influences?"

"Oh yeah, right, about that ..." he began in a tone that was decidedly more guarded. It sounded as if he would have been fine had I left the comment alone. But I made no move to leave and patiently waited for details. "Well, the long story can wait until we have more time. Let's just say that there have been a few developments in my life lately. These are some unexpected occurrences that I didn't really see coming, and I do want to share them with you given, well, you know, everything that has happened."

A few developments? Some unexpected occurrences? My sulky expression and reluctance to leave assured him that this was nowhere near a good enough explanation. But just so there could be no confusion, I pressed a little harder. "Well, don't leave me in suspense, Wilson. How about a preview?"

He took a deep breath and grabbed hold of the wheel while the veins in his forehead throbbed. But just for a moment. Then, all at once, he simply let go. His hands fell back into his lap, and he turned to face me in his seat. The shouts of the kids playing across the street were like cheers that urged him on. "Okay, well, I guess the gist of it is that I've come to the realization that I've grown tired of being alone. I don't want to be alone anymore. I've decided that is where I get into trouble. All of us do, I imagine. So there's that. By the way, you might be interested to know that I've arrived at this realization in large part due to my experiment. I have you to thank for that. I would be absolutely blind if I didn't recognize some themes emerging from the reflections, one of which has something to do with the perils of loneliness. We are not meant to be alone, Owen. Did you know that?"

"Actually, I'm pretty sure I did but—"

"And here's something else you may find interesting. I've traced the emergence of this theme all the way back to that very first day last fall when you came to the garage. Do you remember that day? Ever since that afternoon, I suppose, I have been climbing my way out from under the thrall of being alone. Fits and starts to be sure, but the evidence would suggest that I'm no longer so alone."

Evidence? What evidence?

I knew there had to be more. That didn't really explain the influences. Or Adele. Sure, I had my theories, but I really needed to hear that evidence. But Wilson seemed to want to leave it there. I knew there would not be much more forthcoming. For one thing, his eyes became foggy and glazed. For another, his lips withdrew into a single tight line. And the creases in his forehead fused his eyebrows together, letting me know that he was trailing away on another slipstream of thought. It was *that* look, the one he gets when he is reasoning deeply about something he just heard himself say, measuring the tolerances between the meaning of his words and the current circumstances of his life. Extracting himself from his musings to the point where he could explain matters more fully was, I knew, highly unlikely. And if the past seven months had taught me anything, it was to know when— and when not—to push. There really was a whole long summer in front of us, and there would be time enough for everything … and for everything that needed to be said.

I got out of the car and walked around to the driver's side. My hand rested on his shoulder while I thanked him again for a great afternoon. As he put the key back in the ignition, a wave of relief seemed to wash over him. Nothing more would be asked of him that day. "Would you please tell everyone that I'm sorry and that I look forward to seeing them soon?"

I indicated I would, and we said our goodbyes. The car started up with a roar, and the kids whooped in approval. Wilson acknowledged them with a couple of loud revs before putting the car in gear. Then he rumbled away to work on his lists while I stood on the curb watching him go.

I'd be lying if I said that it didn't feel like something was ending right then and there, like a chapter was closing on the portion of a story in which I had played a part and that whatever might happen next would most likely follow other characters and a different storyline. And I'd be lying too if I didn't admit to feeling both a little sad by that ending and a little grateful too to have gained something of value here at the end of the quest. Wisdom? Experience? Empathy? Whatever it was, one thing was clear; we had made it through stage 3. Together, we would see what followed.

An old Ford Mustang was parked in the driveway as I made my way to the door. The sight of that clapped-out beater, tucked behind the Corolla and resting on four very worn tires, delivered a shock of not immoderate voltage. My older brother had one just like it back in high school, same year even. He bought it against the advice of my parents with the money he earned installing listening rooms with my dad. And just like my brother's, this one looked to be held together by rust and a few stray licks of paint. I was sure there would be sizeable oil stain right there on the driveway when it pulled away in a cloud of blue smoke. It was tempting to stand there and stare and flit back in time to when the Conway boys were ascendant, leaving patches of burning black rubber on the streets of our town. But that was enough time travel for one day. So I just headed inside.

Janey was in the kitchen. One ear was pressed to the phone as she expertly diced some tomatoes. Her "Playing with Fire" apron had come untied at the back, and her long legs looked scorched from the sun. I started to ask about the car in the driveway, but she wouldn't break away and just kept pointing her head toward the porch. That was where I found the girls along with Mike and Reed Riskin sitting around a heaping bowl of guacamole. They were in the middle of some kind of card game, and the four of them were doubled over with laughter as I stepped out onto the deck.

"Oh, hey, Dad," Hannah cried as she slid off her chair and landed cross-legged on the floor. The laughter left her eyes streaming with tears and dramatically gasping for air. Beneath the brim of her hot pink Iowa baseball cap, her face was flushed with sun.

The boys quickly composed themselves and stood up to greet me while Hannah discretely covered the cards with her hat. Then she fashioned a more abstinent tone. "Where've you been all day? Say hi to Mike, and you remember Reed, right?"

"I do. Hey, Mike. Welcome home. And how's the best busboy at Hennigan's? It's good to see you guys." I shook hands with them both and reached for a handful of chips. My instincts told me that I had interrupted something terrific, and it would be better for everybody to just head back inside. I quickly filled a plate with a scoop of guacamole and motioned for the boys to sit down. "I was just over at Wilson's. I finally got a ride in that car of his. He said to tell you guys hello."

"Sounds like fun." The hue that suffused Sara's face was a bit different from her sister's. Its source, I suspected, came from something more than a full day of sun. She had been sharing a chair with Reed when I entered. But now, after standing for our greeting, Reed was left stranded alone in the center, searching around anxiously for an appropriate place to sit. His awkward feints at various chairs forced a rush of tenderness to come over me. The longer he remained standing, hopelessly adrift in the middle of things, the more tenderness I felt for the kid.

Eventually, Sara came to his rescue and patted the other half of her chair. The length of their jeans scraped with a *shoosh*, announcing a whole new kind of arrangement was simmering.

And even as Reed averted his eyes, Sara's flared with defiance. But their militancy was tempered somewhat when the flush in her cheeks deepened some more in keeping with the vines that were blushing on Reed's neck.

"So, Dad," Hannah called out as I was about to head back inside. "Did you hear that Reed is moving into Mr. Lacy's house?" I stopped dead in my tracks.

"What?"

My first thought was that I must not have heard her right. She was still recuperating from all that laughter, and her voice was rough and scratchy. Her words might easily have been misunderstood. But when she repeated the question a second time, there could be no misunderstanding.

"Uh, no. I hadn't heard that at all. Is that even true?" I turned back around, still holding my plate and trying to dampen the shock from my voice. I glanced over at Reed with a mystified look, imploring him to explain.

"Yep, that's true, Mr. Conway," he began, standing up straight and brushing the hair from his eyes. "Small world, huh? Truth is, I could really use a place to stay. Actually the whole thing was Sophie's idea. She kind of made the match, thought it might work out well for both of us. Mr. Lacy and I came to a sort of arrangement. In return for a small rent, I'll take care of a few things around the house. Some of my stuff is already there, but I officially move in next week."

"That … is … incredible. Leave it to Sophie to figure out how to make things work, huh?" My words spluttered out in thick, lumbering clots as I thought about those "unexpected occurrences" that Wilson had just mentioned. This had to be one. And if so, what were the others? Then, in the moment that followed, a couple of obvious things began dawning on me; they rose like revelations, one at a time, beginning with that ratty old Ford out in the driveway. "Wait a minute. "Hold on a second. Reed, is that *your* Mustang out front?"

I knew it was true as soon as I said it. What other explanation could there be? And if I was right about that, then I must have been wrong about something else. No, maybe things weren't quite over just yet. Maybe the boundaries that separate endings and beginnings aren't as neat and tidy as they seem in books. Not nearly as fixed and unbending. Maybe, instead, they are really just fuzzy layers of time through which we continually ebb and regularly flow as we make our way through the stories of our lives. Perhaps the end wasn't right there where I thought it was as Wilson drove off and perhaps there were still pieces to be played or scenes to enact—and influences to be exerted—even now, before this part of the story was over.

"Yes, sir. It is. A '66. I just bought it from a relative of mine who owned it since new. I know it's not much to look at right now, but give me some time. Mr. Lacy's offered to teach me about restoring cars. He says that by this time next year, it's going to be the finest stallion in town. How cool is that?"

"That's way cool, dude," Mike roared as he held out his arm for a fist bump. The girls were beaming.

"It is indeed," I added. "I have no doubt that between you and Wilson, that Mustang will soon be the talk of the neighborhood. Hey, by the way, did you know, Reed, that when I was in high school, my brother had a Mustang just like that, a '66 too, as a matter of fact, and—"

The woeful groans of my two lovely daughters put a quick end to my story. They shooed me back inside with my chips, my dip, and my runny nostalgia so they all could get back to their games.

Later, the six of us crowded into the dining room for a Mexican dinner to officially welcome the girls back home, and the house had to stretch a little more to accommodate the abundance that gathered around our table. But it did so, graciously.

And as night fell and the boys departed, Hannah, Sara, Janey, and I went out back. With nothing more than a single match and a little kindling left over from winter, I managed to get the old fire pit going. Nobody suspected a thing when I came back from the kitchen with all the fixings for s'mores, so I was pretty much a hero for the rest of the night. We counted the stars as they winked on above us. Each new appearance demanded some wine. Antares, Deneb, Vega, and Capella. Altair, Betelgeuse, Canopus, and Bellatrix. There was a time when I used to know them all.

Despite the heat of the day, the night had turned cool, and we gathered in close to the flames. The drifting sparks mingled with the fireflies that merged with the stars until the sky was lit with fire.

While Janey and the girls discussed plans for the morning, I leaned back in my chair and stared up at the heavens. A loose fragment of an old Whitman poem came back to me just then. All I could recall was the end:

> Till rising and gliding out I wander'd off by myself,
> In the mystical moist night-air, and from time to time,
> Look'd up in perfect silence at the stars.

I soon grew dizzy from the torrent and had to shut my eyes. And when the planning was done—and my poem had drifted away with the sparks—I reached for Janey's hand and pulled her to my chair.

She came freely, lightly, an empyreal sprite stripped of unease, and she laid herself beside me.

I held on blindly. At that moment, I had no desire to wander off in perfect silence upward toward the stars. Not anymore. And maybe never again. *This* was where I belonged. Janey and me, tethered to the earth. Tethered to each other. Together. Forever. Tangled up in blue.

Chapter

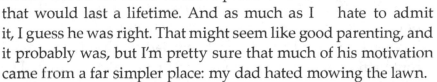

On my twelfth birthday, my father taught me how to mow the lawn. He called it the "gift of responsibility." It didn't come wrapped with a ribbon or tied with a bow; there was no card or note or sign to go along with it. All I had was his word. He assured me that my sour disappointment over not getting a go-kart would soon fade, and I would be left with a far more valuable present—one that would last a lifetime. And as much as I hate to admit it, I guess he was right. That might seem like good parenting, and it probably was, but I'm pretty sure that much of his motivation came from a far simpler place: my dad hated mowing the lawn.

Luckily for him, I took to it immediately, falling in love with the smell of the grass from my very first cut. The sodden Kentucky blue of April, the putting green knit of Bermuda in June, the tawny, dry fescue of fall—my lungs inhaled them all as they lay tamed beneath my Toro. In time, I learned to cut in patterns, usually diagonals but sometimes diamonds, to mimic the outfields I admired on TV. Wrigley was okay, but old Candlestick Park was where a lawn jockey like me could find true artistry.

Neighbors soon took notice of the Conway yard and peppered my dad with admiring praise: "Leland, your lawn always looks so great. Who do you use?"

He'd nod with pride and just quietly say, "My son."

After I was done, he would come out to inspect my work, his shirt unbuttoned and a sweaty bottle of Michelob in his hand. If my effort met muster, he'd reach into his pocket and hand me a crisp five-dollar bill and—if my mother wasn't looking—whatever was left of his beer. He never knew it, and of course I never told him, but I would have happily done the job for free. All I ever wanted was the smell of the grass, his approval, and that ice-cold swig of beer.

The spring after Aaron turned twelve, I taught him how to mow the lawn. Like me, he was a quick learner, but he never really took to it like I had. I remember watching him from the living room window on a steamy August afternoon, furiously running the mower over the same patch of grass in a frantic effort to make everything even. Imperfections were paralyzing to him, and after a couple of months, it was clear that it wasn't meant to be. Then, one day, he asked to quit, explaining that he'd much rather take pictures with his new camera than cut the stupid grass and maybe we could come up with a different plan for learning responsibility.

I still suffer the welts of remorse whenever I recall how wounded I felt by his decision. *He should be like me!*

When I confessed my dismay to my dad, he bluntly suggested I could either accept it and move on or rail like an idiot. The choice was mine, but he strongly advised the former. "Why sweat the small stuff, Owen? Despite what you may think, kids aren't mushrooms. They grow best outside the shadow cast by their parents."

I took his advice and moved on. It was a very good move. And I still love to mow the lawn.

It rained for five days straight after my ride in Wilson's car: drenching, soaking, heavy rains that seeped deep into the center of the earth. When the sun finally broke free early that Saturday, it unveiled a succulent world. The spring rains had baptized the land and brought forth an Edenic profusion of life. Branches swelled and stretched like supplicants, tender vines encroached in tangled plaits, leaves spread wide and flecked cool shade from high above, and the grass stood luxuriant, tall, and thick. Nature's outpouring was unbridled and threatened to ensnare us in rampant tendrils. Something had to be done. So, to thwart the herbaceous invasion, I ventured outside at the first sign of blue sky: rake, clippers, and mower in hand. After all that rain, the grounds needed rescuing from the onslaught of spring, and the grass was the place to start.

I heard it before I saw it. The low, throaty rumble filtered through the air. I leaned my rake against the house and shut my eyes to follow its progress. My head swayed slightly, a blind man listening to Coltrane: "A Love Supreme." The noise grew louder as it barreled down our street: three blocks away, then two blocks, then one. I felt the sound thump in my chest as it curled up the drive. And when the engine shut down, I pictured him there in the driver's seat, grinning that grin with goggles that hung loosely around his neck. So, how can I justify my utter lack of surprise when I opened my eyes on a much different scene?

Both doors swung wide in syncopated rhythm as Wilson and Sophie stepped out of the car. That would have been a most astonishing sight not more than a minute before. But as they made their way toward me down the long, buckled driveway, the two of them together on a Saturday morning, it didn't seem so astonishing after all.

Oh, Wilson and Sophie are here. I took off my work gloves and waved. And when they waved back, there was an uncommon blot of restraint that troubled their faces. I remember being hobbled by the stunning thought that they had come to say goodbye.

"Hey, you two," I said with a calm handshake and casual hug as if greeting them together was as ordinary as oatmeal. "What's up? Going for a ride?"

The question hung in the air a minute too long. Neither seemed ready to respond. Instead, Sophie turned away from our circle and leaned back leisurely against the car, adding a sprinkling of divine conspiracy to the background of a scene that was clearly Wilson's to enact.

So, I turned my attention directly toward him, still waiting for a reply, as he buried his hands in his pockets and glanced at me with a dubious expression. The affirmation he sought from Sophie came in the form of a warmhearted smile. And when he returned his eyes to me, all traces of doubt were gone. "As a matter of fact, Owen, we are. We're heading out now. All the way to the East Coast if the old girl is willing."

"Hey, I told you I was willing—and who are you calling old?" Sophie said with a laugh but without looking up. She was too busy studying some loose pebbles in the driveway, moving them around with the sole of her shoe, and arranging them according to her own private patterns.

I laughed too, but it did nothing to quell the doubt that I now felt rising in me. *Am I being played? Sure, that has to be it. All the way to the East Coast? Now? Right.* I laughed again in a way that let them know that I wasn't about to fall for their prank. They must have concocted this ruse on their way over before setting out for a day trip to Wisconsin.

But when Sophie moved away from the car and twirled her arm like a model, my eyes were snared by the jam-packed interior. Every inch of available space behind and around the seats was loaded with gear. It had all been fitted with an engineer's touch, and I was suddenly forced to consider the possibility that this was no joke after all. Wilson watched as that realization crept over my face.

"Are you kidding? You're going away?"

"Have you ever known me to kid, Owen?"

He had a point there. He was a serious guy.

"And you're going together? Now?" My mind worked hard to absorb the meaning of this remarkable news. There was a lot to consider. At first, it was all red-hot and too bright to see clearly, bursting like flashbulbs one after another right in front of my eyes. But the news cooled surprisingly quickly, and soon the scene began to make some sense. *Oh, Wilson and Sophie are going away.*

"We are," he said calmly. And then he started to explain. "The truth is I have wanted to take this trip for a long time, but things kept getting in the way. I think you know the story there. I just couldn't see my way clear to make it happen. But some of those things have changed recently, and I know you know that too. I now find myself standing apart from something that I barely understand. A part of me I guess that always sought to undermine my better intentions. I know it has always been there, but it feels like I've gained a little distance on it now. A little separation. It's as if I've left something behind, or maybe I've outrun it, or … I don't know. The words are difficult. The point is I feel like I can do this now, and I don't want to miss the chance. And when I asked Sophie if she might be interested in coming along, she actually said yes—and so here we are."

"Road trip, Owen," Sophie said as she took a step toward us, then reconsidered and leaned back once more against the car, not quite done with the pebbles. "I've always been a sucker for a road trip."

"Do you have a plan?" I asked.

"Does *he* have plan?" Sophie chuckled under her breath.

"It's me Owen," he said. "Of course we have a plan. We are going to make our way to Boston through a route of secondary roads that some guys in the MG club recommended. We'll take a few days to get there. And then, well, I'll get to see my kids—and Rachel too. They all know we're coming. It has been way too long, and there are things that need to be said. A lot of things, frankly. Things that have gone unsaid for too many years I'm afraid. After that, we'll head to the Cape. Sophie has never been. We've got a place rented for a few weeks in Truro. And then? Who knows? We're in no hurry. We'll let the car and our desires act as our compass. That last part of the plan is Sophie's contribution by the way."

"That's the part I like best," she said. Finally finished with the pebbles, she came away from the car, out from the shadows, to stand alongside Wilson beneath the bright spotlight of the sun.

She put an arm around his waist and reached up to kiss him on the cheek. "Tell him about the house."

"Oh, yeah. Right. So, I know you heard that Reed is staying at my house. Janey said you heard that from your girls. Well, if you could check in on him every once in a while, I would really appreciate it. The kid is very responsible, and I'm sure he'll be fine, but it would add to my peace of mind to know that you're there if he needs you."

I promised I would.

"And the boys at the restaurant are giving me the summer off, if you can believe it." Sophie added. "They're calling it my sabbatical. But I'm counting on you, Owen, to make sure they don't forget about me. Don't let them screw things up. I love that place, and I want it to be just like it is when we get back."

I promised I would.

"And I can't say for sure exactly *when* we'll be back," Wilson continued. "But we'll be sure to keep in touch along the way. The only thing I can say with certainty is that I will be expecting you to pick me up at eight o'clock sharp on August 17 for the orientation meeting at Middlebrook. You'll be there, right?"

I promised I would.

Promises made—links in a chain that binds us together as we fumble our way through the darkness. For a while, we managed to find a few more things to say, but in my heart, I knew it was time to let them go. Surely, they were anxious to get on the road.

Sophie must have sensed that too because she left Wilson's side and walked over to me for what was undoubtedly billed as a farewell hug. "Thanks, Owen," she whispered.

"For what?"

"For being a good friend and a good man. You can see your hand in all this, can't you? It's there, everywhere. You need to see that for what it is and for what it means."

And when she hugged me again, I couldn't help but notice that it somehow felt different from all the other hugs I had received. Think more sincere, less sassy.

"Oh, and don't be upset with Janey. I made her promise not to say anything. It didn't seem to be my place. We already said our goodbyes, but would you give that girl a hug for me when she gets back? And Hannah and Sara too."

"I promise I will. And look, I really don't know what to say. This is just a wonderful thing that you guys are doing. I am so happy for you both. You're going to have a great time, and I'm holding you to that promise to stay in touch. Send pictures! Lots of pictures!"

They promised they would. Sophie then got back into the car, all satin and silk and smoothness. She pulled sunglasses down from the top of her head and rested a slim, spangled arm on the doorsill, a Hollywood starlet on her way to a grand opening. Glamorous, alluring, and still a little wondrous too. And when she grabbed a baseball cap from the side door pocket, a playful smile co-opted her face. I yelped with laughter at the sight of that gladsome woman sporting a Chicago Cubs hat in Wilson Lacy's car. "This really gets the old man's goat," she chided.

Wilson shook his head, but he could not shake the smile that shone from his face. "So, there's one more thing," he said, his tone taking a more serious turn as he made his way back to the car. It took several minutes of careful rearranging before he could extract a box that was tucked behind his seat. He rested the box on the hood of the car and opened it with great care. I watched as he removed several copies of a book, each wrapped in a layer of fine tissue. He pulled them out one at a time, unfolded the tissue, and opened the front covers until he found the one he was looking for. "This is for you," he said, handing me a copy before returning the others to their box.

The inscription inside was brief, composed in his scrupulous hand.

> To my friend Owen Conway,
>
> With gratitude for your compassion and wisdom and patience. The fact that this moment

exists at all is a testament to all three. I wish someone were taking a picture. It would have made a grand addition to the story.

While doing some research, I came across this quote from the photographer Sally Mann: "Photographs open doors into the past, but they also allow a look into the future." That's a perspective I never could have imagined when my experiment began. And yet, I now know it's true. I'm ready to see about the future.

Odysseus's journey lasted ten years—did you know that? I feel like mine is just getting started.

Ex nihilo nihil fit

Wilson Lacy

I closed the cover with trembling hands. To forestall the turbulence that was surging behind my eyes, I forced my attention on the book. It looked to be a simply bound volume, beautifully encased in cloth-covered boards. In my hands, it felt heavier than I would have expected, more weighted or dense than would seem possible. I did not yet understand why. On the cover was a recent photograph of Wilson standing by his car in front of an exuberant landscape. I recognized the pose. It was a recreation of a similar photo taken over forty years before, the first one in his experiment that he chose to explore when winter had begun to collapse around him: the teenager beside the car. Forty years. A lifetime of moments fenced between two shots. It was an open invitation to those tangled threads—the ones buried deep below that compose the fabric of one's life—summoning them to the surface so that they may reveal the glory of an improbable journey. With a nod to the past, he was beckoning his future. The volume was entitled *A Visual Literacy Experiment: A Structured Examination of Seven Photographs in Search of Meaning and Understanding.*

Sheer Wilson.

"Sophie took that," he said as I continued to admire the book. "She's quite a photographer. She thought it would make a good cover, and I think she's right. Anyways, I thought you might like this. Your hands are on that too. I expect you know that. You'll see, though, that I never did get around to that last entry, so there are some blank pages at the end."

"For the future, right?"

"Yeah, for the future. I'll make sure you get the final installment when it's done, just so you have the whole set, you know."

I thanked him for the book and wished him well. And then, with a suddenness that seems breathtaking in retrospect, they were gone, roaring off toward the seashore that lies at the easternmost end of the world and then headlong into the rest of their lives. The next chapter of the story was already begun.

I stood there with my eyes closed and followed the sound of the car as they left. The rumble grew quieter as they rushed away: one block down, two blocks, then three. Gone. It was easy to envision the road ahead: long stretches of wide-open highway through the flatlands of Indiana and Ohio, then the swells of the Keystone State that undulate and wind through ascending climbs and wooly forests, great complexes of cities that rise and recede and rise again only to forfeit their hand where the land meets the sea. And then the horizon, stretching out forever along the curvature of the earth, tempting them with a future that can never be foreseen yet promises so much, if we only know how to look. That's where I left them, on the brink of the horizon, together.

Wilson has Sophie. Sophie has Wilson.

You never know what may come from a walk around the neighborhood.

I think I like the smell of May grass best. It still carries the clean scent of spring that drains away too soon as the earth goes dry beneath the beat of the sun. I pulled a handful from the ground and held it to my nose. The muddy reek of winter had evaporated. The grass pulsed with the pure, sweet fragrance of spring. It was the smell of rebirth, of resurrection, of new beginnings, and the poignancy was not lost on me. I closed my eyes and breathed again—deeply this time so I would not forget as spring gave way to summer and autumn, and winter—and my mind was assailed by memories: of ball fields and romance and the bitter first taste of beer. Of birdsong and tree climbs and stones skipping on the lake. They burst like photographs, too fast to see, each embodying a thimbleful of truth. But when the volatiles dissipated and the scent was gone, a hazy afterimage remained: of fathers and sons and dreams. I opened my eyes, took another deep breath, and blew the grass away.

I started to push the mower to the front parkway, thinking about a new pattern for the lawn. Maybe something with curves. As I began plotting out a design, a cloud, the first one that day, passed beneath the sun. It took the shape of a bird, or a dragonfly maybe, and sent a shadow to traverse the ground. Along with the deepening dark, a shiver of cold air fell from space. I lifted my head and watched while the cloud fractured the golden light from the sky. Whether it was a reminder or a harbinger or nothing auspicious at all, I couldn't tell for sure. Maybe you can decide. But when the cloud lifted, and the darkness fled, the light that streamed from the sun was changed. Not a remnant of shadow remained as far as I could see, and I raised my arms to the sunlight of summer.

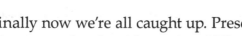

Finally now we're all caught up. Present tense from here on out. How many days has it been since Wilson and Sophie left? I recently lost count. It has been long enough for the emeralds of spring to have faded. Already the first foreshadows of fall have arrived: fringes of olive and russet skirts and verging borders of bronze. It has been long enough for the percolating earth to parch. Great fissures have formed ragged canyons in the ground. They crack the dirt into hard baked clumps that resist the gardener's spade. And it has been long enough for wide tracts of land to transform into golden seas of grass. Milkweed, bluestem, bottlebrush, and rye swell like waves in delicate breaths of air. We are just past the midpoint of summer now, nearing the end of July. The dog days loom. The daylight adheres to everything like gum, and clouds are as scarce as the chill.

Wilson has been as good as his word. He stays in touch along the way. Every few days, another set of photographs appears on my computer. They arrive as email attachments, more often than not with very few words. I'm left to decipher the shape of the story on my own, but that's okay; it is what I do.

In the beginning, just after they left, there were jittery shots of welcome signs passed at each border crossing. Roadside repairs and roadside hotels and slivers of green pools in the back. Rest-stop meals beneath speckled shade and sunsets and sunrises skimming over the long black hood of the car. They pose like tourists beside monuments and landmarks and on trails inside state parks. Strangers, fellow travelers, I assume, zip in and out with no explanation or description or role. From the bleachers at Fenway, they cheer, foamy cold beers in their hands, sandwiched between a cornflower sky and an infield of jelly bean green.

Then came reunions in Boston and Fall River with Nora and William and Rachel. Shy embraces and tearful faces and eyes spilling things to tell. Sublime portraits of Wilson and Rachel as they gaze at the sleeping plum face of their granddaughter. Close-ups of Trevor clearly enchanted by the presence of this big new person in his life, kicking a soccer ball or digging in the park or reading a book or building his Legos or reaching for giraffes at the zoo or asleep in his grandfather's lap.

And just last week, Wilson and Sophie alone at the Cape, walking the shoreline in swimsuits and tans and their bliss. I print a few from each new batch, and for reasons I don't bother to consider, I've taken to hanging them on my wall. I wonder what Wilson is thinking as he prepares to send them on. Does he see how these photographs expose the magnificence of his life, the irrefutable, verifiable, incontestable, elemental magnificence of his life? I like to believe that he does.

I sit in my studio, wilting like spinach in the sultry late afternoon air. A thunderstorm churns in the distance. The rising wind brings a foretaste of rain and maybe a break from the heat. I look up from my computer at a blue flash of lightning and follow the rumble as it scuttles the sky. When I return to the screen, my moment of work is interrupted by the advent of an incoming message. Right on time—five o'clock, every third day, a promise fulfilled with scientific precision.

I glance at the photos pinned to my wall and chase the thread as a prelude to whatever this most recent installment includes. Simmering somewhere in the back of my mind, just as it has all summer, is the rough outline of the trajectory's next phase. I call it stage 4. I'm not quite ready to define it just yet. It is still a little unformed. But I know that it has something to do with the way I feel as I get ready to open this file. I lean back in my chair as a more vigorous peal unwinds. Then, I open my beer and click on the message and wait for the story to ensue.

From: Wilsonlacy@nwu.edu
To: Owen@conwaydesign.org
Date: July 24, 2016
Re: Number 7 of 7

Owen,

I hope this email finds you well. Our time at the Cape is coming to a close. It has been a remarkable trip. I know that you would love it here. Nature's variations continue to astound me, and the beauty that you seek is on display at every turn. The nighttime sky leaves me speechless.

We leave in a few days to take the northerly route through upper New England and Canada. The MG boys were spot-on about the eastern route so we're putting our faith in them once more for the return. With the exception of that faulty fuel pump outside of Providence, the car has been flawless.

Thanks to you and Janey and the girls for the wishes and the lovely gift. That was very thoughtful. Baby Emily is home now, and the family is settling in. There is much to tell that won't translate in email, so I'll leave it there for now. I look forward to sharing it all with you over a beer or two back home. Glad to hear that Reed is getting along well in the house. And in your house too—from what I understand!

I am attaching the final entry on photograph seven. Do with it what you will. I know that I'll never look at things the same way again. Strangely, I find that there is a touch of sorrow associated with that, but mostly this realization brings joy. It's as if the shadows are mostly behind me now, at least for the moment, and the way forward feels less beset. Give our best to Janey and the girls. Let them know that we'll be home soon and hope to enjoy the end of summer with you all. Fall and winter too.

Wilson Lacy
Scientist in Residence
Middlebrook Middle School

P.S. Sophie sends her love. She wants to know if you're following the Cubs this summer. I think I may be in for a whole lot of hurt come October.

A Last Little Addendum

Yeah, I know, you probably thought we were done. I did too for a while. Fair enough. But not quite just yet—a moment more, if you please. I guess you might call this a postscript, a little something extra here at the end. To tell you the truth, I wasn't even sure whether to include this at all. My editors were not so pleased. They thought those last three paragraphs of chapter 18 were a good enough ending. Still, as I think about it now, a whole year out from where we began, the story just doesn't seem complete without this coda. Kind of like a dinner without dessert. Or a concert with no encore. Lightning without thunder. Winter without spring. Something essential was missing. And so, when they finally returned from their trip and the leaves began to turn once again, I asked Wilson if he would let me include this. He didn't hesitate at all. "Sure, by all means, Owen, if you think it might help. Feel free to use it any way you'd like."

Nice guy that Wilson Lacy.

So here it is … Wilson's memoir, the whole enchilada, the results of his experiment, photos and reflections and all. I suppose it might help clarify some things, like the things he was thinking as our story unfolded. Maybe it will highlight the special kind of solace he found from looking at old photos and the lessons he learned about his life. And who knows, maybe you'll even give it a try sometime, to see for yourself the magic that can occasionally happen when you tilt your head a certain way or adopt a peculiar kind of angle to your gaze, when you look anew at those memorable moments, the ones we all have, the ones frozen in time by the snap of a shutter, and find out on your own how that new way of looking can untangle the threads that reside deep below. In any case, I'm happy to include it, just so you have the whole set, you know.

A Visual Literacy Experiment

A Structured Examination of Seven Photographs in Search of Meaning and Understanding

Wilson Lacy

Introduction

A memoir is defined as a "collection of memories that an individual writes about, moments or events, both public and private, that took place in the subject's life." My intent with this project is to compose *my* memoir based on a series of important moments that have occurred during my life. Beyond that definition, I wonder about the motives of the memoir author, about what inspires the sober effort to expose and examine those memories. Do memoirists undertake that effort in a spirit of self-consciousness in order to derive some deeper meaning from one's life? Is it driven by a yearning to weave together a more coherent sense of the assemblage of experiences that, when finally aggregated, depicts the narrative of a life? Or does the author feel that the collected memories and slanted interpretations they arouse might encompass more general notions of life's meaning and—in that sense—be of interest to others? I have no idea.

All I can confidently state is that from the perspective of *this* memoirist, the motivations are purely personal. I seek to make no impact. I do not inflate this process with any outward ambition. Instead, I sit at this keyboard with a singular purpose in mind: to immerse myself in a selection of memories, simply to see where it leads. My hope is that in doing so, I may learn more about those currents that have wound through my life and the debris they deposited along the way. Let the experiment begin.

In the spirit of full disclosure, it is worth acknowledging that this project was inspired by my friend, Owen Conway.

Owen showed up a couple of months ago, and for reasons I still do not fully comprehend—but now no longer question—offered his hand in helping me to understand what he refers to as "the story of my life." I harbor no illusions that I would be sitting here if it were not for him. Without his guidance, I would be facing the turmoil of another long winter with nothing but my loneliness and regrets as companions. Now I have this. I hope he knows that the lifeline he gave me in the form of this idea is clung to with desperation and hope. I suspect he does.

I'll never be a jazz pianist. I'll never appear on the cover of *Sports Illustrated*. I'll never rebuild an old Ferrari. And if I'm honest with myself, I'll never be a novelist. While those ambitions once fueled my passions, the reality is that they will remain unrequited. But that's okay. I had my share. I have stirred with the soulfulness of music made by my own two hands. I have glowed with a string of perfectly fielded grounders on a majestic spring day. I have basked in the fulfillment of driving my MG. And I have sat silently stunned by an elegant sentence formed from the vacuum of nothingness. But there will be no openings at Carnegie Hall, no ticker tape parades down crowded city streets, no blue ribbons at Pebble Beach, and certainly no National Book Awards. Interestingly though, I now sense something hiding in the dark recesses of my long-overdue acceptance of those realities. It skims across my consciousness like gossamer. I wonder how long it's been calling and how I could have missed it all these years.

It's December 2015, and I seem to have hit another rough patch. Held in abeyance for so long, the demons of my depression have descended upon me with a familiar ferocity. For whatever reasons, the chains that had restrained those demons have again come undone, and I find myself toiling through the monochromatic puttiness of despair that is relieved only by the respite of sleep. The fringes of these feelings are tinged with the well-worn outlines of my own familiar sadness. I have fallen. Hard. And it's a struggle to get back up.

I imagine that this endeavor—this memoir—is somehow the residuum of that depression. It is a way to resist the chilly misery that has invaded like a virus and feel the sunlit warmth of hope. I am searching for a better understanding of the themes that have plowed such a fertile field for the demons' rise. I intuitively sense the poignancy of those themes—of their revelatory power—and the potential they hold for unleashing my liberation. And it is precisely that liberation that I seek. This memoir will be my lens to lay bare those themes and manifest that understanding.

Wresting these themes from the firmament of my past will require some heavy artillery. They cling like barnacles to the shady underside of my life, and I don't suspect that they will submit easily. So I will rely on the prima facie of my own lived experiences. I will orchestrate toward my own needs and ends. I will scavenge the past for the grist I seek. I will endeavor to generate evidence of the themes that have wound through my life, and I will follow that evidence—and those themes—wherever they lead.

My plan is to heed Owen's advice and apply the construct of visual literacy to explore a series of significant photographic images. The research literature defines visual literacy as the ability to "interpret, negotiate, and make meaning from information presented in the form of an image." It references a group of visual and interpretative skills we can develop that allow us to simultaneously "see" and "make meaning" through the integration of sensory experiences. When developed, these skills enable a visually literate person to interpret the visible actions, objects, and symbols (e.g., images) that he or she encounters in the environment. In turn, our understanding and appreciation of those images—as well as our lived experiences—are enhanced. Or more simply for these purposes, visual literacy is the ability to construct meaning from images.

I expect that the images selected for this project will trigger flights of my imagination that are inextricably bound to the meaning of the particular moments being explored. Thus, this visual literacy approach will enable me to interpret images from my past and then generate meanings that convey a salient message. I will then quarry those meanings and messages to infer the broader themes that have composed the "story of my life."

The photographs that follow were chosen for the way they resonate with *this* exact instant in time and the harmonic quality they evoked with *this* prevailing purpose in mind. I don't ascribe any universality to these images that might imbue them with heightened meaning or significance. Surely, the conditions that comprised my thinking ten or twenty years ago would have led to the selection of a wholly different set of images to explore. And just as surely, the photos that would focus this inquiry at some point in the future would be a reflection of the unique conditional qualities that impinge at that time.

What this does is infuse an element of temporality into this work that emphasizes the importance of *this* moment. Given the desperation with which I begin this work—that this process will lead to a better understanding of the thematic tides that have shaped my life and, in turn, chart a course toward calmer waters—that seems just as it should. I am anxious to get started.

Photograph 1
Halcyon Days
Early Summer 1974

The lush fecundity captured in this photo reflects the unfolding ripeness of this moment in time. I am bathed in a luxuriant backdrop that seems to thrust me into high relief. I stand on the precipice of transition. It's the summer between the end of high school and the beginning of college. I have blissfully cast off the fretfulness that pervaded my adolescence and, unbeknownst to me, am about to embark on what was to become the true sweet spot of my life: my halcyon days. As with all moments tenuously balanced on the cusp of transition, what comes *after* is simply inconceivable. "What future?" Only the moment matters. My backward glance through time reveals the poignancy of this moment and the knife-edged insistence of the shutter's click. It lays bare the stark demarcation between what came before and all that was to follow.

When I look at my face and stance in the photo, I see the fading scars of that fretful adolescence. They are barely noticeable and mostly healed, inferred more like the presence of an invisible planet from the position of other objects in space. Yet I know they are there. I carried them with me up to the moment that this picture was taken, bending myself to their grotesque contours, and I carry them with me now. Surely it's the nature of adolescence— its inherent storm and stress—to inflict those scars by lobbing a firestorm of tribulation at a time when we are most vulnerable and then demanding that we somehow navigate the incoming fire as a necessary part of growing up. Nevertheless, metamorphosing from those trials reveals the shrapnel damage. As winsome as I appear in this photo— shedding the chrysalis of my own adolescence—I sense the indelible mark of sadness.

Excavating the roots of that sadness seems like an essential focus for this work. There is no evidence in this photo or of my memories of that moment that would lead me to think I felt sad as I stood in front of my car on that radiant summer day. To be sure, the strife I was leaving behind was scorched by a cacophony of fears, self-loathing, and the general bedlam of loud anxieties. The residue it left was like tar, and I can feel it sticking to me today. But my impression is that I was leaving all that behind, that I had unfurled from the trials reasonably intact and was well disposed for the days that were about to follow.

My left hand hints at my impatience with the photographer. "Take the picture already, will ya?" There's an urgency to get on with it so I could sprint headlong toward the paradisiacal future I sensed waiting just around the bend—a future where anything could happen. But just out of sight of the camera's lens, humming on some infrared wavelength, is the cooling of my soft, molten exoskeleton that occurred during that summer interlude, newly extruded from the furnace of adolescence. I barely had time to test its fit, though with each stretch, I discovered some new hue to add to my palette or whiff of sweetness that lay hidden beneath the thinnest veil.

And then, without the least hesitation, I was well and truly in it. I was swept away by a Technicolor intensity that crackled with an infusion of fresh possibility. My senses were inflamed and finely tuned to the resonance that engulfed me. Azure skies and viridian fields stung my skin with quixotic grace. Currents of air carried the scent of young girls' perfume and painted a gallery of dreamy impressions in my mind. And I trembled with an aching, fluttering thrill with each new experience I encountered. For that brief, fleeting moment—that sorrowfully short period of time that followed this photo—I churned with the passions of being alive in a world that overflowed with an inexhaustible catalog of marvels. I burned with the hope that it would always be thus.

I wonder if it's a natural arc in the trajectory of one's life that the accretion of years must dim those passions beneath thickening layers of dust. The corrosive forces of time dull the senses, lulling them into a lazy acceptance of the banal. Eventually, those raw nerve endings that once thrummed so spiritedly became callused with plaque, narrowing the kaleidoscopic vision through which I once viewed my life, and I bemoaned the loss of the new.

Haven't I seen all this before?

It seems reasonable, then, to expect a modicum of sadness when confronted with the loss of the new, when plateaus replace peaks, and the future is robbed of its glamour. The flowing white heat generated by life's surplus of current becomes discharged by amplified needs. It leaves behind a phantom hum of regret and sorrow. Maybe it's the evanescence of those transcendent times, as ephemeral as a mayfly, that induces the sadness. Or maybe the sadness arises out of the gulf that separates the desire to course again with that same boundlessness—to pulse with that same unfettered beat—and the rough-hewn impossibility of its fruition. Or maybe, more simply, it's just the gooey residue of wistful nostalgia congealing as cloying memories of happier times.

I suspect that each of these explanations is somehow in play. Disentangling one from the other in order to uncover the etymology of the sadness seems unprofitable. Instead, as I leave off my entry on this first photo, I seem drawn to the promise of two ideas: (1) Those halcyon days were, in fact, *mine.* They were the precipitate that arose from the spontaneous reaction between *me* and *my life* at that moment. They were *of* me, fomented *by* me, and are indelibly embossed on the permanent record of *my* life. Though often imperceptible, the glow generated from that reaction is with me still and continues to radiate its unadulterated promise, leaving behind the faint trace of what I reckon is a truly blessed life. If only I would listen. (2) Still, there is a quality to this recent sadness that is new—an unbidden welling of sorrow that rises like bile whenever I look at these photos. It is a different species altogether, and I can feel it squirming away from my scrutiny. I peck at the edges, dig at the roots, apply all the forces at my disposal in order to expose its morphology. I'm not there yet, but I believe I may have picked up the scent and am eager to see where it leads.

Entry Date: December 8, 2015
W. L.

Photograph 2
The Moment of Truth
Spring 2008

Propelled by the thrust of a simple leap of faith, the gawky contraption begins its gentle descent, carrying with it the precious cargo of my professional aspirations. Impeded by air and unburdened by mass, it ultimately touches down, at first with a whisper and then with a rush as the shroud of bewilderment is wrenched away. It is precisely that moment—so intentional in its planning, so orchestrated in its execution, and so joyful in its authenticity—that provides the impulse, sowing the seeds of wonder and enkindling the process of discovery. At least that's the theory anyway.

In many ways, this second photo symbolizes the quintessence of my professional life. It lays bare the assumptions, philosophies, and hard-won understandings that have emerged from my engagement with work over the past thirty-five years. It conveys the impression of a well-constructed set of empirical beliefs about the nature of science and the art of teaching upon which a professional identity might respectably be built. And yet, emblematically, I have no recollection of ever endeavoring to cultivate those beliefs, of purposefully setting out to uncover my own ontological system of understanding or establishing a reliable base of knowledge that would yield a kit of practical applications. Still, when I look at this photo, I see that they are there. Those ideas about science and teaching are *unmistakably* there. They provide the coordinates for the "a-has" that are about to transpire from this learning activity. They are what I am. Or, at least, they were what I was.

I can trace the origins of that professional infrastructure to a balmy spring evening during my sophomore year of college. It was in a moment of divine clarity—as perfectly meshed cogs fall in alignment to produce a resounding click that reverberates in waves outward toward the future—that I decided to pursue science as my field of study. I remember trembling with that aching, fluttering thrill as I envisioned the future-bound course of my professional trajectory. Like Kubrick's primordial men in *2001*, that first, tentative contact with my obelisk of ambition sparked a cinematic representation of a future toward which I was forcibly drawn. And so began the evolutionary process of fabricating a professional sense of self.

From a certain perspective, the thread that connects two points of time can appear fragile and kinked, bent with the blunt force trauma of serendipity and fate. The traverse from one point to another unravels with a careless, chaotic invention. Only now, at the end point of this particular thread, can I gain the clearest resolution of the journey's true course. The thread that connected that knowing moment from sophomore year to the dramatic descent of my Mars lander three decades later was a frictionless, adamantine conduit. It propelled me across a professional topography that shimmered with opportunity. And, by some immutable laws of physics, the gravitational field I generated as I sped down that thread attracted the patchwork fragments of a professional identity. I simply became the scientist and teacher I was always meant to be.

So then, what to make of the passage? What does this photograph reveal about the nature of the journey and the emerging themes of this memoir? As I look more closely and consider these questions, I can feel the revelations exfoliate, peeling off in layers of meaning, each with its own attendant apparition. Like ghosts from a Dickensian novel, those apparitions are rattling their chains, clamoring for attention, and groaning for appeasement as I prospect the precipitate of my work.

I can, for example, identify the presence of the Ghost of Inspired Ideas. He is the spirit responsible for this photograph's true iridescence, the spark that infuses this moment with rapturous engagement, forged from the furnace of my own imagination. Throughout my career, I relied on a kind of intuitive engineering to generate ideas designed to achieve a desired end. The precise mechanics of that engineering remained inscrutable, blanketed just beneath my consciousness. I never dared expose it, fearing that it would wither under the glare of my inspection. Instead, I trusted in it as a dependable asset of my professional identity. I knew that, whatever the challenge, the Ghost of Inspired Ideas would, in time, pull from the furnace an idea teeming with potential and sizzling with exultation in equal measures. He never failed me.

It's a bit murkier to discern the handiwork of the Ghost of Lives Touched. His presence is best inferred. From the very beginning, the desire to make a difference in people's lives was the combustible fuel that drove my endeavors. The nature of my work allowed me to engage with others, and those interactions carried the piquant aroma of change: of reforming an outdated perspective, nurturing a virtuous value, or sparking to life some new idea from the spontaneous collision of imagination and reason.

To participate in those transformations was an extravagant privilege, one I was sure I did not deserve. Though their profiles were offered to me in a menagerie of praise, I remained diffident to the temptations they bore. Yet despite my reluctance to acknowledge those offerings, deep down I know that the Ghost of Lives Touched is sated. His contented fatness and greasy grin induce my fulfillment.

Finally, the most diaphanous of these apparitions is the Ghost of Hard Work, the prankster of the group. I imagine him off to the side, quietly chortling with private bemusement that somehow—without the stains of the midnight oil—we pulled it off. But how? And really, how significant could a body of work be without the scars that should have been inflicted by so many years of toil and work?

And suddenly, there it is. Rising to the surface on the buoyancy of his mirth comes the revelatory power of this process. To anyone looking at this picture, those three ghosts are invisible, their leverage easily negated. Who needs them? The photo purrs with enough corporeality to charm the eye of any observer. I have, however, alluded to their collusion in pulling the strings of my professional accomplishments: *he* never failed me, *his* contented fatness, *we* somehow pulled it off. I know those ghosts are there.

But when their spectra are viewed through an alternative lens, I see that these ghosts are not disembodied, shadowy, phantasmal companions greasing the skids of my work. They are indissoluble aspects of me. Somewhere along the way, I seem to have entrusted *them* with the responsibility for *my* accomplishments, schizophrenically tipping the scales of worthiness in *their* favor over *mine* and displacing the possibility of claiming any recompense of my own. That deflection was instinctive, reflexive, and habitual—a safety protocol of old that inured me to the emotional messiness that was bound up with the work. It also abolished any sense of gratification that might otherwise have been mine if I only knew where to look.

So in the spirit of this memoir, let me rephrase: As I traveled the thread of my professional life, *I did* work hard, *I did* impact the lives of others, and *I did* come up with some astonishingly beautiful ideas. Still, it's the past tense of those phrases that seems so troubling now. The ghosts have stolen my share, and all they have left is the void.

Trembling at the terminus of that thread, I am alone, lost, and adrift. I am left wondering where such generativity and productive engagement with the world will now come. And whether it will come at all. And if not, then what is there left to do? The trough left in the wake of that thread is deep. It is filled with sadness, fear, and regret.

Entry Date: December 16, 2015
W. L.

Photograph 3
Upstairs by a China Lamp
August 1978

The air is redolent, perfumed with promise and the inconceivable limitlessness of possibility. An infusion of emotions mixes with the salt air and the sweet mellifluousness in my head to enrapture my soul. By some capricious winds of luck and romance, I've landed here, on the shores of Cape Cod with the blank canvas of my future awaiting a first brushstroke, yet mindful only of my heart's desire. I teeter with exhilaration, drunk on the impression that from this point forward, I can do anything. I can make of my life what I will. My intuition tingles as I sense the opulence of the moment, bestowed upon me like a precious gift, simply for having made it to adulthood. And despite the tendency to flinch from the prospect of being unanchored in such open seas, left alone to face the violent headwinds and turbulent waters of an indeterminate future, I am becalmed by the intoxicating wish only to embark on that voyage—wherever it might lead—hand in hand with the girl on my side.

By any measure, $1/250^{th}$ of a second is an impossibly brief period of time. With a cold, mechanical insistence, the camera's shutter opens to admit an abrupt flash of light that imprints a single heartbeat on film and leaves behind an impression that endures for a lifetime. In comparison, the blink of an eye, the flutter of a hummingbird's wing, a lightning strike all transpire with what feels like an impatient, sluggish lethargy. $1/250^{th}$ of a second.

Out of a vertiginous haze dawns the realization that the fractionally fleeting instant captured in this photo was preceded by more than half a billion similarly fugacious moments that unfolded since that very first glance. Even to this day, I am stunned by the Jenga-like construction of moments that somehow—fantastically, implausibly—coalesced with the two of us here, in *this moment,* side by side around the oilcloth-topped picnic tables firmly anchored in the Wellfleet sand.

The shutter snaps. The chill in this gothic classroom burrows deeply and carries with it the scent of old varnish and wood. Tall windows climb high walls and are pitched with the fathom's deep darkness of a winter night. The only light comes from ancient fixtures, shrouded in dust, that seem a mile away.

We wear the slowly fading freshness of the college experience like novitiates, balanced somewhere between the astonishment of actually being here and a creeping complacency that drapes our postures. Yet not too complacent. We still swell with wonder at the new faces that accompany the start of every new term, secretly scanning the rows to gain our bearings. And there she is, all the way across the timeworn room and as distant from me as two people in the same classroom can be. The most beautiful thing in the world.

The shutter snaps. Another classroom, a few years later, this one betrayed by the stark angularity of its design and lashings of earth tones as architectural expressions of modernity. Early-morning sun filters through the double-pane windows and spills onto the floors, barking the promise of an early thaw.

The rapidly lengthening days of this final spring offer a wistful reminder of the irrepressibly dwindling number of days that are left, suffusing everything with a sun-drenched urgency. Puddles of snowmelt gather under my desk in sympathy with my fluttering heart while I wait and wait. And there she is, walking in, casting her glance to the empty seat on my left, and sealing my love forever. The distance that once seemed astronomical evaporates to a narrow frisson that overwhelms the moment, leaving nothing but white noise in its wake.

The shutter snaps. Moments upon moments link together according to destiny's blueprint. The radiant warmth of the earth sprouts a fragrant carpet of grass to caress our bodies. A makeshift vase of pilfered flowers rests furtively at her door. Walking together across the shimmering campus as time slips through my fingers. And that dewy spring night, awash with honeysuckle and hyacinth and hope, when we found our way through the inky darkness so that I—at last— might lighten my heart and unburden my soul.

The genomic sequence that maps the course of one's life is comprised of countless, fleeting moments, each careening with the others, ricocheting us toward the future. Most are buried in insignificance, lost forever to the backdrops and rhythms that landscape our lives. Individually, they exert the influence of nearly weightless particles, barely detectable, yet by their sheer number, they ooze with the glue that binds the ensemble together. Others are more combustive. These are the moments that fracture the chain of events, disassembling the orderly sequence of things and inserting mutations that cause our paths to veer off in unanticipated, unimagined directions. These are the ones we always remember; their poignancy saturates our memory. They linger with a radioactive half-life, replaying on an endless loop of reverie, haunting our dreams.

I wonder if our seaward glance on that late summer day ever envisioned what was to come as the seemingly endless stream of moments reached out toward the future. How could we have known, with our toes so firmly dug into the sand and our hearts overflowing with the glistening now, that just beyond the rapier-sharp margin of that far horizon, was the chain like confederation of moments that has since made up our lives?

From that vantage point, on that beach, those moments seemed to stretch out forever, unsullied like blank dominoes awaiting the gentlest push to begin their steady fall, an innumerable, inexhaustible profusion of moments to be upon which we would indelibly inscribe our deepest desires and most noble aspirations for what our lives could be.

I imagine myself entranced by the romanticism of such a glittering future, looking out over the roiling water and anticipating the brilliance of all those moments to come, moments of ecstasy and contentment, pain and grief, fulfillment, bleakness, satisfaction, peace and longing, a great, thundering miscellany of moments that would, in time, recite the story of my life. I would embrace them all.

But what I surely could not imagine—from the edge of that windswept beach—is how many of those moments would be mindlessly devoured with an addict's madness, frittered away in a Novocain-induced numbness, blind to the looming reality of an ever-shrinking supply and anesthetized to the poetry that breathes inside every shutter snap.

How could I ever have anticipated the brutal speed with which a single moment becomes a lifetime? Or how that lifetime tows behind it an endless trail of moments, withered by time to fade away until all that remains is the bleached filigree of my dreams? Will there ever be another moment that stakes as glorious a claim on my imagination? Or has my share run dry, leaving me only to mark the moments that remain with a tedious precision until the end? What can I learn from this photograph that might anoint the moments to come with a preciousness steeped in the lyricism of love?

Entry Date: January 14, 2016
W. L.

Photograph 4
Reconciliation
1957

Safely cradled in his arms, I surrender to my father's tender kiss. His eyes are gently shut, letting him finely tune his other senses to absorb the softness of my cheek and drink the milky sweetness of my skin, the ephemeral charms of infancy. He holds me tightly against his chest. Our hearts pulse in fragile synchronicity to awaken the bonds of attachment between father and son and then cement them with everlasting glue.

We are so close that none of the bright light streaming from the bedroom window penetrates between us; no light gap yet exists. And still, with each passing heartbeat, a bit more of a gradually expanding fissure is revealed. Eventually, a small pinprick will appear, allowing a few photons of light to pass through the space that separates us. Then that space will grow, first with a slow, sleepy pace that lets more light pass through until it gapes from the colliding forces between the dreams of a hopeful parent and the inescapable infringement of an unfolding reality. But in this photo, in *this* moment, the strong gravitational field that links us together precludes any such gap. The skies are tranquil, the storms are miles distant, and we are one.

The word *nestle* is derived from the Old English *nestilian*, from nest, and refers to a structure or place made by an adult for the purpose of sheltering its young. It can also refer to a set of similar objects of graduated sizes made so that each smaller one fits snugly into the next size for storage. Both of these definitions seem apt. On the one hand, this fourth photograph shows me nestled cozily in my father's arms, sheltered and secure and completely protected from any dangers or discomfort that the world outside his embrace might impose. Every bit of memory reinforces the belief that the nest my parents feathered offered everything a growing child might need in order to thrive. And, like those Russian nesting dolls, I am, at this point, a diminutive analogue of my father. I fit snugly in his cradle, carrying with me an inescapable legacy as well as an unformed, malleable, and profoundly impressionable sense of self that will, in time, define who I am. But unlike those lifeless dolls, I will soon outgrow this nestled fit, rubbing ever more contentiously against the edges of his confines until the friction I generate leaves me intractable. Time is the lever that pries the gap between parent and child. But for this brief instant, before that lever finds its fulcrum and gains its purchase, I am nestled in a state of absolute preciousness.

No such state can long withstand the contamination that comes from the world beyond the nest. In just a few short years, my own sense of self-awareness—of seeing *me* as separate from *him*—will dawn. And with it will come all the yardsticks, stopwatches, triple-beam balances, spectrometers, speedometers, barometers, and thermometers that would adjudicate the measures of my life. Those scales would soon appear everywhere. Their ubiquity was bound in the cultural cloth that enveloped me, persistently prosecuting my goodness, grading my skill, weighing my thinking, appraising my creations, assessing my appearance, and evaluating my potential. They strangled me with foul, contaminating storm clouds of expectation where every accomplishment only seemed to reinforce the objective truth of an incessant mediocrity.

The weight of those thunderheads was crushing. They brought a hailstorm of tyrannical demands that I would never be able to achieve, leaving me mired in a knee-deep litter of *shoulds*. And now, sixty years on from the moment this picture was taken, I suspect that the meteorological ground zero for the formation of those storm clouds was my father.

I wonder what he was thinking as he held me in this picture. What images streamed through his mind as he envisioned a future for his third and last-born child? Did he dream of an ascendant life that would be well and fully lived, free of deep regret and sadness? Did he yearn to see me grow resplendent where every mark I would most assuredly make could be traceable back to him—and to his father—thus granting a modicum of immortality as a soothing salve against the looming biological imperatives? Or did he just quietly pray that his finespun and tender son would find a way to endure the squalls of life and still have heart to joyously swoon at the color of rose, the scent of fresh-cut grass, and the sounds of a string quartet playing Mozart?

Surely, fragments of each of these tableaus must have quickened his dreams as he held me in his arms that day. But it is the poetry of the third possibility, with its inherent humility—its reasonableness and realism—that resonates most deeply, ringing true with the narrative that I have accrued over all these years. As he contemplated the unfurling of my life, with his eyes so gently shut as I lay nestled in his arms, I imagine him sobered by the difficulties ahead. Difficulties were all he ever saw. I think of him bothered by the pitfalls that awaited my every step, discomfited by the challenges and tribulations that would obstruct my way in such an uncertain and unforgiving world. Symptomatic of his own muted disposition, his love for me felt filtered by a peculiar dark lens that turned an urgent desire for my prosperity into a lifetime of disapproving glances, disparaging remarks, withheld praise, and disaffected shrugs reflexively inflicted every time I failed to measure up.

While the mechanics of this perversion elude me, I recognize their influence in my own adult life. I now know that the brilliance of sunlit love is often tempered by overcast skies, its course altered and its radiance dimmed by all sorts of refractive angles before it ever reaches the ground. And yet that love still brims from its source—in me as it did in him—as boundless and relentless as an ancient waterfall, binding together the elemental nature of our lives and dispelling the ephemera that obfuscate the truth.

The clarity of that truth is revealed by the departing clouds at this particular moment, as I record these reflections, just as it was in this photograph. It is the truth of a cloudless sky and a scintillating sun that dislodges puddled delusions and casts everything in acute relief. It is the truth of a father's love that flows like a river downstream through time.

It is a truth that I have only now been able to acknowledge, tearfully and far too late. And it is a truth that I cling to as a guide for my own efforts at seeking redemption and salvation. Before it is again too late.

Entry Date: January 27, 2016
W. L.

Photograph 5
Searching for Contentment in an Ever-Expanding Universe
May 2012

The universe is always expanding. We hear that all the time. Somehow, enigmatically, the thresholds that encompass all that we know are subjected to irrepressible forces that push at the edges of reality, outward, everywhere, in every direction into the unknown. The perimeter is eternally breached, bending like cheap cheesecloth to accommodate the insatiable laws of physics.

Even while sophisticated telescopes fill our screens with wonders from the farthest reaches of space, still the universe rushes past the hem of our imaginations to suffuse the void with stardust. The parochial viewfinder through which we try to organize our perceptions and assert some reasonable frame of reference is constantly undermined by such pungent imponderables ... by a universe that stubbornly will not be contained.

This fifth photograph captures the rapidly expanding perimeters of my own private universe. It flashes with a concussive force that upset the homey equilibrium that forever held our family unit in a tight, densely packed system of orbits. For so long, those four orbits were profoundly predictable. They obeyed known perihelia and aphelia that swept in gentle arcs. They could be plotted and tracked and reliably modeled in a scale measured by the length of my outstretched arms and carved for eternity on the fascia of a kitchen table.

It seemed that there was nothing outside that system of orbits—nothing beyond the margins—that would tempt reflection, least of all a vast, untidy, magnetic *nothingness* patiently waiting to be sublet by the ever-widening chaos of amplified celestial motions. Photographic imaging of my known universe at that time provides proof that our entire system of orbital mechanics could be safely sequestered within prescribed margins calculated precisely in increments of three-by-five, five-by-seven, or eight-by-ten. But the universe is always expanding.

The eccentric ellipses of our four orbits seeded the skies with trails of heavenly debris. Our circumnavigations induced layers of this star stuff to be gently deposited around our lives like a thick, warm blanket. It sheltered us in its sublime accumulation, sculpting smooth contours out of the rocky effluence around us while conveying a singular shape to our own astronomical model. We skidded through space, bound by a system of gravitational fields and complex interactions designed to ensure that the surfeit of our cosmos would remain neatly confined within well-defined borders. But the universe is always expanding.

Rapidly spinning bodies hurtle through space at unimaginable velocities, indentured to ancient orbits laid down from the moment of galactic conception. Yet, the space through which we travel is not as empty as it might seem. Instead, it teems with objects traveling along their own space-time thoroughfares. These exo-objects—long hidden behind the black veil of space—ensnare us with the allure of their gravitational fields, exciting wobbles in our own orbital paths that magnify in intensity with each revolution. As a result, our paths widen and dilate, abrading—and ultimately rupturing—the boundaries that forever embraced our universe. In time, a new celestial stasis will be achieved with enlarged orbital patterns occurring within the periphery of an expanded universe. But there is a symphonious moment in the cosmological progression of things—a percussive big bang—when the known universe undergoes an expansion event, and it is precisely that moment that is captured in this photograph.

And now, in the aftermath of that seismic moment, a fleecy quietude dampens this vast, new universe. Cosmological shockwaves have jarred our orbits awry, slinging us into the yawning hollow. The density that once packed our lives and held us together has surrendered its matter to the silent vacuum of space. The course of my own heavenly pilgrimage whirls me toward unexplored regions at the edges of this diffuse universe, moving me further from the sunlit center, and I shiver with the chill of loneliness. *Where the hell is everybody?*

The mechanics of celestial motion are as indifferent as they are reliable. They always win out. As I consider their influence in this expansive new universe, I wonder whether a fourth law of Keplerian motion might be in order (i.e., planetary objects traveling along discordant paths may—even in an enlarged universe—periodically converge).

Perhaps that time of convergence is near. And perhaps there are things I can do to set it in motion.

I picture that convergence commencing with a single chime. It radiates a blushing overture into space. The rhythm grows as the astral objects heed the call and angle their orbits toward conjunction. The high-pitched strain of a thousand strings exacts a bounty of expectation as the voyagers make their way through the heavens. Battlements of horns and woodwinds follow to herald the intersection as the four paths merge and venerable patterns are renewed.

The moment is sweet joy.

Yet in the end, those age-old forces of attraction are overcome as the pull of stronger, newer forces scatters us again to the distant corners of space. The rhythm rapidly recedes. It assumes the lowing of a mournful bass, growing more bittersweet with each pass of the bow before trailing off like a comet's tail, leaving behind a silent lamentation in the emptiness of space.

But what if that space is no longer so empty? Surely, any new universe contains wonders of its own, indigenous mysteries that beguile the senses and arouse the imagination. As my eyes adjust to the transcendental light of this new, fresh firmament, glimmers of possibility twinkle above me like galactic jewels. They emit a flash of beauty that travels on a frequency I am just now beginning to see.

Dated: February 25, 2016
W. L.

Photograph 6
The Tendrils of Time
July 1991

You can consider performance from several angles. But whichever aspect you consider most important you will find BSA gives a first-class performance under all conditions. Here is a machine which gives you a real sporting performance combined with economy in running costs ... Small wonder that BSAs are the popular choice.

A "real sporting performance" is an excruciatingly lovely phrase lifted directly from the pages of a period broadside for the 1934 BSA Blue Star. Even the copywriting for this motorcycle weeps an oily patina that feels just slightly out of time. But when this particular Blue Star found its way to me, landing in my garage after an improbable journey across continents and several decades, any pretensions of a sporting performance had long been surrendered to the ravages of time.

Age had exacted a hefty toll from this sporting mount and left behind a patchwork of rust and corrosion as change. And yet, even in this decrepit state, laid bare in this sixth photograph, I succumb to the rakish lean and low-slung stance of its Jules Verne design. Its curves are as irrepressible as those flowing beneath the dress of a bygone beauty queen with the same potency that tempts the senses to imagine what once was.

And so, as I often do, I imagine. I think of it as high summer, sometime between the wars, and I'm standing in a chestnut landscape atop a rise that offers a commanding view of the bucolic English countryside. The sunbaked earth radiates a medley of hay and pastureland, a smell that drenches me in a typhoon of fusty sweetness. The stillness is serene, disturbed only by the beat of a sparrow's wing above me and the solstice-driven madness of the grasshoppers at my feet. A black ribbon of macadam snakes a sweeping pass over stone bridges and heath-covered moors—seemingly without end—past the thatch-roofed farms and verdant glades of a place called Orkney on Trent or Bassenthwaite or Banbury or Swadlincote.

From my vantage point, here on top of this tranquil hill in the time of the Bright Young Things, I can watch the approach of the machine and its rider. The thump of that one large piston grows louder as it strokes its way through a blackened cylinder and advances toward my position.

Once in view, I see the rider, upright in the saddle seat, dressed in tweed and tartan wool, goggles pulled over a knit touring cap, twisting the slender throttle in order to wring every last drop of that heralded sporting performance from his gleaming four-speed iron. He rockets past, destination ahead, the chatter of exposed valves on song as he tucks into a string of velvet curves. And then, with a parting glissade through one last bend, he is gone and the pastoral calm is restored.

I'm a breathless voyeur, standing there on top of that hill, a time-traveling imagist, conjuring up the illusion like candied nectar for the soul. It nourishes my imagination with the stunning realization that one day, eighty years in the future, that will be *my* Blue Star—and *my* hand on the throttle—passed on to me through the bewildering perplexity of time, so that I might curate another chapter in its long and storied history.

I don't need an Elizabethan sled from the ornamented fantasies of H. G. Wells to travel in time. Nor do I need a sleek DeLorean with its flux capacitor power drive. No quantum accelerators that inflect the laws of nature, no phone booths, hot tubs, sensory deprivation tanks, or zebra-striped time tunnels are necessary. The plutonium that powers my time machine comes more simply from the senses: the acrid smell of warm dust riding a current of convection from the glowing glass envelope of a vacuum tube, the reassuring feel of an old hardcover book, cloth boards and foxed pages worn smooth by the woolgathering of many hands, the arresting sound of a beloved song that slows the rush of time to an absolute standstill and unveils the trusty wormhole through which I drift to other places and times, or the fleeting glimpse of a familiar photograph, framed by the hardwood rails of the past, where the interplay of light and shadow induces an hypnotic dreaminess and exposes the hoary drawings, slowly fading, on the cave walls of my mind. These are the triggers that transport me back along the sweep of my life. They bewitch me with a vivid array of celluloid memories pleading to be remembered and inflict a stinging melancholia that pierces my heart with sadness. It leaves me suffering a wistful, blissful longing that is the jet lag of the devoted time traveler.

Memories pleading to be remembered are troublesome things to dissuade, and so, as I often do, I remember. I submit to the unyielding pull of memory and trespass on the past. Scene after scene passes before my eyes, clicking into view one at a time, like the yellowing slides in an old Kodak carousel. Each beckons with a siren's song, imploring me to shed the fetters of the present and dip my soul into the warm, reflective pools of remembrance. I know I shouldn't, but I do. I travel back, and time stands still.

The destinations for my time travels are as countless as the stars. Collectively, they bellow their demands, drawing me back with an extravagant promise. I think I should resist, but I don't. Instead, I gorge on the verisimilitude like a teenage anorexic, hopelessly trying to fill some subterranean need with just enough sustenance to survive until I can return.

But it takes a lot of energy to loiter in the past, and the plutonium eventually gives out. Soon, the profiles of the present are all neatly restored, precisely as they were before. And yet there is a persistent fleece that clings to my soul every time I return—a soothing sheath of dreaminess that I wear like a cape. It enfolds me in heartache and, for a short time, inures me to the vicissitudes of the present. It's the charisma of that heartache that entices me back time and again, dangling a shiny lure of exaltation. As I strike for that lure—as I always do—I'm grazed by the fear of what this all means in terms of my connection to the present.

Does this fixation on the past force some commentary about a ponderous present beset by a long litany of regrets? Or a leaden future? And what about the future? The almanac of moments that draws me back is enchanting; it reads like the memoir of a storied life. But that can't be all there is.

Something in my perspective is changing. I can feel it as sure as the springtime. After all, time machines can travel in two directions. As I think about this lovely old bike and reclaiming its sporting performance, I find myself looking forward again. I rail against the idea that the last entry of this memoir has been written. Or that the story of my life ends here, with photographs already taken and moments already lived. Instead, I cling to the belief that there are moments still to come, future moments I cannot conceive but moments that will hold the same capacity to enthrall. I see them radiating on the edges of the horizon, beckoning my glance forward, exhorting me on. I think I should follow them wherever they lead. Whatever the risk. And I tell myself that I will. While I still have time.

Dated: April 10, 2016
W. L.

Photograph 7
A Handful of Dust
July 2016

I will show you something different from either
Your shadow at morning striding behind you
Or your shadow at evening rising to meet you;
I will show you fear in a handful of dust.

—T. S. Eliot

I stand alone at the end of the world. A thousand miles lay behind me. And ten thousand more stretch beyond those, all the way back to the beginning of my time. They lay along a path that is paved with the impressions of a lifetime of moments. Footprints in clay.

Glancing back along the length of that path induces a familiar weariness that numbs the soul: so many miles, so many moments, so many orbits around the sun, spinning through space at breakneck speed following a path that has been fixed forever and over which I exert little control. And there is something else to be seen in that backward glance, captured there, in the lower corner of this seventh photograph. My shadow looms behind me. It lurks like a yeti, black and foreboding and omnipresent. It seems that no matter how far I travel—even here where everything ends but the sea—I can never outrun it. I suppose I never will. Standing beneath this vast midsummer sky, atop golden bluffs that overlook a dispassionate sea, I still feel the grip of its unrelenting allure. It reaches from the ground with sticky coils to ensnare me in despair, and I am seized by the residue of fear. But something is different now; something has changed. I know the shadow for what it is. I understand its anatomy. I can discern its edges and the darkness within, and I can anticipate its movements. And I know that the shadow is me.

I stood here once before, in this same exact spot, decades ago, and looked out over the same turbulent water to thrill at a lustrous future that seethed with a profusion of moments to come. It would be easy to lose myself in remorse, to yield to the yearning to look back again, to slip away from the mournfulness of winter, and bask once more in the splendor of spring, but I won't. I refuse to indulge the backward glance and the reckoning that always follows: the weighing and calculating and judging and accounting of the bulk of a life that has fallen between these two parallel moments on the shores of Cape Cod. That is shadow talk. It brings nothing but regret. Instead, I'll scan ahead out over the ocean and toward that elusive horizon, here on my ledge at the edge of the world, and my soul will soar with the gulls. For I know that others stand with me, and together we make impressions in the wet sand of the road ahead. I'll even let myself tremble with the prospect of hope that there are miles to come before the evening shadow rises up to meet me.

How did this happen? To what can I attribute this new way of seeing and the lessening of my shadow's pull? How can I explain the vision shift? The scientist in me demands a theory and so, here are my findings.

My experiment is at an end. What began last winter as an exploration of important life themes through a structured examination of several significant moments is complete. The intent of this investigation was to address the persistent feelings of sadness (e.g., clinically, my depression) that had overrun my experience in—and of—the world. The work was informed by two underlying assumptions: (1) The insights emerging from this exploration would reveal essential motifs which, when analyzed inductively, would generate new understandings (i.e., truths, themes), and (2) those understandings would be prerequisite for bringing about an improvement in my condition.

Seven photographs were originally selected as the basis for exploration. The techniques embedded in the visual literacy process were adopted as the core methodology. Approximately two-thirds of the way through the process, one photo was rejected in order to reserve space for a final, future-oriented moment and entry. Anecdotally, this event may have signaled the onset of an emerging shift in perspective, but no contemporaneous observations to that effect were recorded. And, in most cases, the photographs—and my thinking about them—were shared with two other individuals and therefore subjected to external influences. Lastly, it is significant to note that more than three months has elapsed since my last entry. This has provided a useful objectivity that has allowed a fresher examination of content and themes. Prior to this final installment, I reviewed the previous entries and applied a variety of appropriate sampling techniques to qualitatively analyze the data. As a result, I can confidently draw three conclusions:

(1) *There is grandeur in the past.* This theme has been reiterated throughout the previous entries and represents the single most consistent finding emerging from my analysis. As a result, its significance as an outcome of this experiment is unambiguous. The collection of moments that has made up my life is vast and diverse. The seven moments that were selected for this project and the innumerable others that have filled the spaces between prescribe the course of a life that has been nothing less than a sublime journey. I can rest assured in the comforting knowledge that I have indeed had a pretty good run. But to assuage the demons of my depression, I surrounded myself with reminders of other places and other times and gorged on the grandeur of a life already lived at the expense of the life unfolding before me. I see that now for the distortion that it is. And while my shadow still strives to tempt my gaze in order to dwell on the past, I believe I am ready to move on. I will save that dwelling for another day and turn my eyes ahead where there is still so much more to see.

> *Those halcyon days were, in fact, mine. They were the precipitate that arose from the spontaneous reaction between me and my life at that moment. They were of me, fomented by me, and are indelibly embossed on the permanent record of my life. Though often imperceptible, the glow generated from that reaction is with me still and continues to radiate its unadulterated promise, leaving behind a faint trace of what I reckon is a truly blessed life. If only I would listen.*

I'm listening now.

(2) *I am not alone.* It took the kindness of a stranger to remind me of this. For far too long, the shadow was my only companion. It lured me with dark comforts, conjuring up images and sensations that entranced me to walk with ghosts while occluding the infiltration of light. Though I was

certainly complicit, that shadow jealously excluded me from others. It shielded me from the paroxysm of life. I became isolated, bereft of the understanding and compassion of those around me—for far too long. And then a chance collision occurred, and then another, and the trance began to break. I discovered I was no longer quite so alone. I grasped for hands I barely recognized but that fate had put in my way. Holding firm to those hands has forced the ghosts to flee, and I find myself dancing again in the light.

> *Yet, the space through which we travel is not as empty as it might seem. Instead, it teems with objects traveling along their own space-time thoroughfares. These exo-objects—long hidden behind the black veil of space—ensnare us with the allure of their gravitational fields, exciting wobbles in our own orbital paths that magnify in intensity with each revolution. As a result, our paths widen and dilate, abrading—and ultimately rupturing—the boundaries that forever embraced our universe. In time, a new celestial stasis will be achieved with enlarged orbital patterns occurring within the periphery of an expanded universe.*

I am stunned by the love of others.

(3) *There is promise in the future.* I'll claim this last finding as tentative, a working premise to be revisited in time. But as I stand here this morning—in this most immediate of my life's moments—and fix my eyes to the future, I am overcome with a new sense of hopefulness, eager to see what comes next. I swell with something akin to the blustery optimism of a twenty-two-year-old kid who once avowed,

> *I imagine myself entranced by the romanticism of such a glittering future, looking out over the roiling water and anticipating the brilliance of all*

those moments to come, moments of ecstasy and contentment, pain and grief, fulfillment, bleakness, satisfaction, peace and longing, a great, thundering miscellany of moments that would, in time, recite the story of my life. I would embrace them all.

I *will* embrace them all. I will watch my grandchildren grow. I will revel in the discoveries we make together, hand in hand as we walk through a forest or skip along a beach, or gaze upon the stars. I will follow my children as they grow old, and I will do what I can to soothe their pains and lessen their fears in order to nurture their own journeys toward acceptance. I will indulge my passions wherever I find them and share that joy with others who will listen. I will seek beauty and wonder in the smallest things and astonishment and awe in the largest things and in all the things between. I will acknowledge the blessings of every new day as I wake up in the morning beside a woman I love—and who, amazingly enough, seems to love me too. And I will cling to the belief that there are more grand moments to come, moments that are worthy of the shutter's snap, or a place on a wall, or a space in a frame, or a chapter in the unfolding saga of a life well lived, and that there are many miles still to travel before I am nothing more than a handful of dust.

Dated: July 24, 2016
W. L.

Epilogue

The first thing Owen did when he spotted the rare mushroom was to grab the field guide from his backpack. He had a pretty good idea of the species but preferred to consult the manual before confirming the find in his log. There are procedures to be followed after all: systematic, consistent parameters required for proper and reliable identification.

The backpack was a gift from Hannah, her way of saying thank you when she graduated from college last spring. "For all your excursions," the Post-it note card read. Rifling through it is always astounding to Owen, bewildering him with the amount of gear that can be stowed in its three elastic pockets. Energy bars, water, various lenses, and filters. Sketchbooks, pencils, notebooks, and guides. And the handful of chocolate kisses that Janey always provides. In the two years since his mycology interest had flamed, Owen has become adept at organizing his things. It took just a second to locate the reference:

> Cup-shaped, often becoming flattened or irregularly shaped as a result of the clustered growth habit; reaching widths of 10 cm, but often smaller; bright orange and smooth above; undersurface usually whitish-fuzzy, at least when young, but often orange and more or less smooth;

without a stem. Odor none. Flesh orangish; brittle (Kuo, Michael).

That sounds about right, he thought to himself.

Aleuria aurantia. Orange-peel fungus. The first one of fall. He recorded the discovery in his log, noting the date, time, and precise coordinates of the find along with a description of soil conditions, habit, and size. Next, with a selection of colored pencils, he added a sketch of the mushroom. Then he swung the big Nikon around on its padded nylon strap and attached a macroscopic lens, the fifty-millimeter shorty to start. Before he began shooting, he marveled again at the wonders to be found find right here in the neighborhood. This stretch along the tracks that front Jensen Park had become an ideal location for the intrepid fungi explorer.

Besides the candy-orange color, it's the white felt underside that distinguishes this species. In order to photograph it, Owen had to lie on his back. The crust of ground was brittle and unyielding and smelled sharply of frost. He was glad he remembered the fingerless gloves. It was cold for late September, and his breath kept fogging the viewfinder.

After several snaps, he was ready to shift to the cap when a pair of Nike cross-trainers came to a stop right alongside his head. Metcon 3s, he observed. Not much different from his own. As he started to stand, a voice called out from above, "Oh, sorry, didn't mean to disturb you."

"No, no, no problem at all," Owen assured him, brushing the crumbs of earth from his pants. "I must look a little silly lying on the ground taking pictures of things that grow in the dirt."

The man in the Nikes pulled a pair of headphones from his ears and began winding them into his pocket. *"Heat Wave,"* Owen thought to himself. *Martha Reeves and the Vandellas, 1963. A Motown man.*

Now that he could see the man's face, Owen realized he had seen him around before. In fact, Owen had seen him a lot. The nest of steel wool that protruded in tufts from under the old Yankees hat was pretty hard to miss—as was the bright red bandana he always wore on his wrist. Owen would frequently spy him tearing down the sidewalks, arms swinging, hips sashaying, a serious walker for sure. Inevitably, in such a small part of town, there were times when their routes would cross. On such occasions, they would exchange the usual greetings that pass for small talk among the cult of walkers: a nod or a "hey" and maybe a little eye contact. Nothing much more than that.

To Owen, the man in the Nikes had one of those faces that made it difficult to estimate his age, but if he had to guess, he'd say the guy was probably a little younger. Or maybe a little bit older. It really was hard to tell. And then there was this that he suddenly remembered: whenever Owen would see him, he had those headphones plugged into his ears and a distracted look in his eyes, like he was thinking important thoughts as he walked. Of course, none of that did anything to ease the concern that rapidly dawned on them both: neither knew the other's name.

"I'm sorry," the gentleman said. "I don't mean to intrude, but I'm so curious about what you are doing. I sometimes see you around here with that camera on your neck. It looks like you can't get close enough to whatever it is you're photographing. Pardon me, but I've always wondered why that is."

"Well, it's these mushrooms," Owen tried to explain while pointing to the ground. "I guess it's become a hobby of mine. I find them really interesting. Their structure is remarkably beautiful to me. So complex and so simple at the same time. I go around town looking for new ones to find, and then I record them in my books. A nerdier form of bird-watching, I suppose."

The man in the Nikes looked thoroughly perplexed. He gave Owen a skeptical smile before squinting down into the dirt. "Huh? I don't really see it, to tell you the truth," he said after a quick second's glance. "Looks like a mushroom to me. Maybe a nice-color mushroom, but—"

"Here, wait, try this," Owen suggested while passing the camera to the man. "You'll need to bend down a little and then look through this lens. You may have to refocus it a bit, but I'm sure you'll see what I mean."

Gingerly, as if he had never held such an intricate camera before, the man got down on both knees. He was quiet while he adjusted the lens. Then he moved in a little bit closer. "Whoa. Hold on a tick," he remarked before moving in still closer and twisting the lens some more. A gasp of disbelief whistled from his chest. "Wow! My gosh! That is remarkable! What definition. It almost looks like the structure has been engineered. You're right. It is so complex. I never would have guessed." He stood back up, shaking his head, and carefully returned the Nikon.

Owen began to cover the lens and detach it from the camera.

The man in the Nikes continued to look at the ground.

Their feet shuffled nervously in the way of uncertain connections. Self-consciousness finally dawning. For a moment, neither seemed sure about what to say or do next, but that moment soon passed. "Hey, I'm Owen, by the way. I've seen you around a lot too, but, sorry, I don't think I ever learned your name."

"The name is Walter, but my friends call me Walt. Walt Levin. I live over on Ridge."

They shook hands with a straight, sure look in the eye.

"Well, it's nice to finally meet you, Walt. I take it you're a walker," Owen said with a nod to the brightly hued shoes.

"I am indeed. Just coming back from my daily, in fact. Beautiful day. Perfect for a brisk one. How about you?"

"Yup," Owen replied. "I've been walking all my life."

Another moment of silence intervened. And then a few more. The beginning of things can be awkward at first. Everybody knows that. A little chemistry is all that is needed to set off a proper reaction.

Walt turned his head to stare down the street while Owen continued to gather his gear.

When they looked at each other again, Owen noticed a gleam in Walt's eye, a twinkle of pure sapphire blue. It left him with a pretty good idea of what was about to transpire.

"Well, Owen, it looks like you're busy, and I wouldn't want to take you away from your mushrooms, but I was just about to do another few blocks before heading in. If you'd like to join me,

I would sure love the company. Who knows what gems we may find along the way?"

The daylight still loiters at the end of September. Still more summer than fall. The shadows that tumble the ground are no longer the soft shrouds of June, but neither do they bear the severity of November or the stridency of the winter to come. To Owen, the timing felt right. Fortuitous even. An invitation had been tendered and was awaiting a reply.

"Well Walt, it just so happens that you caught me at a very good time. I was just packing up for the day. A short walk sounds terrific. I could really use to stretch these legs. I would love to join you. Can you give me a minute to load up my stuff?"

"Excellent!" Walt replied. His face was scored with delight as he reached once more for his music. "And no hurry, Owen. I've got all the time in the world."

"Me too," Owen said through the dawn of a smile. "Me too."

CPSIA information can be obtained
at www.ICGtesting.com
Printed in the USA
LVHW030054270219
608884LV00001B/33

9 781532 065293